AWAKENING THE SHY NURSE

&

SAVED BY THEIR MIRACLE BABY

ALISON ROBERTS

MILLS & BOON

First Published in Great Britain 2020
by Mills & Boon, an imprint of HarperCollins*Publishers*
1 London Bridge Street, London, SE1 9GF

© 2020 Alison Roberts

ISBN: 978-0-263-27965-8

MIX
Paper from
responsible sources
FSC® C007454

This book is produced from independently certified FSC™ paper
to ensure responsible forest management.
For more information visit www.harpercollins.co.uk/green.

Printed and bound in Spain
by CPI, Barcelona

AWAKENING THE SHY NURSE

ALISON ROBERTS

MILLS & BOON

PROLOGUE

'WHAT'S THAT?'

'Nothing.' Annalise Phillips tried to fold the sheet of paper and stuff it back in the envelope at the same time. Her nonchalance didn't quite work and her younger sister Abby narrowed her eyes suspiciously.

'That's envelope's got a window. It's a bill, isn't it?'

'It's nothing to worry about. I've got everything under control.' Lisa watched as Abby manoeuvred her wheelchair to the other side of the kitchen table. She'd always been able to convince Abby that she could manage and that had turned out to be an accurate prediction for so many years that it had become an automatic and genuine reassurance. So why was Lisa aware of a nasty edge of panic approaching this time?

'Look…' It was good that there was a distraction on hand. 'There's a letter here for you as well. No window.'

'Really?' Abby transferred her laptop from her knees to the table and reached for the letter. 'Oh… maybe it's confirmation of my date to sit my driver's licence.' She grinned at Lisa. 'I still can't believe you managed to find that funding for my modified car. It's the most exciting thing ever…'

It felt good to be able to smile and tap into the glow of having achieved something that had been such a long time coming. Abby didn't need to know that Lisa hadn't exactly found funding from a charitable community support organisation and she had, instead, taken out a huge loan against the house to pay for the modifications the car had needed to accommodate a paraplegic driver. Or that the first repayment of the loan was now due at such an unfortunate time when she was between jobs, having been forced to resign from her nursing home position due to a merger that would have meant she had to move to another city.

'Oh…*oh*, you're not going to believe this…' Abby sounded as though her new car had just been demoted from being the most exciting ever. She handed her letter to Lisa. 'There's a room available at the uni hostel. Ground floor, with an en suite bathroom—one of the ones that are only available to disabled students. And get this… it's an unexpected vacancy because a student has pulled out of her course so I can move in next week!'

'Next *week*?' Lisa took the sheet of paper but she couldn't focus on the words. 'But…but…' She had to swallow hard. She wasn't ready for this after all.

Abby was waiting for her to look up. 'You knew this was coming, Lise,' she reminded her gently. 'I've had my name down for one of those rooms in that hostel ever since I started uni and that's years ago.'

'I know.' Lisa tried to find that smile that seemed a million miles away now. 'And it's wonderful. You're going to be completely independent and I'm so proud of you and…and…would you like a cup of tea?' Lisa got to her feet quickly to escape her sister's watchful gaze. 'Wait, no…we should be having a drink to celebrate, shouldn't we? Have we got any wine?'

'We never got round to opening that fizz when you found out about your new job. You said that seeing as you weren't starting for more than a month, we might as well keep it on ice, but maybe now is the perfect time.'

'Mmm… I think it is.' Lisa busied herself finding the bottle in the back of the fridge, getting glasses down from the high cupboard and then opening the sparkling wine. It certainly seemed like a good idea. Abby wouldn't know that she might be drowning her sorrows instead of celebrating, would she? Or panicking because she needed to find enough money to pay a rather large bill in the very near future?

But, of course, her sister knew her better than that. How could she not, when Lisa had been pretty much her principal carer for as long as she could remember? Her only family since their grandmother had died nearly ten years ago now.

'What's really up, Lise?' she asked quietly.

What could Lisa say? That she was beginning to wonder if she'd made a big mistake applying for that desk job as a junior manager in another nursing home just because it had regular hours and was close to home and would make life a lot simpler? That living alone in this little house they had inherited from Gran suddenly seemed like the loneliest prospect ever and it would give her far too much time to worry about how Abby was coping. Worse, it would be more time to revisit the guilt that it was her fault in the first place that her sister was having to cope with so many more challenges in life?

No. She couldn't go there. They'd agreed long ago that it was so far in the past it was a no-go subject. That you could destroy your future if you didn't leave your past behind…

But she couldn't be dishonest either. 'I'm going to miss you,' she told Abby.

'I'll only be on the other side of town. I'll drive you crazy with how often I visit.'

'And I'm only a phone call away.' Lisa nodded, taking another sip of her wine. 'If…you know…'

'If I fall out of my chair, you mean?' Abby laughed. 'I can manage. It's a long time since I've needed you hovering around like a helicopter parent.'

It was meant as a joke but Abby must have realised it stung a bit because she reached out to touch Lisa's arm. 'It's not that I don't appreciate everything you've done, you know that, don't you?'

Lisa nodded. And took a longer sip of her wine.

'You've been—and still are—the best sister ever but it's time we both got to live our own lives. It's the next step for me and then I'll really be able to have a place of my own. Where I can bring my boyfriend home. Or you can bring yours, at least.'

Lisa's jaw dropped. 'You've got a boyfriend?'

'No, silly.' There was a beat of something very dark in the way Abby avoided her gaze. Avoided allowing a memory any hint of the light of day in the hope that it would stay buried for ever. It was another reason that Lisa felt the need to stay close to Abby to be able to protect her. If she hadn't come home when she had that night, they both knew what would have happened because Abby had been unable to defend herself.

'You'd be the first to know if I did.' Abby's tone was too bright. 'I've been way too busy getting my Master's in occupational therapy to want the hassle of a man in my life again. And now I'm well into my postgraduate course in hand therapy so I'm still too busy but, for heaven's sake, Lise—you're nearly thirty and you haven't had a proper boyfriend yet and it feels like that's at least partly because you think you have to keep looking after me.'

'I have had boyfriends,' Lisa protested. If Abby was determined to deal with her past trauma by burying it, then all she could do was support her. She made her own tone light and bright as well. 'I've had lots of them. There was Michael. And Stephen. And…um… what was his name? Oh, yeah… Geoffrey. I guess he doesn't really count…'

Abby was laughing again. 'None of them count. They were all the most boring men on earth. Stephen wore socks and sandals and the most interesting thing he had to talk about was his worm farm. Michael was so skinny and tall and bald he looked like one of the test tubes in his laboratory and…oh, my God… I'd forgotten about Geoffrey. Wasn't he the one whose mother turned up on your first date?'

The wine was definitely helping because Lisa was

laughing now, too. 'I think he'd booked a table for three all along.'

They'd seemed like such nice men, though. Safe…

'You're right,' she had to admit. 'I have a talent for picking boring men.'

'Being bored is bad,' Abby declared. 'I think that's your problem at the moment. You haven't got enough to do until you start your next job. You should go on a holiday.'

Lisa's breath escaped in a huff of laughter. As if. She'd never been on holiday in her life and she certainly wasn't about to start now. Not when money was so tight it was scaring her.

'What I *should* do is find a job for a few weeks.'

She didn't realise that she had voiced the thought aloud until she saw the frown on Abby's forehead.

'Why? Oh…it's because of my car, isn't it? I *knew* it cost too much…'

'No.' Lisa shook her head. 'It's because I need something to do so I don't die of boredom. I'll go crazy rattling around here by myself for weeks after you move into the hostel. I might end up on your doorstep every day.'

'Can't have that.' Abby feigned horror. 'Fill up those glasses again.' She opened her laptop and started tapping keys. 'I'm going to see what's on offer for a supertalented nurse who only wants a few weeks of work. Hmm…we need a high-end medical locum agency, don't we?'

By the time Lisa had their glasses brimming again, Abby was looking triumphant.

'I've found the *perfect* thing. Tailor-made. It's work but it's a holiday at the same time. And it's legit. This agency—London Locums—is obviously highly rated.'

'What is it?'

'A cruise. More specifically, a Mediterranean cruise. Oh…' Abby's sigh was heartfelt. 'It starts in Spain and then goes to places in the south of France and Italy and some Greek islands before finishing up back in Spain again. How romantic is that…?'

The countries and islands were fantasy destinations. A cruise ship even more of a fantasy but not one that Lisa had ever considered desirable.

'I couldn't do that. Cruise ships are full of self-indulgent people who have too much money and just want to float around having a good time, eating and drinking far too much. It would be disgusting.'

It certainly went against the values Lisa Phillips had embraced since she'd been no more than a child.

'There's nothing wrong with having a good time occasionally.' Abby was watching her sister again. 'It might be fun. They need a nurse in this ship's well-equipped infirmary, just for a two-week cruise, to fill in a gap in a team of two doctors and three nurses. You'll get time off to go on shore at some ports of call and accommodation and all meals are provided. And they'll pay top rates for the right person. Why don't you give this woman a call tomorrow? Julia, her name is…'

Lisa's attention had certainly been caught. Not so much by the idea of shore excursions in foreign parts or shipboard accommodation or even the novelty of working in a completely different kind of environment.

There was, however, something that made this feel like it might be meant to be—probably the words "top rates".

'Show me…' She leaned closer as Abby turned her computer so she could see the screen. 'Oh, wow… they're paying *that* much? And it doesn't start until after next week so I'd be here to help you move.'

Lisa pulled in a deep breath. 'I think you're right. It *is* perfect…'

CHAPTER ONE

WEARING JEANS HAD been a bad idea.

It was much hotter than Lisa had expected in Barcelona and, by the time she climbed out of the taxi after her trip from the airport to the port, it felt like the denim was actually sticking to the back of her legs. Even her short-sleeved white shirt felt too warm, despite her having removed her light cardigan. She could only hope that the uniform Julia from London Locums had told her would be supplied for her temporary job as a ship's nurse was better suited to a late summer Mediterranean climate.

The friendly taxi driver opened the boot of the car to retrieve her small, bright red suitcase. 'Here you go, *señorita*.'

'Thank you so much.' Lisa dug in her bag to find her wallet. 'I don't suppose you know which of the ships here belongs to the Aquamarine cruise line?'

Her driver shrugged. 'It's no problem. See that big round building over there?'

Lisa looked over her shoulder and nodded.

'That's the World Trade Centre. Your ship will be one of the ones berthed around it.'

Lisa could see the massive ships docked around the building. They looked like floating cities and one of them was going to be her home for the next couple of weeks. Maybe those butterflies in her stomach weren't solely due to the nervousness that came from starting any new job. Maybe they were due to something she didn't have that much experience of…like excitement? She could feel a smile tugging at the corners of her mouth as she turned back to pay her driver but for a split second her gaze snagged on what was happening over *his* shoulder.

Another taxi had pulled up. The rear door was open and a man had stepped out. A tall, lean, *ridiculously* good-looking man… He was wearing light, casual clothing and looked as though he'd just spent a very relaxing day of sightseeing and highlighting those streaks of sun-kissed blond in his hair. To add to the impression of sheer pleasure, she saw the long, long legs of his companion emerging from the back seat of the car. Slim, elegant arms went straight around the man's neck as the woman got to her feet and he leaned in to kiss her with a leisurely grace that suggested it was by no means a first kiss and more like a continuation of a sexy, afternoon romp.

'Um… Here you are. Is that enough for a tip?' Embarrassed, Lisa was fumbling with the notes and coins. The embarrassment wasn't just because she didn't know about tipping practices in Spain. It was more to do with what was going on just a few feet away from her.

That *kiss*… It was still going on. And on. For heaven's sake, it was broad daylight. Those two needed to get a room. Again…?

'Enjoy your time before you set sail,' her driver instructed. 'You can walk to Las Ramblas from here in less than fifteen minutes. If you have time, take a tour on the bus. This is the most beautiful city in the world.'

Lisa nodded her thanks for the advice but she knew she wouldn't be exploring Barcelona today. Arrangements for her urgent passport hadn't been finalised in time for her to join the cruise along with all the new passengers in Malaga a couple of days ago so it felt like she was playing catch-up already. She was due on board her new place of employment at four p.m. and that was…she glanced at her watch…less than twenty minutes from now, which didn't give her that much time to identify the correct ship to board. Being late was the height of rudeness as far as Lisa Phillips was concerned.

As her taxi pulled away she noticed that *that* kiss was finally over and the leggy blonde was—reluctantly—getting back into her taxi. As Lisa pulled the long handle out of her suitcase the man lifted his hand in a farewell wave and then turned, his gaze locking onto Lisa's a heartbeat later. He had to know that she'd seen what he'd just been doing but he didn't seem remotely bothered. If anything, that quirk of his eyebrow seemed like nothing more than a flirtatious invitation. Perhaps *she* might like to find out how good at kissing he was?

Lisa could feel colour flooding her cheeks as she snapped the handle of her suitcase into place and then tipped it so she could start dragging it behind her. She'd already had a sneaking suspicion that it wasn't just the sightseeing and unlimited food and drink people took cruises for and that had just been confirmed. Some people clearly found a cruise an opportunity for un-limited sexual adventures as well. A "what happens on board stays on board" kind of thing.

'Can I be of some assistance?'

Oh…dear Lord… The man's voice was just as gor-geous as the rest of him. Deep and sexy and with a hint of laughter that went with his whole, laidback look. It had to be the overly warm air she was dragging into her lungs that was adding to the heat Lisa could feel in her cheeks. And in the pit of her stomach, come to that. A rebellious corner of her brain was melting in that heat as well. Otherwise, why would it come up with the absurd idea that maybe she *would* rather like to find out how good this man was at kissing?

'No,' she said firmly, without looking up, so he wouldn't notice her fiery cheeks. 'Thank you, but I'm fine. It's not heavy and I'm perfectly capable of man-aging by myself.'

'No problem.' That hint of laughter was more pro-nounced now. 'Enjoy your cruise.'

A group of women, in flowing maxi dresses and floppy sunhats were coming towards them. Amidst the giggles, a call came that sounded more like a command.

'Hugh… You must see these photos we took at the beach today. Wait until you see Scout's new bikini.'

He'd already slowed his pace so it took only seconds for Lisa to leave him behind with the young women. Fellow passengers from the same ship, she decided. Hopefully not hers. She quickened her own pace, heading towards the first ship that was towering over her more and more as she got closer. There was a covered gangway sloping up to a door on the side of the hull and a desk shaded by a canopy at the bottom, staffed by uniformed people who might well be able to help her. If this wasn't her ship, they could no doubt point her in the right direction.

Well, well, well… So there were still women in the world who blushed?

Hugh Patterson was intrigued, he had to admit, as he strolled along the marina, having finally extricated himself from the group of overexcited young women that he really didn't have the energy for after a long lunch with his Spanish friend, Carlotta. Well acquainted with the tourist circuit of the Mediterranean for a couple of years now, Hugh had friends in many of the popular cruise ship destinations.

It wasn't just sailors that had a girl in every port these days, he mused. Ships' doctors could be just as privileged and if you were that way inclined, it was the easiest sex life ever because anybody involved knew that it was never going to be anything serious. It was just intermittent fun. Living life for the moment and enjoying every minute of it.

That young woman he'd made blush at the taxi rank had looked as if she needed to learn to let herself enjoy the moment. Fancy being so uptight you wouldn't even let someone help with your suitcase? Or even make eye contact with them when they offered? Maybe it was actually irritating rather than intriguing? Being dismissed like that was not something he was used to.

'Hi, Hugh. Had a good day?'

One of the team welcoming people back on board the ship after their shore excursions saw him heading for the gangway.

'Fabulous, thanks, Simon. I love Barcelona. I had a picnic with a friend in Parc Guell.'

'Oh…lucky you, not having to work today. I don't get a day off on shore until Santorini this time. Or it might be Mykonos. One of the Greek islands, anyway.'

'I know… I'm lucky. We only need one doctor on board at all times when we're in port so, with two of us, we can take turns.'

He did feel lucky. What other doctors got to do their work in what could seem like an endless holiday but still got to practise enough real medicine that it didn't get boring and it was also possible to keep one's skills honed? Okay, he'd probably want to settle down sometime in the future but not yet. Maybe never, in fact. He'd almost done that once and look what a disaster that had turned out to be.

'I'm about to go and take over from Peter now, though,' he added, heading towards the gangway. 'That way he can at least get out and stretch his legs on land.'

Hugh took the stairs rather than the elevator to get to the lobby atrium of the ship, which was one of the most impressive areas on board with its marble floors, glittering chandeliers, huge potted palm trees, and the grand piano that was always providing some background music for the crowds taking advantage of the boutique shops and bars that circled the lobby on several levels.

Except old Harry wasn't playing his usual repertoire of popular classics. He wasn't playing anything at all but standing beside his piano stool, looking down at a knot of people at the base of one of several staircases that curved gracefully between the atrium levels.

What was going on? Hugh's pace increased as he got close enough to see that someone was on the floor in the middle of the group. An elderly woman, who, despite what had to be well over thirty-degree heat today, was wearing quite thick stockings. One of her shoes had come off and was lying beside someone that was crouched at the woman's head.

'Let me through, please,' he said calmly. 'I'm a doctor. What's happened here?'

The crouching person looked up and Hugh was momentarily startled to see that it was the blushing girl from the taxi rank. Right now, however, she was supporting an elderly woman's head in a manner that suggested she knew what she was doing to protect and assess a potential cervical spine injury.

'She fell,' he was told. 'From about halfway down these stairs. Her neck seems to be okay, though.'

'Did you see it happen?'

'Yes... I was almost beside her going up the stairs.'

'Please…' the victim of the fall raised her hands. 'Just help me up. I'm fine… I really don't want to cause such a fuss.'

'We need to make sure you're okay first,' Hugh told her. 'My name's Hugh and I'm a doctor and this is…' He raised his eyebrows at the young woman who had, he couldn't help noticing, rather extraordinary eyes—a golden hazel shade but the edge of the iris had a dark rim around it, as if nature had been determined to accentuate the design.

'Lisa,' she supplied. 'My name's Lisa and I'm a nurse.'

No wonder she was giving the impression of competence, Hugh thought, as he focused on his patient. 'What's your name, love?' he asked.

'Mabel…'

'Is anything hurting, Mabel?'

'I… I'm not sure… I don't think so, dear.'

'Can you take a deep breath? Does that hurt?'

'No…'

'Is someone with you?'

'Frank…my husband…he's coming shoon. We need to shee about our…our…'

Hugh frowned. Mabel might look to be well into her eighties but that didn't mean she might not have been having a drink or two this afternoon. But slurred speech could very well be an indication of something more serious as well—like hypoglycaemia from a diabetic emergency or a head injury, which was not unlikely given the hard marble flooring beneath her.

'Was she knocked out?' he asked Lisa.

She shook her head. 'I don't think so but, if she was, it would have only been for a moment because I was beside her by the time she got to the bottom of the stairs. I tried to catch her but I was just a split second too slow, unfortunately.'

This Lisa might be small but Hugh could imagine her leaping into action to try and help someone. She was still clearly determined to help.

'She didn't just fall,' Lisa added. 'She looked dizzy. She was already holding the railing but she let go and…' Lisa was watching the elderly woman carefully. 'Mabel? Do you remember that?'

'No…pleashe…let me up…'

Hugh was holding Mabel's wrist, finding her pulse rapid but very pronounced, so her blood pressure couldn't be low enough to explain any dizziness.

'Move back, folks.' Old Harry, the pianist, had come down from the stage and was trying to move people further away. 'Let's give them some space.' He caught Hugh's gaze. 'I'll go to the infirmary, shall I? And get some help?'

Hugh nodded. 'Yes, thank you.'

Mabel pulled away from his hand and moved as if she was making an effort to sit up.

'Don't move, Mabel,' Lisa said. 'Let us look after you for a minute, okay?'

But Mabel tried to roll and then cried out with pain.

'What's hurting?' Hugh asked.

'Look…' Lisa tilted her head to indicate what she had noticed. 'That looks like some rotation and shortening of her left leg, don't you think? A NOF?'

Fracturing a neck of femur was a definite possibility given the mechanism of injury and they were often not that painful until the patient tried to move, but Hugh was impressed that Lisa had picked up on it with no more than a glance.

'Try and keep still, Mabel.' Lisa leaned down so that Mabel could hear her reassurance. 'It's okay…we're going to take care of you…'

The warmth and confidence in her voice was as distinctive as her eye colouring. She sounded absolutely genuine—as if she was well used to taking care of people and doing it extremely well. If Hugh were unwell or injured, he would certainly feel better hearing that voice. Mabel was trying to respond but seemed to be having trouble getting any words out and that was when Hugh noticed the droop that was now obvious on one side of her face. Lisa's observations that it had appeared to be a medical event that had caused the fall rather than a simple trip and the other symptoms like the slurred speech now were coming together to make it urgent to get this patient into hospital.

It was a relief to see the other ship's doctor, his colleague Peter, coming into the lobby, with the emergency kit in his arms. One of their nurses was following and she carried a pillow and a blanket under one arm and an oxygen cylinder under the other. Hugh had another flash of relief that they were currently docked in the port of a major city. They might be very well equipped to deal with emergencies on board but someone who was potentially having a stroke and had fractured their hip in a fall would have needed evacuation to a land hospital as quickly as possible. At least they wouldn't need to call in a helicopter this time.

'We need an ambulance,' he told Peter. 'Not just for the NOF. We've got signs that the fall might be the result of a CVA.'

'We'll get them on the way.' the older doctor nodded.

'Mabs?' An elderly man was pushing his way through the concerned spectators. 'Oh, no…what's happened?'

He crouched down beside Lisa, who moved to let him get closer to his wife. Hugh turned to reach into the emergency kit as Peter opened it. They needed to get some oxygen on for their patient, check her blood glucose level, get an IV line in and some pain medication on board and to splint her hip. They needed to talk to Mabel's husband, too, and find out about her past medical history and what kind of medications she might be taking. It was only when he looked back to start talking to Frank that he realised that Lisa had disappeared. Did she think she might be in the way now that the rest of the ship's medical staff were on scene?

It was a shame she'd gone, anyway. He would have liked to have thanked her. And to tell her how helpful she had been.

Lisa should probably have introduced herself to the ship's doctor and the nurse who'd come in with him and she should have offered to keep helping, but after she'd moved to let Mabel's husband get close enough to comfort his wife, the nurse had moved in front of her and it just hadn't been the right time to say anything that might interrupt the focus on their patient so Lisa had let herself slip into the background to let them do their work. She would have expected that good-looking passenger who also happened to be a doctor to stand back and let the people in uniform take over but it almost looked as if he was still in charge of the scene.

Moving further back brought Lisa to the bottom of the staircase and she took a few steps and then paused to watch what was happening. She might be doing this herself very soon, dressed in pale green scrubs with a stethoscope hanging round her neck like the nurse who was currently taking Mabel's blood pressure. The doctor, in a crisp, white uniform with epaulettes on the shoulders of his shirt, was attaching electrodes to monitor Mabel's heart and the extra doctor... Hugh... was sorting something from what looked like a well-stocked kit. IV supplies, perhaps?

She could only see Hugh's profile but she'd been much closer to him only a minute or two ago and she'd been aware from the instant he'd appeared that this was a very different man from the one who might have been flirting with her near the taxi rank earlier.

It wasn't that he was any less good looking, of course. Or even that that relaxed grace that came from an easy enjoyment of his life had vanished. It was more that there was a focus that made it obvious this man was intelligent and he knew what he was doing. Lisa could respect that. She could forgive him for being some kind of playboy, in fact. After all, doctors were just like any other professional people and there were no laws that prevented them going on holiday and letting their hair down occasionally, were there?

Onlookers were being asked to leave the area and make space as a team of paramedics arrived with a stretcher. Lisa found herself in a flow of people that took her to the next level of the atrium but she knew she needed to find an elevator or internal stairway. Not that there was any point in finding the ship's medical centre to introduce herself when she knew the staff were busy here for the moment, but her suitcase would have been delivered to her cabin by now so it would be a good time to find out where that was and freshen up before she went to meet her new colleagues.

She did know she had to go down rather than up. Crew members didn't get cabins with balconies. They were possibly right in the middle of the ship and might not even have any portholes. Lisa had to hope that she wasn't prone to seasickness. Either that, or that the Mediterranean was a very calm sea.

An hour or so later, Lisa was heading for the middle of Deck Two, where a helpful steward had told her the medical centre and infirmary were located. She had showered, swapped her jeans for a more formal skirt and brushed her short waves of auburn hair into a semblance of order. A large red cross painted on a steel door told her that she had found her destination and a sign below that gave the hours the medical facility was open and phone numbers for the nurse on duty for out of hours. So, it was a nurse rather than a doctor that made the first response to any calls?

Lisa's heart skipped a beat as she went into an empty waiting room. She was going to be one of those nurses for the next two weeks, with possibly more responsibility than she'd ever had before if she was going to be the first responder to something major like a cardiac arrest or severe trauma. This time she knew that that internal flutter was definitely excitement. She was stepping well out of her comfort zone here, and… well…she couldn't wait…

'Hello?'

The desk at one side of the waiting room was empty. Lisa peered around a corner and walked a short distance down the corridor. There were consulting rooms, a room labelled as a laboratory where she could see benches covered with equipment that looked like specialised blood or specimen testing machines and a closed door that had a sign saying it was the pharmacy. An open door on the other side of the corridor showed Lisa what looked like a small operating theatre. Surprised, she stepped into it. There was a theatre light above the narrow bed in the centre of the room, a portable X-ray machine, cardiac monitor and ventilator nearby and glass-fronted cupboards lining the walls that looked to be stocked with a huge amount of medical supplies.

A movement in her peripheral vision as she entered the narrow corridor again made Lisa turn, to see the back view of the white pants and shirt of the ship's doctor's uniform as he stood at the desk in the waiting room.

'Hello...' she said again, walking towards him. 'I was starting to wonder if I was all alone here.'

The doctor turned and Lisa could actually feel her jaw dropping. If she'd thought this man was good looking when she'd seen him kissing his girlfriend, it was nothing to how attractive he looked in uniform. Especially *this* uniform, with the snowy, white fabric accentuating his tanned skin and making those brown eyes look remarkably like melted chocolate. He also looked as startled as Lisa was feeling. They both spoke at precisely the same time.

'What are *you* doing here?' Lisa's voice was embarrassingly squeaky.

'It's *you*...' His tone was more than welcoming. It was almost delighted.

They both stopped speaking then and simply stared at each other. Lisa was confused. Why was Hugh wearing the same uniform as the ship's doctor? And, now that they were nowhere near someone who needed medical attention, why was it that the first thought that came into her head as she looked at him was the image of him kissing that woman so very thoroughly? To her dismay she could feel heat creeping into her cheeks.

It was Hugh who finally broke the awkward moment, his mouth curving into a lazy smile. 'You're blushing.' He sounded amused. 'Again...'

Oh, help... So, avoiding eye contact with him out on the pier hadn't been enough to disguise her beetroot-coloured cheeks, then. Lisa closed her eyes as she sighed. 'I'm a redhead. It kind of goes with the territory.' She opened her eyes again, frowning. 'I thought you were a passenger.'

'But you knew I was a doctor. We've just been working together.'

'Yes, but... I thought you were a doctor who was on holiday.' Good grief...the look she was getting suggested that it was Hugh who was confused now. He probably thought that she was an idiot. 'I'm Lisa,' she added. 'Lisa Phillips. I'm a—'

'Nurse,' Hugh put in helpfully. 'Yes, I remember. A good one, too, I think. Thank you for your help earlier. With Mabel.'

'It was a pleasure.' The compliment about her abilities was making her feel far more proud of herself than it merited. 'Do you know how she is?'

'I believe she's doing well. She's scheduled for hip surgery later this evening but the better news was that her neurological symptoms had virtually resolved by the time she reached the hospital.'

'So it was a TIA rather than a stroke?' A transient ischaemic attack could present with the same symptoms of a stroke but they were temporary. A warning signal rather than a critical event.

'So it would seem.' The quirk of Hugh's eyebrow told her that he was impressed by her medical assessment but then his smile reappeared. 'Now...what it is that I can help *you* with, Lisa Phillips? I hope you're not unwell...or injured...'

Along with a very genuine concern in his voice, there was a gleam in those brown eyes that made Lisa remember that kiss all over again. Or rather the moment he'd caught her gaze after the kiss and they'd both acknowledged what she'd seen. There was also an acknowledgement of something on a different level—one of mutual attraction, perhaps? Oh…help… Lisa looked away. Any attempt to return the man's smile evaporated instantly. She'd never expected to see him again and things were about to get even more unsettling.

'I'm a nurse,' she explained.

'Yes, I know. A nurse on holiday.'

'No… I'm here to work. Through London Locums. I believe I'm replacing someone called Amanda who needed time to support her mother who's having surgery?'

There was another moment of startled silence. 'You're our *locum*? Why didn't you say something?'

'Why would I? I thought you were a passenger.'

'But you didn't say anything when Peter turned up.'

'Peter?'

'Our other doctor. And Janet was there—one of our nurses.'

'Well…it didn't seem quite the right moment to be introducing myself.'

'I guess not. Let's do that properly now, shall we?' Hugh was holding out his hand. 'I'm Hugh Patterson. Pleased to meet you, Lisa. I look forward to working with you for the next couple of weeks. And it will be me you're working with mostly because you're filling a gap on my Blue Watch.'

'Oh?'

Lisa had taken his hand automatically but, instead of shaking hers, he simply held it for a moment and then gave it a slow squeeze, and that did it. Like a switch being flicked on, an electrical jolt shot from Lisa's hand and raced up her arm—an extraordinary tingle she had never felt before in her life. It was enough to make her pull her hand free with the kind of instinctive reflex she might have had to touching something that was hot enough to burn her badly.

How weird was that?

And this Hugh Patterson was looking forward to working with her?

'Yes,' he said, as if confirming her silent query. 'I'm Blue Watch. Peter's Green Watch. It just means that we'll be working together. Probably having the same days off as well and you should be able to get some shore excursions if there's space. Do you have a favourite place to visit around the Mediterranean?'

'This is the first time I've been out of England,' Lisa confessed.

'Really?' Hugh sounded astonished. 'You don't like travelling?'

'I've…um…never really had the opportunity, that's all.' Lisa wasn't about to tell him the reasons why. He didn't need to know about her family responsibilities and he certainly wouldn't be interested in hearing about financial hardship. This Hugh Patterson looked like one of life's golden people who never had to worry about anything much. Someone from a completely different planet from her own, which made her wonder how well they might be able to work together. Perhaps he was thinking along the same lines now because the look she was receiving made her feel as if she was being seen as someone very unusual. Someone…interesting?

The prospect of her new working responsibilities pushing the limits of her professional comfort zones were nothing in comparison to how this man was pushing the boundaries of anything she considered personally safe when it came to men.

No wonder she'd snatched her hand back as if she was about to get burned.

Anyone who had anything to do with Hugh Patterson could be playing with fire. Lisa could feel herself releasing her deeper than usual breath carefully. It was nothing to worry about because she never played with anything dangerous. Never had. Never would. That there was even any temptation there was enough of a warning that she wasn't about to ignore.

'I'm looking forward to working here as well,' she heard herself saying with commendable calmness. 'And, if you've got a moment, I'd appreciate a bit of a tour, if you've got time, that is. I'd like to get up to speed as soon as possible—preferably before my first shift tomorrow morning.'

Lisa was edging back a little as she spoke. Even though she had broken the skin contact between them well over a minute ago, she could still feel that odd tingle it had provoked. It was almost as if she could still feel the warmth of his skin, filling the air between them, and when he spoke both his words and his tone made both those impressions even more noticeable.

'No problem,' he said. Those dark eyes were watching her so closely Lisa had the horrible feeling that he

knew about that tingle. That he knew that she thought
he was dangerous.

'Come with me,' he added, with that lazy smile that
was already beginning to feel familiar—the one that
suggested he was finding this all rather amusing and
he intended to enjoy the entertainment as much as possible. 'I'm all yours, Nurse Phillips.'

CHAPTER TWO

OH, DEAR…

It was going to be too tempting not to tease this new colleague a little. There was something about her that made her seem much younger than she probably was. First appearances were giving him an interesting impression of someone being well educated and intelligent but possibly naïve at the same time. Hugh had never had a little sister, but if he had, he was quite sure he'd feel like this in her company. He could appreciate the fact she was gorgeous without being remotely attracted, feel proud of her ability to do her job well and perhaps recognise that there were things he could teach her. That, in the interests of being a kind, big brotherly sort of person, he had a duty to teach her, even.

Like persuading her that life could be significantly more enjoyable if she relaxed a bit? She was so tense. So eager to give the impression that she could cope with anything she might be asked to do. It seemed that this Lisa not only liked to be able to manage on her own when it came to carrying a suitcase, she was determined to get all the information she needed to be able to achieve the ability to manage alone in her professional environment if that should prove necessary.

'So…do you follow a standard protocol for resuscitation in cardiac arrest?' Lisa was clearly familiar with the model of life pack for cardiac monitoring and defibrillation that was on top of their rapid-response/resuscitation trolley. 'Thirty to two compressions to ventilation rate until an advanced airway is secure? Immediate shock for documented VT or VF and then every two minutes?'

Hugh nodded. 'You've got a recent Advanced Care Life Support qualification, I assume? That's one of the standard requirements for working on board a ship.'

Lisa mirrored his nod. 'I've had experience with laryngeal mask airways and administration of adrenaline but I'm not yet qualified for antiarrhythmic drugs or intubation.'

Something in her tone made Hugh curious. Or maybe it was the use of that qualifying 'yet'.

'What made you decide to go into nursing and not become a doctor?' he asked her.

There was a flash of surprise in her eyes that made him wonder if she wasn't used to people asking her personal questions—or that she discouraged them because she preferred to guard her privacy.

The response was no more than a verbal shrug, however. 'Why do you ask?'

'I just get the impression you'd like to be doing more. Like intubating someone in a cardiac arrest?'

Lisa's glance slid away from his. 'I always wanted to work in a medical field,' she said. 'Nursing was the most practical option at the time.' She turned to touch another piece of equipment that was close. 'Does this take digital X-rays?'

'Mmm…' Hugh was still curious but he knew when someone wanted to avoid talking about something. Had Lisa become a nurse because she hadn't been able to afford the time or costs to go to medical school? 'It can be helpful to be able to transmit an image, either for a second opinion—which we can get via internet links to all sorts of international experts—or to get the right treatment available as soon as possible if we transfer someone to a land hospital, by chopper, for instance.'

'Do you go with them?'

'Sometimes they might need a doctor on board if they're critical. If someone local doesn't come with the evacuation crew we might send Tim, who's qualified as both a paramedic and a nurse and covers a lot of our night shifts currently. Or you might even go as a medical chaperone, depending on what else is going on.'

It was a true statement but Hugh was telling her that she might be involved because he wanted to see her reaction and, sure enough, there was a gleam of interest in those amazing eyes at the prospect of being choppered off the ship and back again. A glow of excitement even, and that gave him an odd little kick in his gut. So, she was up for a bit of adventure, this Lisa, even if she was uptight. This was good. It could make teasing her even more enjoyable.

'And do you ever do actual surgery in here? It looks more like an operating theatre than an assessment or treatment area.'

'It is, at times.' Hugh told her. 'We have to be able to deal with every situation you could imagine and sometimes we're out of range of emergency transport for some time. We've got anaesthetic and ventilation gear along with the digital X-ray and ultrasound and a full range of surgical instruments, though I haven't had to use too many of them yet.'

'But you've got a surgical background?'

'I've mostly specialised in emergency medicine and critical care but I've got both surgical and anaesthetic diplomas as well. How 'bout you?' Hugh led the way out of the room. 'What's your background?'

'My early experience was working in A and E,' Lisa said. 'Which I really loved. But my last job as head of a nursing home team gave me a lot of scope for first response and medical assessment and that was interesting, too. I'm...between jobs at the moment, which was why a locum position was ideal.' She had paused to look through the door of the laboratory. 'What range of tests can you do on board?'

It seemed like asking Lisa a question only made him want to ask more—like why she'd gone to work in a nursing home if she'd loved the emergency department so much? And, if she'd had so much experience already, why did she give off this impression of...well, it was almost innocence. Unworldliness, anyway, and that certainly wasn't something Hugh normally came across in the women he met these days. He was curious, he realised. A lot more curious than he usually was when he met someone new.

'Again, we have to be prepared for as many things

as possible. We can test for cardiac enzymes if we suspect a heart attack, infections, arterial oxygen levels and blood glucose levels and a dozen or more other things. Janet's our expert and she can give you a rundown on how to do the tests but it's mostly automatic so it's easy. And, speaking of Janet, she's in our little two-bed infirmary at the moment because we admitted a woman with a severe migraine earlier today for monitoring so let's go there and I can introduce you.'

'That will be great, thank you.'

Hugh watched as Lisa took a last, slow glance back over her shoulder towards the areas he'd already shown her, as if she was mentally cataloguing and memorising everything she'd learned so far, and he was almost tempted to give her a quick quiz but then her gaze ended by catching his and there was a note of surprise there. Or maybe it was criticism because she had expected him to be moving by now and taking her to the next source of information about her new job.

She could turn out to be bossy, he decided, once she had settled in and was confident of her surroundings and responsibilities, but he took the hint and led her towards the hospital end of the medical centre.

"Bossy" was the wrong word, he decided moments later. "Feisty" was probably a more accurate prediction. His internal correction made him smile.

Hugh liked feisty. He liked it a lot.

If he was any more laidback, he'd be horizontal.

But Lisa knew that this relaxed impression of complete confidence with a streak of an impish desire to liven things up a little was just one side of the coin as far as Dr Hugh Patterson was concerned. She'd seen him morph into a completely focused professional dealing with an accident scene and she saw the coin start to flip again as they entered the ship's hospital at the other end of the medical centre. There were two small four-bed wards, one for passengers and one for crew, separated by a nursing station currently staffed by the team's senior nurse. Janet was older, with a friendly face and a Scottish accent but they had no time for more than a brief introduction before Hugh picked up the chart for their inpatient.

'She's responded well to the treatment,' Janet told him. 'She's had a good sleep, her headache's down to a two-out-of-ten pain score and she hasn't vomited since her first dose of anti-emetic.'

Lisa saw the frown line of concentration that appeared between Hugh's eyes as he rapidly scanned the information on the chart of medications administered and observations taken. Then he walked towards one of the only two beds in the room, the frown line evaporating as his mouth curved in a reassuring smile.

'Rita, isn't it? I'm Hugh Patterson, one of the doctors on board. It was my colleague Peter who saw you this morning, yes?'

The woman on the bed, who looked to be in her early forties, was nodding. 'I feel ever so much better,' she told Hugh. 'Those pills have been wonderful.' She was staring at Hugh. 'Have we met somewhere before?'

His smile was charming but fleeting. 'I don't think I've had the pleasure but I'm very glad you're feeling better. I suspect the main thing that's helped was to give you something for the nausea and vomiting and fix the dehydration that was making things worse. This wasn't your first migraine, was it?'

'No, but I haven't had one for ages. I know to stay away from triggers like chocolate and red wine.'

'Are they the only triggers that you know of? Flashing lights and loud noises can do it for some people. You haven't been out partying in the nightclubs on board till all hours, have you?' His tone was teasing.

'I should be so lucky.'

Rita was smiling now. And blinking more rapidly, Lisa noticed. Good grief…was she trying to flirt with her doctor? Batting her eyelashes even? If so, at least Hugh wasn't responding with anything more than a hint of his earlier smile.

'Might be an idea to keep avoiding anything like that for a day or two. I'm sure you don't want to be stuck in here and missing out on any more shore excursions.'

'No…my friends all went out for a horse riding trek today and I was so looking forward to doing that. Oh…' Rita's eyes widened. 'I remember now. I *do* know you. You're *that* Hugh Patterson…'

'Oh?' Hugh was looking wary now. 'Which one would that be?'

'Your mother was Diane Patterson, yes? The District Commissioner for the Windsor pony club and you used to have a three-day event on your family estate every year. I rode in it more than once—oh, ages ago now but I remember you used to be on the quad bike, doing errands like delivering coffee to the judges.'

Wow… His family had an estate in Windsor? Somehow that didn't surprise Lisa. That laidback, making the most of good things approach to life often went hand in hand with extreme wealth, didn't it?

'Mmm… Ancient history.'

His clipped tone made it very clear that he had no interest in pursuing this line of conversation and Lisa dropped her gaze instantly when his glance slid sideways so she could let him know she wasn't interested in hearing personal information like this. She could understand perfectly well why he might be embarrassed at having his family's financial situation made common knowledge and she could sympathise with that. She might be completely at the other end of the financial spectrum but she wouldn't want strangers knowing about hers either.

'We'll be setting sail in the next hour or so.' Hugh was scribbling something on Rita's chart. 'What we'll do is take your IV line out and give you some medications to take with you.' He was turning away from this patient. 'Don't hesitate to call if you're not continuing to improve, though. One of our wonderful staff members will be available at all times.'

His smile became suddenly a lot more genuine as his gaze shifted to catch Lisa's and, for the first time, it was impossible not to smile back. He was making her feel so welcome and as though he really did believe she would be a welcome addition to their team, even though he had only just met her. There could be relief making that welcome more pronounced because he could get away from a conversation he obviously didn't want to have but it didn't matter... Lisa was going to make sure that Hugh wasn't disappointed with his new staff member.

Janet was also very welcoming and, after she had taken out Rita's IV line, dispensed the medication Hugh had prescribed and discharged her, the older nurse took Lisa to find her uniform and then continue her exploration of the ship's medical facilities as she heard about what her duties would entail.

It was during this additional tour that Lisa became aware of a background hum of sound that was new and an odd sensation that something was changing in the air around her. Janet smiled at her expression.

'We're underway,' she told Lisa. 'I love that moment when we leave shore and head out into the freedom of the open sea. It's what keeps me coming back every season.'

Yes. Lisa could recognise that it was the distant hum and vibration of extremely powerful engines that she could both hear and feel, and the realisation hit her that this massive vessel and the thousands of passengers and crew on board were soon going to be far from land and reliant on what suddenly seemed like a very small medical team to deal with any medical or traumatic emergency that might happen.

They were also on the way to somewhere Lisa had never been in her life and the combination of potential adventure and challenge was...well...it was enormously exciting, that's what it was. The hum and sensation of movement was coalescing somewhere in the pit of her stomach in a tingle that was not unlike the one she had experienced earlier today, when Hugh Patterson had been holding her hand, but this was far more acceptable. Welcome, in fact, because it was almost completely a professional kind of excitement.

Whatever this exotic position threw at her for the next couple of weeks, she was going to do her absolute best. She always did, of course, but there was an incentive here that was a little different from anything she'd experienced before. She had to admit that part of that incentive was a little disturbing, however. While it was perfectly natural to want to do her job exceptionally well for the sake of anybody who was ill or injured on this ship, and she'd always had that determination wherever she'd worked, what was different this time was why it seemed almost more important to impress her new boss.

I found your ship online. Looks amazing!

It's totally unreal. There are bars and restaurants open all night, shows like you might see on Broadway, fitness clubs and dance classes—you name it, it's happening on board this ship.

I found a page with pictures of all the important people who had lots of stripes on their shoulders.

They're the officers.

Lisa was curled up on her bunk, typing rapidly in the message box on her laptop screen. Conversations with Abby were both more reliable and a lot less expensive this way than by phone.

The ship's doctors were there too.

They're considered to be officers as well. The nurses get privileges too. We can go anywhere we like on board and not just keep to the crew quarters for meals and things.

Who's the doctor with the beard?

That's Peter.

And who's the other one? The really *really* good-looking one?

Hugh. He's the one I mostly work with.

Oooh... Lucky you.

A string of emojis with hearts instead of eyes made Lisa shake her head before she tapped back.

You're just as bad as every other woman on board. We had four of them in the clinic yesterday, all trying to outdo each other to get his attention and...get this... two of them had come in to ask for the morning-after pill because things had got "out of hand" the night before at some party.

Wow...not the best line to take if you want to get somebody interested, I wouldn't have thought.

Lisa was smiling as she responded.
No. And anyway there are strict rules about the crew fraternising with the passengers.

What about the crew fraternising with the crew???

It was a winking face at the end of Abby's message this time.

Not going to happen.

Why not? Is he single?

I haven't asked him.

Why not?

I'm not interested.

Oh...yeah...right... Why not? Because he's too good-looking? Doesn't wear socks with sandals?

Lisa leaned back against her pillow and closed her eyes for a moment. She'd been busy enough settling into her new environment in the last couple of days so that she could concentrate purely on her work and find her way around this enormous ship. There was a lot of work to do during the often busy open surgeries at the medical centre, which ran for a couple of hours both morning and early evening, where she was responsible for triaging any patients that arrived and dealing with minor cases that didn't need to see a doctor, like small lacerations or medication needed for seasickness.

Between those hours, there seemed to be plenty of administration to take care of, new people to meet and calls to what had so far proved to be easily managed situations in cabins or public areas of the ship.

But now that Abby was teasing her, there was no getting away from the fact that she was not immune to Hugh Patterson's charms, however confident she was in being able to resist them. Not that she'd had to resist them, mind you. He was both charming, friendly and great to work with, but it was patently obvious that she was a curiosity to him and she knew why. She'd seen one of the type of women he was attracted to, for heaven's sake, and she couldn't be more different to the sophisticated, confident and sexy blonde that had accompanied him back to the port in Barcelona.

The woman that he'd been kissing with such...thoroughness...

Oh, no...there it was again. That tingle that she thought she had actually conquered over the last busy days. Distraction was needed.

Lisa opened her eyes and started tapping again.

How are things for you? Do you still like the hostel?

Love it. It's so much easier to be close to campus like this and the food's great. Miss you, though.

Miss you, too. Got a date for your driver's licence test yet?

Next week. And guess what?

What?

I'm going to try out for a wheelchair basketball team. I need some more exercise, what with all the great food in the canteens.
Hope that's not as dangerous as wheelchair rugby.

Lisa hit the "enter" button before she stopped to think that maybe Abby wouldn't appreciate the warning but it had always been difficult not to be overprotective of her little sister.

Sure enough, she could almost hear the sigh that came with Abby's response. And she obviously wasn't the only one who would prefer a distraction.

Stop being a mother hen. Tell me about where you are. Have you been on a shore excursion yet?

Not yet. My watch was on duty for the stops in both Corsica and Marseilles. Next stop is Nice, though—tomorrow—although we actually stop around the corner in Villefranche sur Mer because this ship is too big for the Nice port and we have to take small boats to get in to shore. We dock at dawn and then the ship doesn't sail until about ten o'clock at night and I'm just helping with the morning surgery hours so I've got most of the day and the evening to go sightseeing.

OMG…on the French Riviera? You're living the dream.

I know.

Lisa found an emoji with a huge grin.

I'll send photos but try not to get too jealous.

Don't send a photo unless it's you and that cute doctor alone in some romantic French café. Preferably drinking champagne.

LOL Lisa sent back.

Give it up, Abby. Not going to happen.

But, despite any firm intentions, it was what she was thinking about as she shut down her computer, climbed into bed a bit later and switched off her light. Champagne. Delicious food. An outdoor eatery, maybe shaded with grapevines. Someone playing a piano accordion nearby. And a companion who was only biding his time before taking the opportunity to kiss her senseless. Lisa could actually feel the tension of that anticipation. The curiosity. Desire…?

No. She pushed it away, rolling over to find a cool patch on her pillow. She'd certainly never found a kiss that lived up to that level of anticipation. It was the stuff of romance novels, not real life. It was just easier to toy with fantasy when she was temporarily "living the dream", as Abby had reminded her. Floating on the Mediterranean in a luxury cruise ship. Heading for land in a country that was famous for romance as much as anything else.

And there she was again…imagining being on the receiving side of a kiss like the one Hugh had been giving the gorgeous blonde. Not necessarily with Hugh, of course…just a kiss like that.

Oh…who was she kidding? It had to be Hugh, she realised as she was drifting into sleep. She'd never even seen anyone kissing like that in real life—she'd only read about it, or seen it on a movie screen. But this wasn't real life, exactly, was it? Lisa was already deeply into a very odd mix of real life and fantasy and the lines between the two were already a bit blurred. About to indulge herself by drifting further towards the fantasy side, it was a rude shock to hear the strident beeping of her pager. She snapped on her light and reached for the small device.

Code One, the pager read. Lido Deck.

Lisa was out of bed and hauling on her uniform in seconds. There was no time to even think about what her hair looked like. Her cabin was the closest to the medical centre. She had to go and grab the rapid response trolley and head for the deck that had the swimming pools. Hopefully, someone else from the team would join her quickly but, for the moment, she knew she was on her own.

Her heart skipped a beat and then sped up as she raced along the narrow corridor towards the medical centre. This was definitely real life and not any kind of fantasy and she was on the front line. Lisa had no idea if any of the other medical staff would also be responding to this call, even if Code One was the most urgent kind of summons. She might well be on her own until she found out whether the situation was really serious enough to warrant extra staff at this time of night.

It had to be well after midnight by the time Lisa had commandeered a service lift to get her to the Lido deck as quickly as possible. Heads turned as she raced past people wrapped up in blankets lying on deckchairs. It was a movie night where a huge screen had been lowered on the other side of the largest swimming pool, the deckchairs lined up in rows to accommodate the audience. Red and white striped bags of popcorn got spilled as a crew member in a white hat jumped out of Lisa's way. She passed restaurants that were still open and she could smell the variety of food on offer—from burgers to Indian meals.

There were people everywhere, laughing and having fun, even dancing in the area that Lisa was heading for where there was another pool and two spas, which made it feel quite bizarre to find a knot of crew members and others around a figure that was slumped against the side of one of the spa pools, wearing only a bathing suit.

Lisa could hear that the young man was having trouble breathing as she crouched down beside him, feeling for his pulse on his wrist. It was rapid and very faint, which suggested his blood pressure could be low.

'I'm Lisa,' she told him. 'One of the ship's nurses. Can you tell me your name?'

He opened his mouth but all she could hear was the harsh sounds of him trying to move air through obstructed passages.

'His name's Alex,' someone told her. 'We got him out of the pool because he started coughing and couldn't stop.'

'Are you asthmatic, Alex?' Lisa was pulling open drawers on the resus trolley. She needed to get some oxygen on her patient and probably a nebuliser to try and help him breathe.

'He's allergic.'

Lisa looked up at the young woman in a red bikini. 'To what?'

'Strawberries. He told me when he didn't want to try my strawberry daiquiri.'

'He said he had an adrenaline pen in his pocket,' A crew member added. 'But we haven't found where he left his clothes yet.'

'Okay…' Lisa slipped an oxygen mask over Alex's face. 'I'm going to give you an injection right now,' she told him.

Her own heart rate was well up as she located the drug she needed, filled the syringe and administered the intramuscular injection. An anaphylactic reaction could be a very satisfying emergency to treat if it responded rapidly to adrenaline and the frightening swelling in the airways began to settle, but it could also be a situation that could just as rapidly spiral into something worse—potentially life-threatening.

Waiting the few minutes to see if a repeat dose was needed gave Lisa a chance to take some vital signs and check Alex more thoroughly, and that was when she noted the diffuse, red rash that was appearing all over his body.

'You didn't drink the daiquiri, did you, Alex?'

He shook his head. He was holding the oxygen mask against his face and his eyes, above the mask, were terrified. Even through the plastic of the mask, Lisa could see that his lips were swelling.

'I kissed him.' The girl in the red bikini burst into tears. 'This is my fault, isn't it? He's not going to die, is he? You have to *do* something...'

She did. Nebulised adrenaline was the next step, along with a repeat dose of the drug by injection but, even if that started to make a difference, Lisa was going to need help and, as if she'd sent out a silent prayer, the figure that pushed through the group of spectators was the answer she would have wanted the most.

Hugh Patterson.

'Fill me in,' was all he said. 'I've got some crew bringing a stretcher.'

'Anaphylaxis to strawberries,' Lisa told him. 'Diffuse rash, hypotensive, tachycardic and respiratory obstruction with stridor—oxygen saturation currently eighty-eight percent. First dose of adrenaline was about three minutes ago but there's no improvement.'

'No worries.' His nod let Lisa know that he'd absorbed all the information and he knew how serious this was. His tone was still laidback enough not to alarm anyone else, however. 'Let's get another dose on board. And can you set up a nebuliser as well?'

Lisa drew up the medication as Hugh put a hand on their patient's shoulder. 'We've got this, okay? But we're going to take you down to our medical centre where we've got all the bells and whistles. I'm just going to pop an IV into your arm while we wait for your transport.'

Lisa knew her way around the trolley drawers by now so she was able to hand Hugh everything he needed before he had to ask. A tourniquet to wrap around Alex's upper arm, an alcohol wipe to clean the skin, a cannula to slip into a vein and then the Luer plug and dressing to secure the access. Lisa prepped the bag of saline by puncturing the port with the spike of the giving set and then running fluid through the tubes to eliminate any air bubbles. Hugh was attaching the line to the Luer plug as the crew members arrived with the stretcher and then helped lift Alex onto it.

'Carry that bag, please, Lisa. And squeeze it. We need to get that fluid in fast.'

They moved swiftly through an increasingly subdued crowd of people on the Lido deck, into the lift and then down to the deck they needed. Lisa was relieved that they would soon be in their well-equipped treatment room. She was even more relieved that she had Hugh by her side. They had just been working seamlessly, side by side, to stabilise this patient and she was sure that they would have things under control in no time.

'On my count,' Hugh said to the crew. 'Lift on three. One, two…*three*…'

Alex was being placed smoothly onto the bed as Lisa reached up to flick on the overhead operating theatre light and she caught her breath in a gasp of dismay as it went on. Alex's head had flopped to one side and his chin had dropped enough to close his airway completely. He had clearly lost consciousness.

Hugh heard her gasp and his gaze locked on hers— only for a heartbeat but it was enough for a very clear message to be shared. Their patient's condition had just become a whole lot worse. They were in trouble and Hugh was counting on Lisa's assistance. She could also see the determination not to lose this battle in those dark eyes.

Lisa tilted her head instantly in a nod to let Hugh know she had received the message. That she would do whatever she could to help. That she shared his determination to succeed. And then she took a very deep breath.

CHAPTER THREE

IT WAS VERY likely that other members of the medical staff on board were already making their way to help with a Code One emergency but the non-medical crew members who'd helped transport their patient were dispatched to make sure that Peter knew what was going on. In the meantime, the situation was escalating so quickly that Hugh and Lisa were the only people available to deal with it and they would have to work fast to save this young man's life.

The bag of IV fluid that Lisa had been squeezing to administer it more quickly was empty so she reached for a new one. Fluid resuscitation was an essential part of dealing with anaphylactic shock. As was oxygenation. As she worked to set up the new bag of saline she could see how smoothly Hugh was working to tilt Alex's head back to try and open his airway and then, using one hand, to shift his stethoscope over all lung fields to listen for air movement.

'He's still shifting some air but it's not enough.'

Lisa checked that the clip on Alex's finger was secure and looked at the screen of the monitor, below

the overly rapid spikes of the ECG. 'Oxygen saturation is down to seventy five percent,' she told Hugh.
The automatic blood pressure cuff was deflating at
the same time. 'His BPs dropping again. Seventy-five
over forty.'

'Come and take over here. We'll swap the nebuliser
mask and use an Ambu bag and a hundred percent oxygen. I'll get another IV line in and start an adrenaline
infusion. I'm not going to wait if things deteriorate any
more, though. We'll go for a rapid sequence intubation.'

Lisa could feel the fierce concentration when Hugh
took her place by Alex's head a minute or two later to
try and insert a breathing tube through the swollen tissues in their patient's mouth and throat. A lot of doctors
might have panicked when not only the first but the
second attempt failed. Hugh only looked more focused.
He caught Lisa's gaze as she moved back in with the
bag mask and tried to deliver oxygen to Alex's lungs.

'Oxygen saturation's down to seventy percent,' he
said quietly. 'We're in a "can't intubate, can't oxygen-
ate" situation. Have you ever assisted with a surgical
cricothyroidotomy?'

'No.' Lisa held his gaze. 'Do you want me to find
Tim? Or Peter?'

'There's no time.' Hugh hadn't broken the gaze either.
'You can do this. I'll talk you through it.'

And, within what felt like seconds, when they were
both gloved and Hugh had unrolled another kit, that
was exactly what he was doing as he palpated the front
of Alex's neck around his Adam's apple after swabbing
it with antiseptic.

'I can feel the thyroid cartilage here and this is the cricoid cartilage. I'm aiming for the space between them, where the membrane is, and I've got a good grip on it all so nothing moves.'

With his free hand, Hugh picked up a scalpel and made first a vertical incision and then a horizontal one. Because Alex was now deeply unconscious and this was such an urgent situation, there was no time or need for local anaesthesia but Lisa found herself holding her breath at Hugh's confident, swift movements.

'I can feel the "pop" so I know I'm in the trachea now.' Even his voice sounded calm. 'I'm going to put my finger in when I take the scalpel out but what I need you to do is pick up that tracheal hook, put it at the top end of the incision and retract everything for me.'

Lisa had never been this hands on in such a dramatic invasion procedure but, amazingly, her hand wasn't shaking and she had no problem following Hugh's clear instructions. She watched as he widened the incision, inserted a bougie as a guide for the endotracheal tube that followed and then inflated the balloon around the end of the tube that would help secure it. He attached the Ambu bag to the tube and squeezed it.

'Good chest rise,' he said quietly. 'I'll have a listen to be sure and then we can take that hook out and secure the tube properly.'

Lisa could tell that the tube had been correctly placed because the concentration of oxygen in Alex's blood was already increasing and his heart rate slowing a little. They had got through a crisis that could have killed an otherwise healthy young person and, when

Hugh looked up and smiled at Lisa, while he was still listening to lung sounds with his stethoscope, she knew that he was just as happy as she was.

They had done this together. She could hear other people arriving in the medical centre now, with rapid footsteps coming towards the treatment room, but it was Lisa and Hugh who had done the hard work here. They were the only ones to have shared that rising tension, background alarm of the ticking clock of a limited amount of time available and the nail-biting stress of a dramatic procedure to deal with it. So they were the only ones who got to share this moment of relief. Joy, even.

Along with something else. A knowledge that they could work together this closely under extreme circumstances. That they could trust each other. That they were in exactly the same place when it came to how much they cared about their patients and how hard they were prepared for a fight for something that really mattered. The moment of connection was only a heartbeat before others rushed into the room but the effect lingered as Lisa stepped back to let Peter and Tim close to their patient. It was Tim who was tasked with securing the tube and Peter assisted Hugh in setting up the portable ventilator.

'We'll need transport to the nearest hospital. He'll need intensive care monitoring for a while.'

'Chopper?'

'Possibly. We might be close enough to shore for a coastguard vessel. I'll get hold of the captain.'

'I can go with him, if he needs an escort,' Tim offered.

Hugh nodded his acknowledgment of the offer but his gaze shifted to Lisa, one eyebrow raised. Was he asking if she wanted that drama? Maybe he was even suggesting that they both go to look after the man who had been a patient they had both been so invested in saving. Suddenly, it felt like the connection they had just forged was strong enough to make Lisa feel flustered. Unsure of which way to jump and it was a well-practised habit to find a safe option as quickly as possible. Ignoring the unspoken invitation was a first step. Removing herself from the situation was the second.

'We'll need more details, won't we?' she said. 'I could go back up to the Lido deck where we found him. They might have found his clothes and his medication. He'll need something more than a swimming suit when they discharge him.'

'Good thinking, Lisa.' It was Peter who was nodding now. 'We can get Housekeeping to go to his cabin and pack a few things for him as well. I'll get someone to meet you.'

By the time Lisa got back to the medical centre with Alex's suitcase, she found the entire team were ready to escort their patient up to helipad at the very bow of the ship.

'None of us need to go with him.' Hugh had a clipboard in his hands and must have been working fast to have written up what looked like a very detailed report. 'They're sending an intensive care doctor and a paramedic to take him back.'

'Come and watch,' Janet said. 'It doesn't happen that

often and it's pretty exciting, especially in the middle of the night.'

'Does the ship have to stop?'

'It's already slowing down but I've seen them land even in fairly big seas when the ship is going fast. If it's too dangerous to land, they'll winch the patient up. They're amazing.'

It was an opportunity not to be missed. Lisa followed the entourage and waited with them to watch as the helicopter got close enough to glow in the flood-lit area of the helipad located right at the bow of the ship, overlooked by the bridge, as it hovered and very slowly sank until its skids were on the deck. Two of the French crew ducked their heads beneath the still whirring blades of the aircraft and came to meet Hugh, who was standing at the head of Alex's stretcher, holding the clipboard, raising his voice to give a verbal handover to the new health professionals in charge.

'Bonjour, messieurs. Voici Alex, qui a eu une réaction anaphylactique sévère...'

The fact that Hugh was doing the handover in French was not only astonishing, it completely took Lisa's breath away. That he was already such a charming and good-looking man had been quite enough to deal with in terms of being happy to keep herself at a safe distance. That he seemed to be at ease speaking what had to be the most beautiful language on earth took his attractiveness to another level and, on top of that, there was now that moment of connection they'd shared tonight that made Lisa think that the social planets they inhabited might not be that far apart after all.

Minutes later, she also had to wonder whether the butterflies that had taken over her stomach were due solely to the excitement of standing here as the helicopter lifted off and swung away right in front of her, the beat of its rotors vibrating right through her body. It was quite possible that these unfamiliar sensations had even more to do with the man who was standing right beside her.

It was no wonder that Lisa found it impossible to go back to bed and try to sleep after the tension and excitement of the last few hours. Even though it was nearly three a.m. she decided she needed to go and walk off the adrenaline or whatever it was that was still bubbling in her veins and making her brain race in an endless loop of reliving those fraught minutes of working to save Alex's life. The beat of fear when she'd believed she was facing the challenge alone. The relief when Hugh had arrived. That feeling of someone moving close enough to touch her soul when they'd shared the joy of success and, possibly the most disconcerting recurrent thought, how she'd felt when she'd heard him speaking French so fluently.

Yes…that very odd, melting sensation that was happening every time that part of the loop resurfaced was the best reason of all to go for a brisk walk and get some fresh air outside.

Lisa headed for the stairs that would take her to the deck she wanted that had a running track available. They were right beside a set of elevators and the doors on one slid open as she walked past. She heard the giggle of an obviously inebriated woman and she probably would have heard her voice even if she was halfway up the stairs.

'But you *are* coming to my cabin, aren't you, darling? You promised…'

'Yes, I did. And I will. Oops-a-daisy… I think you'd better hang on a bit more tightly…'

It was the sound of the male voice that made Lisa turn her head and slow her feet enough to count as a long pause. A deep, sexy voice with that note of muted amusement she was rather familiar with. She knew she was staring. She knew her mouth was gaping and she was probably looking as appalled as she was feeling.

For one long, horrified moment she held Hugh Patterson's gaze. And then she all but fled up the stairs because, quite honestly, she couldn't get away fast enough. Not that she had any intention of trying to analyse why she felt so…disappointed? Because she suspected that there might be a corner of her mind that could justifiably taunt her with the notion that she was jealous.

Oh…*man*…

It had been all too obvious what Lisa Phillips had been thinking when she'd seen him holding up that drunk woman in the lift. She probably wouldn't believe him if he told her that he'd found the woman rather too worse for wear when he'd gone back to the bar on the Lido deck to reassure the staff who'd been so worried about Alex, and he'd offered to make sure she got safely back to her own cabin. What was his nurse still doing up, anyway? He had the excuse of having been waiting for an update from the hospital that had taken their patient and then spending time with the staff on the Lido deck, but Lisa should have been in bed long before now.

As if he'd ever take advantage of an inebriated passenger. Or any passenger, for that matter. Okay, it was not unpleasant to have an endlessly changing number of beautiful women who were often remarkably uninhibited in advertising that they'd like to add to their holiday pleasures by including a dalliance with him but he very rarely had any desire to do more than a bit of harmless flirting.

He'd practically been a monk, for heaven's sake— apart from that first cruise when he'd been a passenger and not a crew member, of course, and when he'd needed a lot more than the on-board entertainment to distract himself from the betrayal of the woman he'd believed had loved him as much as he'd loved her. A woman he'd been on the verge of committing to for the rest of his life, in fact.

His friendship with Carlotta, in Barcelona, was the closest he'd come to in any kind of relationship since then and they both knew that it was no more than a friendship with occasional benefits.

It seemed a bit ironic that the first time he'd seen Lisa she'd been watching him kiss Carlotta and he'd been well aware that she'd been somewhat shocked. Well…she'd looked more than shocked when she'd seen him in the elevator tonight. She'd looked positively disgusted, and the worst thing about that was that a part of Hugh's brain could see himself through her eyes only too easily and…he had to admit, it looked shallow.

He looked like a pleasure-seeker with a job that might provide the occasional medical challenge, as tonight had done, but was mostly delivering a kind of private general practice, catering for an elite group of people who were wealthy enough to take luxury holidays. It was also a job that could obviously provide a playground for unlimited sexual adventures.

Hugh didn't like the thought that Lisa would think so little of him. But, then again, he didn't like the idea that she was judging him either. She knew nothing about why he was here or how much satisfaction this job could deliver on a regular basis. She was only here for a couple of weeks anyway, so why the hell should it matter *what* she thought?

But it seemed that it did. Having found a female crew member who had helped him get the passenger back to her cabin and taken over the responsibility of getting her into bed and checking on her later, Hugh didn't go straight back to his own cabin. He needed a bit of fresh air, he decided. A moment to take a breath and dismiss whatever unpleasant vibe that look on Lisa's face had left him with.

It was unfortunate that he chose that particular deck to go out onto. Or that his new colleague had still not retired to her cabin and was looking over the railing at the stern of the ship, watching the moonlight sparkle on the impressive foam of the wake stretching back into the inky darkness of the sea. It was even more unfortunate that, when she finally noticed him walking in her direction, she chose to try and make some sort of negative comment about his sexual prowess.

'That was quick,' she said. She sounded surprised but there was a smile tugging at the corners of her mouth, as if the idea of him being terrible in bed was somehow unexpected but amusing.

'Excuse me?' Hugh stopped. He took a breath, trying to put a lid on how defensive he was feeling, but the lid didn't quite fit. 'I take it that you're assuming I jumped into bed with the passenger you saw me with?'

'The invitation was obviously there.'

'And you think I would have been unable to resist? That I sleep with every woman who offers invitations for sex even if they're not sober or if it might jeopardise the position I hold here?'

Her gaze slid away from his. 'It's none of my business,' she said. At least she had the grace to sound uncomfortable. She might even be blushing, although it was hard to tell in this light, but Hugh wasn't about to let her off that lightly. For some inexplicable reason this mattered.

Maybe that was because he was feeling something other than defensive. Something like disappointment? Working with Lisa tonight and especially that moment when they'd both acknowledged how amazing it was to know that you'd saved someone's life had given Hugh a feeling of connection with a woman that was different from anything he'd ever experienced before.

A chink in his armour even, where he could feel what it must be like to be with someone you could really trust. Someone who could share the important things of life—for either celebration or encouragement to conquer. And maybe he had felt that way because he'd seen himself in a big brother role, which gave Lisa the status of family—someone it was safe to care about.

But she was judging him and his lifestyle now and any glimmer from that chink in his protective armour was nowhere to be seen. Lisa wasn't family. She was a stranger and, while she might be damned good at her job, she was uptight to the point of being a prude.

'At least I know how to relax occasionally and enjoy myself,' he heard himself saying. 'What's *your* problem, Lisa?'

'I haven't got one.'

She sounded as defensive as he had been feeling and Hugh could see that her hands were gripping the railing so tightly her knuckles were white. Was she *scared* of something? Hugh contemplated the ship's wake for a long moment and he could actually feel his negative thoughts getting washed away and disappearing into the night. There was something vulnerable about Lisa. She was the one who needed encouragement right now, even if she didn't realise it. He injected a teasing note into his voice as he turned to lean his back against the railing so he could watch Lisa's reaction.

'Are you a virgin?' he asked.

That shocked expression he'd seen on her face when she'd seen him propping up that passenger in the lift was back again.

'*No*... Of course I'm not.'

'But I'm guessing you don't like sex that much?'

Her breath came out in such an incredulous huff he could hear it over the hum of the engines and the sound of the churning water far below them.

'Just because I don't approve of jumping into bed with total strangers?' Her chin came up. 'I think sex is an important part of a relationship, if you must know. But I also happen to think there are more important things.'

'I'm not talking about a relationship.' Hugh was keeping his tone light. He was curious about how far down the list sex would come on the list of important things in a relationship for her but that could wait for another conversation. Right now, all he wanted to find out was just how tightly this woman kept herself under control.

'I'm just talking about sex,' he added. 'Enjoying a physical activity. Like dancing.' This seemed inspired. Did Lisa ever let herself go enough to dance? 'Do you dance?'

'No.' Lisa was resolutely keeping her gaze on the endless wake, although he had the feeling that she knew how closely he was watching her.

Hugh could feel a frown line appearing between his eyebrows as he leaned a little closer so that he could lower his voice. 'What about eating some amazing meal? Or drinking champagne? Do you like drinking champagne, Lisa?'

She shrugged. 'I've never tasted real champagne.'

Wow…she'd never tasted a lot of things, it seemed. Hugh's annoyance had long since vanished. He was watching Lisa's profile—the way the wind was playing with that short tumble of waves, the freckles he could see dusting her pale cheeks and that delicious curve at the corners of her mouth that looked like an embryonic smile, even though she was clearly not that happy at the moment.

Hugh leaned even closer. So close he could feel the tickle of a windblown lock of hair touch his forehead.

'What *do* you enjoy, then?' he asked.

He hadn't really intended to use his best flirtatious tone that he knew women loved. He hadn't actually intended to be this close to Lisa and he certainly hadn't expected the punch in his gut when she turned her head slowly and he found himself so very close to those remarkable eyes. They were a very dark shade of golden brown right now, with the pupils dilating rapidly towards that intriguing dark rim.

Hugh knew exactly what that punch in his gut was telling him. He also knew by Lisa's reaction that she was experiencing the same thing. Whether or not she was prepared to acknowledge that shaft of desire was quite another matter and Hugh knew he should move before she even had the time to think about it. He should step back, say something about it being far too late to be out and about and escape before this odd moment turned into something they might both regret.

Except he left it a split second too late. Just long enough for his gaze to catch something other than the expression in Lisa's eyes. He could see the way her lips were parting... The way the tip of her tongue appeared to touch her bottom lip. It was mesmerising, that's what it was. Hugh was unaware of any movement from either of them but their faces were even closer now. Close enough for their noses to touch as his mouth hovered above hers.

And then their lips touched. So lightly it was no more than a feather-light brush—not dissimilar to the touch of the wind that Hugh could feel caressing the bare skin on his arms and neck as he bent his head. A scrape of a touch that was also similar to a match being struck and it certainly created a flame. It was impossible not to repeat the action and, this time, Hugh could feel the response.

He might have expected Lisa to be shocked. He was shocked himself, to be honest, but it seemed that even that gentlest of touches contained something far too powerful to be resisted. On both sides. There was nothing for it but to *really* kiss her, Hugh decided as he covered her lips with his own and began a conversation that he might have had a thousand times already in his life but he'd never found one quite like this.

Ever…

Oh…dear Lord…

She'd wondered what it might be like to be kissed by this man from the moment she'd first clapped eyes on him kissing another woman. She'd imagined how it might feel. She'd even dreamt about it but she'd had *no* idea, had she?

It wasn't the first time she'd been kissed by any means but it *felt* like it was.

Who knew that there were such infinite variations in pressure and movement that a kiss could feel like listening to the most amazing music with its different notes and rhythms? That closing your eyes would only intensify other senses and there'd never been anything that tasted like Hugh's mouth and that the silky glide of his tongue against hers would trigger a sensation that felt like the inside of her whole body was melting...

She could feel the absolute control that Hugh had but she could sense the strength behind it and she wanted more. So much more. If a kiss with this man could be like this, what would sex be like?

Any judgement she might have had about people on cruise ships who were intent on finding as much pleasure as possible in the shortest amount of time were disappearing—getting buried under the weight of curiosity. No...make that a kind of desire that Lisa had never, ever experienced before. Hugh hadn't been that far off the mark, had he, when he'd suggested that she didn't like sex that much? She'd never been kissed like this, though. Or felt desire that was more like a desperate need to discover something she might otherwise miss out on for the rest of her life.

It was a subtle change in the engine noise beneath them that finally broke that kiss. Or perhaps it was a need for more oxygen because Lisa knew she was breathing far more rapidly than normal as they pulled apart. Her lips were still parted as well, and her eyes drifted open to find her gaze locking onto Hugh's.

His smile grew slowly. 'I take it back,' he said.

'Take what back?' The thought that he was already regretting that kiss was like a shower of cold water in her face.

'Thinking you were so uptight,' Hugh said. 'Where did you learn to kiss like that, Lisa Phillips?'

She couldn't say anything. Because she'd have to admit that she'd never learned to kiss like that until he'd taught her? Or because she was processing the fact that he'd considered her to be uptight? Lisa could feel herself taking a step back to create some more distance between them.

Was Hugh laughing at her? She couldn't let him know that that kiss had, quite possibly, been life-changing for her when it was probably no more than an everyday occurrence for Hugh. He'd think she was immature as well as uptight, wouldn't he? Had he just been amusing himself all along by kissing her in the first place? Or…and it was a horrible thought…had she been the one who had initiated that kiss? Lisa could feel her cheeks reddening in one of her hated blushes so she turned away so that she could catch the breeze on her face.

'We're slowing down.' Hugh broke a silence that was on the verge of becoming really awkward moments later as the engine noise dropped another note. 'We can't be that far away from docking. I expect we'll have a busy clinic in the morning. When most of the passengers have gone ashore, it gives a lot of the crew a chance to visit us.'

He was talking like her boss, which prompted Lisa to shift her gaze to catch his again. Was he dismissing that kiss as something that shouldn't have happened between people who had to work together? Or was he warning her that it couldn't go any further? It was more like there was a question to be seen in his eyes than a warning, however. Maybe he was wondering if he should say something about that kiss? Or was he waiting for an indication from her that she'd enjoyed it as much as he had? That she wasn't that "uptight" after all?

Well…she didn't have to prove anything. And she didn't want to talk about it either—certainly not with someone who thought sex was just something to enjoy as a physical activity, like dancing or drinking champagne. She'd already let Hugh know how much she disapproved of people who simply jumped into bed with each other for no other reason than giving in to lust.

Okay, she might have just gained a disturbing new insight into how it could easily happen but, now that she'd had a moment to catch her breath, she could remember that she wasn't that type of person herself. That she knew it was dangerous to break rules or step too far outside the boundaries of what you knew was the right thing to do. The safe thing.

Maybe what Hugh was really asking was if she'd like to pretend the kiss had never happened. Or that it was no big deal—which it obviously wasn't for someone like Hugh. It was the first thing she'd ever seen him doing, after all. Perhaps he'd mentioned work because it was a safer topic and a place where they had discovered a professional connection and that was absolutely something Lisa could use as a life raft when her head was such a whirlpool of jumbled sensations and emotions she was in danger of drowning. She grabbed hold of it.

'And it's late,' she added briskly, turning away. 'Don't know about you but I need some sleep before I turn up for work. See you in the morning, Hugh.'

CHAPTER FOUR

HOW THE HELL had that happened, exactly?

Okay, he'd been pushing her a bit after being irritated by that unimpressed comment that he had interpreted as judgement on his performance in bed. Deliberately being in her personal space as well as he'd prodded that barrier Lisa seemed to have between herself and the good things in life, but he'd certainly never expected it to end in a kiss. He hadn't even been attracted to her, given that she was so not his type. Was that what had made that kiss seem so different? Why it had haunted his dreams in the few snatched hours of sleep he'd managed later and why it was still lurking in the perimeter of his consciousness this morning?

Hugh arrived early at the medical centre, despite his lack of sleep, but moving around his familiar environment as he checked that everything had been thoroughly cleaned and restocked in the wake of managing their dramatic case of Alex's respiratory arrest due to anaphylaxis in the early hours of this morning, he was aware of an unfamiliar tension.

He might not understand how that kiss had hap-

pened exactly but there was no getting away from the
fact that it *had* happened and now it felt like it was
going to be more than a little awkward working with
Lisa. Most women he knew would be happy to either
dismiss that kiss as fun but naughty, given they had to
work together, or to enjoy a bit of sexual tension and
have fun playing with it for a while. But Lisa wasn't
like any of the women he knew and Hugh wasn't confident he would know how to respond to a different,
less relaxed reaction.

Sure enough, when she arrived a few minutes before
morning surgery was due to begin, she avoided any direct eye contact with him when he gave her a friendly
greeting and said that he hoped she'd had enough sleep,
given her extended working hours last night.

She merely nodded, still not meeting his gaze as
she reached for a stethoscope to hook around her neck.
'Shall I set up in the second consulting room to do the
initial obs?'

'Yes, please.' So she was going to pretend the kiss
had never happened? That was a bit "head in the sand",
but he could go along with that. And it was always
useful to get an idea of what a patient was presenting with, along with baseline observations that let him
know whether they had any signs of infection like a
fever or any problems with their blood pressure or heart
rhythm. A competent nurse could also deal with minor
stuff herself, like dressing a burn or closing a small
laceration with sticky strips or glue.

It was a walk-in clinic that didn't require appointments and the knowledge, based on experience, that

they might be very busy for the next couple of hours should have been enough to focus Hugh's attention completely on his job.

Except it wasn't quite enough. He was watching Lisa from the corner of his eye as she moved swiftly around the medical centre for the next few minutes, collecting supplies like the plastic sheaths for the tip of the tympanic thermometer, a new roll of graph paper for the ECG monitor and dressing supplies and antiseptic ointments that might be needed to deal with minor injuries that didn't need a doctor's attention. How hard was she finding it to pretend that the kiss hadn't happened?

Was she thinking about it as much as he was? Those unwanted flashes of memory that were strong enough to interfere with anything else he might be trying to focus on? Did she have the same, disturbing idea that it could be tempting to do it again or was she avoiding even looking at him directly because she really was wishing it had never happened in the first place?

He found himself listening in from the treatment room as he made sure the electronic equipment like the X-ray machine was turned on and ready for use, when Janet arrived to help with the surgery by manning the reception area and triaging to get the most important cases seen first.

'Tim's been telling me about all the excitement last night. Can't believe something like that happened when I'm not even on call.'

'It was a memorable night, that's for sure. Possibly a once-in-a-lifetime experience.'

Hugh flicked another switch to turn the steriliser on. Was Lisa making a reference to the case...or the kiss? Not that it mattered, because maybe he agreed with her—on both counts.

'You could be right. I've never seen a cricothyroid-otomy done on land, let alone at sea.'

'I'd never seen one done either and I've worked in ED a lot. It was amazing. *Hugh* was amazing. He saved that guy's life...'

'*We* saved that guy's life.' Hugh couldn't eavesdrop any more when he was the subject of the conversation.

Perhaps it was because she was startled by his sudden appearance or the genuine compliment he was offering that Lisa finally looked at him properly and something in Hugh's gut did an odd little flip as her gaze met his. The last time he'd seen those eyes had been very close up indeed...

'Lisa was first on the scene,' he added, 'and I couldn't have handled his airway later without her excellent assistance.'

'So he actually arrested?' Janet was open-mouthed.

'Close enough. His oxygen saturation got down to below seventy percent at one stage and he was unconscious.'

'Wow...'

'Have you had any update on his condition?'

Lisa shifted her gaze swiftly as he looked back to answer her question. The way she was biting her lower lip was another sign that she was finding any interaction between them awkward this morning and that had the effect of making whatever that was in Hugh's gut flip back the other way. Yep…this was awkward all right and Hugh was aware of a beat of another, unfamiliar emotion.

Guilt? He'd imagined himself in a big brother kind of role with Lisa, hadn't he? Well…nobody would trust him to take on that kind of role again, would they? Had he really asked her if she was a virgin? And suggested that maybe she didn't like sex? How insulting had that been? Plus, he'd told her how uptight he'd thought she was as well and that had been an unkind thing to say. No wonder Lisa had backed off so fast. She probably wasn't looking forward to working with him at all and he couldn't blame her.

'Alex is fine,' he said aloud. 'They monitored him in Intensive Care for the rest of the night but everything had settled by the time I spoke to someone an hour or so ago. They're going to patch up his neck, give him a course of steroids for a couple of days and have advised him to wear a medic alert bracelet and make sure he has his auto-injector within reach at all times. He should be back on board before we sail this evening.'

A late sailing, Hugh remembered, turning to head into his consulting room as Janet moved to open the doors to their first patients. And after this morning's surgery he had the day to himself in one of his favourite parts of the world, which was just what he needed. A chance to relax and soak up some of the very best things in life. The kind of things that Lisa didn't seem to be at all familiar with. That he'd thought he could help her discover. Maybe he could try and step back into that helpful role.

He turned back. 'What are you going to do with your first onshore leave, Lisa?'

If nothing else, he could provide some recommendations for things she could see or do and that might get them past this awkwardness.

'I'm not sure.' Lisa's gaze skittered away from his again. 'One of the team on the excursions desk told me about a walk that was lovely around the Cap d'Antibes but what I'd really love to see is one of the medieval towns.'

'Get up to Eze, if you can. It's an outstanding example of a medieval village. Or St Paul de Vence, although that could still be pretty crowded on a lovely day like this. It's a shame we won't finish in time for you to tag along with one of the organised bus tours. They're always keen to have someone from our team available as medical cover but a taxi probably wouldn't be too expensive. Less than fifty euros, probably.'

The expression on Lisa's face suggested that their ideas of what wasn't too expensive were poles apart. She was the one to turn away this time but he caught the hint of smile that felt like an acknowledgement of his effort to restore their working relationship to its former amicability. Not that it seemed to have worked particularly well.

'I expect I'll just take a walk around Villefranche sur Mer from where the tender boat drops us,' she said. 'Or I can find the bus that goes into Nice. I'll explore the old town and then find somewhere lovely for a late lunch. I'm sure it will be gorgeous.'

* * *

Oh…*help*…

The first time Lisa had been in this reception area and had realised that she was going to be working with Hugh, she hadn't been able to dismiss the memory of having seen him kissing that leggy blonde woman.

Now she was totally unable to dismiss the memory of having been kissed herself. And it was so much more than merely a thought. She could actually *feel* it happening again. The soft press of his lips on hers. The taste of his mouth. The fierce lick of desire that sent an electric buzz to every cell in her body and made her knees feel distinctly weak.

Biting her bottom lip hard enough to hurt helped. So did avoiding any more than a split second of eye contact. Even better was being able to focus on the patients that started arriving within the next few minutes. Hugh had been right—they were in for a very busy few hours and, best of all, there was plenty for Lisa to do in her consulting room and she wasn't being asked to assist Hugh in any way.

An hour in and she was starting to feel a lot more confident that they could continue working together without the awkwardness of that kiss hanging in the air between them. A purely professional exchange presented no problems at all after the first couple.

'This is Elaine.' Lisa handed the clipboard to Hugh as she took her tenth patient into his consulting room. 'She's running a fever of thirty-nine point six, has frequency and pain on urination and the dipstick test was positive for blood in her urine.'

It would be a quick consult for Hugh to double check the history and any other health issues that Elaine had and then prescribe the antibiotics and other medications to ease the discomfort of a urinary tract infection for their patient.

Jeff, the next patient, only needed a certificate to be signed by Hugh to give him a day away from his job as a kitchen hand.

'It's a second degree burn but the blisters are still intact,' Lisa told him. 'I've cleaned it, put antibiotic cream on and a non-stick gauze dressing and I've told Jeff to come back tomorrow for a dressing change so that I can make sure it's not infected. If it's looking okay, I think he'll be able to work as long as he wears gloves and keeps it dry.'

Hugh scrawled his signature on the certificate. 'How's the waiting room looking?'

'Still quite full. I've got someone with chest pain to do an ECG on now, but he's a dancer in one of the cabaret acts and I suspect he's pulled a muscle.'

'It should start to slow down soon.' Hugh handed back the piece of paper and smiled at Lisa. 'You're doing a great job,' he told her. 'Thanks…'

She tucked the praise away as she went back to Jeff to give him his final instructions on how to look after his burn injury today and sort out an appointment for a dressing change tomorrow morning. Hugh's words made her feel good, she decided, but they hadn't undermined the relief of stepping back into the purely professional interactions between herself and her boss. If anything, they were giving what had happened in the early hours of today a dreamlike quality—as if that kiss couldn't possibly have happened for real.

The final patient that came in turned out to be the real test of whether things were back to normal. A tall, brusque Scotsman in his fifties, he was reluctant to admit to having anything wrong.

'But if it gets any worse, I'm not going to be able to do any more of these tours, Nurse,' he said as he limped from the waiting room. 'I can barely put any weight on my foot now.'

His anxious wife was by his side. 'We're supposed to be doing a tour of St Jean Cap Ferrat that includes lunch at that amazing hotel that was in a movie we saw recently. The *Abolutely Fabulous* one? It would be such a shame to miss out.'

Lisa had a look at the sole of the man's foot. He had a reddened area just below his middle toes that could be a deep blister.

'Let me just run a couple of checks and then we'll get the doctor to have a look.' Lisa wrapped a blood pressure cuff around his arm. 'You haven't been doing a lot of walking in a new pair of shoes, have you? Going barefoot more than usual? Could you have had an injury that you might not have taken much notice of, like a stone bruise?'

She went in with her patient to give handover to Hugh a few minutes later. 'This is Gordon,' she told him. 'He's presenting with nine out of ten pain when he tries to put any weight on the ball of his left foot. Vital signs are all normal. He had an injury two weeks ago when he was replacing boards on his deck and fell through a rotten part but he was treated in his local ED and discharged.'

'Oh? What did they do for treatment?'

'Cleaned out a small cut but it wasn't anything to worry about.' Gordon shook his head, dismissing the incident. 'They X-rayed my foot, too, in case I'd broken something but they said it all looked fine. They gave me a tetanus shot and some antibiotics.'

'And it's only started to get painful again now?'

'It's been sore ever since.' It was Gordon's wife who spoke. 'He's just been putting a brave face on it but when he got up this morning it was suddenly a whole lot worse. He almost fell over.'

Lisa had been about to leave Hugh to deal with his patient and go and finish up her own paperwork but he caught her gaze.

'Could you set up the treatment room for us, please?' he asked. 'I think we'll have a look with the ultrasound.'

'Why would you want to do that?' Gordon's wife echoed Lisa's first thought. 'I thought ultrasounds were just for when you were pregnant.'

Lisa had seen that kind of smile on Hugh's face many times already but this time she noticed the crinkles around his eyes as well. It wasn't that he was making fun of a layperson's lack of medical knowledge in any way. This smile held understanding rather than amusement and it was also reassuring. Lisa knew that the people in front of him would be confident that he cared about them. That he was doing what he believed might help.

'There are some things that don't show up on X-rays,' he told them. 'It could be that there's something in your foot, like a piece of glass or a splinter.'

Sure enough, there was something to be seen on the screen as Hugh gently examined Gordon's foot.

'The entry wound's healed over now,' Hugh warned. 'We'll need to do a bit of minor surgery to open it up and see what we can find. Are you happy for us to do that or would you like a referral to an emergency department of a local hospital?'

'I'd rather you did it, Doc. That way we can get it over with and we might make our posh lunch after all.'

'Oh…' His wife didn't look so happy. 'I can't watch. Not if there's going to be blood…'

Hugh's smile reappeared. 'Don't worry,' he said. 'We'll get Janet to make you a nice cup of tea while you wait. Lisa and I have got this covered. We're the A team, aren't we?'

Reopening a wound to explore it for the presence of a foreign body was a walk in the park compared to making an opening in someone's neck to establish an emergency airway. Lisa found herself smiling back at Hugh in total agreement. They most definitely did have this covered and it could prove to be a very satisfying end to their morning clinic. Even better, it seemed that the awkwardness had finally evaporated.

This was fun.

Minor surgery was an unexpected finale to an ordinary clinic but Hugh really was enjoying himself. He'd already known that Lisa was someone that he could rely on in a tense, emergency situation but this time he could relax and appreciate her skilled assistance even more. As he filled a syringe with local anaesthetic, he watched her setting up everything he could need on a tray and then swabbing the skin of Gordon's foot and arranging sterile drapes to protect the area.

'This is going to hurt, isn't it?' Gordon's stoic expression slipped a little.

'Not once the local is doing its job,' Hugh assured him. 'Bit of a sting just to start with. Lisa, can you hold Gordon's foot steady, please?

It wasn't the easiest area of the body to be working on and it was frustrating to be able to feel the tip of whatever it was embedded in his patient's foot but be unable to grasp it firmly enough to extract it. Hugh could feel Lisa watching him as he pressed a little deeper into the wound and opened the forceps a little wider. Then he took a grip and held it and this time he could feel something shift. The dark object slowly came out through the skin and just kept coming. With a silent whistle of how impressed he was, Hugh held up an enormous triangular splinter between the teeth of the forceps.

'Look at that.'

He didn't need to tell Lisa to look. She was staring in disbelief that anyone could have been walking around with something that size buried in their foot. Her gaze only had to shift a fraction to catch Hugh's, given that he was watching her reaction, and he wasn't disappointed. Her astonishment morphed into delight. Or maybe it was just professional satisfaction but it didn't matter because just watching the change was a joy. The note of connection might pale in comparison to the satisfaction they'd shared in getting a secure airway into Alex last night but this was significant in its own way because it felt like that awkwardness between himself and Lisa had gone.

She certainly sounded happier. 'You're not going to believe how big this splinter is,' she told Gordon. 'You've been walking around with a log in your foot.'

Hugh showed their patient what he'd pulled out and Gordon grinned. 'That's a piece of my deck, that is. No wonder it was a wee bit sore.'

'I'm going to clean out the wound thoroughly now,' Hugh told him, 'and then we'll get you patched up and bandaged. You might want to keep the weight off your foot as much as you can today but there's no reason you can't go and enjoy your lunch.'

As he intended to enjoy his own. It was nearly two p.m. by the time Hugh had taken one of the tender shuttles to get into the port of Villefranche sur Mer and he was delighted to find that his arrangements for the afternoon were in place. He picked up the keys to the classic car he'd hired, and when the powerful engine of the gunmetal-grey nineteen-sixties E-type Jaguar purred into life a short time later he just smiled and listened to it for a moment, before pulling onto the road.

It was a sparkling blue day with that soft light and warmth that he loved about the French Riviera. He was going to put the roof of this convertible down and drive up towards the mountains and one of his most favourite restaurants ever. He might even indulge in a glass of the best champagne they had on ice.

Lisa Phillips had never tasted champagne…

The thought came from nowhere but with an intensity that let him imagine exactly what she might look like when she did taste it for the first time. He would see that surprise in her eyes and be able to watch it shift and grow and light up her whole face with the pleasure of something new and delicious. Kind of like the way he'd seen her satisfaction with her work but better somehow. More like what he'd seen in her eyes after that kiss? Until he'd ruined the moment by telling her how uptight she was.

Why had he done that? It was almost as if he'd been trying to push her away as a form of self-protection but that was ridiculous. Even if Lisa had been completely his type of woman, he had absolute control over how involved he ever got with anyone. He wasn't about to make the mistake of falling in love again.

But, hey…maybe he could bring a bottle of champagne back with him as a way of making up for being a bit of a jerk.

Or…

Maybe there was a way he could not only make it up to Lisa but reassure himself just how in control of his own feelings he was.

He was moving slowly down the street now, towards a new group of people who'd just been ferried from the cruise ship by the tender. Heads were turning to admire the car he was driving but he was focused only on the solitary figure amongst them. Lisa was wearing a pale yellow T-shirt, jeans that were rolled up to mid-calf, and sensible-looking shoes on her feet that would be just right for a lot of walking as she explored the medieval centres of either Villefranche or Nice. She was clutching her shoulder bag as if she expected a pickpocket was already following her and, as Hugh got closer, he saw her pause and look around. He could even see the way she was taking a deep breath as if she might be a little overwhelmed by the prospect of a solo adventure but he could sense her determination as well. She was going to make the most of whatever new experiences were in store for her in the next few hours.

His foot pressed on the brake as he made the decision to go with that flash of inspiration he'd just had. The car was right in front of Lisa as he stopped, and Hugh leaned across the empty passenger seat to open the door. Then he put on what he hoped was his most charming smile.

'Perfect timing,' he said. 'Hop in.'

He couldn't see the expression in her eyes because she was wearing sunglasses but he knew it would be surprised. Possibly shocked. Definitely hesitant.

'You won't regret it.' He caught his own sunglasses, pulling them down enough that she could see his eyes. 'I promise…'

CHAPTER FIVE

LISA OPENED HER mouth to say, *Thanks, but, no thanks.*

Getting back to a working relationship that wasn't full of lingering tension had been hard enough in a professional environment where there'd been any amount of distraction. Spending time with Hugh when he was looking like some celebrity about to do a photo shoot with a vintage sports car would take her right back to square one when she'd just been kissed senseless and hadn't known which way was up.

The words didn't emerge from her mouth, however, because another thought occurred in the same instant. Maybe spending time with Hugh could do the opposite and reassure her that she wasn't someone who ever lost total control. There seemed to be a tacit agreement between them that they were both going to pretend that kiss had never happened after all.

Or…and it was quite hard to silence that naughty whisper in the back of her mind that was wondering if accepting this invitation might actually lead to another one of those extraordinary kisses. Trying to stifle that whisper made Lisa take hold of the open door of the car, ready to push it shut. It would be far less stressful to go exploring on her own.

But now Lisa could actually hear Abby's voice in her ear. And see an imaginary message that could be her sister's response to news of what her day out had involved.

You went driving around on the French Riviera in a vintage sports car with the roof down? With that gorgeous man driving? That's more like it, Lise... Live the dream...and remember...don't send me a photo unless you're with him in some romantic French café. Preferably drinking champagne...

She'd want to know about every detail and it would make her so happy. It might even go a long way towards finally erasing some of that guilt that Abby could never quite let go of—that she had somehow held Lisa back from doing what she really wanted to do in life.

It wouldn't hurt to live the dream just for an afternoon. As a bonus it would give her enough to tell Abby about that her sister wouldn't be able to pick up that Lisa was keeping something to herself as she had no intention to confessing anything about that kiss. Or letting it happen again, despite that whisper. She was in control. She'd learned very early in life to stay in control and not be seduced by anything because that was where danger lay.

If she hadn't stopped to gaze dreamily at that doll in the toyshop window that day, she would have been holding onto Abby's hand far more tightly. The toddler would never have been able to pull away with a gleeful chuckle and run straight onto the road...

Lisa had tested her resolve to stay in control countless times since then. This might be another test for her, but it was nothing more than a friendly gesture on Hugh's part because, clearly, he'd already dismissed as unimportant what had led to their awkwardness this morning. Or maybe it was even an apology that it had happened in the first place? If Lisa declined the offer, that awkwardness might be there again the next time they had to work together and she didn't want that to happen. The hand Lisa had been about to use to push the door of this extraordinary car shut pulled it further open instead and she settled herself onto the smooth, red leather of the passenger seat.

'Hold on to your hat,' Hugh told her. 'You're about to get blown away.'

He wasn't wrong. Lisa was blown away by far more than the wind in her hair. It seemed that Hugh knew these mountains and their villages like the back of his hand and Lisa was whisked from one amazing view to another until they finally stopped, hours later, in a walled, medieval town that sat high on a hilltop with what looked like a view of the entire Côte d'Azur. Ancient stone walls gave way to rippling acres of forest and, in the misty distance, the deep, deep blue of the Mediterranean. The same stone was underfoot on the terrace of the restaurant Hugh took her to. Vines scrambled overhead to provide shade and frame the view from what had to be the best table available. Lisa shook her head.

'So, is this what usually happens when you rock up in a car like this? You get the corner table with the best view? Even if you're with someone who's wearing jeans and whose hair must look like a complete bird's nest after being out in the wind like that?'

Hugh just laughed. 'You look great,' he told her. 'This is a very relaxed place and they only care about providing the best food and wine. Plus...' He winked at Lisa. 'I booked this particular table. I've been here before. Several times.'

Lisa could believe that. She could also believe that he hadn't been here alone on his past visits and, without warning, she was aware of a beat of something that felt like...envy? Jealousy, even?

No. How ridiculous was that? She was only here as a colleague of Hugh's but, even if she had been here in a far more intimate capacity as his date, it would be stupid to feel jealous of other women in this man's life. There must have been dozens of them in the past and there would no doubt be dozens more in the future because Hugh obviously liked to play hard. He loved dining out and dancing. Champagne and...sex...

Oh, *help*...

Lisa could feel her cheeks heating up. Looking around for a distraction—any distraction—she found herself watching the maître d' of the restaurant approaching with a white cloth over his arm, a bottle in one hand and two fluted glasses in the other. A waiter was following with an ice bucket.

A short time later, Lisa found herself holding her very first glass of real French champagne.

'Chin-chin.' Hugh held up his glass. He took a sip of the wine but he was watching Lisa over the rim of the glass. Waiting to see her reaction?

She closed her eyes as the bubbles seemed to explode on her tongue and then almost evaporate before she could swallow the icy liquid. As her eyes flew open in astonishment she saw amusement dancing in Hugh's steady gaze.

'I knew you'd look like that,' he murmured. 'Tastes nice, doesn't it?'

'Unbelievable.' Lisa took another sip and then she had to reach into her bag for her phone. 'Sorry,' she muttered. 'I hate it when people take photos of what they're eating or drinking but Abby's not going to believe this without some proof.'

It was exactly the photo she'd requested, wasn't it? The romantic café. The "cute doctor". The champagne.

'Abby?'

'My sister. Well, she's my half-sister, actually, but we're…um…really close. And I know how much she would love this place.'

'You'll have to come back one day, then, now that you know where it is. You can bring your sister.'

How amazing would that be? Lisa would give anything for Abby to have the joy she'd had today of cruising mountain roads in a spectacular car, exploring cobbled streets and vibrant marketplaces and cooling off in the shadows of an ancient cathedral or two. How much harder would it be to do that in a wheelchair, though? Lisa had to blink to clear the sting at the back of her eyes as she took a photo of the frosty flute beside the bottle of what she suspected was a very expensive—probably vintage—champagne. Hugh had already told her, politely but firmly, as they'd come into the restaurant that she was here at his invitation and that this was his treat and he would be highly offended if she offered to pay for any of it.

'Let me take one of you with the glass in your hand.' Hugh reached for her phone and Lisa blinked again, held her glass up as if she was toasting Abby and sent a silent message to her sister.

Here I am... Living the dream...

At least it would be easy to convince her sister that she wasn't on a date with Hugh. Who would go out on a date in a T-shirt and jeans?

She needed to take a picture of the view as well. She didn't let embarrassment stop her taking some of their food either. She wanted to capture every detail for Abby, including the beautifully presented salad Niçoise she had ordered, the steam rising from the ramekin of the boeuf bourguignon that had been Hugh's choice—even the basket piled with sliced baguette.

'So...' Hugh filled Lisa's glass again when he had mopped up the last of his sauce with torn pieces of the crusty bread. 'Tell me about your sister. She must be younger than you, yes?'

'What makes you say that?'

'Well...you're so well organised and you like being in charge.' The corner of Hugh's mouth twitched, as though he was supressing a smile. 'I can imagine you being a bossy big sister.'

Was it a magical side-effect of champagne that made that sound like a compliment? Or maybe it was Hugh's smile.

'I'm six years older,' she admitted. 'It was the perfect age to get a baby sister to help look after and…'

'And?' The prompt from Hugh fell into a sudden silence.

Lisa almost told him. That she'd had to take sole responsibility for Abby on so many occasions that it was like she had been another mother for that tiny baby. That she hadn't done a very good job of it either, because it was her fault that Abby was now facing challenges that would mean it would be so much more difficult for her to end up in a place like this. In a mountain village in France. Drinking real champagne…

She took another mouthful.

'And I love her to bits,' she added quietly. 'I'm missing her and I'm worried about her, to be honest.'

'Why?'

'We've been living together for her whole life but she's just moved into a university hostel and I know that she's going to be fine and that she can cope perfectly well without me. She's amazing, in fact, so I have to get over worrying about her but…'

But Hugh was frowning. 'If Abby's six years younger than you, that makes her…what…about twenty-four?' His gaze was focused intently on Lisa and she could almost see his clever brain putting pieces of a puzzle together. 'Is she…okay?'

'She got badly injured being hit by a car when she was nearly two.' There was no need to tell Hugh that it had been her fault and she'd never stop hating herself for that moment of carelessness. 'She's been in a wheelchair ever since,' she added. 'And she's always needed me. We went to live with our grandmother when Mum died a couple of years later.' Again, Lisa held back on the more sordid detail that her mother's death had been due to an overdose. 'Gran had some health issues of her own so she couldn't really manage the kind of round-the-clock care Abby needed. We always had some help but I did as much as possible myself.' Lisa took a deep breath and reached for her glass of wine again.

'Sorry... I don't usually talk about this stuff. I guess I'm missing Abby because this is the longest time we've ever been apart.' She found a smile. 'I only took this job because she talked me into it. She thought it all sounded very romantic and that it was time I had some fun.'

'And are you?' Hugh was watching her again. 'Having fun?'

Lisa couldn't read his expression but it seemed... serious. Not in that focused, professional kind of way when they were working together. Not in that flirting kind of way, like the first time he'd ever looked at her, and it was definitely not in that intense *I'm about to kiss you* kind of way. This was...just different. A new side of Hugh.

'You don't really think about "having fun", do you?' he added quietly. 'I think that maybe you've always been too busy worrying about and looking after other people to worry about yourself.'

It was a look of respect, that's what it was. Understanding, perhaps, of how much Lisa had sacrificed along the way, from the small things like not going to play with friends after school because she'd needed to get home and help look after her little sister to being excused from school trips that would take her away from home and even her career choice, because if she'd wanted to follow her first dream to become a doctor she would have had to go away to medical school. Nursing training had been available in her own city.

That Hugh might get how hard some of those decisions had been and respect her for making them made Lisa suddenly feel an enormous pride in everything she'd done. For all those sacrifices she had made—and was still making—in order to be there for her sister. Unjustified pride, perhaps, given that it had been her fault in the first place but it was a lovely feeling, nonetheless. There was something else in his gaze as well…was he feeling sad on her behalf? She needed to reassure him. To reassure herself at the same time, or maybe it was to disguise a flash of guilt that he was only thinking so well of her because he didn't know the whole truth?

'Today has been so much fun,' she told Hugh. 'It's quite likely the best day of my life so far.'

His smile was one of pride. 'There you go. All you needed was the example of an expert. And I'm sorry I said that you were uptight. It's not true, by the way.' He took the bottle from its bed of ice again.

'Uptight people don't love champagne.' He reached for her glass. 'And you'll need to finish this because I'm driving soon. I'd better get us back to the ship before it sails.'

Lisa made a face as she took her glass again. 'Tough job,' she murmured, 'but I guess someone's gotta do it.'

Hugh laughed. 'I like you, Lisa Phillips,' he said. 'We might be total opposites but that doesn't mean we can't be friends, does it?'

They *were* total opposites. Hugh indulged in pleasure of all kinds and Lisa had learned to sacrifice anything that could interfere with what was most important in her life—keeping her sister safe. But Hugh could afford to indulge without any guilt, not only because he could obviously afford it financially—going by the personal information that patient with the migraine had revealed—but more because he didn't have anyone depending on him, did he? He was free to enjoy everything and, today, he'd given Lisa her first taste of that kind of life.

And it had been utterly amazing. It wasn't hard to return his smile. 'How could I not be friends with the person who introduced me to French champagne?'

'My work is done.' Hugh leaned back in his chair. 'If only everything in life could be sorted so easily.'

Friends.

It had been hard to persuade Abby that that was all there was to her relationship with Hugh after she sighed over the romantic photos of that mountaintop café.

'Nothing happened? Really? Not even a kiss?'

'Not even a kiss.' Lisa could sound sincere because they were only discussing the French outing, not what had happened the night before. 'Or not a real one, that is. We were running late by the time we got back and we only just caught the last tender so we were laughing about it all and then we kind of had a hug to say goodnight and he kissed me on the cheek.'

'Aha! There's still time, then. Sounds like a perfect first date to me.'

'Except that it wasn't a date. Now, tell me what's going on with you. You had your test today, didn't you?'

And fortunately Abby was too excited over the news that she'd not only passed her driver's licence test but had been accepted onto the wheelchair basketball team to try and pry any more information out of her big sister.

'Oh, and I've got my first real, hands-on session with a patient tomorrow, to practise what we've been learning about wound care and splinting. My case is a guy who broke three fingers in a rugby game. I can't wait. I'm going to feel like I'm a huge step closer to being a real hand therapist.'

'Good luck with that. I'll look forward to hearing how it went. We'll be docking near Rome so reception might be good enough for a video call. Ring me when you're all done for the day. I'll be on duty but if I can't take the call I'll ring you back later, okay?'

Lisa did miss Abby's call the following evening. Even if she'd been aware of her phone ringing, she wouldn't have even been able to fish it out of her pocket. She was running at the time, helping Tim the paramedic push the resuscitation trolley that was kept ready to deal with any sudden collapse that could be due to a cardiac arrest. Hugh was already on scene because he happened to be eating in the same restaurant as the man who had simply fallen sideways off his chair while he had been waiting for his main course to be served.

'It's the restaurant that caters for passengers who think an evening meal with the ship's officers is a traditional part of their cruising experience,' Tim told her as he hit buttons to try and make the elevator work faster. 'They love an occasion to get really dressed up. Usually older people so it could well be a cardiac arrest. Lucky they've often got a doctor hosting one of the tables. Peter and Hugh take it in turns.'

Hugh was wearing a different kind of uniform, Lisa noticed as they raced into the small restaurant moments later. He still had a white shirt but it was paired with black trousers and jacket and even a tie. There were other people standing around wearing similar formal outfits and she recognised one as the captain of their ship, although she'd only met him briefly and hadn't been invited to have dinner at his table yet. Most of the diners seemed to have left the area but staff were looking after a distraught-looking woman.

The unconscious man lying on the carpeted floor was certainly not one of the older passengers Tim had told her about. This man barely looked any older than the doctor who was kneeling beside him, performing chest compressions. Maybe that was why there was a flash of real relief on his face when Hugh looked up to see Lisa and Tim arriving with the trolley.

'Take over compressions, will you, Tim? I've been going for more than two minutes.' Hugh pulled at his tie to loosen and remove it as he straightened up and moved to let Tim kneel. He was shrugging out of his jacket as he scrambled to his feet to get the defibrillator off the trolley. Lisa had already turned it on and taken the sticky pads from the pouch on the side.

'Find some laryngeal mask airways, please, Lisa. We'll need the IV kit and the drug roll. You can set up some saline and make sure we've got adrenaline and amiodarone ready to draw up.'

The next few minutes were controlled chaos. Hugh applied the patches while Tim kept up the rapid compressions until he was asked to stop so that they could identify the rhythm on the screen of the defibrillator.

'It's VF.' Hugh nodded. He pushed a button on the machine and the whine of the increasing charge could be heard. 'Okay, everybody clear. This is going to be a single shock at maximum joules.'

Tim put his hands in the air. 'Clear,' he responded.

Lisa wriggled back from where she was on her knees, unrolling the drug pouch. 'I'm clear,' she added.

The whine changed to an alarm. 'Shocking,' Hugh warned.

Their patient's body arced and then flopped back. He made a sound like a groan despite the mask airway that was filling his mouth and the woman, whom Lisa assumed was his wife, cried out in distress from where she was watching the resuscitation efforts.

'You good to continue compressions?' Hugh asked Tim.

'Yep.' Ideally the person doing the compressions should change every two minutes to keep the energy level high and effective but there was too much to do in a very limited time and Lisa was ideally placed to assist Hugh right now. He needed to get an IV line inserted and the first of the drug dosages administered.

'Draw up one milligram of adrenaline, please, Lisa.'

'On it.' Lisa had put everything he needed for putting in an IV line on a towel. She could watch Hugh moving as she located the ampoule of adrenaline, tapped the top to shift any liquid back into the base and then snapped off the tip so that she could fill a syringe. Hugh's movements were swift and sure. He tightened the tourniquet, felt for only a brief instant for a vein and slid the needle and cannula in only seconds later. By the time Lisa had drawn up the drug, he had secured the line and attached a Luer plug. Lisa handed him the syringe, and the ampoule so he could double check that the right drug was being given.

The first dose of adrenaline made no difference to the potentially fatal rhythm of ventricular fibrillation. A dose of amiodarone was administered, also with no effect. A two-minute cycle was ending so another shock was delivered and Hugh and Tim swapped places for compressions and using the bag mask to deliver oxygen.

'Any cardiac history?' Tim asked.

'No. He's forty-six,' Hugh told him. 'Company director from Canada. His name's Carter.'

'Family history?'

'Clear. No history of congenital heart defects or fainting episodes that might suggest an arrhythmia. He passed a medical recently and his blood pressure and cholesterol were fine. This cruise is the honeymoon for his second marriage. That's his new wife over there.'

Lisa glanced over her shoulder at the woman in a silver evening gown who was standing in complete shock, her hands pressed to her mouth. The ship's captain was right beside her and he was looking just as shocked as it became apparent that this wasn't going well.

At twenty minutes into the resuscitation attempt, with their patient now intubated and receiving continuous chest compressions, another dose of amiodarone was added to the repeated doses of adrenaline and repeated shocks but Lisa could see, every time there was a rhythm check, that the wiggly line of fibrillation was getting flatter and flatter.

News of the emergency must have travelled fast because both Peter and Janet arrived at the restaurant. They now had the ship's full medical team involved and they weren't about to give up but, twenty minutes later, when the line on the screen was absolutely flat, Lisa could tell that the doctors were trying to prepare the man's wife for bad news as they explained what they were trying to achieve with their actions as they still continued the attempt to save Carter's life.

'It's a heart attack, isn't it?' she sobbed.

'It's a cardiac arrest,' Hugh told her gently, leaving Peter to carry on as he went to stand beside her. 'A heart attack is when an artery is blocked and blood can't get to the heart. An arrest is when something is disturbing the electrical current that makes the heart beat. It can be caused by a heart attack. More often it's caused by something that interferes with the rhythm.'

'He's…he's not going to be okay, is he?'

'We've done everything we can,' Hugh said, his tone sombre. 'We've shocked him and used all the drugs we can to try and correct any electrical disturbance and we've kept his circulation going while we've tried but… we're not winning. I'm so sorry…'

Lisa bit her lip, staring down at the pile of discarded wrappers and the sharps bin where she'd been putting broken glass ampoules and needles from syringes. In a case like this, with a younger person involved, it had to be a unanimous team decision to stop the resuscitation. They had probably already gone for much longer than could have been deemed justified but nobody wanted to give up.

Nobody wanted to witness the distress of Carter's new wife a short time later when that decision was finally made. Peter took over caring for her while Tim and Hugh arranged for a stretcher to take him to the ship's morgue. Lisa and Janet cleaned up the mess of equipment and medical supplies and they took the trolley back to the medical centre to restock. It might be unthinkable but this kind of lightning could strike twice in the same place and they had to make sure that they were ready to respond.

'You okay?' Janet asked.

Lisa nodded. But the nod turned into a head shake. 'Not really,' she admitted. 'It's never nice to lose a patient but that was so sad. He was so young. And on his honeymoon…'

'I know.' Janet gave her a hug. 'The only good thing I can see is that he would have been so happy and it happened so suddenly he wouldn't have known anything about it. There are worse ways to go and things like that can happen at any age.'

Lisa nodded again. Her sister could have had a sudden death when she was only two.

'Is there someone you'd like to talk to? Hugh will be back soon. Or we could go and get a coffee.'

But Lisa was reaching into her pocket. 'It's okay,' she told Janet. 'But thanks. I promised I'd talk to my sister tonight and she'll understand.' Glancing at the screen, she saw that she'd missed a call from Abby hours ago now. Would she still be awake? Would it ruin her evening to know that Lisa was upset?

Abby rang straight back when Lisa texted so that she wouldn't disturb her if she was already asleep. It was a video call on her phone so that she could see that Abby was clearly not about to go to sleep either.

'Hey…' Lisa frowned at what she could see on her sister's face. 'What's up, Abby?'

Any thoughts of offloading onto her sister to receive the comfort and reassurance she needed evaporated instantly. Lisa might also be upset but it was Abby who burst into tears and struggled to get her words out.

'It's just… I've had…the most *awful* day.'

'Oh, no…' Lisa suddenly felt far too far away from the person she loved most in the world. All she wanted to do was hug her sister but all she could do was listen. 'Tell me what's happened…'

CHAPTER SIX

WAVE-WATCHING.

The river of churning water between the white waves on either side stretched as far as she could see into the night. How great would it be to be able to gather up any distressing thoughts and throw them overboard to get washed away and simply disappear into that endless sea?

It was an astonishingly therapeutic activity, Lisa decided, having wandered to the stern of the ship when she had finished her call to Abby. It had taken nearly an hour before Abby had started sounding anything like her normal determined and courageous self, but she'd had a real blow to her confidence today when she'd been taking a big step forward to achieving her dream of becoming a specialist hand therapist with her first clinical session.

'He thought I was there for therapy myself,' a still tearful Abby had told Lisa. *'And the look on his face when he found out I was there to treat him... Okay, maybe it might have been justified if I was there to help him learn to walk with a prosthetic leg or how to*

get down stairs with crutches but I was there to dress and splint his hand, Lise. Why do most people only see my wheelchair? Why can't they see me?'

It was so unlike Abby to let something knock her like this but, as Lisa had reminded her, she had a lot going on in her life. She was adapting to living independently in a new environment, coping with an intensive regime of postgraduate study towards her new speciality and…the only family member she had might as well be on the other side of the world. When Abby had finished the call by telling Lisa how much she missed her, it had been Lisa who'd had tears rolling down her face—fortunately after she had ended the video call.

She needed to be home but she wasn't even halfway through this cruise and she couldn't walk out and leave the medical team shorthanded, especially given that she was learning just how intense this job could be. There was a dead man somewhere on board this ship right now, and a grieving woman whose dream honeymoon had become her worst nightmare.

And she didn't really need to be home at all. She didn't need to do what she'd been doing her whole life and fret so much about Abby because she knew that her sister was going to be fine. Abby had already processed why the assumption had been made by her patient by the time she'd finished her conversation with Lisa. She'd forgiven the man for making it and had even laughed about it in the end, polishing up that armour that she'd built as a small child when she'd got stared or laughed at in the playground.

'*I'll show them,*' she'd say. '*I can do stuff too, even if my legs don't work.*'

Lisa lifted her gaze from the movement of the churning water so far below her and looked out to sea. They must be close to the Italian coastline now but she couldn't see it. All she could see was inky-black water below and an equally dark sky above with just the pin-pricks of starlight. This massive ship suddenly seemed a tiny thing in the universe and, as a person standing there alone, Lisa felt totally insignificant.

And unbearably lonely. She wasn't as vital in Abby's life as she had been up till now and her own life suddenly seemed so much emptier, but she couldn't just turn away and take herself in a whole new direction either. She had to be very sure that Abby was safe and that meant staying close. Keeping herself safe.

'Hey…'

The voice behind her made her jump and then spin to see who was greeting her. Not that she needed to see. She'd known who it was as soon as she'd heard his voice.

'Hugh…what are you doing out here?' She was pathetically pleased to see him because it meant she wasn't alone any longer. And because they were friends. She needed a friend right now.

'Same as you, I expect,' Hugh said. 'Clearing my head. It's been quite a night, hasn't it?'

He looked exhausted, Lisa thought. He was still wearing his formal uniform but he had the sleeves of his white shirt rolled up and the neck undone, his jacket was hanging over one arm and she could see the tail of his tie that had been stuffed into a pocket of his black trousers. His hair was rumpled as well, as though he'd been combing it with his fingers. He looked more sombre than Lisa had ever seen him look, too, and that melted something in her heart.

She wanted to give him the hug that she hadn't been able to give Abby but, if she did that, she had the horrible feeling that she might burst into tears and how embarrassing would that be?

'Something like that doesn't happen that often,' Hugh said. 'And, when it does, it's usually someone in their eighties or nineties or with an underlying condition that means they're living on borrowed time. It's a lot harder to take when it's someone so much younger and apparently healthy, isn't it?'

Lisa nodded slowly, dropping her gaze so that Hugh wouldn't see her eyes fill with tears.

But he put a finger under her chin and she had to lift her face and there was no hiding how she was feeling. Hugh's gaze was searching. It seemed as if he was absorbing everything she was feeling. That he wanted to understand because then he might be able to fix something and the impression that he cared enough to do that was almost enough to undo Lisa completely in that moment.

'Come with me,' was all he said, dropping his arm around her shoulders. 'Peter and Tim are covering the rest of the night and I have something to show you.'

Lisa was aware of the weight of Hugh's arm and that her feet were already moving in response to his encouragement. She had no idea what it was he wanted to show her, but the last time she had gone somewhere with him he'd promised that she wouldn't regret it and he'd given her a memory that she would treasure for ever. It wasn't hard to trust him now.

'We did everything we possibly could, you know,' Hugh told her when they were alone in the elevator, going down to a lower deck. 'And you were an important part of that, getting the defibrillator on scene so fast. Even if he'd been in the best-equipped emergency department on land he wouldn't have survived. I'm guessing he had a catastrophic heart attack or a serious, undiagnosed cardiomyopathy.'

'He was on his honeymoon,' Lisa said. 'How sad is that?' She walked ahead of Hugh as the elevator doors opened. 'It should have been the happiest time of his life.'

The huff of sound from Hugh made Lisa turn swiftly and his eyebrows rose at the look she was giving him.

'Sorry… It's not funny at all. It's just that…well, the first time I ever came on a cruise ship, I was on my honeymoon.'

Lisa could feel her jaw dropping. 'You're *married*?' Oddly, there seemed to be a sinking sensation in her stomach at the same time. Because she was disappointed that a married man would be playing around with so many other women, perhaps?

But Hugh was shaking his head emphatically. 'Nope. Never been married. Never intend to be either. One honeymoon was enough and I did it solo.' His mouth tilted on one side. 'Apart from everyone I met along the way, of course, but I did it without a wife.'

'What happened?' The personal question popped out before Lisa could stop it but, as a distraction from her own less than happy thoughts, this was irresistible.

Hugh shrugged. 'I'd gone to my best friend's house a couple of days before the wedding to deliver his suit because he was going to be my best man. That was when I found him in bed with my fiancée, Catherine. It was a no-brainer to cancel the wedding but I couldn't cancel the cruise and I thought, seeing as I'd paid for it all and arranged time off work, I might as well get away for a couple of weeks.'

'So this was before you started working on ships?'

'It was *why* I started working on ships.'

Lisa was so fascinated by this story she simply walked through the door that Hugh had opened but then she stopped and stared.

'This is someone's cabin,' she said.

'It is indeed,' Hugh agreed. 'It's my cabin.'

It was a lot bigger than Lisa's cabin. There was a desk with its surface crowded by a laptop computer, scattered medical journals and a collection of empty mugs. The chair in front of it had Hugh's normal white uniform draped over it. There was a couch and armchairs in front of doors that led out to a generous balcony, a door that obviously led to a bathroom and a double bed that looked rumpled enough to give the impression that Hugh had just climbed out of it.

Lisa's gaze slid sideways, trying to imagine him in pyjamas. Nope... If ever there was a man who would sleep naked, surely it would be Hugh Patterson. The uninvited thought was enough to make her close her eyes for a moment as she willed her cheeks not to start glowing like Rudolph the reindeer's nose.

'Um…' She cleared her throat. 'What was it you were saying?'

Lisa looked about as uncomfortable as she had the first time Hugh had ever seen her, first on the wharf in Barcelona when they both knew she'd been watching him kiss Carlotta and then when he'd met her in the medical centre and she'd known she would be working with him for the next couple of weeks.

But, until she realised he had brought her into his private, personal space, he'd been doing a good job of distracting her from the misery that he assumed was due to their unsuccessful resuscitation efforts this evening. He hadn't seen her with tears in her eyes like that before and he suspected it would take something huge to make Lisa Phillips cry so it had induced an odd squeezing sensation in his chest that meant he had to try and fix things.

'Ah…' Hugh decided to ignore her embarrassment and act like it was no big deal that his cabin was messy and he hadn't even made his bed properly. He walked towards the sitting room corner to open the balcony doors. That way, Lisa wouldn't feel like she was trapped and it was a nice enough evening to sit out there if that helped. 'I was saying that my solo honeymoon was the reason I took a job as a ship's doctor. I had been about to take up a position in a general practice in the nice outer London suburb I'd grown up in. I was all set to settle down and move back into the family home and raise my two point four children—you know, the whole nine yards.'

Lisa was shaking her head. 'You were really in love, weren't you? It must have been absolutely devastating.'

'Better to happen then than when those two and a bit kids were involved.' Hugh kept his tone light. He also needed to change the subject because, like his privileged background, it was something he preferred not to talk about. To anyone. He *had* been devastated. He'd gone on board his first cruise ship feeling totally betrayed and crushed and, for some weird reason, he almost felt like telling Lisa every gruesome detail. Because he knew she would understand? That she would care?

'Anyway...there was an incident on board. Or rather on shore. One of the passengers was riding a donkey on a Greek island and he fell off and dislocated his shoulder. I managed to get it relocated for him and used his clothes to splint it in place, got him back to the ship and then ended up helping to X-ray him to make sure it was all okay.'

Lisa had followed him towards the balcony but now she sat down on the edge of the couch as she listened to his story.

'The doctor I was working with told me they were looking for new medical staff and it all came together. I didn't have to settle in one place or start thinking about real estate or nursery schools. I didn't need to get bored by turning up to the same place every day to do the same job. I could live and work like I was on a permanent holiday and get an endless variety of medical challenges, some of them as big as anything you'd get on land—like tonight.'

Hugh turned away, towards the small fridge tucked behind one of the armchairs. That had been more than two years ago now. It didn't feel so much like a permanent holiday any longer. He was, in fact, turning up to the same place every day to do the same job, wasn't he? And, yes, he was living the dream with all the fabulous places he got to visit and the glamour of being a ship's officer but…sometimes it all felt a bit transitory, with nothing solid to hang onto. Even friends that you made along the way—like Lisa—didn't necessarily stay in your life.

This living the dream felt pretty darned lonely sometimes, in fact…

Empty, even?

'Right.' He opened the fridge. 'This is what I wanted to show you.'

'You're kidding.' Lisa looked shocked. 'Champagne? Tonight—after how *awful* it's been?'

Her voice wobbled a little on the last few words and Hugh felt that squeeze in his chest again. He opened the freezer compartment of the fridge to pick out the frosty glasses that lived there and then went to sit beside Lisa, putting the glasses on the coffee table in front of her.

'Have you heard of Napoleon Bonaparte?' he asked casually.

'Of course. I loved history at school.' Lisa looked surprised at the random question but there was a hint of a smile on her face as she played along. 'Short guy, born in Corsica, married Josephine and crowned himself emperor of France. He was famous for saying that an army marches on its stomach, I believe.'

Hugh nodded. He was removing the foil and twisting the wire around the cork on the bottle. 'He had something to say about champagne, too.'

'Oh?'

'Yep. He said that in victory you deserve champagne but in defeat you *need* it.' As if to applaud the statement, the cork shot towards the ceiling with a satisfyingly loud popping sound. The sound of Lisa's laughter was even more satisfying.

'You're incorrigible, Hugh, you know that?'

'I'd agree if I knew what that meant.' Hugh suppressed a smile as he filled a glass to hand to Lisa. 'But it's a good thing, yes?' He touched his glass to hers. *'Santé,'* he murmured.

'You know perfectly well what it means.' But there was genuine amusement in her eyes before she closed them as she took an appreciative sip of her sparkling wine.

'It's just as good as the first time,' she said. 'Maybe even better. That doesn't often happen, does it?'

'Some things actually get better the more often you do them,' he said, 'And some things you never want to do for a second time. Once burnt, forever shy.'

'Mmm...'

He could feel Lisa's gaze on him and, as soon as he turned towards her, he knew she was thinking about the spectacular crash and burn of his wedding plans. He could feel the moment her thoughts changed from sympathy to something else, though. She was thinking about the kinds of things he had done often enough to become expert in. Like kissing… Any second now, she was going to go back to that assumption she'd made that he fell into bed with every willing woman who tried to attract his attention.

He held her gaze steadily, making a silent statement that she was completely wrong in that assumption. That there were actually very few women he had fallen—or wanted to fall—into bed with.

But… He didn't need that spear of sensation in his body to confirm what he suddenly realised. Lisa Phillips was definitely one of those women and, at this moment in time, it felt like she was the only one.

Stunned by the realisation, Hugh put his glass carefully down on the table as an excuse to break the eye contact but he was a fraction of a second too late. He'd seen the way her pupils were dilating. She not only knew what he was thinking, she was responding to it.

Hugh pulled in a slow breath but he wasn't about to shake off the detour his brain, and his body, were determined to take. He wanted her. He wanted to see that flicker of desire in her eyes get kindled into a flame. Maybe he wanted to tease her in a completely different way from any he would have considered before now— to create enough frustration to be able to make getting tipped into paradise all the more intense. Would the expression in her eyes be anything like the first time she had tasted real champagne?

Would he be making a terrible mistake if he tried to find out? Just proving that Lisa's assumptions about his lifestyle were not wrong? Or was he right in suspecting that she might want this as much as he did?

He turned back to meet her gaze again, knowing that she would see that last question in his eyes. Maybe he didn't really have a choice here, given the way his desire was exploding now that it had been acknowledged. But Lisa did have a choice and he would totally respect that. A cold shower might well be in the cards in his very near future.

Oh…*my*… That *look*…

Lisa had to swallow her mouthful of champagne in a hurry. Nobody had ever looked at her like that. Ever. As if she was the most desirable thing in the entire world. As if he wanted to do a whole lot more than simply kiss her. And every single cell in Lisa's body was not only reminding her of what it was like to be kissed by this man but making a plea to find out what doing more than kissing would be like.

This was, she realised, the first time in her life that she actually, desperately wanted to get really intimate with someone. Oh, she'd had the usual teenage curiosity about sex but that had been mixed with doubt that the experience might not live up to expectations that had been set by some of the books she'd read and she'd been so right. Early attempts had been fumbling and embarrassing. With her more recent choices of boyfriends it had been a lot better. Enjoyable, even, but still nothing like having fireworks going off or the earth spinning on its axis or a herd of unicorns galloping off into the sunset.

She had, with the help of one of those boyfriends, come to the conclusion that the fault lay completely on her side, and in a way that had been a relief because perhaps there was a part of her that had decided long ago that she really didn't deserve that kind of pleasure. Whatever the cause, Lisa had given up believing in any of that hype about how good sex could be—as far as she was concerned, anyway.

Until Hugh Patterson had kissed her the other night, that was...

Lisa could imagine that she was standing on the edge of a precipice here. She could—and undoubtedly *should*—step back onto firm, safe ground. If she let herself fall, there were two possibilities. One was that Hugh would catch her—probably with his lips to start with—and the other was that she would just keep falling, in which case she might crash into an embarrassing heap because he would find out that she wasn't very good at sex, but...

But... There was something about tonight that felt different. Hugh had found her at one of the lowest points she could remember in a very long time. She was missing Abby and worried about her but aware that her sister would actually be able to cope perfectly well without her, which made this a turning point in her life, but it was scary because she couldn't imagine such a different future. She had been gutted by the death of their patient. She'd realised what an insignificant speck she was in the face of a limitless night sky and sea and she'd been feeling *so* lonely.

His company had been a godsend because it was

exactly what she needed to counteract that loneliness. The way he'd held her face up with his finger under her chin and tried to read her face like a book had made her feel as if her well-being was important to him. That he was really seeing her. He didn't know a lot about her life, other than how important her sister was to her, but it felt like he knew more than any man ever had.

He'd shared something personal, too. Physically, as in bringing her into his private cabin, but emotionally as well, by telling her the story of how he'd been betrayed by the woman he'd loved enough to be about to marry. Above all, he'd made her laugh. He'd given her a moment that had obliterated the worry for Abby, fear for the future and the grief for the man who'd died tonight.

Right now, he was silently asking her if she wanted to be made love to and the answer was a cry that came from somewhere very deep in Lisa's soul. She felt astonishingly vulnerable in this moment but…she trusted this man and she'd never before wanted so much to be as close to another person as possible. She needed that comfort. To escape for a little while from any worries or sadness in her world. To know that she wasn't as insignificant as she'd imagined?

She still hesitated, however. Because, judging by that kiss, Hugh was an expert in all things sexual and she…well, he was going to be disappointed, wasn't he?

Oddly, the nerves in her fingers seemed to have stopped working because she made no attempt to hang onto her glass when Hugh gently took it from her and put it down beside his on the table. The nerves in her lips, on the other hand, were in overdrive as he slowly turned back, cupped her chin in one hand and touched her lips with his own in the same way he had the first time he'd done this. Such a feather-light touch, a soft rub, a tiny lick. Infinitely subtle changes of pressure as if her mouth was being not only invited to dance but being led around a dance floor so that being good at it was effortless. A tiny sound escaped her lips as Lisa let herself sink blissfully deeper into that kiss.

It was that tiny sound that totally undid Hugh.

That took him to a place he didn't recognise, in fact. He'd seen the heart-breaking vulnerability in Lisa's eyes before he'd kissed her and that had set off alarm bells like never before because he knew he was in a position to hurt Lisa. But she knew as well as he did that this was only about tonight and he could feel that her need was as urgent as his own. And…what really did something unprecedented to his head—and his heart— was that he could see the trust she was gifting him.

That sound was like the sigh of someone who'd pushed past a final barrier and could see the place they were desperate to get to. And, even more than how much his own body was craving the release of indulging this astonishingly powerful desire, that sound made Hugh want this to be something special for Lisa. She might not be a virgin but there was something that told him Lisa was nervous of sex for some reason. Afraid of it, even? He had given her the joy of her first taste of real champagne. Maybe, if he took things slowly and gently, he could give her the knowledge that sex could be just as good. Perhaps even better…

So that's what he did. He lost track of time but it didn't matter a damn how long this took. He took his sweet time getting them both naked and into his bed and then introducing himself to every inch of Lisa's body with his hands and his lips. He could feel every time she got tense or tried to please *him* by hurrying things along so he would slow her hands. Capture them and hold them above her head for a moment or two.

'Shh… It's all good,' he would murmur to reassure her, before kissing her for as long as it took for her to relax again. 'Wait… We've got all the time in the world.'

Maybe it was the gentle motion of the sea way beneath them.

Or maybe a taste of champagne on top of the emotional and physical fatigue of this evening had put Lisa into a space like no other.

Or—and this was far the most likely—it was because this was Hugh she was with. A man who clearly knew his way around a woman's body. It seemed like he knew *her* body better than she knew it herself. And whenever she had the fear that he was going to discover that she was being a complete fraud and only pretending that she was loving this, he would simply back off. Slow the pace and force her to be patient when all she wanted to try and do was give him the pleasure of the release he more than deserved.

She'd try again in just a minute, she decided. Surely

he'd had enough of trying to bring her to a climax. It wasn't going to happen and the worry was that he would guess that she was faking it, like others had, unless she could be more convincing than she had ever been before. But the flicker of doubt came and went, along with the determination to move and touch Hugh again in a way she was sure he wouldn't be able to resist. She was caught, she realised, in an escalating tension being created by the movement of Hugh's fingers.

She put her hand over his to ask him to stop but he ignored her and, in alarm, Lisa opened her eyes, only to find that Hugh's face was right beside her own and he was watching her. And that was when it happened. She was falling. Falling into wave after wave of the most intense pleasure she'd ever experienced in her life.

Her astonished gasp triggered what she'd been trying to achieve for what felt like for ever to make sure that this was good for Hugh and, even as those extraordinary waves began to recede, she heard his groan of need and then she could feel him inside her and, unbelievably, the new movement was building that tension all over again.

This time, when she unravelled, he was holding her tightly in his arms so she could feel the shudders in his body and knew that they were both falling. He was still holding her as she tried to slow her breathing afterwards, aware of the pounding of both their hearts. Aware that Hugh was watching her again and there was a question in his eyes but a smile on his face as if he already knew the answer.

'Good?' he whispered.

Lisa could feel a smile curving her own lips. 'Unicorns,' she whispered back.

The sparkle of delight in Hugh's eyes and the way his smile widened told Lisa that he understood. That he couldn't be happier that she'd found it magic and the knowledge that he was so happy that she was happy gave Lisa a whole new sensation of falling.

Falling in love?

'So, what do you reckon?' Hugh was still smiling. 'Is sex as good as or better than champagne?'

That's what this had been, Lisa reminded herself hurriedly. Just sex. One of those "good things" in life— like dancing or fine wine. It might have been the best sex she'd ever had in her life but she and Hugh weren't lovers, they were only friends. But that didn't seem to matter right now because Lisa was still under the spell of the magic and it seemed that she was stepping into a whole new world.

'I'm not sure,' she murmured. 'I might have to test that theory again sometime.'

The growling sound that Hugh made was most definitely one of approval. 'I think that's very wise. One should never jump to conclusions about important things. I'm happy to help with the research.'

But Lisa wriggled free as he began to trail kisses down her neck and onto her shoulder. Her world had just been rocked in a rather spectacular manner but reality was making its presence felt and there was suddenly a beat of fear to be found in the knowledge that she had lost control to such an extent. That, for heaven knows how long, the most important thing in her life had been Hugh and what was happening between them. She'd never let desire overwhelm her like that before. It was dangerous because it distracted you and, if you let important things slip from your grasp when you were distracted, it could ruin your life. That she could remember a lifelong mantra she had just ignored but still feel so incredibly happy was confusing, to say the least.

'I need to go,' she said. 'I think it's time I got back to my own cabin and got some sleep.'

Hugh let her slip out of his grasp. 'No problem,' he responded. 'We've got all the time in the world for that research.'

Which wasn't true, Lisa thought as she moved quietly along deserted narrow hallways a few minutes later. They had little more than another week before the fantasy of shipboard life, exotic locations and now mind-blowing sex would have to come to an end. But that didn't seem to matter either. Because, even if tonight was the only night she could ever have with Hugh Patterson, it had been worth it. She wasn't broken after all. She'd just needed a person who cared enough to show her that and, while she couldn't possibly be *in* love with someone like Hugh, she could love him for giving her that. For making her feel that perhaps she *did* deserve that kind of joy in her life.

And, even if it was dangerous to be distracted like that, it had nothing to do with her real life, did it? Abby was safe. Lisa was here, earning extra money to make sure she could maintain that safety for both of them. So the distraction was confined. And limited. It could only last a matter of days, until this cruise was finished and she flew back to her real life. A handful of days was just a blip in anyone's lifetime.

Could there be any real harm in enjoying it while it lasted?

CHAPTER SEVEN

So…sex was one of the things that got better the more often you did it.

Or, she should qualify that, Lisa realised, because it was only sex with Hugh that continued to surprise and delight her on new levels every time. The total opposite to her past experience in relationships, in fact, when sex had become progressively more predictable and dull. Anxiety inducing as well, because she'd known she wasn't performing as well as expected.

She knew why it was so different, of course. Hugh was the complete opposite to anyone she had ever chosen to get close to in the past. The bad boy versus the sensible, safe kind of man. Not that they were in a relationship. They both knew that this was never going to be any more than a friendship and that their time together was limited. Perhaps that was why they were both making the most of it.

Keeping it secret was part of the thrill as well. Maybe that was making it safer to enjoy because it confirmed that this was a friendship with hidden benefits rather than a relationship that carried responsibilities. Or perhaps it really was frowned upon for crew members to hook up, but whatever the reason was, the agreement was tacit and became more enjoyable as the days ticked past. There were a couple of long days at sea as the ship sailed around the bottom of Italy to the Greek Islands on the itinerary and then back again.

They both became very good at the game of working together without betraying how close they were, resisting the urge to hold eye contact a little too long, or engineer moments when their hands or bodies might touch as they moved in sometimes confined spaces. They were being careful not to be seen visiting each other's cabins and spending only a part of each night together, and they could make it appear that they went on shore leave separately but meeting up as soon as they were out of sight.

Like they had for a delightful day on the island of Mykonos, where they had met up at a private beach that was not on the usual tourist radar. There were small fishing boats in the nearby port, pelicans that seemed to be expert in posing for photographs and a waveless beach that was like the biggest swimming pool ever.

And like they had again today as they'd reached the second-last destination of this cruise and it was Blue Watch's turn to have shore leave, having stayed on the ship for the visit to Santorini.

With the cruise ship docked in the port of Salerno as they reached Italy again on the way back to Spain, there had been multiple choices for a day's outing. There were buses going to Naples, to Sorrento with a boat trip to the island of Capri, and a tour that took in both Mount Vesuvius and the ancient city of Pompeii.

They were all destinations that took Lisa's breath away so why did she avoid every one of them?

Because Hugh had offered her something far more enticing. Another day alone with him and somewhere that no one else would be likely to be going.

'I know this walk,' he told her. 'It's called The Valley of the Ancient Mills. And it's right under everybody's noses but they'll be jumping on the buses to go further afield. This valley is quiet and green, and full of the ruins of old mills and a river and waterfalls, and we can walk up the hills towards a gorgeous village called Ravello, but on the way is another little village. I don't even know the name of it but it has a restaurant with a terrace and a view and—'

'Stop…' Lisa pressed her finger against Hugh's lips. 'I'm sold. How could I go past a restaurant with a terrace?'

She couldn't. Not after the most romantic evening ever, in that French restaurant, even though there had been nothing romantic happening between them yet. How much more fabulous would it be to have a setting like that when you were with your lover? Well, okay, she couldn't—and didn't—think of Hugh as her lover and she knew there was a definite limit to this fling and that this outing today would be almost the last, but she was making memories here, wasn't she? And memories could be woven into a fantasy that she could enjoy for ever. A private fantasy. She hadn't confessed the new development in her life to Abby, although her sister had guessed something was going on.

'You just look so...different, Lise. So...happy. I've never seen you kind of glowing like this before.'

'I'm happy you're okay. That that last clinical session was the total opposite of that horrible first one. She won't be the first patient to see you as an inspiration.'

But Abby hadn't been convinced. *'It's more than that. You look like, I don't know, a kid on Christmas morning.'*

'I'm loving this cruise, that's all. I could go to Pompeii on our next stop, if I want. Or walk up to the top of Mount Vesuvius. How incredible is that?'

She had convinced Abby that her excitement was at the prospect of seeing such famous sights but the real reason was far simpler.

'Actually, you had me at the name of the valley,' she told Hugh. 'It sounds very...romantic.'

And it was. It was as green and quiet as Hugh had promised and the shade was welcome in the increasing heat of a late Italian morning. There were wild cyclamen making a carpet of pale pink beneath the trees, the buzzing of bees and bird calls nearby and the refreshing ripple of the river not far away. There were moss-covered ruins of the old stone mills and, best of all, they had this track all to themselves. A private world. Hugh took Lisa's hand to help her up a rocky part of the path but he didn't let go when she was back on smooth ground.

Instead, he pulled her close and kissed her with one of

those slow and, oh, so thorough kisses that Lisa was quite probably getting addicted to because they were a drug all by themselves. She could feel herself floating away within seconds towards that place where nothing else existed. Just herself and Hugh and the promise of absolute bliss...

But Hugh broke the kiss too soon this time, albeit reluctantly.

'We need to keep going,' he said. 'We've got a bit further to go and this weather's not going to last.'

'I heard that there was stormy weather coming but I thought it was a few days away yet.'

'The big storms probably won't catch us until we're somewhere between Sardinia and Malaga on our way home but it's going to get overcast later today and will probably rain by tomorrow.'

Lisa didn't want to think about arriving in Malaga, which was when she would be leaving the ship to fly back to England. 'I hope the sun lasts while we have lunch on that terrace,' she said. 'I can't wait.'

'I hope it lasts a bit longer. If we've got time and enough energy, we can walk further up to Ravello and go exploring and then get a taxi or bus back to the ship. There's an amazing old villa in Ravello called the Villa Rufolo and it's well worth visiting.'

'You know so many places to go.'

'I've done it so many times. Too many, perhaps. I usually try to find something new to see at every destination but...' he smiled at Lisa. 'It's actually a lot more fun sharing the things I already know with you because... I don't know...it makes them more special.'

His words made Lisa feel special. In fact, knowing

that Hugh was getting genuine pleasure from sharing things that he liked with her was giving her an even stronger connection to this man who had the most gorgeous smile in the world. It gave her a bit of lump in her throat, to be honest.

They finally left the beautiful valley and its mills behind and followed a path that gave them wonderful views past forests and lemon groves and terraced fields of tomatoes to where the town of Amalfi nestled right beside the sparkling blue of the Mediterranean. The path led through stone archways that were charmingly decorated with old wicker baskets and unusual-looking utensils.

By the time they reached the restaurant, they were ready to rest and enjoy a meal. They both ordered an *insalata caprese*—a salad of delicious slices of fresh local tomatoes, mozzarella cheese and basil leaves that was drizzled with olive oil. It came with a basket of fresh, crusty bread and was the most perfect-looking lunch Lisa had ever seen. She had to take a photo of it for Abby.

Hugh ordered Prosecco as well.

'Think of it as Italian champagne,' he told Lisa, with a wink. *'Saluti, cara.'*

Cara. Didn't that mean something like *darling* or *sweetheart*? Lisa touched her glass to Hugh's and met his gaze over the top of the glasses. The warmth in those brown eyes and the echoes of the endearment he had just used stole her breath away and it was at that moment that Lisa realised she was in trouble.

She had known right from the start that this was temporary. That it was just a shipboard fling that was going to end very soon and it was highly unlikely that she would ever see Hugh Patterson again. But she also knew that it was not going to be easy. At this moment, if felt as if it could very well be devastating.

Because she'd fallen in love with him. It had probably happened, without her even realising, that night when he'd managed to make her laugh when she'd been feeling so awful. When he'd taken her to his bed and changed her life for ever. When she'd mistakenly analysed her feelings as lust rather than love, but this was so much deeper than anything purely sexual. Lisa wanted the closeness and connection they'd discovered to last for ever. She wanted, in particular, to freeze this moment in time when it felt like she could fall into that gaze and never want to come up for air.

Maybe it was an omen that a shadow noticeably darkened this idyllic scene as a first bank of clouds drifted overhead to obscure the sun. It was Hugh who broke that eye contact to look up at the sky.

'Uh-oh,' he murmured. 'Maybe that storm's on its way a bit quicker than they predicted.'

'Mmm.' But Lisa wasn't thinking about bad weather as she made a concerned sound and even suppressed a shiver. She was thinking of something that was going to be a lot less pleasant to endure.

Saying goodbye to Hugh…

Had Hugh really thought that Lisa Phillips was uptight and controlling?

That she wouldn't trust anyone else enough to even help her carry her suitcase?

That she was the complete opposite of the type of women he could ever be attracted to?

Oh, man…how wrong could a person be?

As if she'd picked up on his thought by telepathy, Lisa turned from the window of the bus to catch his gaze. There was awe in those amazing eyes, thanks to the view down the mountainside to the town of Amalfi they were heading back to, but there was also a bit of fear at the speed at which the bus driver was taking these hairpin bends on the narrow road.

'I guess he knows what he's doing,' she muttered. 'He must have done it plenty of times before.'

That was so like Lisa, wasn't it? She might be afraid to some degree and she might be determined to excel in everything she did but she was still prepared to trust someone else, which gave her a very endearing, almost childlike quality.

She trusted *him* now. On a very different level from anything he would have imagined them sharing.

He had wanted a certain level of trust from Lisa as soon as he'd realised they were going to be spending a lot of time together for a couple of weeks. He'd wanted to tease her and make her a little less 'uptight'. He'd wanted to show her that there were things in life that were meant to be enjoyed and she was missing out on most of them.

What he hadn't realised was that sharing those things with her would make them so different for him. He'd been drinking champagne and having sex with beautiful women, travelling to amazing places and just getting the most out of his life for a very long time now, but doing exactly the same things with Lisa was like doing them himself for the very first time because they felt *that* different.

The bus was leaning as it took another bend and Hugh could feel the pit of his own stomach dropping as he looked over Lisa's shoulder to the drop below the side of the road. The bus seemed to be clinging to the road by the edge of its tyres but Lisa's squeak of terror was half excitement and the way her fingers clutched his arm so dramatically made him smile.

Maybe this was what it was like when you had a child, he thought, and you got to see the world all over again from their perspective. You could experience the sourness of a lemon perhaps as you laughed at the face they made. Or the joy of feeling your body fly through the air that was enough to make you shriek with glee when someone pushed you on a swing for the first time. Perhaps what made this so different with Lisa was that it was an adult version of rediscovery.

The sex had been a revelation every single time. So familiar but so new as well—as if everything had suddenly become colour instead of just black and white. The joy on her face today, when she'd had to stop and simply gaze at the beauty of that walk past the ancient paper mills, and her eyes closing in bliss when she'd had her first mouthful of that mix of tomatoes and cheese and basil…

Hugh had never tasted a salad that good himself and yet he'd eaten an *insalata caprese* countless times before. It wasn't that those astonishingly bright red local tomatoes had that much more flavour. Or that the olive oil was especially good. Hugh knew that it was being with Lisa that was making things so different and that was more than a little disturbing.

Because it was true that she wasn't his "type" at all. That when he had first met her, when he had actually been with the sophisticated Carlotta—who was exactly his type—he wouldn't have dreamed of asking Lisa out. The notion that he might be able to make love to her time and time again and feel like he could never get enough of her would have been a joke. If he'd had a premonition that doing something as ordinary as sight-seeing with her could be so delightful he would have known he needed to stay well clear. He had invented what he thought of as his type because those women were safe. They didn't want loyalty or commitment or to risk betrayal any more than he did.

It had been too long, hadn't it? He'd become complacent and hadn't realised that it was even possible for anyone to get past his protective barriers. He'd considered himself to be completely safe from feeling like this again. That *pride* in being the one to provide something that gave joy to someone else. That desire that had nothing to do with sex but was a wish to keep providing things like that. To protect someone and cherish them.

That was what falling in love was all about, wasn't it?

He'd started out seeing Lisa as someone who could be the little sister he'd never had. How could this de-termined but naïve, petite, shaggy red-haired woman with unusual eyes and freckles to match their hazel brown have become the most beautiful person Hugh had ever known? He'd been in love once before but how he was starting to feel about Lisa had the potential to blow that past love out of the water and make it barely worth remembering.

That was a little terrifying, he had to admit.

Except that Lisa was nothing like Catherine, his ex-fiancée, was she? This was someone who had actually sacrificed probably more than she was letting on in order to care for someone she loved—her sister Abby. Lisa would have that kind of loyalty to anyone she loved, if she ever let someone in to that degree, and she wouldn't lie about how she felt either. Or, if she tried, he would be able to see immediately that she wasn't being truthful because he could read her face like a book now thanks to watching it so carefully in her unguarded moments.

And that meant he could trust Lisa. On a level that he'd never thought he would ever trust a woman again. But what, if anything, should he do about that? There was a clock ticking here. In a matter of only a couple of days this woman was going to walk out of his life and back to her own. If he didn't want that to happen he would have to make some big decisions in a hurry. But not yet… He might recognise that he was feeling the way you did when you fell in love but that didn't mean it had actually happened yet, did it? Or that Lisa even felt the same way.

They were nearly back at sea level now, passing the first houses of Amalfi, and they'd need to hurry to get a taxi back to Salerno and back on board the ship in good time before they left the port. There would be no time for a while to give such a serious matter the amount of thought it needed and Hugh could feel himself releasing his breath in a sigh of relief as they climbed down the steps of the bus. He could just stop thinking about it and enjoy the present for a bit longer. He'd lived this way for long enough to know that it could work.

The smile on Lisa's face as she skipped a step to catch up with his long stride was enough to make it well worth thinking only about the next few hours. Getting back on board, an evening surgery, dinner and then… Hugh held Lisa's gaze for a long moment as he sent a silent invitation for her to come to his cabin later tonight. The way her smile faded as the colour in her eyes changed from golden brown to something more molten was enough to let him know that the invitation had been received and accepted.

He couldn't bring himself to break that gaze. He opened his mouth and he knew that the words that were about to come out would change everything.

Three little words.

I love you…

They were there. In his head. On the tip of his tongue. But something stopped him. Maybe it was the tiny frown line that appeared between Lisa's eyes when she heard a sound from her phone. She dived into her bag to find it.

'That's Abby texting me. She was going back to the house to check things for me today. I hope everything's all right.'

Hugh could sense that Lisa's attention was a very long way away from him now. She was back in her real life for the moment. Away from her working holiday fling. In a place he would never belong.

'Everything okay?'

'She's stressing because she's found a pile of mail behind the door and she's wants to know if she should open it. I've told her to leave it where it is. I'll deal with it all when I get home.'

Her glance was apologetic, as if she understood that her real life had nothing to do with him. Or that she didn't want it to have anything to do with him? Hugh took a deeper breath and he could feel his mind clearing noticeably. He was certainly going to miss Lisa when she left the ship in Malaga but he could cope if he had to and that would be a lot easier than grappling with concepts he had given up even thinking about a very long time ago. Things like settling down to a more ordinary job somewhere. Getting married. Having a family.

Good grief... Hugh turned away from Lisa and hurriedly raised his arm to flag down a taxi. Had the thought of getting *married* actually entered his head in that flash of muddled thoughts? The sooner they were back on board his beloved ship and in his familiar environment the better. He had to put a stop to this before he did something really crazy.

Like asking Lisa to marry him...

Something had changed but, for the life of her, Lisa couldn't put her finger on quite what it could be.

They'd had such a lovely day together with that walk up through the valley and the delicious lunch and then exploring the mountain town and that crazy bus ride back to the coast. She was quite sure that Hugh had enjoyed the day as much as she had but he seemed a little edgy when they opened the medical centre for the evening surgery. Was it because the wind had picked up as the ship had eased out into more open sea? Lisa could feel the gentle roll of bigger swells beneath them, although she wasn't finding it alarming at all.

'Is it likely to be a problem, getting a storm while we're at sea?'

'Hard to say. Sometimes the captain can navigate around the bad weather and modern ships have stabilisers that help a lot, although it's surprising to a lot of people how rough the Mediterranean can get. Usually they just blow past with nothing more than a lot of people getting very seasick or complaining that some decks and the swimming pools are closed. Thanks for the reminder. I'd better check our supplies of anti-motion-sickness medications.'

'What do you use?' Lisa followed him into the pharmacy room.

'We give out the usual over-the-counter remedies to anyone who asks and they're also available in many of the shops if there gets to be too much of a queue here. The shops also have things like different forms of ginger and peppermint, which we often advise people to try. Other advice includes eating something, like dry crackers, getting some fresh air on the balcony or deck or going to the centre of the ship where it's more stable.'

'And if it's serious?'

'We've got good stocks of promethazine and meto-clopramide.' Hugh shut and locked the glass-fronted cupboard he'd opened. 'And plenty of saline if some-one gets really dehydrated. Here…' He scooped a lot of small packages out of a drawer to hand to Lisa. 'Let's keep these supplies of Dramamine at the front desk. If they're mild cases you can dispense this and send them home when you're triaging.' He glanced over his shoulder as he led the way out of the pharmacy. 'You're not worried about this storm, are you?'

'Um…no…' But Lisa bit her lip. 'I did find some videos online, though, that looked a bit scary. Restaurants with all the tables and even a piano rolling one way and then the other and taking people out on the way.'

Hugh was smiling. 'Have you seen that movie with the ship and the iceberg? That's a good one, too. It's just as well that we don't get many icebergs in the Mediterranean.'

Lisa loved that smile so much. She loved the way there were crinkles of amusement on either side of those gorgeous brown eyes but, most of all, she loved that he was checking how she was feeling about some-thing and was trying to make her laugh to ease any worry. She *did* laugh and, suddenly, whatever tension had been in the air this evening evaporated, along with any nerves about stormy weather. She was with Hugh. They could handle whatever came their way.

Including a patient she was worried about the moment she walked into the medical centre and had to snatch a breath even while she was introducing herself.

'You're sounding very wheezy, Michelle. Are you asthmatic?'

The young woman nodded. 'It's not getting better… so I thought… I'd come in…'

'Good thinking. Come with me.' Lisa led her straight to the treatment room. 'I'm just going to check your blood pressure and heart rate and the oxygen level in your blood.' She put the clip on his finger. 'Have you been using your inhaler?'

'Yes…lots…'

She got Michelle to blow into a peak flow meter as well.

'What do you normally blow?'

'On a good day…four hundred.'

She was down to a lot less than three hundred now.

'I'm sure the doctor will want to start a nebuliser at least. Let's give you another pillow or two to keep you a bit more upright and I'll go and find him.'

Hugh was with another patient who had run out of his high blood pressure medication a week ago but had thought it wouldn't matter until he'd started getting bad headaches, but one look at Lisa's face and he stood up.

'Wait there, Jim,' he told his patient. 'I'll be back very soon. We're going to admit you to our little hospital here for a while so we can keep an eye on you while you have some intravenous medication to bring your blood pressure down in a controlled manner.'

Jim's wife had come to the appointment with him. 'I told you it was serious,' she growled. 'Don't you dare move. I'm going back to the cabin to get your pyjamas and toothbrush. You're going to stay here until the doctor says you're okay.'

Hugh was right beside Lisa as she sped back to the treatment room. 'I'm worried that her asthma isn't responding to her inhaler. She's not speaking more than three to four words per breath and her oxygen saturation is down to ninety-six percent. Respiration rate is twenty-five, heart rate is one twenty, and peak flow is not much more than fifty percent of normal for her. Do you want me to set up a nebuliser?'

'Absolutely. We might need to start some IV corticosteroids as well. And get an arterial blood gas measurement.'

By the time Hugh had listened to Michelle's chest, Lisa had a nebuliser mask ready, with medication in the chamber and oxygen running through at a high enough rate to produce a good vapour. She slipped the elastic over the back of Michelle's head and rearranged her pillows to make it more comfortable for her to sit upright.

She worked with Hugh to find and hand him everything he needed to set up an IV line and then the more difficult procedure of inserting a cannula into an artery in Michelle's wrist so that they would be able to get a far more accurate indication of how much circulating oxygen she had in her blood. It couldn't be something that Hugh had to do very often but he made it look easy, from putting in some local anaesthetic to find a vessel that was much deeper than a vein, inserting the cannula and then controlling the spurt of blood under pressure as he attached and taped down the Luer plug. He filled a tiny, two-ml syringe with the arterial blood.

'I'll page Janet or Tim to pop in and show you how to use the benchtop ABG analysis,' he told Lisa when he headed back to his other patient a few minutes later. 'We're also going to need a hand for a while. Might see what Peter's up to. I need to get Jim's blood pressure down so we'll have two patients that need close monitoring for some time.' He held her gaze. 'We could be in for a long night.'

'I wasn't planning on being anywhere else,' she responded.

Except that was only partly true. She might have been planning to be with Hugh tonight but it hadn't occurred to her that they might not be able to leave the medical centre and spend any time alone together. Not that it mattered. Except that that was only partly true also. There was no question that their patients had complete priority while they were on duty, but they only had a very limited number of nights left that they could find that kind of private time so losing one of them was actually quite a big deal. It felt as if there was a giant clock nearby that might be invisible but Lisa could hear the loudness of its ticking slowly increasing.

She was the kind of person you would want right by your side in any crisis but Hugh had already known that, hadn't he? It was one of those trustworthy things about Lisa Phillips. Like the way she had devoted herself to caring for her sister. And the way she not only always gave a hundred and ten percent in everything she did but she did it with intelligence and good-humoured grace even when she had to be rather tired by now.

Hugh was feeling a little weary himself. They'd put in quite a few miles of uphill walking today and work had been full on ever since the start of the evening surgery. They'd been kept very busy, despite calling in the extra team members, until the surgery hours were over. Now he and Lisa were alone in the medical centre and ship's hospital. Janet had gone to bed and Peter and Tim were going to be on call for anything else that happened on board overnight.

Jim's blood pressure had responded well to the intravenous medications and had dropped slowly enough not to cause any complications. Hugh wanted to keep him under observation till morning but he didn't need to be wakened for another check for an hour so he was sleeping peacefully. His wife had gone back to their cabin.

Michelle's condition had, thankfully, started to improve once the extra medications had taken effect. Hugh wasn't going to let her go in a hurry either. He was going to keep a very careful eye on her blood oxygen levels, which meant another arterial sample needed to be taken soon and they would continue to give her both oxygen and nebuliser therapy every few hours.

The roll of the ship was more obvious now as the night wore on. It didn't bother Hugh at all—he rather liked a bit of rough water, in fact, and he had been pleased to see that it didn't seem to be affecting Lisa either. He was concerned about what her level of fatigue must be like by now, though, so he went to the tiny kitchen in the medical centre on the other side of the reception area and put the electric jug on to boil water so he could make Lisa a mug of coffee.

He left the door behind him ajar because this room was not much bigger than a cupboard and, as he gathered the mugs and spoons he needed, he could hear that someone had come into the reception area. He turned his head so that he could see through the crack of the door, hoping that it wasn't a new patient arriving. It wasn't. Lisa had obviously come out of the treatment room so as not to disturb Michelle by taking a phone call.

'I can't talk long,' she was saying. 'I'm monitoring a patient. What on earth are you doing up at this time of night anyway?'

Hugh heard the soft ping of the jug announcing that the water had boiled. He should step out of the room, he thought, and let Lisa know he was nearby. But he hesitated, probably because it was a little disturbing how much he wanted to step closer to her, having heard that note of anxiety in her voice. The urge to protect this woman and to fix things that might be a problem for her was getting steadily more pronounced.

'I told you not to open that mail, Abby.'

There was a note of something like panic in Lisa's voice now, even though she had lowered it, and that need to try and make things better for her was so powerful it squeezed his chest tightly enough to be a physical pain.

'It's not a problem, okay?' Her voice was firm now

after a short silence. 'I'm dealing with it. That's why this job was such a great idea.'

Hugh could feel a deep frown creasing his forehead. What wasn't a problem? And why would being on this cruise be a way of dealing with it? Was there something she'd needed to get away from for a while? Or some*one*?

'It's only money,' he heard her say then. 'I've got this—I've got a plan. Don't worry. Look, I'll be home in just a couple of days and I'll explain everything. Now, I've really got to go. Talk soon, yeah?'

Lisa had her back to the kitchen door and she walked back to the treatment room as soon as she'd ended the call so she had no idea that Hugh had been eavesdropping.

He couldn't tell her, of course. Which meant he couldn't ask her what kind of problem she had or what the solution she was planning was all about. If it was money she needed, he had more than enough. He could help...

Or maybe not. Maybe he shouldn't try to find out what was going on and risk getting sucked into an even deeper involvement in Lisa's life.

It had been the mention of money that was changing things. Setting off warning bells that he couldn't ignore, despite the fact that they were taking him straight back to a place he had no desire to be. Back to those dismal days right before the wedding that had never happened. Back to the time when he'd lost both his fiancée and his best friend in one fell swoop.

Back to the worst moment of all. When Catherine had

turned away from him to walk out of his life for ever with the words that were going to haunt him for ever.

'I never really loved *you*, Hugh. I just loved your money.'

CHAPTER EIGHT

THE STORM BUILT through the night.

By the time daylight broke, the huge ship was riding some dramatic swells that only seemed to get bigger as the day wore on. The Lido deck was closed and the view from the windows was of a such a dark grey sea it was almost black, so the contrast of the white foam of countless breaking waves was even more breathtaking. The feeling of your stomach dropping when a swell had been crested was alarming and the crunch of the change at the bottom before another climb was also breathtaking. Wind howled through windows that weren't closed tightly enough and people were tilted sideways as they negotiated corridors around the ship.

It was like riding a roller-coaster in very slow motion and Lisa had never wanted to ride any kind of roller-coaster. Or do any thrill seeking, for that matter. Hugh, on the other hand, was actually enjoying this.

The medical centre was busier than Lisa had ever seen and, despite having only managing to catch a few hours of interrupted sleep after caring for their inpatients overnight, she and Hugh were there along with

Peter, Janet and Tim, dealing with not only the normal kind of workload but minor injuries that were arriving at an increasing rate due mainly to falls caused by the ship's rolling. They were also handing out huge quantities of anti-motion-sickness medications, trying to reassure overly anxious passengers, and they still had their inpatients.

Michelle seemed to be well over her frightening asthma attack but, for everybody's peace of mind, they were going to keep monitoring her for a few more hours. Jim's blood pressure was down to an acceptable level and he could be discharged as soon as a crew member was available to make sure he got back to his cabin safely.

On top of what was keeping the medical centre so busy, they were also fielding calls to various parts of the ship. Tim had just rushed off to a cabin where it sounded like an elderly person had fallen and hit their head to cause a frightening amount of bleeding when another call came in.

'It's in the gym,' Hugh announced. 'Another fall but they're having trouble breathing so I might need a hand.'

Lisa came out from behind the desk instantly. She was on Hugh's watch so it was obvious that she was the one to accompany Hugh.

But he wasn't even looking in her direction. 'Janet?'

Janet put her hands up in front of her. 'Not unless I have to. I'm okay here but if I go forward and that high I'll get sick.' She was the one to turn to Lisa. 'You're not prone to motion sickness, are you?'

'Haven't noticed anything yet.' Lisa tried to smile but there *was* a knot in her stomach that could turn into nausea down the track. Anxiety about the storm had just been augmented by anxiety about why Hugh had chosen Janet to go with him rather than her.

'Be a good test for you, then.' Hugh still wasn't looking at Lisa as he picked up another one of their first response packs. 'The gym's right at the bow. And we need to cross the Lido deck if we want to get there fast. Here, put this on.' He handed Lisa a bright yellow sou'wester. 'Even if it's not raining, there's enough spray to get you soaked almost instantly.'

They needed to get there fast if someone was having difficulty breathing and that meant running up the stairs to avoid both waiting for an elevator and the risk of getting caught if there was a power outage.

There were people pressed against windows as they reached the interior part of the Lido deck and the collective cries of mixed awe, alarm and excitement only added to Lisa's anxiety.

'You ready?' Hugh had his shoulder against the door that led to the deck. 'Brace yourself.'

They only had about twenty metres to go to get to the outside entrance of the gym on the other side of one of the swimming pools. Lisa was unprepared for the blast of wind as she went outside, however, and could feel herself losing her footing. She could get blown overboard, she thought. Or into a swimming pool that currently looked like something out of one of those horrific videos she'd seen where the grand piano was flying across a room. The water in the pool was tipping towards one end and then sloshing back to form a small tsunami that spilled out and washed across the deck with enough force to send deck chairs sliding into a heap against the railing.

For one terrible moment Lisa thought she might be going to drown and all she could think of was that she wouldn't be there for Abby when she was needed in the future. It had been bad enough not to have been there for her sister the other day when the upsetting incident with the patient had happened but at least she'd been able to talk to her and it had been enough. Not being there in any form would be even more of a failure than having been responsible for Abby's injuries in the first place.

How could she have been so irresponsible to have put herself in danger like this?

Except, in that same terrible moment, Hugh reached out and caught Lisa's arm. He was leaning into the wind and she could feel how stable his body was. He'd done this before. He was, in fact—judging by the grin on his face and the sparkle in his eyes—loving every moment of it.

Nothing could have demonstrated more clearly that they were—as Hugh had commented on during that, oh, so romantic dinner when they'd decided they could be friends—total opposites when it came to their approach to life.

But… Lisa was clinging to Hugh until they reached the doors that led to the relative safety of the gym. Opposites attracted, didn't they? Sometimes they could even make a long-term relationship work. If both sides wanted it to work, that was.

It was feeling more and more like Hugh was losing interest, however. Something was very different today but it wasn't until they were halfway through assessing the crew member in the gym who'd lost his balance and gone rolling across the floor to land against the metal handles of a piece of equipment that Lisa realised what it was.

The feeling of connection had vanished. As suddenly as a switch being flicked off.

Ever since their first night together, they'd been playing that game when they were working together. Frequent eye contact that was held just short of being a beat too long. Accentuating the kind of situations that meant they came into physical contact with each other, like their hands brushing when Lisa helped to shift the crew member's shirt to expose the painful area of his chest.

The tingle had gone. That awareness. Something was broken and Lisa didn't know what it was but it scared her. Okay, she'd known that her time with Hugh was coming to an end and it would be difficult but she'd thought they would make the most of it for as long as possible and then part as close friends. That they could stay in touch and might even see each other again one day. But maybe that was breaking some unspoken rule. That what happened on board ship simply ceased to exist when the cruise was over, and perhaps Hugh was thinking it was a good idea to wind things down as preparation so he wouldn't have to deal with tears or something when they said goodbye.

Or maybe what was really scaring her was being out in the open sea in weather like this. She could understand now why Janet had wanted to stay in the centre of the ship. Right up at the bow like this made the falling into the trough of a swell even more stomach-dropping and she could see the impressive wall of spray that came up to flood a lower deck when they hit the bottom of the dip between waves.

'Try and take a deep breath for me,' Hugh told their patient as he gently palpated an area where bruising was already becoming evident.

'Can't.' The young man's voice was strained. 'Hurts… *Ow…*'

'Sorry, mate. I think you might have cracked a rib or two. Let me listen to your chest and then we'll give you something for the pain and get you down to the clinic so we can so some X-rays.' He unhooked the stethoscope from around his neck. 'You didn't hit your head as well, did you?' He looked up at another member of the gym staff. 'Was he knocked out?'

The other personal trainer shook his head. 'He just went flying, along with a bunch of gear. We've closed the gym now, which is a shame, because we're going to be stuck at sea for an extra day. Have you heard that Sardinia's been cancelled? We're heading straight back to Malaga.'

What a way to end a cruise.

You had to feel sorry for the passengers but, for

Hugh, it was a blessing. He loved being flat out like this, facing a challenge that threatened to tip them past the point of being able to cope. He loved the thrill of riding waves like this but, best of all, it was the perfect excuse to totally ignore the mixed messages in his head concerning Lisa.

He was being given the chance to step right back and see what was going on from a perspective that wasn't getting sabotaged by spending personal time with her. Just being alone with Lisa was enough to make him want to trust her. Enough to make it preferable to block his ears to any alarm bells ringing. It was a bonus that fate was going to ensure they didn't get a chance to make love again because that would be even harder to resist and might make him want really stupid things, like being able to wake up with her in his bed for the rest of his life.

How could you feel so strongly about someone you'd only met a couple of weeks ago? He didn't really know Lisa at all, did he? Not that it probably made much difference in the long run. He'd known Catherine for two years, for heaven's sake.

As another bonus, there were the other medical staff around. It was Tim who helped Hugh glue the scalp wound that he'd found on the patient who'd been bleeding in her cabin. Peter took the X-rays that confirmed the broken ribs that the personal trainer had suffered but had also been reassuring that there was no underlying injury like a punctured lung.

He also X-rayed a Colles' wrist fracture that came in a little later and Lisa was tasked with helping splint the arm with a plaster slab underneath which kept her well out of Hugh's way for some time.

He hadn't missed the occasional puzzled glance that came his way from her from time to time but it was as though he wasn't actually in control of the growing distance between them. It was simply happening and he wasn't exactly enjoying the process himself.

He was missing Lisa already.

The medical staff took turns to have meal breaks by themselves or had food delivered by room service to ensure that they were caring for their inpatients, that someone was available at all times to see people that turned up at the clinic and that they had enough staff to respond to calls from other parts of the ship as well.

That would need to continue overnight, although the forecast was that the weather would have settled by the time they were due to dock in Malaga tomorrow morning. Even if that was the case, however, everybody was going to be exhausted by the time they reached their final port but at least Hugh and the rest of the team would have a couple of days off before a new cruise began—a three-week one next time—and Lisa would be heading home and would no doubt have plenty of time to rest before going back to her real job.

And her real life that didn't include him. Maybe it couldn't include any permanent relationship given that her sister was her first priority. Ironically, that was one of the things he loved about Lisa. The thing that made him feel like she was completely trustworthy and that was what was doing his head in enough to make it impossible to sleep when he was given a break in the early hours of the morning.

Instead, he went walking around the ship because, finally, the seas around them were subsiding. He might as well get a coffee, Hugh decided, because there was little point in trying to sleep for what was left of the night. They would be busy as soon as they docked as well, making arrangements for transport for the people who needed hospital care, like the woman who'd broken her wrist.

There were staff in the bar on the Lido deck that was now open again and it seemed like something was drawing Hugh into it.

'Just a coffee, thanks, mate.'

'Bet you've been busy, Doc. It's been kind of a wild ride, hasn't it?'

'You're not wrong there. Just as well you were closed for the day, I think. You've had enough drama in this bar for one cruise.'

Hugh took the coffee but decided not to stay on the bar stool to drink it. The reminder of the drama in this bar early on in this cruise was a reminder of something else and he was too weary to cope with any addition to the confusion he had going on in his head. It had been right here when he'd first properly worked with Lisa Phillips as they'd responded to the crisis of Alex's anaphylactic reaction. He'd never be able to come into this bar again without thinking of her, would he?

He walked to the edge of the deck instead and stood by the rail. He could see down onto a lower deck from here and there were obviously plenty of crew working overtime tonight to start the clean-up process that was part of the aftermath of bad weather. The kitchens and dining rooms would be even worse than the decks. Hugh had already treated a few lacerations from people dealing with bucketloads of broken glass. The deck chairs were one of the main issues outside. They got blown around or washed into corners to end up in a tangled heap. Someone was walking around one of those piles right now. A small figure in a bright yellow sou'wester.

Lisa…

Was she on the way to a call or just getting some fresh air? Hugh leaned over the rail, tempted to call out. Tempted to invite her to come and have a coffee with him just because he wanted to be closer to her. As he opened his mouth, however, he saw Lisa turn suddenly and then stoop to pick something up from amongst the jumble of deck-chair legs.

It was a wallet. He might be well above Lisa and it was the middle of the night but she was standing directly beneath a light so it was easy to see just how full of notes that wallet was when she opened it to have a look, and then touched the wad of notes as if trying to estimate its value. Hugh could also see the astonishment on Lisa's face and the way she instantly looked around, as if she expected the owner of the wallet to be nearby. Or was she wondering if anyone had seen her? The only person on that section of the deck was a crew member who had his arms full of folded deck chairs and he was walking away from Lisa to join his colleagues so he hadn't seen her. She looked over her shoulder again and then, with what almost looked like a shrug of her shoulders, Lisa folded the wallet and slipped it into the pocket of her coat.

He knew perfectly well that Lisa wasn't stealing that wallet. That she would be taking it to someone who would know what to do about finding its owner. He knew that with the same conviction that he knew how much she loved her sister. What that little scenario did do, however, was give Hugh a glimpse of an escape route back to a safe place. Because he had buttons that could be pushed quite easily when it came to women who cared too much about money—buttons that had clearly already been primed by overhearing that conversation Lisa had had with her sister. And because that button being pushed automatically pushed another one, that made him also easily remember the pain of making oneself vulnerable by loving someone so much that they had the power to break your heart.

That kind of pain was what was very likely to happen if he allowed this fling with Lisa to get any bigger than it already was. He could get hurt again. And, if that wasn't enough to convince him to pull the plug on what was happening between them, there was something else that was even less acceptable. Lisa was going to get hurt. And, okay, she might be going to get hurt anyway but this was about damage limitation now, wasn't it? For her sake even more than his own. Because that's what you did when you cared enough about someone else. They would both get over this. It had just been a shipboard fling, after all.

It wasn't exactly the end to this cruise that Lisa had imagined or that she would have wished for.

She was on deck as dawn was breaking and this massive ship was edging into port at Malaga. In a matter of only a few hours, she would be walking down the gangway and away from the most extraordinary job she'd ever had.

Away from the most extraordinary man she'd ever met.

She'd hardly seen him since that storm had peaked and they'd gone to that call in the gym together. She'd known that something had changed but she couldn't understand why. Unless she'd been completely wrong in the kind of man she believed Hugh Patterson to be? Maybe that very first impression of him had been the correct one. That he was one of those shallow, wealthy, pleasure-seeking people who were up for unlimited sexual adventures with no intention of getting involved or thought of hurting others along the way.

No…that wasn't going to work. She knew perfectly well that Hugh was one of the most genuine and caring people she'd ever met.

In fact…that was Hugh walking towards her right now and the expression on his face was exactly that. Genuine. Caring. She knew that her own face must be showing a lot of what was happening inside her. Joy in seeing him but puzzlement about why he'd apparently been avoiding her. A need to snatch any last moments they could enjoy together but sadness in knowing that they *would* be the last.

Maybe Hugh could see all that and maybe that was why there was no need to say anything. Why he took her into his arms as she turned away from the rail towards him. Why he kissed her with such...thoroughness...

But it felt different. So heartbreakingly tender it could have been a final farewell.

Somebody walked past, which was enough to make them break the kiss, but Lisa couldn't bear to move out of the circle of his arms yet so she put her head into the hollow of his shoulder, where she could hear the beat of his heart. The way she had done many times now, when they were in bed together and desire had been sated, at least temporarily.

'I feel like I haven't seen you for so long already,' she murmured. 'I was missing you, Hugh.'

'I was up here a few hours ago.' Hugh's voice was a rumble beneath her ear. He sounded incredibly weary. Almost sad, in fact. 'I saw you on the lower deck. It looked like you'd dropped something?'

'Not me.' Lisa closed her eyes so she could soak in how it felt to have Hugh's arms around her like this. 'Somebody must have lost their wallet in the storm. It's crazy how much money some people carry around with them.' Not that Lisa wanted to talk about this. There were far more important things she wanted to talk about. Like whether or not she might ever see Hugh again. 'I...um...handed it in.'

'Oh...' It seemed like Hugh's grip tightened around

her for a moment but then he let her go. 'Of course you did.'

There was something odd in his tone. Something that made Lisa look up to catch his gaze, and she couldn't interpret what she could see in his eyes but it looked as if it was mostly something sad. Disappointed even?

Perhaps he was feeling the same way she was. That she was about to lose something very precious. Lisa took a deep breath and summoned every bit of courage she had.

'I'm going to miss you, Hugh,' she whispered. 'I… I love you…'

He held her gaze. She could see the way his face softened as he smiled. 'I'm going to miss you, too, Lisa. It's been fun, hasn't it?'

Lisa swallowed hard. *Fun*?

He wasn't going to say it back, was he?

Because he didn't feel the same way. He'd just been having *fun*… Already she could feel the rush of blood to her cheeks. The heat of mortification…

Hugh broke their gaze to look over the railings of the deck. 'We'll be finished docking soon,' he said quietly. 'Our cruise will be officially over.'

And the cruise wasn't the only thing that would be officially over, obviously. Lisa was cringing inside now and she knew she must be the colour of a beetroot by now. She'd just told this man she loved him and he was about to tell her that he never wanted to see her again?

'I know,' she said quickly. 'And it'll be time to say goodbye. These cruise things…well, they're like holiday flings, I guess. Better to leave them as a good memory than turn them into dust by trying to make them into something they're not, yes?'

Why on earth was she trying to make this so easy for him? Or was it that she was just trying to make it less painful for herself? To give herself a chance to get away before he could see just how devastating this was for her?

'Especially for people like us.' Hugh's tone seemed to hold a sigh of relief. 'You're a family person through and through. It's been hard for you to be away from your sister, hasn't it? Me—I could never stay in one place for long.'

Or with one person. Lisa could easily add those unspoken words. She'd known that right from the start. Had she really thought that maybe she would be the one to change his mind?

She really did have to escape.

'I'd better go and start packing.' She actually managed to sound cheerful. Excited about the prospect of going home, even? 'I'll come down to the clinic to say goodbye properly before I go onshore.'

Hugh wasn't in the clinic when Lisa went in to make her farewells. He had intended to be there, of course—it was the polite thing to do—but he'd left it too late because he'd gone back to that bar on the Lido deck now that he was off duty, to do something he would never normally do at this time of day.

'Another coffee, Doc?'

'No. I've been up for so long it doesn't feel like morning any more. I'll have a glass of champagne, thanks.'

Because, in defeat, you needed it?

So here he was, watching the swarm of people leaving the ship far below him, with his glass almost empty, and that was when he realised he'd left it too late to say goodbye properly to Lisa Phillips, because he could see her on the pier, dragging her bright red suitcase behind her as she headed for the taxi rank.

She'd told him she loved him.

And he'd had to exert every ounce of his strength not to say it back. If he had, they would have stayed there in each other's arms, making plans for a future together that could never have worked. This was the life he loved and he was nowhere near ready to give it up. Lisa would never want to work on a cruise ship on a more permanent basis because that would take her away from her beloved sister. A sister who needed her to be close because she was disabled. He couldn't compete with that although Lisa might have agreed to work at sea with him if he'd asked. Because she loved him and he could feel the truth of that in a way he never had with the woman he'd almost married.

And he loved her which was why he'd pushed her away. Because if you felt like that about someone, you did what was best for them, not for yourself. He could never ask Lisa to give up caring for her sister to be with him. No matter how much she loved him, a part of her would be miserable and that would undermine everything. He would hate himself for making her miserable and maybe she would even hate him in the end. And, if he'd given up the life he loved in order to be with her, he would have been miserable and the end result would have been the same. It could never have worked so it was better this way. It just didn't feel like it yet.

It was easy to recognise Lisa down there on the pier but Hugh knew she wouldn't be able to spot him. It felt like she could, though, when he saw the way she stopped and turned to stare up at the ship for the longest moment.

It felt like a piece of his heart was tearing off.

CHAPTER NINE

ABIGAIL PHILLIPS WAS increasingly worried about her older sister.

She could understand that there would be a period of readjustment from the excitement of that amazing couple of weeks she'd had working on a cruise ship and then having to settle into a new job as a junior care home manager but it had been another couple of weeks now and, as far as Abby could tell, this new job was a complete disaster.

She'd never seen Lisa looking so miserable.

In an effort to cheer her up, Abby had not only picked up their takeaway dinner, in what they'd agreed would be a weekly tradition now that they weren't living together, she had a special gift for Lisa.

'Put the food in the kitchen and we'll heat it up soon. Come and sit in the lounge with me. I've got something for you.'

An advantage to being in a wheelchair was that you could tuck things in beside you and keep them hidden. It was a little harder with the bottle-shaped something that Abby had on her left side but she'd hidden that with her big, soft shoulder bag. The small, flat package on her right side had been easier to conceal.

Lisa opened the wrapping and then froze as she stared at what was inside the package. Abby's heart sank like a stone.

'It's that French café,' she said. 'The one you sent me the picture of. I thought you'd like a memory of being in the most romantic place on earth.' And that was why she'd chosen a silver frame with heart-shaped corners for the print of Lisa, sitting beneath grapevines, with the most beautiful view in the background, holding up a glass of champagne in a toast, she'd later labelled *Here's to living the dream!* when she'd sent it to Abby. Seeing even an echo of that kind of joyous smile on her face was what Abby had been aiming for this evening. What actually happened was that Lisa burst into tears.

'Oh, heck…' Abby manoeuvred her chair and put the brakes on so that she could transfer herself to the couch and put her arms around her sister. 'I'm sorry… I've done the wrong thing, haven't I?'

'It's not you.' Lisa was making a valiant effort to stifle her sobs. She scrubbed at her eyes and sniffed. 'I…love the photo…'

'It's that new job of yours, isn't it? I know you hate it.'

'It's not that bad.'

'But you hate it, don't you?'

'I just need to get used to it. Being in an office that doesn't even have a window instead of working with any patients myself, you know? The closest I get is helping the family fill in their pre-admission forms or organising medical appointments for the residents that can't be managed in our treatment rooms.'

'You'd rather be back on that ship? Dealing with exciting things like that guy who stopped breathing? Going to romantic places like this café?'

But Lisa was shaking her head with such emphasis that it was almost despair and Abby finally twigged.

'Oh…my God,' she breathed. 'You *did* have a fling with that cute doctor, didn't you? That was why you started looking like a kid on Christmas morning.'

Lisa caught a slow tear that was trickling down the side of her nose. 'It was a really bad idea. I knew what he was like. The first time I ever saw him he was kissing another woman, for heaven's sake.'

'He *cheated* on you?' Abby could feel a knot of anger forming in her gut. Whatever the guy had done, he'd hurt Lisa and that was unforgivable.

'You can't cheat on someone if you're not in a relationship,' Lisa said. 'And we weren't. We both knew it was only going to last as long as the cruise and, no, I know that he wasn't interested in anyone else while he was with me. He just…switched off being interested in me at the end. Like it hadn't been anything important…or even special…'

Abby watched as Lisa screwed her eyes tightly shut to try and ward off any more tears. 'You fell in love with him, didn't you?' Her own heart was breaking for Lisa. 'You went for the first non-boring guy ever and you fell for him.'

Lisa nodded miserably. 'It was entirely my fault. I knew it wasn't safe. I knew I was playing with fire and there was a good chance I'd get burnt. And that's exactly what happened.'

'Takes two to tango,' Abby muttered.

'It wasn't as if it was anything that could have become something more and we both knew that. That day, in that café in the picture, we'd agreed we could be friends even if we were total opposites and then…and then he made me laugh when I was feeling really crap.'

Abby shook her head. 'Yeah, that'll do it. What is it that's so powerful about someone making you laugh?'

'Maybe it's because it's something that shows you want someone to feel better. And that there has to be a connection, whether you've known it was there or not, to make it work.'

'Hmm…you could be right.' But Abby frowned. 'Why were you feeling so crap?'

'We'd lost a patient. A cardiac arrest in a guy who was on his honeymoon. We tried to resuscitate him for nearly an hour but we were never going to win.'

Abby's eyes widened. 'You never told me about that.'

'Well, you were having a hard time yourself. It was the same day that you'd had that patient assume *you* were a patient as well, not his therapist.'

'Oh…so you were already feeling bad and then I heaped all my crap on you and you spent your time trying to make me feel better but didn't even let me know how you were feeling so I couldn't try to make *you* feel better.' Abby really was angry now. 'How do you think that makes *me* feel?' She reached to pull her chair closer, intending to get off the couch and away from Lisa before they revisited an argument that would ruin the evening—the one about how Lisa had always done too much for Abby, who was never allowed to reciprocate in any meaningful way. 'And, as for that guy, what was his name?'

'Hugh…' Lisa's voice was a whisper.

'Yeah… *Hugh*… Well, he's just a bastard and you're better off a million miles away from him. Man, I wish I could tell him exactly what I think of him.'

It wasn't possible to shift herself onto the cushion of her chair until she'd pulled her shoulder bag off the cushion. Oh…and that bottle of champagne. She would have hidden it from Lisa but it was too late. She'd seen it and she was crying again. But she was laughing through her tears and suddenly that made the prospect of a big fight evaporate instantly. It was Lisa who put her arms around Abby this time, to give her a fierce hug. They'd been through far worse times than this and survived. They would always survive because they had each other as support, even if the giving had always been too heavily weighted on Lisa's side.

'How did you know?' Lisa asked when she finally pulled herself free of the hug and wiped her eyes.

'Know what?'

'That, in defeat, you need champagne.'

'What on earth are you talking about, Lise?'

Lisa got to feet. 'I'll find some glasses,' she said. 'And then give you a wee history lesson about Napoleon Bonaparte.'

* * *

'It's lovely to see you, Hugh. Or it would be, if you weren't looking so…wrecked.'

'You mean I look older?' Hugh shrugged. 'It's the end of a three-weeker and we had some challenging passengers on board. Hypochondriacs, mostly. Very demanding ones.'

He hadn't enjoyed the last three weeks nearly as much as he usually enjoyed his job but maybe that was due to the fact that he'd enjoyed the previous cruise so much more than normal—up until the end of it, anyway. Because he had been sharing it with Lisa and that had made everything seem new and far more meaningful. He'd taken her to some of his favourite places. Worse, he'd taken her to his bed and the effect of sharing that with Lisa had been the same. New. Far more meaningful.

But he'd been right to let her walk back to her own life without the complications that would have come if they'd tried to keep their connection. Lisa wasn't the kind of woman who'd be happy to see him for an afternoon here or there when he happened to be in London. She deserved someone who could offer her the same kind of loyalty and commitment that she would give to someone she loved. The kind she was already committed to giving to Abby who—as she'd said herself—was the most important person in her life.

It should have been a lot easier than this to have turned back to embrace the lifestyle that had been so perfect for the last couple of years. Not much more than a month ago he'd been looking forward to spending an afternoon with Carlotta in Barcelona. He could remember how much he had enjoyed kissing her and maybe that's what he really needed to distract him. Hugh raised his hand to signal the waiter that he was ready to pay the bill for their lunch. Now they could go somewhere more appropriate for some more intimate time together.

He found what he hoped was a seductive smile, although it felt rather more that he was leering at his companion.

'You, on the other hand, look as gorgeous as ever, Carlotta. Shall we go somewhere more comfortable?'

'Of course…' But Carlotta was looking at his full glass. 'You don't want to finish your wine first?'

'I think I might have gone off champagne.' There were too many memories associated with it now, that was the problem, and every one of them included Lisa Phillips.

So many wonderful memories, like the way she would glow with the pleasure and wonder of a new experience, like tasting champagne for the first time or soaking in a fabulous view or enjoying a delicious meal or…or…dear Lord…the way she used to look when she was coming apart in his arms…

Man, it was hot here today. Hugh was wearing an open-necked shirt and yet he had an urge to loosen his tie or go in search of a sea breeze. Was his face as red as it felt? Surely he wasn't blushing, the way Lisa had been unable to prevent herself doing so furiously when she was uncomfortable or embarrassed. Like the way her cheeks had gone such a bright colour after she'd told him she loved him and he hadn't said it back...

Okay...knowing that he'd hurt Lisa wasn't such a good memory. But neither was the one that sprang to mind when Hugh opened his wallet to extract a note or two to leave a tip for their waiter. It was sad, he decided as he put his hand on Carlotta's lower back to guide her between tables, that it only took one less than happy memory to take the shine off so many of the better ones.

Carlotta slipped her arm around his waist as they left the restaurant and it was enough for him to stop and turn towards her. She put a hand on his cheek then and raised her face to kiss him. But Hugh found himself breaking the contact of their lips almost instantly. Lifting his head with a jerk.

'I'm sorry,' he said. 'But I can't... I don't know what's wrong with me today.'

'I think I do.' Carlotta's smile was knowing. 'I don't know who she is, but I think it's finally happened. You've fallen in love.'

Hugh shook his head. 'Nope. I did that once and it was the biggest mistake I ever made. I wouldn't be stupid enough to do it again.'

Carlotta's gaze was full of sympathy now. 'Oh, Hugh...it's not something you can stop happening. You can fight it, of course. Walk away from it even. But you never know...walking away from it this time might be an even bigger mistake than choosing the wrong person the first time.' She touched his cheek again before walking away with a wave. 'Thanks for lunch, Hugh. And best of luck…'

It wasn't far back to the ship and Hugh walked briskly despite the heat of the Spanish afternoon. Simon was at his usual place at the bottom of the gangway, although it was only staff he was welcoming back on board today. The passengers from this cruise had all disembarked this morning.

'Hey, Hugh…how's it going? Happy to have a day off?'

'I've got a few days off this time. I'm thinking of grabbing a flight to London and visiting my folks.'

By the time he reached the marble-floored atrium, where Harry's piano was deserted and silent, the idea of escaping the ship for a few days had become so appealing that Hugh went towards one of the desks where he knew someone could help him make his travel arrangements. Everyone on board relied on Sally to answer any questions because she'd been in the business for so long she seemed to know everything. If she couldn't give you the answer herself, she always knew where to find it.

Hugh wasn't the only one with a query this afternoon. The ship's captain was ahead of him and as Hugh got closer he was startled to hear what the captain was saying.

'I'm sure her name was Lisa. She was wearing scrubs under her sou'wester, so I assume she was working in the medical centre. It was the night of that storm.'

'Oh, I remember.' Sally nodded. 'That was some

storm. Now…let me look and see if I can find who she was.'

'Lisa Phillips,' Hugh told them. 'She was just a locum nurse—only with us for the one cruise.'

Just…? Lisa could never be "just" anything. She was an extraordinary human being, that's what she was… and Carlotta was right. He *was* in love with her. She had been in love with him and had been brave enough to tell him. And he had thrown that back in her face. Even if he'd had good reason, which he'd believed he did, it was a horrible thing to have done. He hadn't even said goodbye to her, had he?

'Well, I need her address,' the captain said. 'I've got a rather large cheque to forward.'

Hugh blinked. Sally looked curious as well. 'Whatever for?' she asked.

'Someone lost their wallet during that storm. This Lisa found it and handed it in. Well, she bumped into me and asked me where she could find someone from Security and I said I'd look after it for her. We tracked down the owner once things had settled down and, after he got home, he was so impressed that the wallet had still had a rather ill-advised amount of cash in it that he thought the person who'd found it deserved a reward.'

Hugh's breath caught in his throat. Lisa not only deserved an apology from him, she deserved the reward of that cheque. And… it gave him a perfect excuse to see her again.

He cleared his throat. 'I'm about to head to London

for a day or two,' he said. 'I could deliver it personally, perhaps, if she's not too far away?'

'Marvellous idea.' The captain handed him the envelope. 'Get some flowers to go with it, lad, and tell her that we all appreciate her honesty. She's done our reputation a power of good.'

Sally was beaming. 'Let me find her address in the system for you. Ooh, I'd love to be a fly on the wall when you turn up on her doorstep. Won't she be thrilled?'

Abby glared at the man on the doorstep.

She hadn't needed his introduction.

'I *know* who you are,' she said. 'Lisa's working late but even if she was home I'm pretty damn sure she wouldn't want to see you.'

Mind you, this ship's doctor was a lot cuter in real life than in that photo on the website. He also had a massive bunch of flowers in his arms and an expression in those rather gorgeous brown eyes that looked… nervous?

The flowers—and the man—were getting rapidly wetter as they stood there in the pouring rain but Abby suddenly had misgivings about whether sending this unexpected visitor instantly on his way was the right thing to do. Hadn't she wanted the opportunity to give him a piece of her mind about how he had treated her sister?

'You'd better come in for a minute,' she said ungraciously. 'I don't want those flowers dripping all over my lap.' Abby swung her chair around and headed for the kitchen. 'Put them in the sink,' she ordered. 'I'll deal with them later.'

He did as he was told, which was gratifying. But then he gave her a grin that was cheeky enough to disarm her completely.

'And there I was thinking that Lisa was the bossy sister,' he said.

Abby couldn't help a huff of laughter escaping. 'She is. It's actually very out of character for me to be rude but…'

'But…?'

'I don't like you,' Abby told him bluntly. 'You've made my sister miserable.'

'I'm really sorry about that. Maybe this will cheer her up.'

Hugh took an envelope out of his pocket and handed it to Abby, who opened it. Her jaw dropped when she saw the amount the cheque was written out for. By the time Hugh had explained what it was for, she had a lump in her throat that made it difficult to swallow.

'She only took that job on the ship because she was desperate for a bit of extra money,' she told Hugh. 'Because of *me*… She got a loan to get a specially modified car for me but it was a real struggle for her to meet the payments, especially when she had to find a new job after being made redundant. She even missed a mortgage payment on the house—I opened a threatening letter from the bank when she was away, which was really scary. Anyway…' She put the cheque back into its envelope, so that Lisa could get the same surprise that she'd had. 'I shouldn't be telling you any of this but I guess it's just as much my fault as yours that she's miserable now.'

He didn't say anything but when Abby looked up, she could see how carefully he was listening. How important this was to him. He also looked as though he was concerned for Abby. Perhaps he could sense how close she was to crying?

'You'd better sit down,' she said. 'Would you like a cup of tea?'

'You knew about me, didn't you?' she asked a short time later as she put a mug of tea on the kitchen table in front of Hugh.

'I knew you'd had an accident when you were very young that left you in a wheelchair. That your sister is about six years older than you and is completely devoted to you and that she was worried about not living with you any more.'

'Did you know that she's my half-sister?'

Hugh nodded. 'She did tell me that. In almost the same breath that she told me how much she loves you.'

'So she didn't tell you that we had different fathers because my mother had drug and alcohol problems that meant her relationships never lasted? That Lisa was more of a mother to me than our mother ever was, even though she was only a kid herself? That she's always blamed herself for my accident because she wasn't holding my hand tightly enough and I escaped and ran out in front of a car?'

Again, Hugh said nothing. He looked as though he had no idea where to find the words he might need but Abby wasn't going to help him. He needed to know more.

'For her entire life she's put me first,' Abby said quietly. 'She's done it out of love but she's also done it out of guilt and that's something that's really hard for me to live with. She was only a kid herself, for God's sake. She's got nothing to feel guilty about but she chose her career so that she could stay close to home. She wanted to be a doctor but that would have meant going to a medical school away from home so she did nursing training instead.'

'I kind of guessed that.' Hugh nodded.

'She never went to parties when she was a teenager. Never spent money on herself or took a gap year to do any travelling. She took over the mortgage on this house when Gran died and said it was worth it because it would keep us safe. I reckon she chose her boring boyfriends because they were safe options that weren't going to interfere with her life. I don't believe she's ever been in love either. Until now. Which means this is her first broken heart and…and it might be *my* fault she met you in the first place but that…that's down to *you*…'

Again, Hugh nodded. 'It might not be my first broken heart,' he admitted. 'But it feels like it is. And I can't argue with you because it is down to me. I've wrecked the most amazing thing I've ever found and I have no idea what to do about it. I'm sure you're probably also right about Lisa not wanting to see me.'

'Are you saying what I think you're saying?' Abby waited for Hugh to meet her gaze so that she could gauge how genuine he might be. 'That you're in love with Lise? That you really *want* to be with her?'

'For the rest of my life,' Hugh said softly. 'I'm never going to meet anyone else like your sister. I don't think there *is* anyone else in the world that lights up when she's happy quite like Lisa does. I want to see her that happy for the rest of *her* life. I want to be the one who creates some of that happiness.'

'Oh, my God…' Abby could feel a tear sneaking down her cheek. 'That's exactly what I want for her, too.'

'I'm not.' Hugh held up his hands in a gesture of surrender. 'And I realise now that being with Lisa is more important than a lifestyle that isn't exactly compatible with a long term future. I understand how important you are to her, too. I totally respect that. I love that she loves you that much.'

Abby swiped at the moisture on her cheeks. 'I'm perfectly capable of being independent, thank you. I've *told* her that. I've told her that if she wants to go and have an exciting job at sea instead of the one she hates so much here, then I might miss her but I'd be fine. I need to be independent.' Abby had found a shaky smile. 'You'd be doing me a favour if you persuaded her to go sailing off into the sunset with you for a good, long while. You can always settle down later, you know.'

'I don't think I'd be able to do that.' Hugh was shaking his head. 'She's a determined woman, your sister, and I've hurt her. It's going to take something pretty special to get her to even listen to me, isn't it?'

'Hmm…' Abby had no doubts at all about how genuine Hugh Patterson was. She could also see exactly why her sister had fallen in love with this man. But he was right. Lisa thought she had played with fire and been burnt. She wouldn't be keen to go anywhere near that heat again.

Her gaze drifted over to the flowers in the kitchen sink. And then it lifted to the window sill above them, which was where Lisa had put the small framed photo that Abby had given her last week. She turned slowly back to her guest. Biting her lip couldn't stop the smile that wanted to escape.

'I think I might have an idea,' she said.

CHAPTER TEN

'I CAN'T BELIEVE I let you talk me into this.'

'Shh… I'm busy.'

Lisa had to smile at the expression on Abby's face as her sister closed her eyes for a moment. It was sheer bliss, that's what it was.

'You don't look very busy.'

'I am. It's a big deal, you know—this living the dream stuff.'

'I know…' Her voice cracked with the emotion of it because this was exactly what she'd dreamed of for Abby, only a matter of a few weeks ago. For her to be here. In this exact spot. At this precise table, in fact, that had the best view from the terrace.

Not that she'd made it easy. Even after the astonishing good fortune of Abby winning those tickets for a weekend in the South of France in some radio competition—on top of that amazing reward that had been delivered with some flowers on behalf of the ship's captain—Lisa had initially totally refused to give in to Abby's plea to experience the most romantic place on earth. She'd even taken that photograph off the kitchen windowsill and hidden it in a drawer so she didn't have to think about it every time she caught a glimpse of the image.

'It's the last place on earth I'd want to go,' she'd said. *'I can't believe you'd even ask.'*

'It's not as though you were there on a date,' Abby had pointed out. *'It was before you hooked up with Hugh, remember? You were there as friends and you look so happy in that photo. It might help.'*

'How?'

'Oh... I don't know. Like one of those reset things you can do on the computer. Where you can pick a time when you knew things were good and have all your settings revert to what they were then.' The look on Abby's face reminded Lisa of when she'd been a small child and had desperately wanted something that she couldn't have or do because the wheelchair had made it too difficult. *'Please? For me?'*

So, of course, in the end she had agreed. When had she ever not agreed to something that Abby wanted so much?

She'd even let Abby choose her outfit. A floaty red dress sprinkled with tiny white flowers, white sandals and a little white flower on a hair clip. They might have very different shades of red hair themselves, with Lisa being a dark auburn and Abby much more of a strawberry blonde, but it had been a pact from when they were both children that they would wear red whenever they liked.

Abby's eyes opened again. 'Where's that champagne?' she asked.

'Relax. I'm sure it's on its way. We've got plenty of time. The car isn't coming back for us for hours. Have you decided what you want to eat yet?'

'I need some more time—it all looks so good. And I need to go to the loo before I think about it any more.'

'Oh…' Lisa's chair scraped on the stone of the floor. 'Of course…'

Abby's eyebrows shot up. '*You* need to go to the loo, too?'

'No… I thought…' Lisa sat down with a sigh. 'Sorry…'

'No problem.' Abby's smile was forgiving. 'And if I hadn't already checked out that they had a disabled toilet available I would probably be very grateful for your assistance. As it is, I can manage perfectly well on my own. So *you* relax. I'll be back soon.'

Watching her sister expertly manoeuvre between the tables, heading back to the reception area inside the café, Lisa managed to let go of the underlying anxiety that this might not have been a good idea. Abby had managed the travelling with ease and she was revelling in everything they had packed into this short getaway already. It had been such an amazing prize that had not only included a luxury hotel in Nice but a chauffeur-driven car for any sightseeing they had wanted to do.

Relaxing for a few minutes as she waited for Abby to return wasn't difficult. It was even warmer than it had been the last time Lisa had been here so the soft breeze drifting over the canopy of the forest beneath the café was more than welcome. The shade from the grapevine running rampant over the pergola was just as welcome and the play of shadows from the sunlight finding gaps in the leaves was delightful. It would make it harder to see when Abby was coming back, although Lisa could see a waiter standing beside the bar, putting a bottle into an ice bucket. Their champagne? She hoped that Abby would return in time to see it being opened because that pop of the cork was all part of the magic, wasn't it?

Or it had been the last time.

The first time.

From the corner of her eye, Lisa could see the waiter approaching the table now. He had a white cloth over his arm, the bottle in the bucket in one hand and two fluted glasses in the other. It was impossible not to drift back in time. To remember what it was like when those thousands of tiny bubbles exploded in her mouth and then evaporated into delicious iciness. To remember opening her eyes to find Hugh staring at her with an intensity that had taken her breath away all over again.

The same way he'd looked at her when they had been making love…

She could even hear an echo of his voice—*'I knew you'd look like that'*—with that note of happiness because *she'd* been so happy.

Oh, help…

She wasn't going to cry, Lisa told herself firmly. She wasn't going to let anything spoil this for Abby. But where *was* Abby? She was taking such a long time—maybe she did need some help after all. Lisa had to peer past the waiter to try and see if Abby had appeared again yet.

'Don't worry, she's fine.'

Lisa's jaw dropped in total disbelief as she recognised the voice of the waiter and looked up.

Hugh's smile was reassuring but the cork shot from the bottle with a sound like gunfire that made Lisa jump. He caught the escaping foam in one of the glasses.

'It was all part of the plan.' Hugh's smile had disappeared as he slid into the seat on the other side of this small wrought-iron table.

'I've been a complete idiot,' he said quietly. 'Do you think you could ever forgive me?'

This was overwhelming. Lisa suspected she might look like a stone statue because that was how she was feeling. There were just too many feelings that were too powerful.

How much manipulation had gone on to entice her here for what had clearly been a set-up? For someone who'd kept such tight control of everything in her life, including herself—in order to keep Abby and herself safe—the idea that she had fallen for it was somehow shameful.

Knowing that her beloved sister had been in on it and had kept the secret so well was so surprising it was hurtful.

The fact that it was happening here, in what she herself had described as the most romantic place on earth, had the potential to take the magic away and make it simply a stage set and not real at all.

But running beneath that horrible mix of impressions that made her want to get to her feet and run was something else. A bright, shiny thread of what felt like hope. That something precious was about to be offered to her and all she had to do was to be brave enough to accept the gift.

Finally, she found her voice. 'Um…whose idea was this?'

'Abby's,' Hugh admitted. 'Although I have to say I thought it was brilliant and you know why?'

'Why?' There were plenty more questions to ask about how and why Abby had been colluding with Hugh but they could wait. There was something far more compelling about the expression in those brown eyes Lisa loved so much. Whatever he was about to say was so important he wasn't going to let her look away.

'Because this was where you had your first taste of champagne. Where I saw that joy of it in your face. And maybe I didn't realise it at the time—okay, I probably would have run a mile if I *had* realised it—but I think that was the moment I started to fall in love with you, Lisa.'

Oh, yes…that shiny thread of hope was glowing now. Shining so brightly that it was casting a shadow over everything else.

'I told Abby how much I was in love with you. That I want to see that kind of happiness in your face as often as possible for the rest of your life and that I want to be able to do whatever I can to create that happiness for you.' Hugh's voice cracked a little. 'And you know what she said?'

Lisa shook her head. She couldn't get any words past the lump in her throat.

'She said that she wants exactly the same thing. We're friends for life now, your sister and me.'

'Oh…' There was no stopping the tears that were determined to escape.

'She told me about what happened,' Hugh said gently. 'That you've always been so determined to look after her and keep her safe. That you've held onto guilt for something that wasn't your fault.'

'But it was,' Lisa whispered. 'It was…' She swallowed hard. Maybe he didn't know the whole truth—the worst thing about her. 'There was a doll. In the toy shop window. A really beautiful doll with curly yellow hair and I was standing there, wishing with all my heart that I had hair like that and that I could take that doll home with me… That was when it happened. I let go of Abby's hand.'

'You didn't let go, sweetheart,' Hugh said softly. 'Abby pulled because she wanted to run. She took you by surprise. You were only a little girl yourself and you should never have been given that responsibility in the first place. You've always had too much responsibility and you've taken that on with a grace and determination that's amazing. But don't you think it's about time to forgive little Lisa? To stop denying her the good things in life because you decided so long ago that maybe she didn't deserve them?'

Lisa blinked as her tears evaporated. How on earth could Hugh know those things about her when she'd only fleetingly given them any head space?

'You're allowed to want things just for yourself,' Hugh added. There was a twinkle in his eyes now. 'The things that make you feel good. Or to feel loved.' He picked up the bottle and began to pour a glass but when he held it out towards her, he paused, looking at her over the rim—like the way he had when she'd taken her first ever sip. 'Things like champagne,' he said. His fingers brushed hers as she accepted the glass and his words were a whisper that only she could hear. 'Or making love…'

Oh…*my*… Surely everybody in this café could see the glow that was about to reach Lisa's cheeks. But happiness like this was such a fragile thing, wasn't it? Irresistible but terrifying at the same time.

'I know.' Hugh was smiling at her. 'It's scary, isn't it? That was why I was such an idiot. I used my memories of the disaster that was almost my first marriage as a kind of shield to make sure I never took that kind of risk again. I took that shield out and polished it up when I realised I was getting in too deep with you. I was scared, too. I thought I'd get over missing you after you left but you know what?'

Lisa could feel her lips curling into a smile. 'What?'

'I just missed you more every single day. Until I finally realised that I had to trust my instincts. To trust *you*. As much as you were trusting me when you said you loved me. I'm sorry I got that so wrong… I wasn't ready, that's all…'

Lisa nodded. She could understand that. She could understand how hard it was to trust.

'I've never believed that the things I wanted just

for myself were safe,' she told Hugh, her voice wobbling. 'They were just distractions and that made them dangerous.'

'I blame that doll,' Hugh said. 'With the stupid yellow hair.' His tone changed to something far more serious. 'You'll always be safe with me,' he said, 'if that's one of the things you want.' He drew in a deep breath. 'I love you, Lisa. Can you trust that? Can you trust *me*? Take that leap of faith?'

It was Lisa's turn to draw in a new breath. 'Could you hold my hand? So we could jump together?'

Hugh took both her hands in his. 'Always,' he murmured.

For the longest moment, they soaked in that connection. There would be time for the kind of intimate physical connection they knew would come later but the skin on skin of their entwined fingers was all they needed for this moment. The gaze on gaze of their eye contact was so deep it was a connection that felt like their souls were touching.

Nobody interrupted them but they were, after all, in the most romantic place on earth so perhaps a couple who were totally lost in each other's eyes was only to be expected. It had to stop eventually, of course, because a celebration was called for. Hugh filled the second flute with champagne. And then he reached into the inside pocket of his jacket and took out a third glass. He turned his head before he began to fill it, nodding towards the reception area of the café. Seconds later, Abby was rolling towards their table with the happiest smile Lisa had ever seen on her face.

'So you did it?' she asked Hugh. 'You proposed?'

'Oh, no…' Hugh handed Abby a glass of champagne. 'I forgot about that bit.'

Abby put her glass down. 'No champagne allowed then. Get on with it.'

Lisa laughed. '*Abby*—you can't say that.'

Abby scowled. 'But it was part of the plan.'

'It was,' Hugh agreed. 'And I had it all planned—apart from the ring because I'd want you to choose exactly what *you* want. But I just missed the perfect opportunity, didn't I?' He arched an eyebrow at Abby. 'A *private* opportunity.'

'It's not too late,' Abby said. 'Don't mind me. I want to read the menu again anyway.'

Lisa was still smiling. 'You don't have to do what she says.'

But Hugh had caught her gaze again and her smile faded. 'We never said a proper goodbye, did we? That last day of the cruise?'

'No…' It wasn't something Lisa really wanted to remember. It was a bit shocking, in fact, to have a reminder of how broken-hearted she'd felt, walking away from Hugh.

'There was a good reason for that, even if neither of us knew it at the time.' Hugh was still holding her gaze. He'd taken hold of her hand again as well. 'I never want to say a "proper" goodbye to you, Lisa Phillips. I want you to be in my life for every day I'm lucky enough to get. Will you marry me?'

Oh… Lisa was so ready to take that leap. Straight off the edge of that cliff, and she could do it without hesitation because Hugh was holding her hand. And she knew he would always be there to hold her hand.

'Yes,' she said softly.

'What was that?' Abby raised her head from the menu. 'I didn't quite hear it.'

'Yes,' Lisa said, more loudly. She was laughing again. So was Hugh. 'Yes, yes, *yes…*'

EPILOGUE

Two years later...

IT WAS NEVER going to get old, hearing the pop of a champagne cork. Not that they did it all that often but it always made Lisa smile. Perhaps that was because there was always that moment when she would catch her husband's gaze and know that they were both remembering that first time.

And celebrating their engagement, and later on their wedding, all in the same place, on the terrace of that magical café in the South of France. It was one of those private moments when so much could be said with nothing more than a fleeting, shared glance. It was fleeting, because they were here for something—and someone—other than themselves.

'Happy house-warming, Abby.'

'Thanks, Lise. I can't believe I'm here. That I actually have this incredibly cool apartment that's been custom built just to make life easier for me. And it's all thanks to you.' She raised her glass but then grinned. 'Oh… I almost forgot. You're not even going to have a taste, then?'

Lisa shook her head, her hand protectively smoothing the roundness of her belly. As if acknowledging the touch, her baby kicked against the palm of her hand.

Abby touched Hugh's glass with her own instead. 'It's thanks to you, too, bro. If you hadn't given me the heads-up that my dream job was coming up at your hospital, I wouldn't have thought about moving at all.'

'You're going to love it at St John's Hospital. I'm coming up to a year in the emergency department there and I'm still loving it.'

'Hey, it's a specialist hand therapist position in a team that's so good, people come from all over the country to get their surgery and start their recuperation. I still can't believe how lucky I was to get the job.'

'Why wouldn't you?' Lisa was beaming proudly. 'We're not the only ones who think you're the best. And it's Gran we should toast as well. If she hadn't made a good choice when she bought that little house decades ago, it wouldn't have sold for enough to make it possible to do a makeover like this on this apartment.' She looked around at the sleek lines and open spaces that made it so easy to live in for someone in a wheelchair but it still had the character that went with the old building it was part of, like the high ceilings and feature fireplaces.

'Best of all, you're a lot closer to us now,' Hugh put in. 'For, you know…those babysitting duties that are coming up.'

The ripple of laughter was comfortable. So was the teasing. They were a family unit now and about to welcome the first of the next generation.

'It's just a shame you're not having twins,' Abby said. 'Or triplets, even.'

'You're kidding, right?' Lisa shook her head. 'Why would you wish that on me?'

'You've got all those bedrooms in that mansion of yours. You'll need to have a few more kids to fill them up. How are your parents doing, Hugh? Do they like their downsized life in Central London?'

'They're hardly ever there. It's ironic that when Lisa and I gave up working on the cruise ships, they decided that it was their favourite way to travel. They're on their way to Alaska as we speak.'

Hugh had come to stand behind Lisa and he put his arms around her, his hands over hers on her belly. The kick this time was stronger and Lisa glance slid sideways to find Hugh had done the same thing. It was another one of those private moments and it was so filled with joy that she couldn't look away.

'Oh, get a room,' Abby growled. 'No, wait…that's how this happened, wasn't it? I'll consider myself warned.'

It was a joke but Lisa could sense something in her sister's tone that made her move to give her a hug. A note of longing, perhaps? She knew Abby was thrilled with her new life that included her dream job and the perfect apartment but Lisa wanted for Abby the kind of happiness she had found with Hugh. Because it made life about as close to perfect as it could get.

'It'll be your turn one of these days,' she murmured as she wrapped her arms around her sister. 'You just wait and see…'

* * * * *

SAVED BY THEIR MIRACLE BABY

ALISON ROBERTS

MILLS & BOON

CHAPTER ONE

IT CAME OUT of nowhere.

A sickening crunch. A thump as the back of Abigail Phillips's head hit the headrest and the car lurched as the engine stalled. The fear that worse was about to come made Abby her screw her eyes shut for a few seconds and grip her steering wheel as if her life depended on it. Was her car going to get hit again and go spinning off into oncoming traffic or the nearest lamppost?

But there was only silence now and her car was just as stable as it had been before the crunch, when Abby had been the first to stop at this red traffic light. She'd only been rear-ended, she realised, and it was probably no big deal. She'd love to jump out of the car and go and inspect any damage to the vehicle that was her pride and joy but that wasn't going to happen. What she did do was take a couple of deep breaths and try to control the way her heart was still hammering against her ribs. Instead of slowing down, however, it completely missed a beat when someone rapped on her window and gave her another fright.

Her eyes flew open. There was a face at her window now. A very concerned-looking face.

'Oh, my God…' she heard him say. 'I'm so sorry. Are you hurt?'

He tried the door but it was locked. Abby wasn't stupid—she knew to lock her door and keep herself safe from something like carjacking. She also remembered some advice she'd heard about never admitting culpability at the scene of an accident because of potential legal ramifications. Either this man had never heard the same advice or he was just too honest not to admit something was entirely his own fault and then apologise for it. Abby liked that enough to make her reach for the switch to lower her window so she could talk to him.

'I'm fine,' she said. He had blue eyes, she noticed. Very, very blue eyes and a tangle of dark lashes that any woman would envy. There were a lot of little creases at the corners of his eyes, too. As if he spent a lot of time smiling. Or focusing on something very small.

He certainly wasn't smiling right now.

'Are you sure? Can I check your neck, at least? I'm a doctor.'

They were only a couple of blocks away from where Abby worked at St John's Hospital so it was quite possible he'd been heading in the same direction. Not that Abby had ever seen him in the hospital corridors or cafeteria. She could be quite sure of that because she would have noticed him. He was rather an attractive man.

Okay…make that *very* attractive. Those intensely blue eyes beneath black hair that was tousled enough to suggest that he didn't bother looking in a mirror very often, along with a bit of designer stubble, was a combination that made it unlikely that Abby's heart rate was going to slow down anytime soon. Especially when he was looking at her like that—as if it was absolutely critical that she wasn't injured.

And then he reached into the car to slide his hand beneath her long hair, which was loose at the moment, to touch her neck.

'Does this hurt at all?' he asked.

'No…' It didn't hurt. Quite the opposite. She'd never had a man's hand cupping the nape of her neck before, Abby realised, and it felt rather nice. More than rather nice, in fact. He had gentle hands but she could tell he knew exactly what he was doing and it was sending odd little spirals of sensation right down her spine.

Abby wasn't at all sure that it was appropriate to be feeling that tingle when this was the purely professional touch of a doctor checking for a physical injury but it felt like something far more personal. Had she avoided letting any men this close to her for so long she'd forgotten that it *could* be something rather nice?

'Try putting your chin on your chest. Very slowly. Stop if it starts hurting.'

The traffic lights had changed but Abby wasn't going anywhere. A car driver tooted irritably as he pulled out to get around the obstruction the two cars were making. Someone else rolled down their window and shouted.

'Everything okay? Want me to call an ambulance?'

'I think we're okay,' the man shouted back. 'But

thank you.' He turned back to Abby. 'Look over one shoulder and then the other. Carefully…'

Abby did as she was told. The second direction sent her gaze back to him.

'No pain?'

'No pain,' she confirmed.

'And nothing else hurting at all? Can you take a deep breath? Oh, God…that's the first thing I should have asked.' His grimace was so like a face palm that Abby almost laughed.

He was so worried about her but she was quite sure she was fine. It had only been a little bump, really, and it probably hadn't even done much damage to her beloved car. The relief came in such a strong wave that Abby felt slightly light-headed. Happy enough to make a joke.

'I really am fine,' she told the stranger. 'Except…'

'Except…?'

'I can't move my legs.' Abby kept a straight face. 'I don't think I'm ever going to walk again.'

The way the colour drained out of his face made her realise that her attempt at humour had backfired.

'Sorry… Maybe I should have said I'll never play the violin again.'

The poor man was looking bewildered now.

'You're supposed to ask if I could play the violin be-fore,' Abby said helpfully. 'And then I say "no" and it's, you know…funny…' It clearly wasn't funny, though, so Abby offered up her brightest smile and used her hand to indicate what was folded up and fitted behind the passenger seat of her modified car.

Her wheelchair.

He wasn't slow, that's for sure. It took only a split second for him to realise that she was paraplegic and that she'd been making a joke about it. His breath came out in a strangled sound—as if he didn't know whether to laugh or cry.

He chose to laugh, albeit shaking his head and catching Abby's gaze at the same time. She could feel her smile stretching into a delighted grin. She was enjoying this, she realised. How inappropriate was that? Especially when she heard the blare of a siren trying to get through traffic that had been slowed down enough to be turning into the kind of traffic jam nobody wanted at peak rush hour. The flashing light of a police motorcycle could be seen threading its way through the traffic and Abby knew there was going to be even more of a hold-up while they sorted this minor accident out.

She was going to be late for work—something that she never allowed to happen—but, strangely, she was actually quite pleased she had an excuse to stay here a bit longer. With the blue-eyed stranger whose face had just become even more attractive when he'd laughed.

Good *grief*… Noah Baxter had just rear-ended the car of some young woman who was already living with a probable spinal injury that had made her paraplegic, standing in the middle of a traffic jam he was responsible for, and he was *laughing* about it?

Not just a wry chuckle either. It was a real laugh that came from somewhere deep in his gut and it felt like…

…it felt like he'd just stepped back in time, that's

what. To a life that was so utterly different to the one he led now. A life where things were funny and tender or stupid and you could simply enjoy the absurdity. Where laughter had been such a normal part of life that he hadn't given it a second thought—never imagining for a moment that even the desire to laugh would be obliterated in a matter of only two terrible days.

A police officer was getting off his bike and coming towards them.

'Anyone hurt here?'

'No.' It was the young woman in the car who spoke first. She still had a twinkle of amusement in her eyes after making that joke about never walking again. Hazel eyes, he noticed now, in a pale face that was framed by long waves of golden red hair. A rather striking-looking woman, in fact. And that smile…it was astonishingly contagious. Noah found himself smiling again as well.

'It was entirely my fault, Officer,' he said. 'I'd been looking for a street sign to make sure I was going the right way and I braked a second too late. Do you need my details?'

The police officer was scanning the road around them. 'What we need to do is clear this obstruction. Nobody's hurt?'

'No.' Both Noah and the attractive redhead spoke together this time.

'Any damage to the vehicles?'

'I don't think so.' Noah hadn't noticed a bumper lying on the road or anything when he'd rushed to the car in front to see if anyone had been injured. Now he followed the police officer to see that there were only very minor bumps and scratches. No big deal at all.

'No need to write this up, then,' the police officer decided. 'I'm going to start directing the traffic. If you can both move your cars and get going, that would be very helpful.'

Noah nodded. He went back to the car in front. 'There's very little damage,' he said. 'Probably not worth losing a no-claims bonus with our insurance companies for either of us. And there's no reason for the police to be involved.'

'Oh...thank goodness for that. I love this car.'

'He wants us to move our cars and head off asap. Are you sure you're okay?'

'I'm sure. Are you?'

'Yes.' Although there was an odd knot in his gut. Left over from that unfamiliar laughter? Maybe it was also responsible for Noah to do something he hadn't done in more than a decade. 'Can I have your phone number?' he asked. 'Just in case...?'

In case of what? That he'd want to check that symptoms of whiplash hadn't become obvious? Or that her insurance company wouldn't cover the damages if she decided to make a claim? Or...simply because he'd like to see her again? Was her smile this time, as she held his gaze for a heartbeat longer than he might have expected, because she was thinking that she might like to see *him* again?

'Just in case you decide you do want to make an insurance claim and you need my details,' he added hurriedly. He always kept a small notepad in his shirt pocket, with a pen attached. A leftover habit from his days as a junior doctor when there had been just too many things to remember at times and keeping notes of anything important had been vital.

She was telling him her phone number. And then she turned the key in her ignition and started her car up again.

'Oh…' she said, catching his gaze again as she slid the car into gear, using controls that were attached to her steering wheel. 'My name's Abby, by the way.'

'Noah,' he responded. He was smiling again, too, as he slipped the notepad back into his pocket and got into his own car. How weird was this? He'd had a stupid, thankfully minor, accident that was a disruption he certainly didn't need on his way to a meeting with the new colleagues he would be working with in a matter of days and yet it felt like the best thing that had happened to him in quite a while? Like…a few years?

The police officer was overruling the traffic lights to direct vehicles. He waved Abby through the intersection but then put his hand up to stop Noah going through yet. He watched Abby's car getting further and further away and then the indicator went on and she turned, disappearing from his line of sight.

He still had the remnants of that knot in his gut.

Yeah…it was weird all right…

The routine was so well rehearsed, Abby could go through the steps without even thinking about it. Her disabled parking slot, on the ground floor of the hospital's parking building, was extra wide, which made it easy to open her driver's door and leave it wide open. The special controls on the central console allowed her to move the car seats. She could tilt the back of her own seat and then pull the passenger seat forward to make it easy to lift out the folded frame of her chair to put it on the ground beside her door.

The wheels, which were removed for transport, came out next and Abby clicked them back into place, pulled the bar at the back of the chair that unfolded it and then locked the brakes on.

It took less than sixty seconds after that to manoeuvre the chair into the best position, put the cushion on the seat, sling her shoulder bag over a push handle, lift her legs out of the car and then, with one hand on the cushion of the wheelchair and the other on the car seat, Abby used her upper body strength to swing herself into her chair. She pressed the remote to lock her car as she turned her chair and started rolling towards the parking building's exit. She was ready for her work day and she was only a few minutes late, despite the delay caused by that minor accident.

Abruptly, Abby stopped and then swung her chair to go back to her car. How on earth had she forgotten to go and check the damage? Because she'd been thinking about a pair of dark, blue eyes with crinkly corners, perhaps, and that tingle of *something* she'd felt when they'd met her own gaze, not to mention that other tingle that his hand on her neck had generated?

About a name that was unusual enough for him to be the first Noah she'd ever met? Wondering how soon he might ring her?

She would know it was him as soon as he spoke because his voice was etched into her memory as well. Abby could hear an echo of his voice right now, telling her that there was very little damage to her car as she inspected the rear bumper. He was right, there was only a scratch or two and one small dent that she traced with her fingers. It really wasn't going to be worth either the hassle of the paperwork or losing any discount in the cost of her insurance policy.

It wasn't the first ever scratch in that shiny red paintwork. She'd had the car for over two years now after all, and Abby had knocked the side more than once with the frame of her wheelchair but she still needed to get less precious about this vehicle. The problem was that it had been—and still was—such a big deal in her life.

Her older sister, Lisa, had gone into huge debt to cover the massive cost of a car with the kind of modifications Abby needed because she'd understood how life-changing it would be to have this kind of independence. She would also understand how unsettling it was to have been involved in an accident. She took a photo of the damage and texted it to Lisa.

Oops. Got rear-ended at a traffic light. Not the best way to start my day, huh?

Lisa's response pinged in almost instantly.

OMG. U ok??

All good. Need to get to work now. Will come down and see you later.

Come now. Just to be on the safe side.

Both Lisa and her husband worked in St John's Hospital's emergency department now, although Lisa would be leaving before too long to start her maternity leave. Abby loved both her sister and her brother-in-law dearly but she wasn't about to go and visit them. She had far too much work of her own to get on with. She shouldn't have sent the message at all—she could have told Lisa about it later—but maybe she was still a little shaken up and had needed to touch base with her only family.

No need. Stop...

Abby found a picture icon she'd used in the past—a little helicopter. It was a private code that told Lisa she didn't need a parent any more, especially of the hovering and overprotective type. She followed it with a smiley face, however.

Lisa had been a parent to her all her life. Six years older than Abby, she'd filled in the gaps left by a mother who had been unable to cope and had then died, leaving a grandmother to step in. It can't have been easy for either of them after the accident that had left Abby in a wheelchair when she'd been little more than two years old. For good measure, Abby added a heart to finish her message.

She propelled herself out of the elevator, through the doors of the parking building and onto the footpath. She was reaching to push the button that would activate the lights for the pedestrian crossing when someone beat her to it.

'Let me do that for you, love.'

It was never going to go away completely, was it? That beat of awareness of what could happen when a man assumed that her lack of physical ability gifted him the opportunity to take total control. She'd learned to deal with it, of course. To subdue fear and protect herself by becoming even more fiercely independent and not worrying about bruising anyone's feelings by rejecting unwelcome advances. She'd even learned to do it quite politely so she bit back a retort that, actually, her hands worked perfectly well, which was why she was using a manual rather than an electric wheelchair, and instead she gave the man a tight smile, her sweet tone disguising a slightly sarcastic thank-you.

He was probably in his early forties, wearing jeans and a T-shirt under a jacket and carrying a laptop bag. It must be her morning for good-looking men, Abby decided, although this one had blond hair and looked like he might enjoy spending his downtime surfing or skiing or something. Anyway...she preferred dark hair. Especially with blue eyes...

The lights changed and Abby moved onto the pedestrian crossing. To her dismay, the man walked out ahead of her holding up one hand, not unlike the police officer who'd overridden the traffic lights to clear the jam, as if the drivers might be considering taking off before the lights went green again and running a poor defenceless disabled person over. It was obviously done to be of assistance to Abby but it made her feel like everybody was staring at her and unwanted assistance had always been a pet peeve from a very early age. One of Abby's earliest memories was trying so hard to climb into a swing and pushing her sister's helping hands away.

'Go 'way. I can do it by myself...'

It was nothing like someone taking sexual advantage of her disability, of course, but it was on the same spectrum as far as Abby was concerned, and while she had learned to deal with the aftermath of that appalling incident, it was never going to be forgotten.

She sped up on the other side of the road, eager to disappear into the steady stream of people already heading into what was a large, busy regional hospital, but the blond man was keeping pace.

'Hey...could I buy you a coffee or something?'

'No.' Her negative response came out as being curt this time. Rude enough to make Abby feel a little ashamed of herself so she offered another tight smile. 'Thanks, but no thanks. Don't think my boyfriend would approve.'

'Oh...' He looked comically disappointed. 'I should have guessed. See ya.'

Not if I see you first, Abby thought, but she let her breath out in a sigh as she took the corridor that led both to the hand clinic and, further on, to the emergency department. She didn't have a boyfriend—it was just one of the more polite ways she had to brush off any interest that men showed in her. Especially men who saw her disability before they saw anything else about her.

She hadn't brushed that Noah off, though, had she? She'd not only given him her phone number, the thought that he might ring her was creating an unfamiliar ripple of sensation that was…oh, help…embryonic excitement? Whatever it was, it was enough for Abby to fish in her shoulder bag to retrieve her phone as soon as she reached the clinic. It was also enough to feel disappointed that she hadn't missed any messages or calls yet and that, no, her phone wasn't on silent.

It had been a very, very long time since she'd felt that "waiting for a call" anxiety but it only took Abby a matter of moments to put two and two together about why she wanted to hear from the man who'd driven into the back of her car this morning. He hadn't seen her disability, had he? He'd been shocked to see her wheel-chair, which meant that when he'd met her, he hadn't been influenced by any kind of social stereotyping or personal prejudice about disabled people.

He'd only seen *her*. Abby Phillips. A specialist hand therapist, which was something she was very proud of being, although he didn't know that yet. Mind you, she was also a twenty-six-year-old virgin, which Abby was definitely not proud of being, but thank goodness she was the only person who knew that.

And why on earth had it occurred to her to think of *that* right now?

Abby opened her locker to get her white coat off the

hook and then she went to the mirror to brush her hair and scrape it up into a ponytail that wouldn't get in the way of her work this morning. It was the touch of her own thumbs on the back of her neck that gave her the answer to that question. Because she was thinking of the touch of someone else's hands on her neck. Of how it had made her feel. She wanted Noah to call because she was attracted to him. Possibly more attracted than she'd ever been to anyone else. Ever…

Could this possibly be, perhaps, a case of love at first sight?

Abby caught a glimpse of the grin on her face as she turned away from the mirror.

A kind of "watch this space" grin…

Talk about being thrown in at the deep end.

It was specialist hand surgeon Noah Baxter's first day on the job at St John's Hospital and his very first call was to the emergency department for a serious injury to someone's hand. He'd met quite a few of the senior members of his departmental staff the other day but this was his first visit to the ED. The first person he encountered was a nurse who was obviously quite well along in her pregnancy. She greeted him with a friendly smile.

'Can I help you?'

'I've been paged for a consult. By a Hugh Patterson?'

The nurse's smile widened. 'I know him well. I'll let him know you're here.' She turned and went swiftly in the direction of one of the closed resuscitation rooms.

A tension he hadn't actually been aware of started to

recede the moment she turned her back. It wasn't anything to do with meeting new colleagues or not knowing what he'd been asked to come and see. It was just that he still hadn't got to a stage when he could see a pregnant belly and not feel a pang of loss. Maybe he never would, but he'd become very good at distracting himself by deliberately noticing something else.

It was her hair that snagged his attention now. Red hair, quite dark. Nothing like that vibrant red gold shade on the woman whose car he'd bumped into the other day on the way to his first visit to St John's. That shade of hair had proved quite memorable.

Too memorable.

Which was why he hadn't yet called that number he'd requested from her. He'd intended to, of course, on more than one occasion in the last few days but when he'd been about to press the call button, he'd just been unable to do it.

Because he really wanted to…

Which was quite ridiculous. He was a single man in his mid-thirties. If he was attracted to a woman he shouldn't be short of the confidence to do something about that. But that was the whole problem, wasn't it?

He *was* attracted to someone. For the first time in years. And he didn't want to be, any more than he wanted to be affected by seeing a pregnant belly. He never wanted to be attracted to anyone again because he knew where that road could lead. Been there, done that and once was more than enough.

Still, it was inexcusable that he hadn't made contact yet and, at the very least, given her his insurance company details. He didn't actually need to ring and hear her voice for that either. He could simply text her the details and he would do that, Noah decided—just as soon as he had a moment to spare later today.

One of the department's consultants emerged from the resuscitation room and strode swiftly towards Noah.

'Hugh Patterson,' he introduced himself. 'And you're Noah Baxter, yes?'

'Indeed.' He shook Hugh's hand.

'We're delighted to have you at St John's. The word is that you're the best in the field. I think that's what our patient might need today.

Noah raised an eyebrow. 'No pressure, then?'

Hugh's smile had a grim edge. 'Come and see. Not pretty. Patient's a thirty-eight-year-old gentleman who got his hand caught in some food-processing machinery a couple of hours ago. Crush injury to several fingers and partial amputation to his thumb. It took a while to get him free. And it's his dominant hand.'

"Not pretty" was a good description for what Noah found when he lifted the dressings on the man's hand. His fingers and—more importantly—his thumb were all mangled enough for it to be impossible to tell exactly what was, or was not, salvageable, despite the help of the X-rays illuminated on the screen behind the head of the bed. Even if bones could be wired or plated together, there might be too much damage to nerves, tendons and tissues to make reconstruction possible.

'I can't look.' The patient, Steve, had his head firmly turned away and his uninjured hand shielding his eyes.

'Don't touch it…' His breath came out in a sob, '*Please* don't touch it…'

Noah glanced at Hugh. 'He's got a good level of sedation and ten milligrams of morphine on board. Might need a top-up?'

'I'll be as gentle as I can be, Steve,' Noah told him. 'And I don't need to do much at the moment other than assess what's going on with your blood vessels and nerves. I can already see that we need to take you up to Theatre and get things cleaned up. I'm just going to touch your wrist, here, and the palm of your hand, okay? I want to see what's happening with the blood supply.'

'I can't lose my hand, Doc…' Steve sounded desperate now. 'I can't lose my job. I've got three kids and it's hard enough as it is…'

'I know…' Noah's tone was gentle. 'Try not to panic, Steve. We're going to do everything we possibly can to save your hand, okay?'

He put his fingers on Steve's wrist to occlude the radial and ulnar arteries at the same time as he squeezed gently on the palm of the badly injured hand. Releasing one artery at a time give him good information about the patency of important vessels. Even while he was conducting this test, Noah was gathering other impressions. The colour and temperature of this hand was poor compared to Steve's uninjured hand, which meant that the sooner they got him to Theatre the better to debride these injuries and repair blood vessels. An inadequate blood supply could mean complications in delayed healing, fibrosis and infection.

With the injured hand covered again with sterile dressings, an operating theatre being set up, additional assistance from orthopaedic, vascular and neurosurgical staff requested and Steve's panicked wife arriving in the department with a baby in her arms, Noah had a few minutes to pull up a chair, introduce himself properly and talk through what he was going to do.

'So we'll do our very best to save whatever we can,' he finished up. 'Especially with your thumb because it's so important in achieving useful function of your hand, but we won't know how much we can do until we can see exactly what the damage is. And there are risks, as I've explained. Are you happy to sign the consent form or do you have any more questions?'

Steve's wife, Pauline, was still looking terrified. 'They told me when I arrived that you're the best in the country for hand surgery, Mr Baxter. One of the best in the world so we'll leave it up to you.'

Steve had his uninjured hand covering his eyes again and his voice was choked. 'I need my hand,' he managed. 'How am I going to be able to work, otherwise? Or look after my family…?'

Pauline shifted the baby to one arm as she reached to touch Steve's shoulder. 'We'll manage, babe,' she told him. 'I'm sure Mr Baxter is going to be able to save your hand…' Her glance at Noah was a plea that was made even more eloquent as this young couple's baby began crying as she turned back to her husband. 'But whatever happens, we're going to get through this. I love you…'

'You'll have to sign the form for me,' Steve was

clutching his wife's hand now and there were tears on his cheeks. 'You know how useless I am with my left hand…'

He was confident, that's for sure, but maybe that came with the territory of being renowned as the best in the field.

Fancy being about to start your first surgery in a new hospital, leading a large team of people he'd only just met, and this Mr Baxter had given permission for the gallery to be open. Word had spread like wildfire, of course, but staff in the hand clinic were well up in the priority list, and Abby had been thrilled that she could go and watch because her next appointments were with inpatients and they could be fitted in later in the day. She was more than happy to skip her lunch break, if necessary, to compensate.

That the operating theatre gallery had rather steep stairs could have been an issue but one of the orthopaedic registrars, Alex, who was in the clinic when the news came through, had smiled at her.

'Let's go early,' he'd suggested. 'And get the good seats up front.'

Abby appreciated the unspoken part of his suggestion—that they could tuck her wheelchair out of the way before there were too many people around to notice and that Alex would carry her up the awkward entrance to the gallery that had certainly not been built with disabled access in mind. This wasn't the kind of self-important and uninvited assistance like someone directing traffic on her behalf. This was help that was there automatically from someone who knew her well. Someone who knew how much she loved watching the initial repair on a hand she might well end up working on herself further down the track.

So, here she was, in a front row seat that gave her a great view into the theatre below, where there were at least a dozen people busy setting up for what would undoubtedly be complex and lengthy surgery. Abby had a clear view of one of the television screens, too, which would give a close-up view of the microsurgery needed to repair tendons, blood vessels and nerves.

The patient had been anaesthetised and was lying with his arm and hand positioned on a side wing of the operating table. Nurses and registrars were busy making sure that everything was ready for the stars of the show—the surgeons. There were trays of instruments being checked, lights being positioned and headsets with both cameras and magnifying technology being readied.

All they needed now was the lead surgeon and he came in from the scrub room, already gowned and masked, with his gloved hands crossed in front of him to prevent him touching anything not sterile.

He nodded towards the team of people waiting to work with him and then he glanced up towards the gallery. Just the briefest glance that raked the packed seating available and acknowledged the people who were interested in what he was about to do. Only his eyes were visible because he hadn't yet had the headgear placed but there was something familiar about his face that made Abby frown as she tried to focus more clearly.

'Who's that?' she asked Alex. 'Mr Baxter or one of the orthopaedic guys?'

'Yep… Noah Baxter. Let's hope he's as good as they say he is.' Alex glanced up at the screen above them, which was filled with the close-up image of the mangled fingers. 'That hand's a mess.'

A bit like Abby's head right now, then, and it was going to take a breath or two for her to get it back under control. Her excitement at being able to observe such major surgery had evaporated. Replaced by something that should have been anger but, pathetically, felt much more like a surprisingly sharp disappointment.

Noah…of course it was. She would never forget those eyes.

She hadn't been about to forget him at all, for that matter. *Or* forgive him.

He hadn't called her. He had probably never even intended to.

CHAPTER TWO

HE COULDN'T HAVE missed that hair.

Not in a million years. Certainly not when she was sitting in the front row of this operating theatre's gallery because the edge of the pool of light over the central table reached far enough to catch the golden glint and make it shine like some kind of halo.

It hadn't seemed like a big deal when he'd agreed to have the gallery open. Noah was quite used to having colleagues, medical students or other interested staff members who worked in the field observing his work but the last person he would have expected to see was the woman he'd met when he'd bumped her car the other day.

The woman who'd made him laugh…

Abby.

Not that he was about to wonder why on earth she was here, acknowledge her in any way, or let her presence interfere with his focus on his work, but…in the split second before he shut it down, Noah was aware of a beat of something like dismay. Embarrassment, even, because he hadn't yet followed up after that accident to give her those insurance company details or check that she hadn't shown any symptoms of injury later.

There was nothing he could do about that right now, however, so Noah had to dismiss it as completely irrelevant. He had a microphone, as well as the magnifying lens and the camera that would transmit the close-up images to the screens, built into his headset. There were plenty of people other than Abby who would be listening to everything he said and Noah enjoyed both teaching and explaining what he was doing for the non-surgeons in his audience.

'This thirty-eight-year-old gentleman had an altercation with machinery approximately two hours ago. We know there were no cutting blades involved or any belts or chains, no exposure to extreme heat, cold or chemicals, and the extrication was time-consuming but fortunately without major blood loss so our patient is haemodynamically stable.

'We now have to convert a dirty and contaminated wound into a clean surgical field. We're doing this, firstly, by using a solution of saline, iodopovidone and hydrogen peroxide. I'm also a fan of rigorous scrubbing with a brush, keeping in mind that our aim is to get the wounds clean with the least possible amount of tissue damage.'

He had registrars and nurses helping with this decontamination and Noah realised he hadn't quite shut down that awareness of that particular member of his audience. That would change very soon, however. He was not only extremely well practised in a focus on his work that shut out anything else in the world, he had used it as his personal salvation for years. Nothing was about to undermine that ability.

'The second step of creating our clean surgical field is a meticulous and thorough debridement of any non-viable tissue, foreign bodies, shredded tendon pieces or avulsed nerve and also any bone pieces that don't have an attachment to tendon or muscle. Have a look at the way the fingers are lying, here.' He touched the tips of the fingers, which were lying flat. 'You can see from the disruption to the cascade position of progressively more flexion in the fingers that we're dealing with some damage to the flexor tendons.'

This was it. He was well into the zone of being unaware of anything irrelevant. He was still capable of keeping his audience informed at every step, however, no matter how long the surgery was going to take.

'The fractures of the index and small fingers are so comminuted I'm going to use mini-external fixators. These will be removed in about six weeks...'

'The best way to achieve a precise reduction of the fracture in this finger is a low-profile ladder plate...'

'The thumb is our main concern, here. The primary aim for the treatment of any hand injuries is for our patient to end up with a functioning hand and, as I'm sure you all know, the opposition and pincer mechanism and the sensation for grasping are the most important aspects for useful function. Fortunately, our man is not diabetic and is a non-smoker, which is to his advantage as far as healing is concerned.'

The thumb was, unfortunately, the most seriously injured part of this hand and could well need further surgery, including tendon transfers. The blood vessel and nerve repairs were also more challenging and Noah was happy to work alongside the specialists that were already a part of St John's surgical staff.

After a long, tiring stint in Theatre, he had a lot of people to thank. He knew they would be playing catch-up with their own workload for the rest of the day, having taken the time to assist with this emergency surgery.

For his own part, Noah stayed in Theatre to supervise the splinting of Steve's hand and arm. He knew the gallery was emptying above them but he could sense how slow it was, with people wanting to chat as they filed out of the tiered seating towards the doors. He wanted to look up. Now that the surgery was completed, the questions were filtering back into his mind.

Why was Abby here?

How, exactly, had she managed to use those stairs to get into a front row seat?

He got the answer to that question as he followed his patient's bed out of the double doors towards Recovery. Stripping off his gloves and mask to ball them up in one hand, a sideways glance showed Abby being lowered into her wheelchair from the arms of a young man. As she positioned her feet on the footplate and unlocked her brakes, the man who had been carrying her stepped aside and she looked up—straight towards Noah.

No…make that glaring, rather than looking, but she broke the eye contact almost instantly. Her chin rose and she swivelled her chair and took off. The determined push of her hands as eloquent as any signal of dismissal.

Noah could feel a bit of an internal cringe going on.

'Who's that?' he asked his registrar. 'In the wheel-chair?'

'Abby Phillips. One of the therapists in the hand clinic. Don't be fooled—that chair doesn't stop her doing anything. She's one of the best.'

Noah simply gave a single nod to acknowledge the information. Or maybe it was his agreement that she could probably do anything she chose to do. He didn't say anything because he was thinking too hard. As a specialist hand therapist, Abby was going to be an important part of the team of people he would be working with. It was all very well to repair hands with clever surgery but it was the aftercare and especially the therapy his patients received that could determine the success of their outcomes.

He could very well be working closely with Abby before long and he would undoubtedly need to speak to her, probably in the very near future, so it was unfortunate that she was clearly not going to be happy to see him again. His potential excuse of having mislaid that piece of paper with her phone number on it was not going to cut the mustard, was it?

Maybe some flowers would help?

Noah stepped into the specialised recovery area to help settle his patient for the intensive monitoring he would need as the anaesthetic wore off completely. Steve's wife would be able to come in soon and Noah could give them both the good news that he hadn't had to amputate any of his fingers but also a warning that only time would tell how well the thumb would be able to heal.

A last thought about Abby slipped into his head before he refocused to check the limb baselines on Steve's hand. Flowers were inappropriate because, even with his briefest acquaintance of Abby Phillips, Noah could be quite certain that she wasn't the kind of woman who might be impressed by tokens like flowers or chocolate as a form of apology. She was...*different* and he would have to come up with something a lot more original if he wanted to make amends.

This was good.

Exactly what Abby had needed.

She could feel perspiration trickling down between her shoulder blades, the muscles in her arms were screaming a protest and she was gasping for breath but Abby wasn't about to slow down—especially when her peripheral vision showed how quickly her opponents were closing in on her.

The effort it took to propel a wheelchair with one hand while dribbling a basketball with the other was huge. Which was why this activity was what Abby had needed so badly after her work day. The shock of discovering that the man who had rear-ended her car was the rock star specialist surgeon that they had been so delighted to have attracted to St John's had been overwhelming.

No. It had been crushing, that's what. And it had had nothing to do with his profession. The crushing had been gradual but relentless over the last few days, being added to bit by bit each time she checked her phone and with each extra day that had gone by without Noah calling her. Had she really thought she'd been attracted enough to the man to believe she might look back on that encounter and tell her future children that it had definitely been a case of love at first sight?

At least the aftermath of the final blow to that cringeworthy notion—that he'd never intended to call her at all—had been firmly dispatched by the physical exertion and need for absolute focus on this fast-moving game of wheelchair basketball.

Needing a bit more speed and a change of direction, Abby put the ball on her lap. She could now use both hands to manoeuvre the chair for two pushes before she had to dribble the ball again, pass it to another member of her team or attempt to shoot a goal. She could feel the rise of tension around her and the increase in decibels from encouragement being yelled. Someone grabbing the push ring of her sports chair's steeply cambered wheel prompted a split-second decision and Abby took the ball in both hands, before she could be pulled off her line, aimed for the hoop and put every ounce of her remaining energy into trying to score a goal.

The cheer from the team's substitutes on the side of the court was the best sound Abby had heard all day. She'd done it. Scored a goal from outside the semicircle around the opposing team's basket, which made it a three-point goal. It meant, that in the last seconds of the fourth and final ten-minute session of the match, she had taken her team to a win.

'Way to go, Abby!'

There was a lot of shouting and cheering from the audience in this gymnasium as well, but there was one voice she could recognise amongst them. Lisa had come with Abby to watch the match tonight. As soon as Abby had showered and changed she was going to drive Lisa back to her house, stopping to pick up a takeout meal on the way. A once-a-week, easy meal together for the sisters had become a family tradition ever since Abby had moved out of the house she'd shared with Lisa after their grandmother's death. They took turns with whose house they went to. They also took turns to choose which variety of food.

'It's my turn to choose,' Lisa announced as Abby came out of the changing rooms, still combing her loose hair with her fingers to help it dry. 'I'm craving Thai food. Or possibly pizza.'

'I think you'll find it's my turn,' Abby countered. 'And I want fish and chips.'

Lisa laughed. 'No, you don't. What you really want is just the chips and mushy peas and gravy.'

Abby nodded. 'This is true but I deserve it. Apart from winning this game, my day kind of sucked.'

'Oh? How come?'

'It's a long story and I need food. Possibly wine. It's Friday night, after all.'

'I guess that swings the vote to fish and chips. There's a wine shop right beside the chippie.' But Lisa looked thoughtful. 'There's a pizza place there as well and we do need to get extra food. I just got a text from Hugh to say he'd invited someone home for a drink after work and they're still there. You don't mind that it's not just us, do you?'

'Of course not. But let's go. I'm starving.'

'Where's your sports chair?'

'Coach is bringing it.' Abby led the way to her car. 'If you can open the hatch, that would help. I'll get myself sorted.'

She was in the driver's seat with her folded wheelchair stowed when the team coach came out with the angled sports wheelchair. He lifted it into the back hatch of her car.

'That was an awesome game, Abby. I still wish you'd think about trying out for the Paralympic team.'

Abby shook her head. They'd had this conversation before—privately. 'You know how important my job is to me and I just don't have the time for the extra training or travel.'

She had to have the conversation all over again with Lisa as they headed home and explain that, as much as she loved her sport, she loved her work even more and she wasn't going to jeopardise either her position in such a great clinic or the progression of her skills. It was almost turning into an argument by the time she pushed herself up the ramp that Lisa and Hugh had installed by the front steps of their gorgeous old country house.

'But surely you could do both?'

'I don't *want* to do both.'

'Hey…' Hugh came out of the kitchen to meet them.

He took the pizza boxes off Abby's lap. 'What are you two arguing about?'

'Abby's coach wants her to try out for the Paralympic team.'

'Wow…' Hugh turned to take the wrapped parcels of fish and chips from Lisa.

'I'm not going to do it.' Abby did not appreciate what felt like building pressure. Plus she was very hungry after all that exercise. Hangry, that's what she was. She pushed ahead of both Hugh and Lisa to roll swiftly into the enormous kitchen of this old house, which was where they always ate.

And there, standing in front of an ancient Welsh dresser that had shelves laden with old blue and white china as well as random ornaments and photos, with a beer in his hand and looking quite at home was Noah Baxter.

'Oh…no… Not *you* again…'

Hugh was right behind Abby. 'You two know each other?'

Noah was looking as appalled as Abby's tone had been. 'Ah…we've met,' he said cautiously.

'Yeah…' Abby's breath came out in a huff that didn't quite reach laughter. 'You could say we bumped into each other the other day.'

She was still holding Noah's gaze so she saw the flash that acknowledged the humour in her words. Not that he was about to laugh but she could remember exactly what it had sounded like when he *had* laughed the other day, as easily as she could remember how it had made his face light up. Unfortunately she could also remember just how attracted she had been at that point.

'Oh…*no*…' Lisa echoed Abby's first reaction. 'Don't tell me it was that accident you had on the way to work?'

'Yep.' The only good thing about this incredibly awkward situation was that Abby hadn't told her sister about that instant crush she had developed. Or admitted that she'd been obsessively checking her phone like some dreamy teenager ever since.

Hugh was the first one to actually laugh. 'I had no idea,' he said. 'There I was just being welcoming to a new staff member that I'd only met this morning. But maybe this is a good thing. You can both kiss and make up before you have to work together.'

Abby had to avert her gaze swiftly. The very idea of kissing and making up was…oh, help…something she had no intention of thinking about right now, although she had a feeling it might very well come back to haunt her later.

Hugh put the food down on the big, wooden table and then shifted a chair out of the way for Abby. 'Come and dig in,' he said. 'While it's still hot. Abby, can I get you a glass of wine?'

'What do mean, work together?' At least Lisa had forgotten about the coach's encouragement for Abby to take her sport to the next level. She was staring at Noah. 'You were called in for a consult this morning, weren't you? For that guy with the awful hand injuries?'

'This is Noah Baxter,' Hugh told his wife. 'St John's

new specialist hand surgeon. We got so busy after that I never got a chance to tell you.'

'Mmm.' Abby took the glass of wine Hugh had poured for her. 'The famous Mr Baxter. I couldn't believe it was you when I saw you walk into Theatre.'

'And I couldn't believe it was you when I saw you in the front row of the gallery.'

'You got to watch the surgery?' Hugh sounded envious. 'Lucky you.'

Noah was on the other side of the table now and this time he was the one to catch and hold her gaze. Neither of them responded to Hugh's comment. Abby could feel the muscles around her eyes tightening.

You asked for my number... And then you didn't call me...

I know... I'm sorry...it was unforgivable...

The silent exchange made a little shiver run down Abby's spine. Who did that? How could you hear words that hadn't even been spoken like that? Or had he said them out loud? No, she was sure he hadn't—it was just a coincidence that Hugh was giving Noah a sympathetic glance.

'Don't worry, mate. She'll forgive you before too long. It's not as if any real damage was done. It wasn't worth even thinking about making an insurance claim.'

Abby wasn't so sure about no damage having been done but she wasn't thinking about her car.

Noah was making a face as he sat down opposite Abby. 'I was trying to think up something I could put on Abby's desk by way of another apology,' he confessed. 'But I didn't think flowers or chocolates would cut the mustard.'

Abby sneaked a quick glance at him as he took a plate from Lisa. His assessment was correct. But how could he have been so sure that she wouldn't have been impressed with flowers or chocolates? The same way that he could send such an eloquent message with a glance, perhaps?

'The only thing I could think of,' Noah continued, 'was maybe a punching bag with a photo of my face on it.'

That did it. Or maybe it had been those first sips of her wine. Whatever it was, the antagonism in the room evaporated as Abby laughed and Noah grinned at her. Something else took the place of the angst and it was a little disturbing to realise that it was probably the flames of that crush flickering back into life. It was a feeling that got stronger as the group started to relax over their casual meal and Noah became less and less of a stranger. He was watching, fascinated, as Abby piled her plate with hot chips and lined up her small pots of mushy peas and gravy to dip them in.

'I see you're into healthy food, then?'

'Says the man who's stuffing his face with a pizza that has four different types of cheese on it. That's a heart attack on a thin crust.'

'I'll burn it off. Not that I've found any good local running tracks yet.'

'Where are you living?' Lisa asked.

'I've been given a room in the staff quarters for now.

I want to get properly settled into my new job before taking any time out to hunt for real estate.'

'It must be something about working exclusively with hands,' Lisa said to Hugh.

'What must?'

'Refusing to take time away from work to do other important things. Like finding a home. Or exploring a sporting talent that could be so brilliant you might win a gold medal on a world stage.'

'Oh…don't start that again,' Abby groaned. 'I'm not going to try out for the Paralympic team. I'm exactly where I want to be, doing exactly what I want to do. Basketball is just my sport. Exercise. Stress relief.'

'Oh…that's right. You said your day had sucked. What happened?'

Oh…help… Abby concentrated on loading mushy peas onto her chip so that she could avoid catching Noah's glance.

'It just got overly busy for a while,' she muttered. 'But that's what happens when you sneak off to watch some complex surgery.'

If Noah had guessed that he was the reason Abby had told her sister that she'd had a bad day, he gave no sign of it now. In fact, he was ready to offer his support.

'I totally get the fascination with working with hands,' he said. 'Obviously. It's an extraordinary field to be in. I couldn't imagine taking time away to do anything else.'

'Really?' Hugh was interested. 'I love the variety of the work I get in Emergency and never knowing what body part is going to come in needing treatment next. Maybe I just have a low boredom threshold.'

'Nothing boring about hands,' Noah said. 'Not that I'm into the kind of inspirational quotes that you see everywhere these days, but I do have a framed quote that I keep on the wall of my office. From a German philosopher, Immanuel Kant.'

'Oh…' Abby's eyes widened. 'I bet I know which one.'

And then they both spoke together.

'*The hand is the visible part of the brain.*'

Oh…this time the exclamation was silent. Because the sudden feeling of connection was a little overwhelming. Noah understood, didn't he? He had the same passion.

Hugh and Lisa shared a look. 'We're going to hear all about the magic of opposable thumbs again, aren't we?'

Noah's lips twitched. 'Well…half of all hand functions do require the thumb.'

'And, apart from the brain, what other body part can do so much?' Abby added. 'And perform such complex tasks? They let us create art and play music, read Braille if you need to or talk with sign language. Hands—and arms—are far more important than legs and feet.' Her voice trailed off as she realised she was preaching to the converted. 'They can give you your independence…'

She could feel the intensity of the look Noah was giving her without lifting her gaze to meet it.

'I'm not surprised to hear that you're so good at

your job,' he said quietly. 'With a passion like that you must inspire your patients to get completely invested in their recovery.'

Abby shrugged off the compliment. 'I've heard a few good things about your work, too,' she said. 'It was fascinating to watch the microsurgery today. I hope I get a chance to work with him down the track.'

'He will need to start some gentle therapy in the next day or two,' Noah said. 'We'll be having a team meeting that will include your clinical director on Monday morning. Perhaps you can get involved right from day one?'

'I don't get to choose my patients but I'll keep my fingers crossed.' And not just because it would be such an interesting case, Abby thought. It would also mean that she would be working on the same team as Noah and it would be an opportunity to learn so much. She was smiling as she spoke but Noah didn't notice. He was looking at his watch.

'And, with that reminder, I really need to head back. I said I'd be up on the ward later this evening to check on his post-op progress.' Noah got up from the table. 'Thank you so much, Hugh, for the invitation and to you as well, Lisa. I'm sure you were looking forward to coming home for a quiet evening that didn't include entertaining new colleagues.' His smile was warm. 'How long till the baby arrives?'

'A bit over a month,' Lisa told him. 'I'm not stopping work until I have to, though.'

'How exciting.' But Noah's tone didn't match his words and he was already turning away with no more than a nod in Abby's direction. 'I'm sure we'll meet again soon, Abby. Have a great weekend.'

Hugh went with Noah to the front door. Lisa and Abby exchanged a look.

'What was that about?' Lisa murmured. 'He seemed to be having a great time and then suddenly he couldn't wait to get away.'

'Guess he was thinking about his patient and that put him back into a professional zone.'

'Who's in a professional zone?' Hugh was walking back into the kitchen.

'Noah. He just switched off. As though he'd had more than enough of our company.'

'Ah…' Hugh sat back down at the table. 'I was surprised that he accepted my invitation to have a drink, to be honest, after I'd heard the gossip.'

'What gossip?'

'I went up to the ward before heading home, to see how the surgery had gone on Steve—the guy with the hand injury. I was in the corridor, trying to find his notes in the trolley, and I could hear the nurses in the office, chatting. And, yeah… I don't usually take any notice of that kind of stuff but…' Hugh sighed. 'It was why I invited him home for a beer. I thought he could use a friend.'

Abby was hanging onto every word Hugh was saying, her curiosity so sharp it felt like a door was being slammed in her face when he stopped speaking.

'And?' she demanded. 'You can't stop there…'

'I don't like gossip. Even if the story's true.'

'What story?' Lisa was as interested as Abby. 'Come

on, hon. You can't not tell us. Abby's going to be working with the man.' Her gaze slid sideways. 'I even got the impression that they might quite like each other now that they've got over the fact that Noah crashed into her car.'

But Hugh was shaking his head. 'That's just it. One of those nurses was saying how cute she thought the new surgeon was and the other one said she'd worked with him up north and there was no point in thinking that something might happen even if he *was* single.'

'Why not?' Abby asked.

'He's gay?' Lisa suggested.

Hugh shook his head. 'His wife died a few years ago. Some tragic accident, like a fall down some steps, with a head injury that was so catastrophic she was in cardiac arrest by the time she arrived in the ED. Love of his life, apparently.'

'Oh, no…that's tragic.'

'That wasn't even the worst of it. She was pregnant. Far enough along for them to do a post-mortem Caesarean in Emergency. The baby only lived for a day or two.'

Abby and Lisa exchanged another glance. No wonder Noah hadn't seemed that interested in Lisa's pregnancy. Abby was actually finding it hard to take a breath because her throat had tightened up and there seemed to be something so heavy pressing on her chest that she put her hand there to see what it was.

'Anyway…he threw himself into his work and that was it. His personal life was out of bounds and he never socialised with anyone. So…' Hugh reached out to touch Lisa's hand as he smiled at her. 'I'm glad he agreed to come home for a drink. And I think you're right. He does like our Abby and why wouldn't he? They both share the same passion for the same kind of work.'

It was true. That shared passion had given them a genuine moment of connection. But maybe they had something else in common as well, Abby thought, and that was a handicap that affected every aspect of their lives. Hers might be very obvious but being in a wheelchair was only the external aspect of the challenges she faced. Noah's handicap was completely invisible because it was purely emotional but Abby was very well aware of how crippling that could be and her heart was breaking more than a little bit for him.

She'd always had the unwavering support of her sister to face all the hard stuff in her life but who did Noah have? Especially now that he'd moved to a new area and a new place of work. Did he want real friends in his life or were other people always required to stay within the boundaries of a professional relationship? And… Abby released the breath she'd finally managed to take in a long, slow sigh.

Even if he did have family or friends in his life and thought that was all he wanted to have, was he still lonely sometimes for something more?

Like she was?

CHAPTER THREE

THERE WAS A heavy silence in the room.

The four people behind this closed door were all aware of how serious this discussion was going to be. The man in the bed, with his injured hand elevated in a sling. His wife, sitting on his other side, holding his uninjured hand between both of hers. The surgeon who was in charge of his treatment. And... Abby.

'I've brought Abby along with me to talk to you today, Steve,' Noah told their patient. 'I know she started working with you after your first surgery and has been hoping—like we all have—that the second surgery on your thumb would restore an adequate blood supply.'

Steve nodded slowly but he managed a smile for Abby. They'd got on well from the first, very gentle passive therapy that she had begun with him.

'Looks like you've faced a few challenges yourself,' he'd told her. 'I'll bet you're the best person around for this job.'

But it was Abby who'd been the first to notice the signs that the second surgery had failed. That the discoloration in Steve's thumb was the first indication of tissue death, nearly two weeks after the day she'd observed his initial surgery. The same day that she'd found out that she'd met Noah Baxter before. She had her suspicions that their new hand surgeon had something to do with her being assigned to Steve as his therapist but that only made her more determined to do the best job she could. It was very disappointing that they'd reached this point.

'As you know, your fingers are healing very well,' Noah continued. 'We did our best to restore an adequate blood supply to your thumb but I'm very sorry to say that it hasn't worked well enough.'

'But you can do another operation?' Pauline's tone was tentative. 'And fix it?'

It was no wonder that she was looking more and more tired, Abby thought, what with having to juggle babysitting or manage the travelling across the city with three children under five in order to make her daily hospital visits. Abby's relationship with her patient and his wife was still new but she could see that the recent extensive tests and this extra consultation had clearly raised stress levels considerably for both Pauline and Steve and her heart went out to the young couple.

'An adequate blood supply is vital to any part of the body,' Noah said. 'The blood carries oxygen and nutrients and antibodies to fight off infection. Without it, the cells can't survive and the tissue starts to die. That's what is happening with your thumb, Steve, and why those colour changes are happening.'

Even though it was only a couple of days since Abby had noticed the change and her alert had led to a barrage of tests for Steve, the tip of his thumb was already such a dark shade of red/brown that it was almost black.

'The risk of leaving dead tissue attached is that it can get infected and, if that infection travels to the rest of the body, it can cause sepsis, which can be very serious.'

'So I'm going to lose my thumb, then.' Steve's voice was wooden. 'And that means I'll never work again.'

'Oh, that's not true,' Pauline said quickly. 'There are lots of jobs that don't mean you have to use your hands so much.'

'Not the kind of job I love,' Steve said quietly. '*My* job. Where I get to work with my hands—growing stuff. With the best crowd of mates I've ever known… I'd go mad if I had to work in an office or a warehouse or something.'

Abby had heard a lot about Steve's work in the last couple of weeks. He worked at a hydroponic farm where they grew salad vegetables like lettuce and tomatoes and cucumbers. He mostly worked with the propagation and harvesting of the plants in the greenhouses. He'd just been helping out in the packing department for a morning when he'd had his horrible accident with the machinery. She also knew that Pauline had given up her part-time work after the arrival of their third baby and that things were financially tight.

'You are going to lose *this* thumb,' Noah confirmed. 'But it doesn't have to mean that you don't have *a* thumb.'

Both Steve and Pauline looked bewildered. Noah glanced at Abby and she could read the invitation to contribute to this discussion as clearly as if he'd spoken aloud. They'd only been working together for a couple of weeks with limited contact away from anything professional but, already, Abby was getting used to this ability of his to communicate silently.

It had been there from pretty much the first moment she'd met him, she realised. From when she'd seen the understanding that she'd been making a joke about never being able to walk again flash across his face. When she'd seen the appreciation in his eyes of her attempting humour in what could easily have escalated into a more stressful situation. When she'd heard him laugh…

'I think Mr Baxter asked me to come with him to talk to you today because I've had experience of working with a case like this,' she said. 'My patient was a lot further into his rehabilitation when I started working with him because he'd had his surgery and early rehab in another hospital, but he'd lost his thumb in a farming accident after getting caught up in rope when he was trying to deal with a stroppy bull. He was already back at work when I met him and he was really proud of what he could do again. He told me he'd been freaked out at the idea of his new thumb at first but it was the best thing he ever did.'

Abby opened a folder she had on her lap and took

out a photograph. 'This is a picture of his thumb, six months after his transplant.'

'Oh, no…' Pauline looked horrified. 'He got someone else's thumb? Like a kidney transplant?'

'No. Look…' Abby showed them another photo, this one of both the man's hands side by side. 'Can you see a difference?'

'The thumb with the scar is a bit fatter,' Steve said. 'And the nail looks different.'

'It was his big toe,' Abby told them. 'That's where it was transplanted from. Actually, "transferred" is a better word to use.'

'It's a surgery that's been around for a surprisingly long time,' Noah added. 'But our techniques are improving all the time and the results can be very, very good.'

'But what does his foot look like?' Steve shook his head. 'I don't like this. My feet are important too. I'm on them all day. I want to be able to play footie with my boy down the track. Or take my family for a walk on the beach.'

'With therapy and gait training, you won't be disabled at all,' Abby assured him. She wanted to tell him just how much more important hands were than feet but she restricted herself to a smile. Steve had, after all, considered the fact that she was in a wheelchair as a point in her favour as his therapist.

'The left foot is usually the best choice,' Noah put in. 'Simply because you can lose a bit of push power without the big toe, and that means, with an automatic car, your driving isn't affected—by having to jump on the brake unexpectedly, for example.'

It was just a flash of a glance at Abby but she knew he was thinking of a moment when he'd needed to jump on his brake—in that split second before he'd bumped into the back of her car. Which meant he was thinking of her as a person, not simply as a colleague, and that gave her a frisson of something that had nothing at all to do with this patient.

As she laid out more photos for Steve and Pauline to look at and Noah explained the procedure and the option of using a second toe instead of the big toe, along with the pros and cons, Abby found herself remembering that moment herself. And feeling curiously happy that it had happened.

Okay…that crush—and the ensuing disappointment that he hadn't called her—had been a bit silly but she was over that now. Meeting him properly and learning about the tragedy of him losing his wife and baby had put Abby in a very different space.

A safe space.

Because she didn't have to think about things that she'd avoided thinking about for such a long time.

Like sex…

Like how hard it might be for her to face—and overcome—a barrier that had been in place for several years now so that there was actually the possibility of a sexual encounter.

And, if she got that far, would she then have to worry about how different—and possibly disappointing—it might be for someone who was used to being with able-bodied women to be with someone whose legs looked so different? Who couldn't move in the same way? Who could, in fact, be far too passive for it to be a remotely exciting or satisfying experience?

It was better this way. To have a professional relationship with someone who could teach her so much. And to develop a friendship where they could both relax and enjoy each other's company. Where they could make each other laugh. It might, in fact, be enough for her to get past the barrier that had pretty much stopped her forming a meaningful relationship with any man. The subtle nod of Abby's head might have been an agreement with herself but it looked as though she was agreeing with what Noah was saying now.

'So, using the second toe means less deformity on the foot, but the big toe will look so much more like a thumb—as you can see from the photos that Abby's shown you.'

'What about the surgery?' Pauline asked. 'Would you do the transplant at the same time as taking off the thumb or does that have to heal first?'

'It's better to do the transfer at the same time than delay. That way we can be sure we're matching things up as well as possible and can attach nerves and blood vessels more accurately. The surgery itself is long. It could take between eight and twelve hours.'

'The rehab is long, too,' Abby warned. 'To get a good result you have to be willing to face some pretty rigorous and time-consuming therapy. There's six weeks to allow for bones to heal. We'll be doing therapy during that period, of course, to keep everything mobile, but the really intense work will start after that.'

'How long did it take for that chap?' Steve pointed at the first photo Abby had shown them. Till he got back to his work on the farm?'

'Six months,' she told him. 'And he had really good sensation in his thumb and enough range of movement and strength to do most of the things he needed to do in his job.'

Steve closed his eyes and lay back against his pillow. 'I dunno,' he muttered. 'It just seems…really weird. It's doing my head in.'

'I understand.' Noah got to his feet. 'We'll leave you to think about it. Maybe write down any worries or questions you might come up with and we'll talk again later. I'll come and see you tomorrow morning before my ward round. Or you can page me anytime and I'll come as soon as I'm free.'

'I'll be available too,' Abby promised. 'Though I'm sure Mr Baxter will be able to answer a lot more questions than I can.'

She could feel Steve watching he as she turned her chair and headed for the door. Could he see how important her thumb was, perhaps?

Maybe Noah was watching her as well and thinking along the same lines.

'Keep in mind that the thumb is the most debilitating digit to lose as far as hand function is concerned,' he said quietly. 'And that the benefits of a toe transfer far outweigh the risks.'

Noah walked with Abby as she headed back to her office.

'I've got an outpatient clinic starting in fifteen minutes,' he said. 'Maybe I can scrounge a cup of coffee in your staffroom?'

'Of course. You're as much a part of the staff of the hand clinic as anyone else.'

She showed him where to find the mugs and the biscuit tin when they arrived back in her small corner of this large hospital. 'Do you think Steve will agree to the surgery?'

'I hope so.' Noah sat down on one of the armchairs in the room. 'It can take a bit of time to get your head around the concept, though.' He shifted a bag on the low table between chairs to have a space to put his mug.

'Oh…that's mine,' Abby said. 'I wondered where that had got to.'

He handed her the bag, frowning as the blunt point of a thick needle pierced the plastic.

'I'm learning to knit,' Abby explained. 'And it's harder than it looks. I suspect I left it in here and forgot about it on purpose.'

Noah was grinning at her.

'What's funny?'

'The idea of you knitting,' he said.

'I'm about to become an aunty. I thought maybe I should learn how to make a pair of booties or something. I know…' she made a face. 'It's not really me, is it? I know it's got trendy but I still feel like I'm doing old-lady stuff.'

'It does seem about as likely as… I don't know… me playing wheelchair basketball.'

'That wouldn't be a strange thing to do. You'd love it.'

'But I'm not in a wheelchair.'

'You don't have to be, apart from when you're playing. Able-bodied people are allowed.'

'Really?'

'Why not?' Abby shrugged. 'The wheelchair is just a tool. Like using ice skates or a bicycle or something.'

'But it doesn't seem fair. Don't able-bodied people have an advantage?'

Abby smiled. 'No. They just think they do—until they have a go. The only difference is that they have higher points.' It was time she went back to her office and reviewed patient files for the people she would be working with for the rest of the day but stealing a few minutes to keep talking to Noah was irresistible.

'Players get classified according to their level of disability,' she explained. 'The total number of points allowed on the court at any time, adding up the five players, is fourteen. It's all about control of trunk movement. If you have little or no control, you score one point zero. If you have complete control in all directions, you score four point five. As an able-bodied person, you'd score four point five.'

'How much do you score?'

'I'm a four point five, too,' Abby told him. 'My spinal injury was low lumbar so I'm really very lucky. I even got to avoid the total lack of bladder and bowel control that most paraplegics have to deal with.' She bit her lip at the expression on Noah's face. 'Sorry... too much information?'

'No...not at all.' Noah was smiling now. 'I was just thinking that I might like to try the basketball—especially in weather like this when it's too wet to be pleasant getting out for a run. If you didn't set out to wipe the floor with me, that is.'

'Come along, then.' The idea that Noah might want to join in the sport she loved so much was making Abby feel astonishingly happy. 'Tomorrow's a training session and newbies are always welcome. It's friendly and relaxed. I'll send you the address for the gym and you can use one of the extra sports chairs that are stored there.'

'You said this would be relaxing.' Noah could feel his soaked shirt sticking to his back and he knew the muscles in his arms were going to be complaining tomorrow.

'I said relaxed, not relax*ing*.' Abby was waiting for the moment he lost control of the ball as he tried to bounce it and move his chair at the same time. She swooped as soon as he did and then she was off, showing him how it was done as she rolled almost the full length of the court before taking aim and scoring a goal.

He could use both hands to propel the chair now and the physical effort was actually very welcome. This was far more interesting than simply going for a run because he needed to use his brain as well as his body. The effort involved was also exactly what he'd needed after a frustrating end to his day. Steve had decided against the toe transfer and wasn't ready to sign a consent form for an amputation either. He was upset and miserable and refusing to talk to anyone, including his wife. When Abby had arrived for his therapy session she'd been told, very rudely, to "get lost".

Not that she'd taken it personally. 'I'll try again tomorrow,' she'd told Noah. 'We'll win in the end, you'll see. I'm going to have a quiet word with Pauline and see if we can work together to persuade him that it's the best thing to do.

He was feeling a lot more optimistic himself now, as if Abby's determination and confidence was contagious. Although she'd just demonstrated that she was far more capable than him, she hadn't wiped the floor with him as he'd had his first go at her sport. Like her teammates, she'd been patient. And generous. And the amount of laughter on court had been even more contagious.

Noah hadn't felt this good in what felt like for ever. He knew he was beaming as he finally unstrapped his legs and got out of the chair.

Abby rolled up beside him. 'What's the verdict?'

'Great exercise, in good company, with so much fun thrown in? What's not to love?'

'This weather?' Abby had to raise her voice to be heard over the sudden drumming of hail on the roof of the gymnasium. A crack of thunder a few seconds later made her groan. 'I hope it stops before we get to the car park. It's times like this I'm envious of people who get to hold an umbrella and run and jump into their cars as fast as possible.'

'I've got a massive umbrella in my car. If it's still raining, I can help—with the chair or something?'

The offer was matter-of-fact and wasn't making any assumptions about what Abby was, or was not, capable of managing for herself. It reminded Abby of their first meeting. That, while he might recognise that something was more difficult for her, he saw *her* before he saw a disabled woman.

'That would be great. It'll probably blow over by the time we're out of the showers but, in the time-honoured tradition of welcoming newbies, I'd be happy to shout you a beer in the local pub.'

The storm hadn't blown over by the time Abby found Noah waiting for her by the main doors of the gym. If anything, it was worse. His umbrella was threatening to blow inside out and she barely heard her phone ringing over the noise of the heavy rain. She stayed under the shelter of the foyer to answer the call when she saw it was her brother-in-law's number. Hugh might talk to her on Lisa's phone but he never called himself. The beat of alarm intensified when she heard a voice she didn't recognise on the other end of the line.

'Who is this?' Abby demanded. 'And why have you got Hugh's phone?'

Noah's glance was sharp. Nobody could have missed the level of anxiety in her tone.

'I'm Greg, one of the consultants in ED. Hugh threw his phone to me and asked me to call. He's just rushed upstairs to Maternity with Lisa.'

'Oh, my God…what's happened? Is she okay? Is the baby okay?'

'They're fine. The baby's just decided to arrive early, that's all. In fact, it might have been born in the lift. Lisa was asking for you…'

'Oh…no… If you can, tell her I'm on my way.' Abby didn't wait for Noah to hold his umbrella over her as she propelled herself outside. 'It's Lisa,' she called over her shoulder. 'She's in labour. I've got to get to the hospital.'

'What about your other chair?' Noah was struggling to keep his umbrella the right way out as he caught up with her.

'Coach will sort it. There's plenty of room for storage.' Abby's car was in one of the first parking spaces but, as she approached, her heart sank like a stone.

'*No*…not now. *Please*…not now…'

Her rear tyre was as flat as a pancake. Noah had the umbrella over her head but enough rain was being blown sideways to feel miserably cold. For one horrible, scary moment Abby had no idea what to do. Noah, however, was completely calm.

'My SUV,' he said. 'You won't even need to fold up your chair. It'll fit into the back, no problem. We'll sort your car later.'

The only relief that could be bigger than not having to think of a way out of this problem would be to know that both Lisa and the baby were fine. Abby was more than happy to let Noah take charge. She transferred herself into his passenger seat with a bit of extra effort because it was higher than the seats in her car and strapped herself in as Noah stowed the chair in the back. He drove as swiftly as the appalling conditions allowed and then they reversed the procedure and made a dash from the parking building to the hospital entrance. Even well inside the huge building, they could still hear the crack of fresh thunder as they reached the bank of elevators. There was certainly no missing the way the lights flickered, went out completely and then came back on.

They flickered again as Abby pushed the button for the second floor where Maternity was located and Noah frowned.

'Might not be safe to use these,' he said.

'Isn't there an emergency generator that comes on if there's a power outage?'

'Yes, but it's prioritised to cover critical areas first, like Theatres and ICU. Might take a while to get to a lift.'

As if to add weight to his warning, the lights flickered again. A security guard was coming down the corridor towards the emergency department.

'Don't use the lifts,' he told them. 'We don't want anyone trapped if the power goes out completely.'

Abby shook her head. This couldn't be happening. His sister was two floors above them and there was no way she could get any closer without using a lift because the only other way up was the stairwell on the far side of the elevators.

Noah had followed her despairing glance. Then he caught Abby's gaze and it was another one of those silent, fast-as-light exchanges.

I could carry you up the stairs. Is it that important to get there fast?

Yes...it's the only thing that's important right now...

The offer had been impulsive.

Done without thinking about any potential consequences but it was the right thing to do and Noah wasn't about to second-guess the plan. He called to the security guard, who turned back.

'Could you find a safe space for a wheelchair for a while? We need to use the stairs.'

'No worries, mate. I'll put it in ED Reception.'

He waited while Noah lifted Abby from the chair into his arms and then whisked the chair away. There was certainly no turning back now, although it felt awkward as he bumped the firestop door open with his back and then faced the staircase.

'You might regret this.' Abby's voice sounded as if it was hard to keep her tone light. 'I'm not exactly a featherweight.'

It wasn't the weight of Abby in his arms that might make Noah regret his offer. It was far more likely to be the feel of holding a woman this close because... because the last woman he'd held like this had been his wife, Ellen. But it was okay, because this was an emergency and all he had to do was get her to Maternity and then find out where her sister was, and the physical effort, on top of what he'd already done this evening, was enough to drive anything else from his awareness.

Like the way her arms were wrapped around his

neck, holding on for dear life, and the softness of her breast pressing against his arm. Or that smell of…what was it…something like apple blossom? It had to be her shampoo or soap. Surely nobody's skin could smell that good naturally?

There was a nurse near the labour ward's reception desk. 'Abby? We were told to look out for you. Come with me…' She took off, without giving Noah the chance to ask if they might have a wheelchair available. He couldn't exactly slow down and look for one himself either, which meant that when they got to the room Lisa was in, there was nothing for it but to carry Abby inside. Which also meant that Noah was suddenly in a space he really didn't want to be in—with a young mother sitting on a bed, her husband perched beside her with his arm around her shoulders, looking down to where she was cradling their newborn child in her arms.

He could actually feel the emotion that was taking over Abby. The tension that was exploding into something else. That kind of wonder and joy that had been almost missing for him when he'd first seen his child because he'd been inside such a dark cloud of horror at the same time. He'd felt flashes of it, however. Enough to recognise that Abby was overwhelmed by it now. Enough to know that he didn't want to be dragged back into his own past like this.

Gently, he put Abby down into the armchair in the room and stepped back, ready to excuse himself and let the family have this special time together. He wasn't needed any more. Hugh could sort out getting Abby's chair back and helping to deal with the flat tyre on her car.

But Lisa wanted to thank him for making sure that Abby had got here. And Hugh was taking the tiny bundle out of Lisa's arms and was giving it to Abby and… the expression on her face was…well, it was so raw and so powerful that the breath caught in his throat. Noah could actually feel his throat tightening so much it was painful and there was a sting at the back of his eyes that he recognised from long ago.

He had to get out. Now. Before he could get sucked into that feeling of loss. Of being confronted with something he'd wanted so much but could now never have. A family of his own. He was aware of something else as well. He could see—and feel—the love between the people in this room and, right now, especially between Abby and the tiny person she was holding in her arms like the most precious thing to ever exist. A collage of at least a dozen thoughts flashed through his head in the fraction of time it took for him to smile and turn away.

Meeting Abby Phillips and the way she'd made him laugh. Seeing her hair lit up like a halo that day when she had been sitting in the gallery above his operating theatre. That she had known his favourite quote and spoken it with him with such feeling. The fierce determination that was obvious so often but really unleashed on a basketball court but the way it was tempered by generosity and patience.

She was an astonishing person and, in this heart-melting moment, Noah's only—and fervent—wish was that Abby would never have to suffer the heartbreak of losing someone precious to her, like her sister or that brand-new baby, because she deserved so much more than that. She deserved every happiness that life could possibly provide, in fact.

CHAPTER FOUR

'HEY…GUESS WHAT?'

Abby looked up to see Noah poking his head around the door of the treatment room. Her patient, sitting beside her at the table, was still staring at her hand as if willing it to move. Abby nodded and put up her index finger, signalling to Noah that she would be able to talk to him in a minute.

'Try this one, again, Audrey. Relax your fingers and thumb and make an "O" by touching your thumb to your index finger. Straighten your fingers and then touch your middle finger. Straighten again and repeat for each finger. I'll be back in a sec.'

Turning her chair, she rolled towards Noah, happy to interrupt this session with a patient because it was almost finished anyway but more, because she hadn't seen him for a couple of days—ever since her niece had arrived so unexpectedly on that stormy night—so she hadn't had the chance to thank him for his help.

The night was a bit of blur, to be honest, but there were two memories that stood out. One was the feeling of holding that tiny baby in her arms, the astonishing amount of love she could feel for someone she was meeting for the very first time, and the total conviction that to become a mother was most definitely something she wanted in her own future. The other memory… well, that was the way she'd felt when *she* had been held in someone else's arms. Noah's, to be precise.

She'd been held in the arms of a countless number of people in her lifetime. Not so much these days, of course, but it did happen occasionally—like when Alex, the orthopaedic registrar, had helped her negotiate the tricky access to the operating theatre gallery. Noah had only been offering the same kind of assistance and, while it had actually been happening, Abby had been too stressed about seeing her sister to acknowledge how different it had been.

It was only much, much later, when all the drama of that night had settled down and her flat tyre had been taken care of by a car rescue service and she had been back home and safe in her own bed that she'd realised just how strong that memory was. If she thought about it, she could still feel the strength that had been in his arms, despite the workout he'd just given them on the basketball court. She could feel his muscles working beneath where she'd been hanging onto his neck and she could smell his warmth and that masculine undertone that could have been the lingering scent of an aftershave but which she suspected was purely his own. She had also felt the tension when he'd carried her into Lisa's room and she'd known why when she'd seen the expression on his face just before he'd escaped.

Okay…make that three memories because she

wasn't about to forget that haunted look on Noah's face as he'd left Lisa's room in the maternity ward. How hard had it been for him to carry her into that room when it had to have triggered memories of a very different birth of a baby? No wonder he'd been avoiding her for the last couple of days and pulling the mantle of his professional life around him like a protective cloak. Interrupting a therapy session wasn't the most professional thing to do, mind you, and Noah wasn't looking at all haunted now. He was, in fact, looking almost as happy as he had when he'd come off the basketball court the other night.

'He said *yes*.'

Abby grinned back. 'The last time someone told me that and was looking this happy was when a friend came into my room at my uni hostel in the middle of the night to tell me about proposing to her boyfriend.'

Noah blinked and Abby had to give herself a mental shake. What a stupid thing to say. Noah probably wanted to avoid memories of proposals and marriages about as much as being close to newborn babies.

But he was still smiling. 'Steve,' he added. He was holding a clipboard in his hand that had papers attached to it. 'He's signed all the consent forms. I thought you might like to come to the team meeting later this afternoon when we start planning the surgery.'

'Oh…that's wonderful news. I'll start making my own treatment plans for after the surgery. If I'm still going to be his therapist?'

'As a matter of fact, he said that was part of the deal.' There were crinkles at the corners of Noah's eyes, even

though his smile was fading. 'He said that was what
had changed his mind was the conversation he'd had
with you and Pauline this morning. About…babies?'

Abby's smile was a bit misty. 'I was telling him
about the excitement of the other night. About how
amazing it was to be holding a brand-new baby. And
Pauline was helping Steve to hold *his* baby and we reminded him of all the things he'd be able to do with
her more easily if he had a new thumb. Like giving
her a bath or holding her hand to walk her to school
or…' Abby's voice trailed away. Was she rubbing salt
into a wound that Noah was always going to have, by
reminding him of his own loss? He didn't seem upset,
though, even though that smile had vanished.

'Five o'clock, then? In the conference room?'

'I'll be there.' She still hadn't had the chance to
thank Noah for his help the other night but this wasn't
the time either. He was already disappearing through
the door and, behind her, Audrey was sounding frus-
trated.

'I can't do it. I can't make my thumb touch my ring
finger and it's miles away from my pinkie.'

Abby turned back to her patient. 'It'll come, don't
worry. Just think about how far you've come since the
cast came off your wrist. This is something you can
practise at home and every time you do it, you'll be
getting a little closer to making it happen. Now…let's
try something else…'

Places at the long, oval table in the conference room
were full by the time Noah had hooked his laptop up

to the data projector ready for his presentation. He turned to the group and their conversations faded instantly. For many of the people here—the same mix of surgeons and senior ancillary staff that had been involved in Steve's earlier surgeries—the procedure he was about to discuss would be a first and there was a distinct air of professional interest in the room. A hum of excitement, even, and he could feel the intensity of their focus on him. Especially Abby's...

'So...big toe transplantation has proven itself to be the ideal form of thumb reconstruction in the case of traumatic thumb loss,' he began. 'It has a single interphalangeal joint just like the thumb and, for most people, the length and appearance of the big toe is not dissimilar to their other thumb.'

The photograph he put up was the one that he and Abby had shown Steve when they'd been telling him about the option of this surgery and that felt a lot longer ago than a couple of days. It wasn't so much that so many things had happened but that they'd dragged him back to such a traumatic episode of his personal history. Why was it that the time period to deal with difficult things seemed to stretch out but the most enjoyable things went past in a flash—like that first attempt he'd made at playing wheelchair basketball?

'As you all know,' he continued, 'Steve is a father to three children, the youngest of whom is just a baby. He's fortunate enough to have a strong and supportive marriage, he has many years ahead of him to provide for his family and he's extremely motivated to work hard towards a successful outcome and, preferably, to return to a job he loves that requires a good level of hand function.'

He could feel a reflection in the room of his own investment in the upcoming surgery for Steve. This was going to be a very long and technically demanding procedure but it was an intriguing solution to a major issue and everybody here knew what a huge difference it could make, not only to a young father but for his whole family.

As Noah clicked through and discussed slides that labelled the tendons, nerves and blood vessels that would need to be dissected free of the foot and left attached to the isolated toe for the implant surgery, he could feel a faint echo of what he'd said about Steve sitting there in the back of his mind. It was quite astonishing, in fact, that he could be giving a seamless presentation like this and that part of his brain could be aware of something that had nothing to do with anatomy or surgical procedures or anything to do with his patient at all, really. Except it did, didn't it? It was the core of the reason they were all here and why they were so passionate about their work.

It was that notion of family, that's what it was.

Noah wasn't consciously thinking about it, of course, but he could feel it—like a vast space behind an open door. And that door was only open as far as it was because he'd had to confront his own loss of family all over again the other night, and he hadn't been prepared for that at all. He hadn't been prepared for that close physical contact when he'd been carrying Abby either—or the disturbing dreams it seemed to have triggered for the last couple of nights—but it had been the unexpected proximity to Lisa's baby in the first few minutes of its life that had really done his head in.

He pressed the arrow button on his keyboard to bring up a new diagram. A photograph this time of a foot with lines drawn on it with a marker pen. It took only a split second to push that button but it was long enough for one of those momentary flashbacks that he'd never been able to get away from, especially if he saw the tiny face of a newborn or heard that distinctive warbling cry. He'd got very good at pushing the flashbacks away, however, and, without missing a beat, Noah dealt with that image in his mind by flicking it away as if it were no more than an annoying fly near his face. How weird was it, though, that just a glimpse could still carry the weight of unbearable emotions that were associated with that image of Ellen, lying there on a bed in the emergency department.

The consultant in charge of her attempted resuscitation was looking up at the clock to record the time of death. The looks that were exchanged amongst the crowd of people in the room were acknowledging that they'd failed but also that there were two patients involved here. The decision to do something that was too horrific to even contemplate—a post-mortem Caesarean—was being made in that instant and Noah could only grapple with the way his heart was being so completely torn between grief and hope as he saw that tiny baby coming into the world and struggling to take her first breaths.

And then…as they always did—the unwanted images and echoes of associated feelings vanished and it had all happened so fast that nobody would ever guess they'd been there. Except… Noah looked up as he took a breath to talk about this new photograph. His gaze happened to catch Abby's and he had the oddest sensation—like the softest touch on the back of his neck—that made him wonder if she might see more than he realised.

'These lines are the markers for the initial incision,' he said, turning back to point to the screen. 'As you can see, it extends well in to the first web space. We need to leave sufficient flap length to let us close up with minimal shortening of the first metatarsal. These next photos will demonstrate the dissection that needs to happen to identify the arterial branches, the extensor tendon and a dorsal vein…'

There would be two teams working in Theatre, one to harvest the toe and then repair the foot and the other to prepare the site on the hand and then do the implantation.

'When the implantation team is ready, that's when we ligate and transect the dominant artery and vein on the toe. The sequence for implantation is, as you'd expect—bone, extensor tendon, flexor tendon, nerves, artery, vein and finally the skin.'

Noah flipped through slide after slide that covered the rest of this surgery and answered any queries that the team came up with. One of the last was from an ICU consultant.

'How long do you expect he'll need to be in the unit?'

'Three to five days. We'll need to keep a close eye on limb baselines with the help of a Doppler signal and continuous pulse oximetry. It's going to take a few days at least to get all our ducks in a row for a major surgery like this so we've got plenty of time to meet and put a more extensive plan in place. I'll try and get to everyone involved so that we can discuss any details that this overview might have missed.'

There were nods around the table and people began gathering any personal items like notepads and phones. This meeting was almost over.

'Just to finish up,' Noah continued, 'I'd like to—belatedly—welcome Abby Phillips to this meeting. Rehabilitation in a case like this is of huge importance if we're going to get a successful outcome. Do you have any comments you'd like to make, Abby? Or questions to ask?'

'I understand that gentle mobilisation can start as early as three to four days after the procedure if the bone fixation is stable and that starting active exercises will depend on the strength of the tendon repairs. The real work of strengthening and vocational therapy will start at about the two-month mark, yes?'

Noah nodded. 'Let's sort out a time for us to meet before you head away. Same goes for everybody else—I've got my diary here. Thank you for taking the time to come to this meeting and I look forward to working with you all again.'

Abby seemed perfectly happy to wait while he made arrangements to talk through the case in more detail with the various specialists involved and, for his part, Noah felt curiously happy that she was here and waiting for him. He was getting to know his new colleagues now and they were great people to be working with but Abby definitely stood out from the rest of them. She stood out from everyone he'd ever met in his life, to be honest.

He'd never met anyone who used humour the way she automatically did to diffuse any potential tense moment. She'd done that within minutes of meeting him, joking that she might never walk again after that accident, and she'd done it again today, when she'd told him he was repeating the words of someone who'd just proposed to their boyfriend. And she'd done that because she recognised that there was tension between them. Because he'd been avoiding her—avoiding anything other than purely work—after what had happened the other night.

Noah knew perfectly well that hospital grapevines worked between cities as much as departments. That everybody at St John's had probably heard about his tragic backstory within a very short time of him walking through the doors, and he was quite used to the occasional glance coming his way that varied from curious to being full of pity. It was rare to get one that made him feel that someone actually understood how hard it had been, however, especially when it could acknowledge a struggle with no hint of pity or OTT admiration, and he'd received a glance exactly like that in the last moment before he'd escaped Lisa's room in the maternity ward.

Abby had already got past his usual barrier that kept him from engaging in social events with the people he worked with by persuading him to go to that basketball training session but that hadn't been exactly social, had it? It had been exercise and stress relief and he'd been attracted to the idea because it was just so different from anything he'd ever done before. New ground—and new ground was the best because it was guaranteed not to trigger flashbacks of any kind.

Finally, they were the only two people left in the conference room and Noah found himself deliberately relaxing. There was a huge amount of preparation for the gruelling stint in Theatre that Steve's surgery would entail and, from experience, he knew that he needed to make the most of any downtime before that.

'How's your diary looking for meeting times?'

'A lot emptier than yours, I expect.' She was smiling at him. 'It's a big challenge, isn't it?'

'I love a challenge.' Noah was smiling back. 'I suspect you do as well.'

'Story of my life. I'd probably get bored in no time without one.' Abby's tone was light but there was something serious in her gaze. 'Having said that, though, there are the occasional challenges that can make me feel kind of vulnerable and I had one of those the other night—with that flat tyre and then the power cuts. I've been waiting for a chance to thank you for helping me.'

Noah tried to shrug off the thanks. Already, he was waiting for a flashback and preparing himself to find a distraction.

'And, what's more, you managed to do it without reminding me that I have limitations,' Abby added. 'There's not many people who can step in like that and let someone like me keep their dignity.'

Noah had found a new smile. 'I think you'd keep your dignity in any situation. From what I've seen, you own whatever you choose to tackle.'

It was Abby's turn to shrug something off. Maybe she didn't like compliments?

'Anyway… I was trying to think of a way to say thank you but, I dunno, I didn't think flowers or chocolates would cut the mustard.'

That made Noah's breath come out in a huff of laughter. 'Touché,' he murmured. 'We do have that in common, I guess.'

'So I came up with the idea of offering to cook you dinner,' Abby continued. 'It's not common knowledge but one of my splinter skills is that I'm a fabulous cook. I've thought about entering one of the television chef competitions, in fact.'

'Oh?' Noah was impressed. Was there anything Abby wasn't good at? 'I can't cook to save myself. I usually end up getting those ready-made meals from the supermarket. Some of them are surprisingly good, mind you.'

Abby waved a hand dismissively. 'Can't compete with made from scratch. So, that's a yes, then? We could kill two birds with one stone and talk about Steve's rehab and that way you'll have more time in your schedule for any extra meetings you might need.'

'You mean tonight?'

Her glance held a glint of amusement this time. 'No time like the present. I often find if you give yourself too much time to think about something, you'll just come up with a whole bunch of reasons why it isn't a good idea. Unless you've got other plans?'

How did she know that he was already formulating a polite reason why he couldn't have dinner with her tonight? The same way she knew he didn't have anything on his agenda for the evening, other than to spend hours going over his plans for Steve's surgery? She probably knew why he would back away at the speed of light from a dinner invitation from a single woman, too, but that clearly wasn't going to be a barrier in a friendship that suddenly felt remarkably safe. Different.

New ground.

'No other plans,' he heard himself saying aloud. 'And a home-cooked meal does sound like a treat. Give me your address and a time and I'll be there.'

Abby hurriedly threw the packaging from the ready-made meals into her rubbish bin before speeding to her front door when the bell rang.

'I didn't realise you lived so close to the staff quarters,' Noah said. 'Walking distance.'

'It's a great location.' Abby nodded. 'But I just loved the building for its character. High ceilings like this give it such a feeling of spaciousness.'

So did having minimal furniture, of course, polished wooden or tile floors throughout with no rugs to break the smooth surface, and wider than normal doors to accommodate her wheelchair.

'I love it.' Noah belatedly remembered that he had a bottle of wine tucked under his arm. 'Hope you like red?'

'It'll be perfect with our dinner but I have to say I'm a bubbles girl. Can I interest you in a glass of Prosecco to start with?'

Noah was smiling. 'Somehow that doesn't surprise me.'

'Sadly, I've developed a taste for French champagne.' Abby led the way past the doors leading to her bedroom and the bathroom, into the open-plan kitchen living area of her remodelled ground-floor apartment. Two couches marked off the corner where her gas fire flickered within its antique iron casing. A dining table and chairs separated that corner from the kitchen.

'And that's sad?'

'Only because it's out of my budget. I blame my sister, Lisa. And Hugh, of course. Remind me to tell you the story of how they got together sometime.'

'I'm guessing it involved French champagne?' But Noah wasn't waiting for confirmation. He was looking up at the ornate cornice of the plaster ceilings. 'This is amazing. You've got a chandelier even.'

'I have excellent taste,' Abby agreed. She opened the fridge and took out the chilled bottle of sparkling wine. 'I know it's a work night but we don't have to drink it all.'

'I make it a policy to find at least a bit of time to relax when I've got a big surgery coming up. If you don't charge your batteries beforehand it can be a struggle to stay focused for what could be a twelve-hour stint.'

'I'll bet.' Abby handed him the bottle. 'Could you do the honours? I'm just going to check on the oven.'

'Whatever it is smells delicious.'

'Beef Wellington,' Abby told him, relieved that she had a good reason not to be meeting his gaze. 'Just individual-sized ones.'

'I'm impressed.' Noah was eyeing the work surfaces of her kitchen now. 'If I tried to make something that complicated, my kitchen would be a complete bombsite.'

'Ah…' Hadn't Abby heard somewhere that if you wanted to make a lie convincing, the best thing to do was to add in at least an element of truth? 'Well, I have to admit, these were prepared earlier. I had them in the freezer for when I needed a nice meal in a hurry.'

The cork came out of the bottle with a pop and Noah poured the wine into the two glasses Abby provided. He scooped up the cork, wire and foil and headed for the rubbish bin before Abby could stop him but, to her relief, he didn't notice what she'd put in the bin only minutes ago. Even so, she decided it would be a good idea to distract him further.

'Let's sit at the table for now. I printed off a rough outline of a rehab plan for Steve before I left work.'

'Really? That was only an hour or so ago. You did a plan, came home, got changed and whipped up a gourmet dinner and you don't even look out of breath.' He held his glass up in a toast. 'Very impressive.'

'Hmm.' Was it her imagination or was there a note of amusement in his voice?

It was a bit distracting that he'd noticed she had changed her clothes as well. While favouring a more formal skirt and blouse under her white coat at work,

Abby was always keen to get into her favourite leggings and a comfortable sweatshirt as soon as she got home. Was Noah feeling less comfortable because he'd noticed the difference? Or because he was in her home and not in an impersonal space like the gymnasium where they'd last met out of work hours? She could fix that. Abby pushed a thin sheaf of papers towards Noah.

'It's only a rough outline, so far,' she explained. 'I was focusing on the sensory rehabilitation because of how it can speed up the axonal regeneration.'

'That's true. And it's a critical element. Not just for repairing the axons but because it helps interpretation of the altered sensory impulses reaching the central nervous system.'

Yes—it seemed that a professional discussion was ironically exactly what Noah needed to relax out of work hours. Abby took a sip of her wine as she watched Noah begin to scan her pages. He had a few questions, some excellent suggestions and genuine praise for her outline.

'There's a great article I came across in a neurology journal recently about the sensory, emotional and cognitive factors and their interplay in the perception of pain. It was directly related to sensory rehabilitation. I could find it online for you if you like.'

'That would be awesome. But let's eat first. No… don't move,' Abby ordered. 'I'll get everything. I hope you're hungry.'

She ferried plates and cutlery to the table and the bowl of salad from the fridge. She handed Noah the bottle of red wine and a corkscrew before getting the food from the oven and transferring it to a pretty serving platter.

They ate in an appreciative silence to begin with.

'This is *so* good,' Noah finally said. 'Perfect.'

'I'm so glad you like it.'

'Love it.' Noah had almost finished the large puff-pastry square filled with beef, mushroom and chicken liver pâté. 'In fact, it's been one of my favourite meals from the gourmet section of the supermarket for a long time.'

Abby closed her eyes. 'Uh-oh,' she murmured. 'I'm busted, aren't I?'

'So busted,' Noah agreed. 'But they're a great range of ready meals, aren't they? I rather like the cottage pie as well.'

'Oh, me too. And have you tried the chilli con carne?'

'Delicious. Not quite as good as the spaghetti carbonara, perhaps.'

They were both laughing by now.

'And there I was,' Noah said sadly, 'believing that you were some sort of domestic goddess and that you had splinter skills that I could never dream of competing with.'

Abby bit her lip. 'I did *think* of cooking something from scratch,' she said. 'But that would have been cruel. My splinter skill of cooking is on a par with my ability to knit.' She caught Noah's gaze, aiming for an apologetic glance but knowing she was finding this too funny to carry it off. 'But you wouldn't have come if I told you what a crap cook I was, would you? And I really did want to do something to say thanks.'

'It wasn't necessary,' Noah said. 'And I would have come even if it was just beans on toast. I like you, Abby Phillips.'

'I like you, too,' Abby responded lightly. 'And I'll be totally up front and confess that I also didn't make the salted caramel cheesecake ice cream I got for our dessert. Would you like to sit by the fire and relax with it?'

'Sounds perfect. Why don't we have some more of those bubbles with it as well? It's not as if I have to drive home.'

'And I don't even have to walk home.' Abby grinned. 'I like the way you think, Mr Baxter.'

Like…it was the second time she'd used that insipid little word in less than a minute. As she got the ice cream from the freezer and pulled bowls from a cupboard, Abby could see Noah walking towards the other side of this big room to put the Prosecco and glasses on one of the low tables beside the couches.

He looked right at home here, with his height not at all out of place beneath her high ceilings. At home and relaxed and…just as gorgeous as she'd remembered him being when she'd allowed herself to play with the delicious fantasies that her initial crush had created.

Which had been all very well when they were just that—fantasies. How much of a relief had it been, though, to discover that Noah wasn't ever going to want to be more than a friend? To back off from having to confront an anxiety that had been buried for years? Those deep, dark doubts about whether someone would find her as attractive as someone able-bodied and, worse, whether that fear of being unable to protect herself enough might resurface and make it impossible for her to go that far?

It had still been easy, despite having Noah in her own home, thanks to the formality of being at a table and the professional element that talking about Steve's upcoming surgery and rehabilitation had provided. But this…transferring herself from her wheelchair to one of the squashy, feather-filled pillows of her couch, in front of a flickering fire, with not only a bowl of the ultimate comfort food in her hands but another glass of bubbles…well…this was a rather different kettle of fish, that's what it was.

By the time he was scraping the last of his ice cream from the bowl, Noah had made a decision.

'I really need to get serious about finding a place to live that isn't just a room in a place that feels like it's part of my work environment,' he told Abby. 'I'd forgotten how important it is to be able to completely switch off sometimes.' He put his bowl on the table, swapping it for his glass of wine, and then he leaned back into this gloriously comfortable couch and let his breath out in a contented sigh. 'Somewhere like this would be perfect.'

'I do love this apartment,' Abby said. 'I had to move in with Lisa and Hugh for a while because there was so much work needed to renovate this place and make it wheelchair friendly, but it was such a relief to settle in here. It's taken twenty-six years but I feel like I'm finally living completely independently and I love it. The only thing missing is…maybe a cat. If I can find a ginger one, that is.'

'Why ginger? Oh…wait…' Noah shook his head. 'It's the family hair colour, isn't it?'

'Don't let anyone tell you you're not a smart man, Noah Baxter.' Abby handed him her bowl to put on the table and gave him both a smile and a nod when he offered her the other glass of wine he'd poured.

'And the newest family member—was Lisa's baby a boy or a girl?'

'A girl. She's been called Amy—after my gran.'

'And does she have red hair? I didn't notice the other night.'

'She's almost completely bald, so we can't tell yet.' Abby took a sip of her wine and then put her glass down. 'But I'm sure you don't want to be talking about babies. I… I'm sorry you got thrown into that situation. I know it can't have been easy for you.'

So she did know his story. Of course she did. He'd known that already, hadn't he? There was still no hint of pity in her eyes, though. Just understanding.

'It's fine,' he said quietly. 'It was a long time ago and life moves on. You find ways of coping. It wasn't that it upset me…it was more that I didn't want to intrude.'

It was a perfectly reasonable excuse for having excused himself so quickly that night but Noah was quite sure that Abby could sense everything he wasn't saying. She was still holding his gaze and it was a more intense version of the glance he'd caught as he'd slipped out the door when she'd been holding baby Amy. And an element in that look mixed with everything else this evening was providing—the welcoming feeling of home that this apartment had, sharing a meal and simply being able to relax in the company of someone who was trustworthy.

The result of that alchemy was something poignant that made Noah very aware of what would always be missing from his life because it was something that wasn't out of reach, it was more that he didn't have any desire to make the effort of reaching it. Maybe he wasn't even capable of stretching that far now.

He needed to break that eye contact. 'You see too much,' he murmured. 'I hope you're not going to tell me that telepathy is another one of your splinter skills.'

'I've never thought so.' Abby's voice was just as quiet as his. 'Until now.'

He still couldn't look away. Whatever it was that made it so easy to communicate with Abby worked both ways, didn't it? There was only one reason that she wanted a cat in her apartment and that was because she was lonely. She had the same empty space in her life as he did and, while Noah had accepted long ago that he would always have to live with that, Abby deserved better.

She was an absolutely stunning young woman and… and the way she was looking at him—the way it felt like she was touching something so deep that no one else could even see it—was pulling him in. Quite literally. Noah could feel himself leaning closer and closer to Abby.

And what happened then seemed as inevitable as taking his next breath.

He kissed her.

CHAPTER FIVE

DEAR LORD, BUT this man could kiss…

Abby had never been kissed like this before. Right now, it felt like no woman on earth had ever been kissed quite like this—with electrical currents of something fierce and totally irresistible that kept rippling through her body and, astonishingly, it actually felt like they were reaching parts that had been deprived of significant sensation her entire life.

She was so lost in this kiss, in the feel and taste and warmth and just how *alive* Noah's lips and mouth were, that Abby had no idea of how long it had gone on for. It was the tiny sound she made as she realised things were moving to the next level, when Noah's hand slipped down her arms and then brushed her breasts, that made it all come to a crashing halt. Noah jerked back as if he'd suddenly woken up.

For the longest moment, they both stared at each other. Abby was trying to catch her breath. Noah was pressing his fingers against his lips, as though he was trying to capture any remnants of that extraordinary kiss. Or perhaps he was stopping himself from kissing

her again. Abby wanted to catch his fingers in her own.
To bring them to touch her own lips. But she couldn't
move and she couldn't look away.

'Sorry…' His voice was slightly muffled. 'I didn't
mean…'

'You don't have to be sorry,' Abby said. 'And it
doesn't have to mean anything…but…'

Another tiny pause without breaking that locked
gaze and then Noah's eyebrow quirked—a silent re-
quest for her to finish what she was saying.

'But I liked it,' she said softly.

'Me, too…' But Noah was the one who broke the
eye contact. 'Which feels weird because I was starting to think I'd never even want to kiss anyone else
like that again.'

Abby could feel a stillness in the room. As if they
were both caught in a moment of time that could prove
to be momentous. Life changing?

'That's a good thing, then,' she said carefully.

'Why?'

'Because I get the feeling that you're like me. That
you might be lonely in a way that a friend or family
can't be enough to fix and…and it would be sad to feel
like that for the rest of our lives, wouldn't it?'

That got Noah's attention. His direct look was accompanied by a frown. 'I don't understand,' he said.
'You're gorgeous. Funny. Intelligent. A force to be reck-
oned with both on and off a basketball court. Surely
you're only single because you're choosing to be?'

It was Abby's turn to break the eye contact. 'Yes…
and no…,' she muttered. 'It's an old story and not one

I particularly want to dredge up tonight. I'd rather talk about you. If anyone's got a legion of potential partners waiting in the wings, it's got to be you.'

Noah was silent for a moment. 'I can't go there,' he admitted. 'I'm not ready. And it's been so long now, maybe I never will be.'

'Because you think it might be a disaster the first time?' Abby gulped the last of her wine. 'Tell me about it. It's not just the emotional risk—sex can be scary, right? I should know. I'm twenty-six and I've never... Oh... God...' She put her hand over her eyes. She hadn't drunk *that* much wine, surely? 'That's *way* too much information... I have no idea why I just told you that. Nobody else knows. Not even my sister...'

The silence was a lot longer this time. Abby could feel herself cringing.

'Sorry...' she muttered. 'I think I do know what you mean, though. We don't know each other that well yet but there's something there that...that's different. I feel like I can trust you and...and I really did like that kiss...'

When she risked a glance she found that Noah was watching her carefully. He held her gaze as soon as he caught it and when he reached out and touched her cheek so gently with his finger, it almost brought tears to her eyes.

'So did I,' he murmured.

His finger slipped from her cheek to trace a line to the back of her neck which he cupped with his hand. Slowly...agonisingly slowly, he bent his head to cover her lips again with his. But this time it was a more controlled kiss. It wasn't about to spiral into what Abby genuinely wanted—which was a lot more. More than a lot more, in fact. For the first time ever, despite every fear that might be trying to creep in from the back of her mind, she really did want it all.

He could feel exactly what Abby wanted through the touch of her lips and way her hands were shaping his shoulders and then his chest. He could even taste it and hear it in the way she was catching her breath and it was breaking his heart because…

Because she was amazing and she was trusting him with something so huge he didn't want to go there. Perhaps the reason she was still a virgin had something to do with her disability but not in the most obvious way. Noah had caught a nuance of something dark. That Abby was scared of sex because something had happened to scare her and that was…so sad. More than sad. The idea that someone could have treated her badly made a curl of anger stir in his gut.

When he broke this kiss, he cradled her head in the dip below his collar bone. 'Don't be scared of sex, Abby,' he said. 'I don't know what your story is and you don't have to tell me but it *can* be wonderful. You shouldn't let it hold you back from a relationship.'

'But… I might be crap at it,' Abby whispered. 'Like I am with cooking. Or knitting.'

Noah smiled. 'It's not like that. You can't be bad at it. Not if you're with someone who cares.'

'It's a bit…different for me, though.' He could hear how difficult it was for Abby to get these words out as she paused to swallow hard. 'I mean…wouldn't it be… I don't know…*boring* to have sex with someone who can't move half her body?'

Oh, man… How could someone like Abby ever think that being with her could possibly be boring?

'Sex is about a lot more than what goes where and how you move,' he said softly. 'Most of it happens in here.' He touched his head. 'And, if you're lucky and you're with someone you're in love with, it happens in *here.*' This time he touched his chest over his heart.

'I'll have to get past the first time to find that out. And that first time will have to be with someone I could really trust.' Abby's head moved against his chest as she slid an upward glance at him. 'Like you.'

Noah had to close his eyes as he felt that sharp tug on his heartstrings. He lifted his hand to stroke her hair. 'I've never even really thought about being with any-one since Ellen died,' he told her. 'At first it was grief and then it was because I wasn't interested in anything other than my work. As I said, it's been a long time. So long, I couldn't be sure if I could go through with it. Now that you've mentioned it, it could well be a di-saster waiting to happen.'

He could feel the tension increasing in Abby's muscles—as if she was gathering her courage?

'That makes two of us, then,' she said. 'And…don't you think it would be good to know? For…um…future reference? So that—if we ever wanted to—we wouldn't need to be nervous about whether or not it's even pos-sible?'

'You mean like a trial run?'

'Exactly. No big deal…just a "friends helping each other out" kind of thing.'

It was a bad idea. A very bad idea. So why was his body trying to tell him something very different? For the first time in so long, things were falling into place, like a jigsaw puzzle. How attractive Abby was. How much he liked her company. How incredibly soft and delicious her mouth was. Oh, yeah…there were parts of his body feeling things that were intense enough to be bordering on pain.

'It's a bad idea.' At least his brain was being sensible. 'Not only because we have to work together. Your first time should be something special. With someone you're in love with and who's in love with you. So that it's making love and not just sex.'

'That's not going to happen.'

'You might be surprised.'

Abby shook her head. 'I'd be too nervous to let it happen.'

Noah could see those nerves in her eyes now. More than nerves. There was a hint of real fear there.

'What happened, Abby?' His voice was no more than a whisper. 'Did someone hurt you?'

Those glorious soft, brown eyes were shining as if tears were gathering. 'They tried to.' Her voice was as quiet as his. 'Someone I'd made the mistake of letting into the house after a first date. He was laughing that I couldn't run away. If Lisa hadn't come home a minute or two later, he would have…would have…'

Her voice was shaking. Noah put a gentle finger on her lips.

'I get it.'

He didn't need to know the details. He'd heard enough to know how scared she'd been and he could understand why she'd never gone there again. Anger towards the stranger who'd done this was strong enough to cause a wave of unpleasant heat but something else was even stronger. That Abby was trusting *him* to exorcise those ghosts of the past? He had to swallow past a lump in his throat. He already thought enough of Abby to believe she deserved the best things that life had to offer but she was going to miss out on so much if she couldn't learn that being close to someone didn't need to be terrifying. It was a gift that she was asking him to provide.

And…as unlikely as it had seemed before he'd met Abby, his body was continuing to wake up. Telling him that he, too, was missing something in his life that was important. He didn't have to think about falling in love with someone or getting married again but…well…sex was just a part of a normal life, wasn't it? And he really wanted to kiss Abby again. To touch her. To make her feel special. To…hopefully…take them both over the edge. This was totally different from any sexual experience he would have ever had before.

New ground.

But he shook his head. 'We can't. I don't carry anything these days. Protection, that is.'

'There are condoms on the top shelf of my bathroom cupboard,' Abby told him. She even found a hint of smile. An embarrassed but mischievous kind of smile. 'I know…but Lisa looks in there sometimes. I didn't want her thinking I didn't have any kind of sex life, you know?'

Okay…that smile did it. Or maybe it was the humour behind a statement that covered an issue that was huge but that she was dealing with all by herself. The courage of this woman blew him away and Noah was responding to that on both an emotional and physical level as he kissed her yet again. He pushed himself up off the sofa a minute or two later.

'I'll be right back,' he murmured.

'So…how did it go?'

'Sorry…what?' Abby looked up from the bundle of sleeping baby in her arms to meet her sister's gaze. Surely Lisa wasn't reading her mind? How embarrassing would it be if she'd guessed what Abby was thinking about right then—that last night had been so much better than the first time she and Noah had been together.

Not that that first time on the couch had not been good. He'd been so reassuring about how attractive she was and so gentle, letting Abby set the pace and encouraging her to show him how to help position her legs and make it all possible but, if she was really honest, there had been elements of both awkwardness and…yeah…remnants of fear and the kind of momentary flashbacks that had always been enough to make sure she never went that far again.

But not last night. Oh, no… They'd used her bed last night and there'd been laughter involved. Jokes about just needing a bit more practice to make sure that

Abby was confident with her new splinter skill. And the balance between caution and passion had changed. They were more comfortable with each other's bodies. More ready to take risks and…well…they'd paid off.

If Abby had ever wondered—and, of course, she had—whether the amount of sensation she had in her lower body could allow a partner to generate that ultimate release of sexual tension, then she'd certainly found out last night.

Did it show in her face or something?

Lisa was shaking her head at Abby's apprehensive expression. 'For heaven's sake… I'm the one who's sleep-deprived and has mush for brains. I mean that surgery that is the talk of St John's at the moment. The toe to thumb thing. How did it go yesterday?'

'Oh…' Abby let out a relieved breath. She would no doubt tell her sister about this new development in her personal life very soon but she wasn't ready to just yet. It was too new. Too…precious?

No, that wasn't quite the right word. It wasn't as if she and Noah were in a relationship or anything. This was purely a friendship, albeit with a bit of a crush on her side, and the sex had been only supposed to be a one-off—an experiment to see if either of them was ready or even capable of enjoying it. And then it had been another one-off last night—just to see if improvements in technique could be made.

'The surgery was amazing. *Noah* was amazing.' Abby couldn't keep the note of pride from her voice. 'I only got to watch part of it but it was incredible. There was a huge team in Theatre—I've never seen so many people involved in one operation but they all worked together seamlessly. And some of what they did was just mind-blowing—joining those tiny nerves and blood vessels together. So delicate and painstaking. Like a form of art, really…'

'Hmm…' Lisa coming towards where Abby had positioned her wheelchair. 'Noah Baxter has certainly impressed you, hasn't he?'

Abby's shrug was muted because she had her arms full of baby Amy. 'He's very good at what he does,' she said. 'Everybody knows that.'

Not everybody knew about everything he was so good at, though. She was the first woman Noah had made love to since he'd lost his wife. That made it special, didn't it?

Made Abby special?

No…she couldn't start thinking like that, although it was hard not to. Especially after last night, when her trust in Noah had been taken to a whole new level. When they could make each other laugh, even in the midst of something that felt so significant.

So life-changing.

The baby stirred in Abby's arms and whimpered. Both women were instantly focused on the infant and Abby knew that Lisa's interest in Noah Baxter, or even Steve's much talked about surgery had faded. As she was rocked, Amy settled back to sleep, her tiny mouth pouting and then relaxing again and even curling up at the corners.

'Look at that…she's smiling.'

'It's too early.' Lisa shook her head. 'They don't smile until they're about six weeks old. Must be wind.'

But baby Amy seemed to want to prove her mother wrong by repeating her facial twist and, this time, Lisa reached for her phone. 'Hugh's not going to believe this,' she said. 'Try rocking her again and I'll take a video.'

But Abby had to pause to drop a soft kiss onto her niece's head. 'She's so adorable,' she told Lisa. 'I think I want one.'

'Be careful what you wish for,' Lisa warned. 'I've never been so tired in all my life. She'd being an angel right now but it's a different story at three a.m., believe me.'

Rocking didn't produce anything like a smile this time. Instead, Amy woke up and let her mother know in no uncertain terms that she needed attention. Her cries got rapidly louder as Lisa took her from Abby's arms and settled into another chair to feed her.

'How can something that adorable make a noise like that?'

'It's worse at three a.m.' But Lisa was smiling as she nestled Amy into the crook of her arm and helped her latch on to her breast.

'I take it back,' Abby decided. 'Or at least I'll postpone it a lot longer. I don't want one yet.'

'You can enjoy this one,' Lisa told her. 'So much better when you can go home when you've had enough. In the meantime, could you get the nappy-changing supplies? She's going to need some clean pants after this.'

Abby moved towards the bag of nappies and wipes that were being kept downstairs to save a trip up to the nursery on the first floor of this huge, old house. She was quite happy to postpone parenthood. She needed to follow her sister's example and find the perfect man to father a baby, anyway. At least she was confident that that could happen now. She had, after all, found the perfect first lover in a physical sense, hadn't she? It was such a shame that Noah was nowhere near ready to consider a "real" relationship but that was simply the way things were and Abby totally respected that. She was envious of a love that was so strong it could continue after death, in fact, and never be replaced. Just the kind of love she would have to hope that she, too, could find one day.

'Fantastic.' Noah could feel his smile stretching enough to light up his face as he observed the small but controlled range of movement in the thumb that had only ever been a big toe before. 'Exactly what I would be hoping for at this stage of your intensive therapy, Steve, and it's only been two weeks of stepping up the pace.'

'A bit over ten weeks since my surgery.' Steve nodded. 'I'm even walking without much of a limp now.'

'Show me?'

Steve was sitting at a table in a treatment room of the hand clinic, with Abby beside him. His wife Pauline was in a corner of the room, the baby on her lap and a toddler playing with some toys at her feet. Noah had seen them through the window in the door as he'd passed so he'd come in, just to offer encouragement to his patient. And, okay, maybe because it was an excuse to spend a little bit of time with Abby at work. He caught her gaze as Steve stood up to walk the length of the room and back, automatically cradling his injured hand with his other arm to protect it as he moved.

Noah could see Abby's satisfaction in her patient's progress in her eyes. He could also see the pleasure that his surprise visit was creating and, on a level beneath that, how strong their friendship had become.

He'd never met anyone with whom so much communication could happen with a glance that lasted only a heartbeat or two, and it still surprised him even though he'd had more than a couple of months to get used to it. Kind of like the way that sex with Abby still surprised him every single time—because there was always something a little different about it? A new note of discovery or depth or maybe just…delight. Something new, anyway.

Something different enough to have made flashbacks almost a thing of the past and to make it feel like Noah was genuinely moving forward with his life in some way. And, whatever it was, neither of them had quite had enough even though the "one-off" joke had worn off so long ago that neither of them bothered bringing it up now. It wasn't as if they saw each other that often. Once a week at the most—usually after a training session for wheelchair basketball at the gym—and nobody would guess there was anything more than friendship between them if they saw them together at work.

Although Noah found himself turning his head,

aware of Pauline's steady gaze, and there was a look on her face that made him wonder if she might have guessed there was more than something strictly professional in his relationship with Abby. Steve certainly wasn't aware of anything other than showing the two main medical professionals still involved with his case how well he was now walking. He had supportive strapping and a shoe insert on the foot where the toe had been removed but his work with a physiotherapist was adjusting his gait enough to make any change almost indiscernible.

'That's brilliant,' Noah told him. 'I can see how much effort you're putting into your rehabilitation.'

'It's my job,' Steve said. 'Until I can get back to my real job, that is. And I need to do that as soon as I can. The benefits aren't enough, you know?'

'We're managing.' Pauline spoke up. 'I'm not going to say it's easy but we'll get there.'

Steve nodded. 'It's helping being at home again. I'm not about to lose my motivation when I've got the kids in front of me all the time.'

'How's the sensory rehab going?'

Steve and Abby shared a glance. 'Not so great,' he said. 'I can't tell the difference between sandpaper and cotton wool if I've got my eyes closed.'

'We're putting a bag together,' Abby added. She waved her hand at a tray of small objects on one side of the table that included a marble, coin, strip of the hooked side of Velcro and some soft fabric. 'For homework. It can be a game with one of your older children, Steve—where they let you feel something with your eyes open and then again with your eyes closed when you try and guess what it is.' She smiled at the toddler sitting by Pauline's feet. 'You could play that game with Daddy, Lucy, couldn't you?'

Pauline ruffled her daughter's curls. 'She could. And her big brother, Mack, would just love it, too.'

Her smile at Abby made Noah realise that bonds were being formed that were wider than simply between a patient and his therapist. There was gratitude there as well. Because the whole family was being included in the therapy for a beloved husband and father? He'd always known that Abby was good at her job but this was a reminder of just how special she was—in so many ways.

Steve's smile was wry. 'Mack *will* love that. Something he can beat me in until we can play footie again.'

'You can also try and get them out of the bag yourself,' Abby told him. 'It'll be good exercise for your whole hand. Let's give it a try now, shall we?'

Pauline looked up to catch Noah's gaze as Abby gathered the objects to put them into the bag and she was still smiling. In fact, there was a hint of a gleam in her eyes that suggested that if he'd been right in his suspicion that she thought there was possibly something going on between himself and Abby, Pauline approved of it.

He needed to dispel any notion that had the potential to turn into an unwelcome rumour. This clearly needed a more definitively professional note.

'I'll leave you to it,' Noah told them, a little more abruptly than he'd intended, as he turned to leave. 'But

I'm glad I saw you today, Steve. I'll look forward to the next progress report when you come into Outpatients. Keep up the great work.'

'What's up, Abby?' Lisa had a concerned frown on her face. 'You don't look so great.'

'I dunno. Maybe I overdid it at training last night. Or maybe I've just gone off mushy peas. How did I ever like something that looks like it's been pre-chewed?'

'Is everything else okay? Like with…you know who?' Lisa lowered her voice as she looked over her shoulder to where Hugh was peering into the fridge in the hope of finding a beer to go with his takeout curry.

Abby frowned. She had confessed a while back to her "friendship with benefits", but had made her sister swear that she wouldn't breathe a word, even to her husband. It was for that reason she'd been relieved that Hugh hadn't invited Noah again to share their weekly family takeout night. It had been a one-off. Like the sex had been supposed to be?

Abby sighed as she stared her pot of mushy peas. Even if Hugh was also sworn to secrecy it might only take a meaningful glance at the wrong time to start some gossip at the hospital and that was the last thing Abby wanted. Because she knew it would be the last thing that Noah would want. Look at the way he'd rushed out of the room when Pauline had been watching them a little too closely that time he'd come in to see how Steve's therapy was going.

Or maybe it was because she still wasn't ready to stop their intimate time together. At some point in the

last few weeks, even though she had been quite determined to keep that crush under control, the dreams
had started to creep back and the idea that she might
have actually started to fall in love with Noah Baxter
on the day she'd met him was also refusing to be entirely shut down. It was a worry and that was probably
adding to whatever it was that was upsetting Abby's
normal approach to life.

'We're completely out of anything to drink. Beer *or*
wine.' Hugh sounded disappointed. 'And it's the first
night that Amy's gone to sleep early enough for us to
have dinner together properly.'

'There's an off-licence five minutes away,' Lisa told
him. 'Go and get something. We can keep the food
warm. It's Friday night and Abby looks like she could
do with a glass of wine.'

But Abby shook her head. 'Not for me, thanks.'

'Not even some bubbles?' Hugh was grinning as
he reached out to touch Abby's forehead. 'You're not
coming down with something, are you?'

'Go,' Lisa ordered. 'The sooner you're back, the
sooner we can eat.'

'Don't bother keeping the peas warm,' Abby said
as Lisa collected the containers to put in the oven. 'I
don't think I'm even hungry any more. Maybe I'll go
home and let you and Hugh have a romantic evening
together. You never know, you might get enough time
for more than dinner.'

'Are you kidding?' Lisa flopped back into her chair
and closed her eyes. 'I'm too tired to even *think* about

sex these days. I have no idea how people get round to having a second child.'

Abby smiled but it was her turn to frown. Was she doing enough to help her sister in this happy but stressful time with a new baby? Because she was focused on Lisa's face she saw the moment her eyes suddenly opened again to glance at the pot of mushy peas and then catch Abby's gaze. She also saw the expression of something like alarm.

'You're not pregnant, are you? That could be why you've suddenly gone off something.'

'Of course not. Don't be daft.'

'Well…it's not as if it's not possible. You're the one who's getting some action in that "good friendship" of yours.' Lisa used her fingers to create quotation marks.

Abby glared at her. She didn't like her sex life being referred to as nothing more than a bit of "action", even if that was exactly what it was supposed to be. 'I'm not stupid, Lise. We've always used condoms.'

'Not that supply from your bathroom cupboard, I hope.'

Abby's glare deepened. What on earth was Lisa referring to now? And they'd only used hers the first time, anyway.

Lisa shrugged. 'Hey, it's not my fault they fell off the shelf when I needed some dental floss. And I'm a nurse, remember. I'm trained to notice expiry dates. Those condoms of yours expired way before you even moved into that apartment.'

They *had* been around for a long time. Because they'd never been used. But Abby shook her head.

'It wouldn't make any difference. We all know some things last way beyond expiry dates.'

'And we all know some things can fail occasionally.' Lisa's voice was quiet now. 'I've got some pregnancy test kits somewhere in *my* bathroom cupboard. Maybe you should take one home with you. Just in case. And you don't need to worry, I'm not about to say anything to Hugh.'

She didn't need to worry?

She'd thought that rumours of how far their friendship had gone would be the last thing Noah would want?

How wrong was it possible for someone to be?

Back home in her own apartment later that evening, in the privacy of her own bathroom, Abby was staring at what she held in her hands. At the tiny plastic window that was showing two distinct lines. At the helpful print beside the window that had an image of a single line beside the words "Not Pregnant" and one of the double lines with that single word "Pregnant" beside it.

A word that was sounding repeatedly in Abby's head right now. Like a bell. One with a tone that was deep enough to sound menacing. She had no idea how long she sat there listening to it before making the effort to move, taking the evidence of what she'd just discovered so that she could hide it in the kitchen rubbish bin. She was shaking her head as she went.

She'd known that losing her virginity might change her life.

A sound like wry laughter escaped her lips as she reached the kitchen.

She hadn't been wrong, had she? Neither had Lisa. Her sister had been more right than she'd realised when she'd told her she needed to be careful about what she wished for when Abby had said she thought she wanted a baby, although admitting that was not going to give either of them any kind of satisfaction.

And as for telling Noah…

Well… Abby couldn't even begin to think about that. At least she had a whole weekend to start trying to get her head around this before she had to go back to work. Probably even longer before she was breathing the same air as Noah, but it wouldn't be long enough. She was never going to be ready to deliver news that she knew would be devastating for him. He had trusted that, even though they had carried on for longer than intended, what they had was no more than a temporary arrangement. Friends helping each other out as a favour so that they would both know it was possible to move into a new stage of their lives when the time was right.

That time was not now.

Not for Abby and most definitely not for Noah.

CHAPTER SIX

IT SEEMED THAT the more you looked for excuses, the easier it became to find them, but the point at which it became obvious that something was being avoided was inevitably going to arrive. And there was only so long you could put off doing something that you knew had to be done, no matter how hard you knew it was going to be.

It was no big deal to avoid seeing Noah that next week. All Abby needed to do was to say she was too busy to go to basketball training, which was partly true because she'd been tasked with starting an update on all the information pamphlets that the hand clinic made available for their patients. Currently, she was working on an activity list for people recovering from injury or surgery on their hands so that they would know what was permissible when instructed to keep to light or moderate activities, as well as the information given to people facing surgery for carpal tunnel syndrome.

Abby had convinced herself that there was no great urgency in telling Noah. She'd only done a home test and even Lisa had said that she should not only repeat it but have a more definitive blood test done.

She also needed more information before she would be able to answer the questions that Noah would undoubtedly have—like how far along in her pregnancy she was. Abby had no idea, but if she was at a really early stage, she might have to consider whether or not she needed to tell him at all, given his tragic history and how this could affect him. It was obviously going to affect their friendship and, while it was new, it was something that Abby didn't want to lose.

The possibility that she might decide she simply wasn't ready for parenthood because of her age or career or disability or the fact that she was lacking a life partner might be something she didn't want to consider yet but it would have to be faced soon. Time was not her friend right now.

She could legitimately claim that she was too busy treating a patient to stop and talk to Noah on an occasion when he happened to visit the clinic in the days before the appointment she had booked. She knew that he'd been told that she was at a doctor's appointment the following week when she'd missed the team meeting about new patients but she also knew that none of her colleagues had any idea that her appointment was with an obstetrician rather than any of the more usual members of the medical team that had looked after her for most of her life.

It was, therefore, more than a little disconcerting to find Noah, with a worried frown on his face, at the door of her office later that same afternoon. As she stared at him, unable to find a smile, he came inside and closed the door behind him.

'I just came to check that you're okay,' he said. 'You missed the team meeting.'

'I'm fine,' Abby told him. Which was true. Pregnancy wasn't an illness, after all, and she had an echo in the back of her mind reminding her that being less than truthful was far more convincing if at least a part of it was accurate.

'But you had a doctor's appointment today.'

'Just a check-up.' Abby turned to rearrange the papers on her desk. The element of truth thing might be forgivable when you were trying to pass off a store-bought meal as home cooking but she was running out of excuses now. She had all the information she needed.

And Noah needed to know the real truth. Even if she was still having trouble processing everything she had learned today herself. In a way, it was a relief that she was already past the point where an option to make this all disappear would have been relatively straightforward but that was shocking in itself because she was that much closer to her life changing for ever. To becoming a mother...

'I have something for you,' Noah said.

Abby tried to smile as she took the manila folder from his hand. She had something for him as well but, for the life of her, she couldn't find the words she needed to drop the bombshell that his life was also about to change for ever. She couldn't find the courage to deliver those words either. Maybe that was because work was definitely not the right place? With an inward sigh of relief, she focused on the distraction immediately at hand.

'Oh…these are the photos we talked about a couple of weeks ago.' When everything had been as it should be in her world. Better than that, in fact. She'd had it all. Her wonderful job and apartment. A demanding sport to keep her fit. A new niece to treasure and a new friendship that was so special it was also something to be treasured.

'We had a carpal tunnel day surgery session this morning. I had someone from Medical Illustrations come up and take the photos of the endoscopic procedure, which is what the majority of patients will have here now. I'd only consider open surgery if there's a tumour or some other growth to deal with. Or scar tissue from a previous injury or surgery perhaps.'

Abby nodded. She was sifting through papers on her desk to find the relevant pamphlet she'd been tweaking.

'Have you got a minute to check some of the text I've changed? Oh…and I wondered about using a different anatomical diagram to identify the ligament that gets cut.'

'That diagram is fine,' Noah said, as he pulled a chair closer and sat down beside Abby. 'But I'd label it the transverse carpal ligament rather than the flexor retinaculum. This information is intended for laypeople, yes?'

'Mmm…' The word "information" was reminding Abby of what she had to share and she bit her bottom lip as she watched Noah scanning the rest of the text in the updated pamphlet. This wasn't an appropriate time. Not that there was ever going to be a *good* time but Noah, especially, was someone who preferred to keep his personal and professional lives completely separate. She couldn't say anything. Not here. Not now.

'That's a good description of endoscopic surgery, saying that there's a tiny camera through one cut and the other one is used to guide the instrument that cuts the ligament. One of today's photos will be ideal to go with that paragraph. I'd add in a bit about it only needing local anaesthetic and it being a day procedure.'

'What about risks?'

'I can give you some percentage data. Basically, there's more risk of nerve damage with an endoscopic procedure rather than open surgery but it's almost always temporary and recovery time is less. On average, people are back at work about nine days sooner. And there's much less risk of scar tenderness.'

'I won't go into too much detail. That's something patients can discuss with their surgeons. It'll vary so much between cases anyway—like how much time they're going to need off work. I've said it can be anything from one to eight weeks depending on whether it's a dominant hand and how much repetitive manual work is required.'

Abby was about to point out one of the introductory paragraphs of the pamphlet where there was information about the non-surgical treatment of carpal tunnel syndrome, such as steroid injections, splints and ultrasound, that would be tried for some time before surgery was considered, when she became aware that she was being watched. Closely.

'Are you sure you're okay, Abby? You do look a bit pale.'

'Do I?'

'Mmm. And, I may be wrong, but it feels as if you've been avoiding me lately. Have I said something to upset you?'

'No…not at all…'

'Then what is it? You can tell me, you know. We're friends, aren't we?'

Oh, boy…being under the intense gaze of those dark, dark eyes was doing something weird to Abby's stomach. As if the butterflies that came with sexual attraction were being buffeted by powerful currents generated by a churning sensation that could well become nausea. It was unbearable, in fact, and the words that Abby had been finding impossible to form suddenly came rushing from her throat into her mouth and beyond with such force that it was astonishing they escaped as no more than a whisper.

'I'm pregnant…'

They were so close. She could see the moment that Noah's brain processed her words. She could see the shaft of shock and then pain that followed almost instantly. Was he remembering the last time someone had told him he was going to become a father? The joy that had become such an unbearable tragedy a few months later?

She was doing this to him. She was causing this pain and Abby hated herself for it. More than that, she wanted nothing more than to wrap her arms around Noah so that she could do her best to absorb that pain for him. To protect him. To promise that she would do anything to try and help.

And it was in that moment that Abby realised just how much she loved Noah. This wasn't the kind of love that came from friendship—even one that happened to include some pretty amazing sex. It certainly didn't come from a transitory crush. This was the kind of love that came from a place that included the permanence of family. From caring so much about someone that you would choose to spend the rest of your life with them.

This was about being *in* love.

And it was heartbreaking because she could see so clearly what she had known all along—that there was no way Noah was ever going to feel the same way about her. He was looking so shocked right now.

Appalled, even…

'But…we were careful…'

Abby closed her eyes. 'It might have been that first time. My secret stash had been in the cupboard for a long time. Years. I'm so sorry… It didn't occur to me that they might have gone so far past their expiry date—'

'The *first* time?' Noah had clearly only heard her first sentence. 'But…but that's more than two months ago.'

'I had a scan this afternoon,' Abby admitted. 'It looks like I'm into my second trimester so it would fit. I'm a bit over thirteen weeks.'

Noah was looking at her now as if she'd stepped into this room from another planet.

'I had some spotting,' she told him. 'My period's

usually light and my cycle's not that regular anyway. It didn't even occur to me until…'

Until Lisa had wondered why she'd thought the mushy peas looked so horrible…

But she couldn't say that. Because it reminded her of the night that Noah had been there to share a take-away dinner on his first day working at St John's and he'd joked that she was into healthy food. The night that connection with their passion for their work and their friendship had been born. A friendship that had rapidly led to a whole lot more and was now tumbling down around them into such a total disaster that Abby knew she was about to burst into tears.

Noah looked just as upset. He was as white as a sheet and the pamphlet he'd been holding was slipping from his hand to hit the floor and slide towards Abby's wheelchair.

It was the knock on her door that broke that awful moment as they stared at each other with neither of them knowing what to say next. Abby ducked, to hide her face from whoever was about to come into her office, holding onto her wheel so that she could lean down far enough to pick up that pamphlet.

'Ah… I'm so glad you're still here, Noah.' It was Alex, the orthopaedic registrar. 'I couldn't borrow your expertise for a second opinion, could I? I've got a chap in my clinic outpatients and he's got a post-surgical complication. A wound breakdown that I don't like the look of at all.'

As Abby straightened, she could see the effort that it took for Noah to replace something intensely personal with the mantle of professionalism. She could see the remnants of that private pain being swept from his face and replaced by a mask that would reveal nothing before he turned towards the door.

'Of course, Alex.' Only Abby would notice the extra effort that went into pushing himself to his feet—as if even that ordinary action was physically painful. 'Your timing is perfect, in fact. Abby and I have finished our discussion for the moment, haven't we?'

He didn't wait for a response or even look at her as he joined Alex at the door and then disappeared down the corridor. He was right, of course. There would be plenty of time to discuss other things in the weeks and months to come.

Clearly, Noah had already heard a lot more than he wanted to for now. Abby didn't realise she had been holding her breath until it came out in a long sigh. At least the first step had been taken and she had told him. She knew it would have brought back terrible memories for him and that he was hurting but this would be the worst of it, surely? When he'd had time to get over the shock, they could talk again. In the meantime, Abby needed someone else to talk to.

Her big sister. The closest thing to a mother she'd ever had, in fact. Lisa had been six years old when Abby was born and right from the start she'd been her guardian. After her accident, Lisa had pretty much centred her life around her younger sister. It was time to tell her everything because she really needed to be with someone who would be on her side. Who loved her unconditionally, as much as she loved them.

Abby gathered up the photographs Noah had brought and the outlines for the updated pamphlet and stuffed them into her laptop bag. Not that she was likely to do any work this evening but looking like she intended to work at home gave her an excuse to leave her office a little early. And this way she wouldn't have to face Noah again just yet. The least she could do for him right now was to give him some time and space to get his head around what must feel like his worst nightmare.

If only this was simply a bad dream and he was going to wake up soon.

As a form of escape, Noah had focused so completely on Alex's patient that it was quite some time before anything personal had a chance to cross those barriers and fill his head. An ultrasound and other tests on the young man who'd had orthopaedic surgery on his arm and hand following a motorbike accident showed that he had developed blood clots that were compromising blood supply enough to cause the wound breakdown. Not only that, the wounds were now infected and urgent treatment was needed if the patient wasn't going to lose significant hand function. Noah even stayed to work with the orthopaedic team in Theatre to remove the clots, debride the wounds and repair them.

So it was already late by the time he left the hospital and went to his room in the staff quarters where there was no escaping the fact that what Abby had told him was not going to evaporate like any normal nightmare. This was a small, stark room in comparison to Abby's spacious apartment but Noah hadn't yet found the time or inclination to go searching for more permanent accommodation.

Maybe, deep down, he'd known he might not be staying here that long. How could he stay now that he was faced with the one thing he'd been determined never to go through again? This wasn't new ground any more. This was history repeating itself in the worst possible way. The prospect of fatherhood, with all the responsibility and implications for the future that that entailed, along with the fear that came with knowing exactly how catastrophic it could be when things went wrong.

But then again…how could he *not* stay here? It was his baby that Abby was carrying. His child. As much as a huge part of him wanted to flee, he could never, ever contemplate running away from that reality.

But even the thought of becoming a father again was tearing his heart into pieces. He could remember that fierce joy and rush of love that had managed to puncture a numbing grief when he'd been allowed to hold his tiny infant in his arms for just a brief moment before she had been whisked away to the neonatal intensive care unit. And he could remember the agony of being allowed to hold her again as she'd taken her final breaths, when all those wires and tubes had been removed because it had been so obvious that nothing more could be done to keep her alive.

Oh… *God*…

He couldn't stay shut in here with thoughts that were

threatening to overwhelm him more than they had in years now. A full-on session of wheelchair basketball training would have been ideal to quash such unbearable memories and burn off emotions Noah didn't want to have to deal with but that wasn't an option tonight. It might never be an option again, in fact, because it felt like his friendship with Abby and everything that had come with that had just exploded in a fiery crash he hadn't seen coming.

What he could do was what he'd done in the past to relieve stress and that was to run. Hard and fast, for as long as he could before exhaustion forced him to stop. Within minutes, Noah had changed and he was pounding the pavement that circled a local park—trying, but failing, to outrun the thoughts circling in his head.

This pain was never going to go away, was it? The reminders were far less frequent, of course, and the pain was less raw but it was something he'd never forget. Something he'd never, ever want to experience again, and the only guarantee that that could never happen had just been taken away from him. Shards of memory were repeatedly piercing whatever mantle of protection that hard exercise like this could normally provide.

He could remember everything in a kind of reverse order. The funeral where Ellen had been buried with her tiny baby in her arms. Those terrible hours in the neonatal intensive care unit. The trauma of his wife's death and the shocking way their child had been delivered. The excitement in Ellen's eyes as she'd told him she was pregnant. But there'd been a question there as well, because it hadn't exactly been a planned pregnancy. She had wondered if he was going to be just as happy about it as she was. Whether it was the right time.

There'd been more than a question in Abby's eyes today. Like the way she'd understood what it had been like for him to be in Lisa's room so soon after the birth of her baby, it seemed that she knew exactly how hard it was going to be for him to be told he was going to be a father again. She had been feeling his pain and it was hurting her as well because…because she cared about him? *Loved* him, even?

He cared about Abby too. Not in the same way as he'd cared about Ellen, of course—he could never love anyone like that again—but he had absolute admiration for Abby and she was the closest friend he'd ever had. Because he'd never had a friendship that included sex before? Well…that had clearly been a mistake, hadn't it?

Except that it still didn't feel like a mistake. It had been so different. So… No… Noah couldn't think of a word that could encompass how it had made him feel to be with Abby. To feel that connection that was unlike anything he'd found before. To feel the trust that had blossomed into an eagerness to learn everything he could teach her about enjoying her body. To give as much as she was receiving and to do it with humour and a tenderness that had touched him in far more than a purely physical way.

He hadn't even asked her how she was feeling about the news today. Or if she was okay physically. Or what the implications of pregnancy and birth might be for a paraplegic woman. As he kept running, Noah tried to remember whether Ellen had had anything that had been a physical problem in her pregnancy but that period of his life was oddly blurry now. Instead of seeing Ellen in his head, he kept seeing Abby. Images that were brightly coloured instead of faded pastels. A living person rather than a ghost?

And he'd just walked out on her. As if he was the only one whose life was going to be changed for ever. How selfish was that? It was Abby who was going to be dealing with a lot more than he would have to and she was going to face more challenges than most pregnant women or new mothers.

Noah not only had a responsibility to a baby he wasn't about to turn his back on, right now he had even more of a responsibility to the mother of his child and, by the time he'd completed his third circuit of the park, Noah knew what he had to do. What the right thing to do was. He might have learned to shut himself away from grief but he wasn't about to try and bury guilt as well. Nothing could change what had given him so much grief but at least he had the power to change what would create guilt. He went back to his room to shower and change and then he walked the short distance to Abby's apartment and rang her bell.

He rang it again but there was still no answer.

He could see there were no lights on in her ground-floor apartment either.

She wasn't home. As Noah stood there, wondering where Abby might be and how long it might be before she came home, he could hear his stomach growling and remembered that he hadn't bothered eating this evening. It would be sensible to go and find some food but he wasn't going anywhere because it was far more important to talk to Abby. To tell her that he was going to be involved in their baby's life as much as she wanted him to be. That he would do everything he could to support her as well.

Noah sat down on the step beside the wheelchair ramp. He was going to wait until Abby came home because he didn't want her to spend the night thinking he had simply walked out on her and the future she now faced.

His commitment had been made and he wasn't about to walk away from anything, no matter how hard it might be.

He still looked shell shocked.

But there was something about the tilt of his head and the way he got to his feet so deliberately as Abby approached that told her he was in control again and that he was going to face whatever lay ahead with dignity, kindness and probably the kind of humour she had learned was something they both used as a defence against the more difficult challenges life could throw at you. She felt so proud of him at this moment it made her want to cry. How could you not fall in love with a man that was this courageous? This honourable?

This life challenge was a doozy but Noah was here. He might have been here for some time while she'd been with Lisa, just waiting for her to come home, and that made her heart squeeze painfully because it felt like he really cared—about her and not just the baby or whatever arrangements needed to be made for the future.

'You'd better come inside,' Abby told Noah. 'I'm so sorry. I had no idea you would be here. I went to visit Lisa and Hugh.' She led the way up the ramp. 'I thought you'd need time to…to think about things.'

'I did,' Noah agreed. 'And I still do. I'm sure you do as well. But we're in this together, Abby, and I wanted to make sure you knew that.'

There was no wine tonight. No firelight. Even the sexual attraction that had brought them to this situation seemed to have been snuffed out like a candle in an unexpected gust of wind. They avoided the squashy couches in the living area and sat on either side of Abby's kitchen table.

'How are you?' Noah asked. 'I'm sorry I didn't ask earlier. That should have been the first thing I checked on. How you're doing. How the…baby's doing.'

'I'm fine. Everything looks normal. They'll do another scan in three or four weeks. You can come with me if…if you want to.'

She could see the muscles in Noah's throat move as if it was difficult for him to swallow. 'Of course. If I can…' He cleared his throat. 'Are there any problems you might be facing because of your…your…?'

'Disability?' Abby's smile was wry. 'It's not a dirty word, Noah.'

He still looked so pale, she thought. The lines around his eyes were so much deeper. She wanted to touch him and offer comfort but she knew how unlikely that was to be welcome so she pushed her hands down to hide between her hips and the low sides of her chair as she curled them into fists.

'There are some things that may be a problem,' she admitted. 'As the baby grows it'll put pressure on my bladder, which may change the way I can manage. I might get bladder spasms and a urinary tract infection could trigger premature labour.'

Noah was nodding. He was finding this easier, wasn't he? A medical scenario to think about instead of an emotional one.

'I could get increased pressure on venous return from my legs so it puts me at increased risk of a deep vein thrombosis. I might have to wear some of those very sexy compression stockings.'

Her attempt at any kind of humour was falling flat. A bit like first time when he'd been so worried about whether she'd been hurt in that minor car accident and she'd told him she'd never walk again. Her heart was squeezing again as she remembered seeing him for the first time. Already starting to fall in love with him…

'Apart from that, it might interfere with my centre of balance in later stages and I'll need to adapt, but I've got plenty of time to get used to that.'

'You'll need help,' Noah said. 'Maybe I can help by organising a housekeeper? Or…someone to help *you*…?'

'I'm still perfectly independent,' Abby told him. 'And that's the way I intend to stay.'

This felt like Noah was seeing her disability as a

barrier—maybe for the first time? He hadn't even seen
it to start with. He hadn't let it interfere with their professional relationship in any way. Or their friendship.
Okay, he'd needed to get used to a different kind of sex
life perhaps, but that hadn't seemed to lessen the satisfaction he'd got from their time together and that reassurance had been just one of the gifts he'd given her.

Oh…if only he'd reach out and touch her now. Or
better yet wrap her in his arms and take her to bed.
Not for sex necessarily, but just to lie there and have
this discussion like two people who cared deeply for
each other and wanted a future together.

She could hear the sharp tone that came into her
voice. The kind of prickly, defensive response that had
always made men back off. 'If I do find I need help I
can organise it myself, thanks. I also have a supportive
family with Lisa and Hugh. I won't be the first disabled
woman to have a baby, you know.'

Abby could feel Noah becoming cautious. Not
knowing what to say.

'I wasn't suggesting you couldn't cope, Abby. I…
just want to help…'

'Because I'm *disabled*.'

'No…' Was he going to become angry if she kept
pushing this? 'Because I'm involved. Because I *care*…'

Not enough… Abby tried to push the silent cry
away. Was she trying to find a way to push Noah away
as well? To make herself believe that it didn't matter
that he wasn't in love with her and never would be? To
protect her heart as much as possible?

'I'm tired,' she said. 'I think it would be better if you

left. I'll see you at work, obviously, but we both need time to get used to this. We can talk about other things some other time. I'll keep you posted on any medical appointments and, if you want to be there, that's fine.'

Noah got slowly to his feet. 'I'll be there.'

'I won't be going to basketball training sessions any longer. Not until after the birth anyway.' Abby followed Noah to her front door. 'There's no reason for you to stop going, though.'

'I won't be going either.'

Noah paused for a heartbeat on the step. When he turned, the expression in those dark eyes made Abby realise that he'd put up barriers. The kind she'd seen him use in his professional relationships at work where he gave nothing away, but it was something new when they were alone together. And it hurt. Knowing that he needed to protect himself from her broke Abby's heart that little bit more.

But surely the bond of their friendship was still there?

When Noah paused again at street level, looked back and raised his hand in farewell, the way the corner of his mouth lifted in a half-smile gave Abby a beat of hope that she was right. That at least a part of that friendship might be intact. That the reason he wasn't going to continue with a new sport that he really enjoyed was because she wasn't going to be there with him.

They also had a new bond that would be there for the rest of their lives.

It wasn't the kind of bond either of them would have chosen and it felt fragile and difficult. But it was there.

And perhaps it was something they could both build on—if they did it carefully?

CHAPTER SEVEN

'DO YOU WANT to know if it's a girl or a boy?'

Noah felt his breath catch somewhere deep in his chest. No. He didn't want to know. This was hard enough, sitting in this dim room with the ultrasound technician on the other side of the bed Abby was lying on. He hadn't seen Abby lying down for weeks now and it was…poignant. He missed that closeness they'd had. That friendship that had been strong enough to allow intimacy.

He had focused on the screen as soon as the scan had been started but he watched it with a clinical interest as he tried to make sense of the blobs that came in and out of focus. That was the head, of course…and there was the line of tiny vertebrae that made up the spine…

'I think I do,' Abby said. 'What about you, Noah?'

It didn't matter what he thought. This was about Abby. About supporting her in whatever way he could.

'Up to you,' he said. 'It might make it easier to… I don't know…think about names or what you'll need in the way of baby clothes.'

He and Ellen had known they were having a girl.

There'd been a huge box of tiny pink clothes to donate to a charity when he'd finally cleaned out their house to move away.

Abby's head swivelled back towards the technician. 'Can you tell?' she asked.

'Sometimes it's easy.' She nodded. 'If it isn't it could be either because baby might have his legs crossed but when he hasn't…'

'So it's a boy?'

'It is.'

'Oh…' Abby's gaze was riveted to the screen so she didn't see that Noah had to close his eyes to absorb this piece of news.

A boy.

His son…

He opened them as the technician moved the transducer to focus on the baby's heart.

'Here's the cross-section, four-chamber view of baby's heart. I'll turn on the sound so you can hear it, too.'

Abby gasped as the sound filled the small room. And then she grinned. 'Sounds like a dog's chew toy after the squeaker's broken,' she said. But when her gaze slid away from the screen to catch Noah's, he could see something that was very different to humour in her eyes.

He knew exactly what it was that had brought Abby to the verge of tears because he'd felt it himself that first time. The absolute wonder of a glimpse into a new life that was forming. A new person. Their *child...* Noah was braced for a flashback and needing to distance himself for protection but something else seemed to be happening in his head—and his heart?

This was different.

New ground. Not just because this was Abby he was with and not Ellen. Not just because the baby was a boy and not a girl. Maybe it felt so different because he was standing back and it felt like he was watching this happening to someone else through a barrier but there was a thread of something that he might be able to catch—like when you were trying to remember something that had happened in a dream. Noah wasn't sure what it was but he did know it was worth catching. It was something good.

'I'll turn on the Doppler,' the technician said, 'so we can see the direction of blood flow in the heart.' Coloured blobs now appeared on the screen, moving in time to the rapid beat. 'No obvious turbulence or reverse flow,' she said moments later. 'And nothing crossing the septum. It's all looking reassuringly normal.'

Normal...

That had something to do with whatever nebulous feeling Noah had been aware of.

A normal family?

He was still pondering the odd mix of feelings the appointment had generated when he was walking beside Abby as they left the ultrasound section of St John's X-ray department.

He could feel a new—strong—connection to Abby now. A connection to the tiny being whose heart function he'd just been watching. His son. Abby was the mother of his son, which made them…a family.

And families should be together if that was at all possible.

He could make it possible. Only this morning, he'd been idly clicking through offerings on a real estate website as he'd eaten his breakfast and he'd come across a house that was not far away from where Lisa and Hugh lived. Abby's extended family. A real house, not an apartment. With a garden that was big enough for a small child to have adventures in. He could make an appointment to view the house. He could take Abby with him to see what kind of changes would need to be made to make it wheelchair friendly. They could make it work. Couldn't they?

The doors of the lift slid shut after the only other person got out at the next floor.

'Abby?'

She tilted her head up, her eyebrows raised in a question mark.

Noah took a deep breath. 'I think we should get married.'

'Oh, my God… He asked you to *marry* him? Noah *proposed* to you?'

'Not exactly. He said he thought we *should* get married. That he'd found a house not far from here where we could all live together happily ever after.'

The ironic tone in Abby's voice made Lisa's heart sink. 'So what did *you* say?'

'Well…nothing right then. Someone else got into

the lift. But we went for a walk outside. In that strip of park behind the hospital that's got that creek running through it. I've never spent much time there because the paths aren't great for wheels but it's really quite pretty. There are daffodils out at the moment.'

Lisa's nod was impatient. 'I don't want to hear about the scenery…' She adjusted baby Amy in her arms so that she could latch onto her other breast. 'I want to know whether we're planning for a wedding as well as a new baby in the family.'

'No…' Abby made it sound as if she'd asked an obviously stupid question. 'Of course not.'

Making sure Amy was latched on and sucking properly was a good excuse not to say anything for the moment. To weigh up whether she should say what was becoming an increasing concern to both herself and Hugh—that the change in Abby's *joie de vivre* in recent weeks had more to do with Noah's distance than adapting to a major life change or the inevitable challenges that motherhood was going to present.

'*We're not a couple,*' she'd been telling them right from the start. '*We're just friends and it's never going to be more than that. And, yeah, we're having a baby together, but that makes it good that we're friends. Better than being strangers or bitter divorcées, yes? Much easier, if you ask me.*'

But Lisa wasn't so sure about that. Because she knew her sister.

'Talk to me, hon,' she said softly. 'Is it such a bad idea to marry someone that you're in love with?'

Abby's jaw dropped. 'I never said I was in love with him.'

'You didn't need to.' Lisa could feel the weight of the baby changing in her arms as Amy slid into sleep. She moved her daughter so that she was upright on her shoulder and began to rub her back. 'I know what it feels like, remember? I was in love with Hugh and then we split up and I had worst weeks of my life. I tried to convince myself that I'd get over him. That it was partly because I was trying to get used to that new job and life would get back to normal eventually…and then you decided to sort things out.'

'Ha…' Abby shook her head. 'You were such a misery guts I had to do something. It was painfully obvious that you needed to be with Hugh and when he turned up on the doorstep, it was just as obvious he felt the same way. So that was when we hatched the plan to get you somewhere irresistibly romantic so he could tell you how he felt and persuade you to spend the rest of your life with him.'

'Maybe Noah feels the same way and he's just not ready to admit it. It took Hugh some time to realise how much he was missing me.'

Abby shook her head. 'We talked about that. I said that having a baby together wasn't a good enough reason to get married. That I couldn't marry someone that wasn't in love with me. And he said…' Abby paused for a moment to clear her throat and take a new breath—as if she was fighting off tears. 'He said that he couldn't offer that. To anyone. Ever. That he believes that he's not capable of feeling like that ever again but…but that he does care. A lot. That he would do his best to be a great husband. And father. That…um…friendship was actually a good base for any kind of long-term relationship and that maybe it would last longer than a lot of marriages.' A sound that was halfway between a sob and laughter escaped. 'Especially when the sex was great…'

'Oh… Abby…' A piece of Lisa's heart was breaking. She'd only ever wanted happiness for her sister and Abby had tackled every challenge in her life with such determination and good humour. She so deserved to be in the happiest part of her life, like Lisa was. 'It's not enough, though, is it?'

Abby shook her head. 'It would be settling for something less than ideal, that's for sure. I suspect it would eventually destroy whatever friendship we've got. We might end up hating each other.'

Lisa's sigh was heartfelt. 'You deserve so much more than that. You need someone that's going to totally adore you. Someone who can't live without you any more than you want to live without him.'

Abby nodded this time as a tear escaped and rolled down her cheek. 'Like you and Hugh,' she whispered. 'But that's never going to happen.'

'You don't know that.'

'But I do.' Abby's eyes were shimmering with more tears. 'Because I can't imagine feeling like this about anyone else. And it's *Noah's* baby that I'm having. No one else could ever be the real father.'

Baby Amy chose that moment to release a loud burp and this time it was a genuine huff of laughter that came from Abby.

'You said it, Amy.' She was still smiling through her tears as she reached out. 'Enough self-pity,' she announced. 'It's time I had a cuddle. I haven't even told you the most important thing that happened at that scan. We found out that Amy's getting a boy cousin. I hope she doesn't boss him around as much as you bossed me.'

'I never bossed you. You were far too bolshie to let that happen.'

Abby's inelegant sniff advertised that her tears were done with. 'Might have been better if I had let you be in charge, huh?'

The reference to what had caused Abby's disability in the first place—pulling her hand from her big sister's grasp and running into traffic—was a reminder of so many other things. Like the guilt Lisa had always carried that had made it difficult to step back far enough for both the sisters to forge their own futures.

But that had changed in the last couple of years. She had met and fallen in love with Hugh. Abby had embraced her independence and her life had been an inspiration for any young woman, disabled or not. But now she had met and fallen in love with Noah and was faced with a future as a single parent. What were the chances that Abby's future could end up being as happy as Lisa's?

She handed over her baby. A cuddle was definitely what Abby needed. She just wished there was more she could do. She looked at her sister's head bent over her niece and could imagine that she would look just like this in a few months, holding her own infant. Only she would be looking even more beautiful bathed in that unbelievable glow that came from nowhere as you held your own baby for the very first time. Surely that would melt whatever barriers Noah Baxter had around his heart if that was what was keeping him from giving Abby what she needed?

Because broken hearts *could* heal. Sometimes, though, she knew it felt safer to leave the bandages on and the only way of finding out whether healing had occurred was if they got ripped off, but that wasn't something that could be forced. It was generally up to fate as to whether it happened or it didn't happen and usually you didn't even see it coming because, if you did, you'd protect whatever it was that was safely cocooned beneath its bandages. It was only afterwards that you realised that it had happened.

Like falling in love could be for people who'd been hurt in the past.

Could seeing your baby be just as powerful?

Lisa could only hope so. That it might prove to be powerful enough to be the miracle that could dissolve the barriers that were fragmenting Abby's life.

Things were coming together.

Slowly but surely.

A bit like the surgery Noah was completing, the crick in his neck and having to blink away blurriness occasionally as he peered through the magnifying glasses, letting him know that he'd almost reached his limit for the precise and painstaking reattachment of nerves, blood vessels and tendons in the small hand on the table in front of him as he reattached the ends of two fingers that had been amputated by a door.

The poor mother of this child had had no idea the three-year-old girl had poked her fingers into the crack and that, by opening the door further, she had caused the horrific damage. She was always going to feel guilty, even though it could never have been deliberate, but Noah could help by doing the best job he could in attaching the fingertips and children were amazing in the way they could heal. There would be scars, of course, but he was confident that, in years to come, the function of these tiny fingers would be just as good as if the accident had never happened.

Would the mother's guilt fade as well?

Noah could strip off the headpiece as his registrars took over the splinting and bandaging of the hand and the anaesthetist began to reverse the anaesthetic. It was only then, as Noah could see things that weren't magnified enough to let him work on precise structures that would have been invisible to the naked eye, that he realised what a beautiful child this little girl was, with her tumble of golden curls and dark lashes that lay on chubby, pink cheeks.

Three years old.

The age his own daughter would have been if she'd lived.

Not that Noah let himself think of things like that for more than a microsecond. Or even let them become anything more that something that was registered in a deep part of his brain—like a newspaper headline when you had no intention of reading the article beneath. He knew how to cope. He simply focused on something else. Something immediate and real. It was a form of mindfulness that worked well.

'Leave the tips of the fingers completely exposed,' he told his registrar. 'We need to be able to check the colour and temperature and capillary refill in the nail beds. Let's top up the hand block as well. I don't want her in too much pain when she wakes up. I'm going to go and talk to the parents.'

Noah checked the wall clock as he left Theatre. He still had time to get to his appointment and then make it to his dinner date with Abby. Not that it was any kind of "date", of course. They hadn't even kissed since they'd found out about the pregnancy.

It had taken months to even get to a point where friendship wasn't strained and awkward but it was finally happening and Noah knew it had a lot to do with his modus operandi. The mindfulness of having a focus that was real. Palpable. Preferably with a time limit that meant it needed constant attention, like the huge project he'd taken on in the last few weeks when he'd finally taken possession of the house he'd purchased after Abby had refused to consider his offer of marriage.

'You don't have to live in it,' he'd told her. 'But we're going to be co-parenting and I want you to be able to visit comfortably so I need your input for the changes that need to be made. I need the name of the architect you used to renovate your apartment, too, because I want this house to feel like that. Like…home…'

The appointment this evening was to get the plans the architect had drawn up and then it was his turn to provide dinner at Abby's place. He'd found a new range of ready-made meals and it felt good to be tapping back into something that had given them another connection in the first place. A block that was the same but different and one that might fill another gap in the foundation of the friendship they were rebuilding.

It was also something so tangible it could be tasted, which made it as good as the paper plans they would have to focus on to discuss. It wasn't that he was trying to avoid emotional involvement or anything, it was just being practical. Being positive and taking one step after another into the future without letting something get in the way—like being dragged back into a past that no longer existed.

Like concentrating on being able to see those tiny fingertips that needed to heal instead of thinking about a little girl who had never had the chance to grow up. Planning practical changes to a house so that someone in a wheelchair could navigate easily between rooms and even floors, and not think of how different things could have been if his life had stayed on track. Supplying a meal that would hopefully tempt Abby to eat properly because she'd been looking a bit too pale and tired when he'd seen her in the hand clinic a couple of days ago.

He'd waited until Steve had shown him just how much progress he was making with his new thumb and had shared the exciting news that he was starting work again next week, but when he'd left her office, Abby had brushed off his concerns by telling him she was fine. She always said that, though, didn't she? Abby was more of a master than he was in finding positive things to focus on and facing any twists and turns in her life with the kind of courage he wished he had in such abundance. It was one of the things he admired so much about her but it could be a barrier as well.

He had the distinct feeling there were things going on that she simply didn't want to talk about but he was hardly in a position to expect more when they were still finding their feet in a new relationship. A friendship without the "benefits". Two people that needed to find a way of being able to be parents together when the changes were derailing the lives they had both been living.

But it felt like things were finally coming together.

Maybe tonight they could find their way back to a level where they could really talk about things. The way they had that night, which seemed for ever ago, when they'd both talked about how they didn't think it would be possible for them to make love to anyone.

That was ironic enough to make Noah smile but there was sadness mixed in with the amusement. Life could change in a heartbeat, couldn't it? With a trip on a staircase. Or a kiss that just made you want more. That gave you a glimpse of everything you'd ever wanted but knew you couldn't have any more.

Oh…man…

Sometimes the mindfulness thing didn't work so well. It was just as well he could see his young patient's parents in the relatives' room outside Theatre now. And they'd seen him. They were on their feet and they looked terrified.

His smile was reassuring this time, with no hint of any sadness.

'Good news,' were his first words. 'It's all gone just as well as we could have hoped.'

'He's thought of everything.'

Noah's smile was bright enough to be almost a beam but Abby couldn't return it with anything like such enthusiasm. She was getting used to the way the elephant in the room could be ignored and she knew that Noah was only looking this happy because he had something to talk about that had nothing to do with the baby.

'Look at this. Lowered workspaces in the kitchen and laundry.'

'You're over six feet tall, Noah. You should be having your workspaces raised, not lowered. I hope you realise that I'm not planning to come over and do your laundry anytime soon.'

Oh, dear… Abby knew she sounded tetchy but, dammit, she was feeling tetchy this evening. It wasn't so much the elephant in the corner of the room right now—it was more that elephant that was pressing on her bladder.

'Excuse me… I need to go to the loo.'

It was the second time she had ducked off to the bathroom since Noah had arrived and taken over, putting the foil-covered boxes from the latest gourmet ready-made meal service he had discovered into the oven and then spreading the architect's detailed plans all over the kitchen table.

The worst thing was that this house that Noah

was about to spend a fortune on to make wheelchair friendly was a smaller version of the rural mansion that Lisa and Hugh lived in. A perfect family home. The kind Abby would have dreamed of living in, if things were different.

But they weren't different. Okay, she and Noah might be in a better space now, having had more than three months to get used to the idea of becoming parents, but they were never going to recapture the kind of connection that they'd found when their friendship had begun. By the time she came back from the bathroom, Noah's smile had vanished completely and she could tell he was treading carefully again.

'I don't expect you to do any laundry,' he told her. 'I'm quite happy to have a housekeeper available but I'm just thinking of the future. I don't expect you to give up a career you love and I certainly don't want to give up mine.'

'I don't see what that's got to do with the height of worktops in your house.'

'What if I want to go to a conference sometime? And it's your turn to do the childcare but it's better to be at my house because it's closer to his school or he's got a hut in the garden that he likes to play in. And he gets muddy and you want to throw his clothes in the wash. Or cook him dinner.'

Abby was staring at Noah. 'Why is he always "him" or "he" when you talk about our baby?'

'Ah...because he's a boy?'

'He needs a name.'

That shut Noah up. Abby could see the shutters

come down in his eyes. He'd flatly refused to discuss any choice of names because he said it was far too early and, anyway, he'd be happy to go along with whatever she chose, but sometimes it was better to wait and see what a baby's personality might be like.

Why wasn't it enough that her baby's father was committed enough to be planning for the future with such thoroughness being given to every possible scenario? Because it was at the kind of superficial level that came from someone keeping an emotional distance?

They'd talked about houses and gardens and child-care and schools—everything that could be needed to provide for a child's happy upbringing except for what their baby needed the most. Parents who loved each other as well as their child. It should be getting easier to get used to this but, if anything, it was getting harder.

There were moments when Abby wondered if she'd made a huge mistake in dismissing the idea that she and Noah could get married and live together to raise their little boy. It would be better than this, wouldn't it? This…longing to be touched. To be cherished… and becoming more and more aware of the distance between them.

Maybe it was pregnancy hormones getting to her. Of course it wouldn't be better. It would be soul destroying to live with someone and love them as much as she loved Noah and to be reminded, every single day, that she could never take the place of the woman he had truly loved. And she was tired as well. The extra weight Abby was carrying was making everything harder, even a simple transfer from her chair to her car or bed or a couch, but she needed to change her position more frequently because there were some pressure areas on her skin that her medical team were concerned about. So she was moody and sore and tired and Noah didn't deserve to be on the receiving end of it all.

'Sorry,' she muttered. 'It's been a long day.'

'You must be hungry. I reckon you'll like what I found today at Gourmet to Go.' Noah stood up and moved to the bench to picked up the discarded wrapping for the foil packages in the oven. 'How good does this sound? Chargrilled organic chicken breasts in a red pepper sauce, served on mushroom risotto with a side of green beans cooked to al dente perfection?'

'Mmm…' Abby tried to sound appreciative, even though she didn't feel at all hungry.

'Okay…' Noah was giving her that intense look, as if he was trying to decide whether something was wrong. 'There's a salted caramel crème brûlée for dessert if that's more exciting.'

'Sorry. I'm not very hungry, that's all.' Abby had her hand on her belly—an automatic reaction to feeling her baby move. She knew better than to offer to let Noah feel that movement—not after it had been dismissed in the past with the same kind of denial that discussing baby names had received.

This didn't feel like a normal sort of kick or wriggle—everything suddenly felt oddly tight—but then her ability to feel in her lower body wasn't exactly normal either, was it? It was probably just her bladder complaining again. It certainly felt as if she needed another trip to the bathroom. Or, oh… God…was it too late?

Noah had seen the expression on her face. 'What's wrong?'

'I…um… It's nothing… I just need to go to the loo again.'

But Noah was in front of her chair as she started to move. 'This isn't normal,' he said. 'What's going on?'

He put his hand on Abby's forehead and it felt deliciously cool but Noah swore softly.

'You're burning up,' he said. 'No wonder you look so tired. You're *sick*…'

'It's probably just a virus.'

'You've been running off to the loo every ten minutes. Sounds more like a UTI to me.'

Abby closed her eyes. 'You could be right,' she murmured. 'I did wonder if it smelt funny the last time.'

Noah flicked the switch off on the oven. 'We're taking you into ED,' he said. 'You need to be checked and started on some antibiotics.'

'I need some clean clothes. I'm…a bit wet.'

Even as she said the words, Abby realised it was an understatement. She was more than "a bit wet". There was fluid dripping from the cushion of her chair to puddle on the floor. Too much fluid for it to be coming from a very recently emptied bladder.

Noah was clearly thinking the same thing, but if he was worried it wasn't showing on his face. Abby had never seen him look quite this calm.

'I'm calling an ambulance,' he told her. 'I think your waters have just broken.'

CHAPTER EIGHT

'WHERE'S NOAH?'

'I saw him when we arrived.' Lisa bit her lip. 'He was talking to one of the doctors in the ward reception area. I overhead mention of…um…was it magnesium sulphate?'

Hugh nodded. 'They're planning to add it into what they're giving Abby to try and slow down or prevent premature labour. It's been shown to protect brain development and reduces the risk of complications like cerebral palsy.'

Abby closed her eyes. This nightmare wasn't going to go away anytime soon. The drugs she was being given to slow her contractions didn't seem to be working either. And now the beeping of the monitor beside her bed that was recording the baby's heart rate seemed to be slowing down when her belly tightened for longer periods.

Hugh was watching the monitor. 'You've had the second of the corticosteroid injections to help baby's lung development, yes? It's been more than twelve hours since you came in.'

Abby nodded. 'Why?' She fixed her gaze on her brother-in-law. 'You think I'm going to deliver this baby, don't you?'

'You need to be prepared for that.'

'But it's too early. I'm only twenty-nine weeks.' Abby was fighting tears. 'This is my fault. I should have picked up on the signs of a UTI. If I'd started antibiotics earlier, this might not be happening.'

'This isn't your fault, Abby.' Lisa took hold of her sister's hand. 'And you're in the best place you could be. St John's neonatal intensive care unit is second to none and…and babies survive way before twenty-nine weeks these days.'

'She's right.' Hugh's voice was gentle. 'The odds are totally on your side. Your baby's got more than a ninety percent chance of making it if he is born now.'

But Abby couldn't stop her tears. 'But he's not just my baby. He's Noah's baby too and…and how can I ask him to be here when he's already lost a premmie baby? Even if I really, really need him to be here…'

'You don't have to ask. I'm here, Abby.'

Everybody's gaze flicked towards a door they hadn't heard opening. Behind Noah stood the obstetrician in charge of the team who had admitted her and there were other staff members behind him. Because the information from the monitors in this room had been transmitted to the central desk as alarms had begun sounding?

Lisa and Hugh shared a worried glance. 'Do you want me to stay?' Lisa asked Abby.

Abby shook her head slowly, her gaze fixed on

Noah's as he walked towards her bed. This was the person she needed with her. The father of her baby who was about to come into the world too soon. Someone who could understand, only too well, how scared she was at this moment. Maybe he was even more scared because he knew what it was like to go through something this traumatic and yet he was here.

He was here for her and Abby had never loved him more for being brave enough to go through this again.

For giving her his hand to cling to as things began happening around her and any control had to be ceded to people who knew what they were doing.

Lisa and Hugh slipped out of the room as more people came in, pushing equipment like an incubator and trollies and more monitors. Just minutes later, the only people here with a connection that was more than professional were Abby and Noah, and it had to be obvious to everyone how close their personal connection was—they were holding hands tightly enough for their knuckles to be white.

So many things were the same as Noah watched what was happening a short time later.

Those tiny limbs that looked as fragile as twigs as they waved in the air in protest at what so many people were doing to him as they prepared to cannulate umbilical vessels and put the smallest size of breathing tube down his throat. A chest that was so small it was half covered by an ECG electrode and the miniature ribcage so visible with the struggle for each breath. The time it took to get the tube down that narrow airway and get the settings for the ventilator perfect. The woollen hat that looked five sizes too big that was slipping down over the baby's closed eyes as he was snuggled into the incubator. Wire after wire that came snaking away from that tiny body to be attached to every monitor available.

That sensation that something sharp was piercing his heart was the same, too. The knowledge that this tiny human was part of him. Was his *son*. And the fear was the same. Knowing all too well how precarious the next hours and days could prove to be for this new life. It was a fear that had to be somehow locked away securely enough for Noah to be able to stay strong. For Abby. And for the baby.

It helped that many things were so different at the same time.

He could focus on the fact that the mother of his child was not lying in front of him, having already lost her battle for life. Abby was very much alive, still hanging onto his hand as if it was the only life belt on a terrifyingly rough sea. She had tears on her face but… yes…she had hope in her eyes. And a love that was making them shine like nothing Noah had ever seen before. Of course it was love for the baby she had just brought into the world but when Abby looked up to catch his gaze, it felt like he was included in that love. Or could be, if he wanted to be.

Which he didn't. Or rather couldn't because that was what everybody really wanted, wasn't it? To be loved like that? But how could he let Abby feel this way about him if he couldn't offer her the same level of connection? Being loved could become a burden if it was one-sided and, if he couldn't feel the rush of that depth of feeling in this moment, it seemed unlikely that he ever would. Either it was still too soon for Noah or he'd been through something so traumatic he'd genuinely lost the ability to let go enough to love anyone like that.

And that was both heartbreaking but…kind of a relief at the same time because it meant that he could stay strong. That he could care very much but not be destroyed all over again if the worst happened.

'I'll go with him,' he told Abby, although he hadn't let go of her hand yet. Or maybe it was Abby who hadn't let go of his. 'They're going to take him to NICU now.'

She pulled her hand free. 'Go,' she agreed in a whisper. 'He needs one of us to be with him. Just…' Another tear rolled down her cheek. 'Just…in case…'

Noah wanted to stay. Not just because he couldn't quite suppress the flash of fear at the thought of being present as the only parent if the worst happened. He wanted to stay here to make sure that Abby was being well looked after. To try and comfort her in some way and reassure her if he could. To care for *her*. Because he could this time? Because she was still alive?

But part of him knew he had to be with that tiny scrap of humanity that was their child, no matter how hard it was.

His head was such a mess that the only way he could take control was to take all those feelings and push them back. To slam a door on them and then lean on it with enough force to stop these confused thoughts and feelings that were so powerful, it almost felt as if he was physically being torn in two.

Oddly, though, it felt like Abby was still holding his hand as he followed the medical team surrounding the incubator out of the room. And it did kind of feel like a life belt and he certainly needed one. This was history repeating itself in the worst possible way. Was this another life that was going to be measured in no more than hours?

The first forty-eight hours should have been the hardest.

Abby knew that every time Noah came to the NICU where she was sitting, hour after hour, beside their baby's incubator that he had to be remembering the last time he'd done this. That he was probably reliving the tragic finale to that terrible time. When two days became three and then four and finally a week—when some of the wires and tubes had gone and she was expressing breast milk every few hours so that it could be fed to her baby, Abby had expected the tension might ease a little but, instead, it was getting worse.

She had turned her wheelchair to the wall this evening because she had discovered it was the best way to feel as if she and her baby were alone and as close as they were allowed to be. Abby still hadn't been able to hold him in her arms but she could do this—she could put her hand through the porthole of the incubator and put her fingertip on the palm of that tiny hand and let him close his fingers and hold on—the tiniest fingers imaginable but they could hold on with a strength that never failed to give Abby hope. That made her love him more and more with every passing day they were together.

Facing away from the rest of a unit that was busy but carefully quiet and without harsh lighting to protect these vulnerable babies meant that Abby didn't see Noah come in but she was aware of the change in how the space around her felt. Because she was getting used to him coming in at this time of day, when his work responsibilities were dealt with, or was it deeper than that in that it somehow felt safer when he was here—as if their baby could get more strength by having both his parents nearby?

Abby didn't move. She kept her gaze on that tiny hand still gripping her fingertip but in her peripheral vision she could see the movement of her baby's chest wall, and knowing how hard he was still working to breathe made it hard to keep the wobble out of her words. Behind that was a blur of golden fabric—a soft security blanket that had a small, toy lion and its front paws attached to one corner. The cuddly blanket stood out as one of the only personal items amongst all the medical paraphernalia.

'Did they show you the test results? The echocardiogram and the ECG?'

'Yes.' Noah positioned a chair beside Abby and sat down. He rested a hand on the top of the incubator and leaned closer, as if he was trying to see their baby through the jumble of wires and tubes and sticky tape and the oversized hat and nappy. 'A patent ductus arteriosus is not an uncommon heart defect in premature babies. It only becomes a significant problem if enough blood is bypassing the lungs to reduce the flow to the rest of the body, which can damage other organs like the intestines and kidneys.'

'If the medications don't help it close, they're talking about him needing surgery.'

'I know.' Noah was quiet for a moment. 'But it's a procedure that can be done by catheter now, even for someone as little as this. That wouldn't be nearly as scary as open chest surgery.'

It was Abby's turn to say nothing. It would still be terrifying.

Inside the incubator the baby moved, stretching legs so that his tiny feet were in the air. One hand also rose but the other was still gripping Abby's finger.

'Look at that,' Noah said softly. 'He's not letting go, is he?'

'He's a wee fighter,' Abby whispered back. She blinked back a tear, shifting her line of vision to the soft toy in the corner of the incubator. 'Our wee lion.'

The silence was longer this time. Until Abby audibly caught her breath which made Noah catch her gaze.

'Leo,' she murmured. 'It's the perfect name for him, isn't it?'

He was a week old but the name tag on the wall behind him still read simply 'Baby Phillips/Baxter' and there'd been too much else to think and feel and worry about to make choosing a name a priority. Especially when Abby knew that it had been something Noah had wanted to avoid. Even now, his gaze was sliding away from hers and she could feel the way his body was tensing—preparing for him to get up and go?

'You said that sometimes it was better to wait and see what a baby's personality was like, remember?'

Noah was nodding slowly but he was still starting to move away.

'Leo.' It sounded like he was testing the name as he looked down at the baby. Abby could see the muscles in his throat move as he swallowed. 'Yes…it's perfect.' But he glanced at his watch. 'I've got a patient I should check on. I'll have to go.'

Abby couldn't keep the wobble from her voice this time. 'Me, too. I… I have to go home tonight. Apparently I'm too well to have a bed in the ward now.'

'Oh…'

Noah clearly understood how hard it was going to be to become like the other parents in the unit who could only come in to spend the day with their babies, even if that day could stretch to ten or twelve hours.

'Are you going to stay with your sister?'

'She suggested that but I'd rather be in my own home where things are, you know…a bit easier. Lisa offered to stay with me there but she's busy with Amy and I don't want to wear her out.' Reluctantly, Abby was disengaging her finger and taking her hand away from the warmth inside the incubator. 'It's not as if this is going to be over anytime soon and I might need her even more later.'

'Let me help,' Noah said. 'I could come home with you and…and cook dinner, at least.'

Oh…there it was, just for a heartbeat. That silent

communication that seemed to have vanished behind some kind of barrier a long time ago—about the time that Abby had discovered she was pregnant? Anyway... it was still there—just well hidden. This flash of connection acknowledged the only "cooking" either of them was likely to do was to turn on the oven to heat food that someone else had prepared far more expertly than they could.

Not that Abby felt remotely hungry but the offer was too good to turn down because it would provide what she needed far more than food and that was the company of the man she loved. The father of the baby she loved and who now, finally, had a name that they had chosen together and it made it feel as if they were even more of a family. A family that couldn't be together for more than fractured moments but every one of those moments felt too precious to waste right now.

'I'd love that,' she told Noah. 'I'll go and pack up my stuff in the ward. Come and find me when you're ready to go home.'

Home...

That's what it felt like, following Abby through the front door of her apartment. A comfortable, familiar space that he liked to be in. With a person he liked to be with. It was good to have something to do as well. To put a meal together from the wealth of supplies he found in both the fridge and the freezer.

'Someone's been shopping for you. And they cleaned up the food we left in the oven the night that... Leo decided he was going to arrive early.'

It felt strange to say their baby's chosen name aloud again. Who would have thought that a name could be powerful enough to change something that felt huge. Scary even… Just three letters but it made his son more *real*, somehow. A small person with a name that reflected his courage.

'Lisa's been in and out.' Abby told him. 'She had to come and get things I needed, like fresh clothes. And I wanted something to go in Leo's incubator right from the start so it didn't look quite so clinical. I'd bought that lion lovey blanket ages ago to give to Amy but then I kept it because I thought it was so cute. I hid it away because… I don't know…maybe I knew how much I wanted to have a baby one day.'

She hadn't planned on having one this soon, though, had she? Or with someone who couldn't give her the kind of love she absolutely deserved. There was a heavy feeling in Noah's chest, like a stone that was gradually getting bigger, but he tried to ignore it and stay cheerful. Supportive.

'Maybe we should go with a lion theme for his nursery?'

'It might be a good idea in your house. To go with that jungle of a garden you've got out the back.'

This made where he was feel less like home. There was a jarring note to be found in thinking about separate living arrangements that needed to be made but… that was the way things were, wasn't it? As much a part of what they were dealing with as the fact that he couldn't offer what he felt he should be able to offer to the mother of his child.

Abby was coping somehow so Noah had to follow her example, that was all there was to it. He mentally added finding a landscape gardener to the list of things he needed to get organised. He would give the go-ahead to start the alterations to his new house in the next few days as well, he decided, as he collected the plans still scattered on Abby's kitchen table. The more he had to supervise, or better yet to do himself, the easier it would be to cope with the stress of what the next days or weeks might throw at them. And the better he could cope, the more he would be able to do to support Abby.

He only had to catch her gaze to see just how she needed him right now, no matter how bravely she was facing up to this new challenge in her life. This had to be the hardest part so far, being forced to be away from her baby, unable to reassure herself by listening to the steady beat of those monitors or the touch of his hand. She still looked far too pale. Too stressed. Too...scared.

He went to her and crouched down a little, putting his hands on the wheels of her chair so that he wasn't looking down at her.

'How 'bout curling up on the couch for a bit? I'll go out and see if I can find some chips and gravy and mushy peas at the local chippie and we'll have a picnic on the coffee table.'

There was something warm in those gorgeous, soft, hazel brown eyes now. Gratitude that he was trying to do something that might make her feel better? No...it was more than that. It reminded him of the way she'd looked when he'd gone into the NICU this evening—when little Leo had been holding onto her finger. It was a look of love, that's what it was, and the longing to be able to feel that and gift it back to her was so strong it was actually a physical pain.

Or maybe the pain was coming not from a longing for something that he couldn't have but because he was hitting that barrier so hard. The one that made it impossible to feel that kind of love again because the flip side of that coin was a loss that was too unbearable to risk. Whatever…his heart was aching. For himself but more for Abby, and without thinking Noah offered his arms. It was a reflex action, wasn't it—to find something physical to do in order to strengthen whatever protection was needed from something emotional? Abby, surprisingly, accepted his silent offer to carry her to the couch so that she didn't have to make the effort of moving and transferring herself. She lifted her own arms and wrapped them around his neck as he lifted her body.

Holding Abby in his arms hadn't been his brightest idea, though. To feel the shape of her body against his, the warmth of her skin—the scent that was uniquely Abby's—was too much of a reminder of how close they had been back in the days when it had seemed safe because they had only been "good friends". But nothing was really safe, was it? And he might be doing his best for both Abby and his son at the moment but Noah felt like a failure.

They both needed more from him and he simply didn't have it to give. And this wasn't fair. On any of them.

'I'm sorry,' he murmured, as he put Abby gently

down on the soft cushions of the couch. It had been this couch where they'd made love that first time, which only made the memories stronger and increased the guilt that he'd made a serious error of judgement that was going to affect the lives of other people as well as himself. Abby deserved so much more than Noah could offer.

'What for?'

Noah had already turned away, fishing in his pocket for his car keys. He looked back just long enough to meet her gaze.

'Everything,' he said.

CHAPTER NINE

YOU COULD GET used to almost anything.

Like having to tap the sole of your baby's foot when the apnoea alarm sounded to warn that he'd stopped breathing for too long. Like making the most of the small things that you could do to help the nursing staff care for your baby, such as washing his face with the softest of muslin cloths or changing a disposable nappy that looked too big even though it was far smaller than any newborn size you could buy in a supermarket.

You could even get used to the roller-coaster of the hope that came with good news and the despair and fear that seemed to follow—sometimes only hours later. Things could change in a heartbeat—as they had today when Leo's apnoeic episodes had increased in frequency to the point that the decision had been made to go ahead with the surgery to correct his heart defect.

But even in a downward swoop of this journey, there could be a sudden, unexpected lift. A moment of pure joy, in fact. Like right now, when Abby was being allowed to actually hold Leo for the first time as they disconnected some of his monitors or changed them to a portable version so that he could be taken up to Theatre where his neonatal cardiology team were already preparing for his arrival.

"Holding" wasn't quite the right word for what she was doing, Abby thought. She had undone the buttons on her shirt and the nurses had lifted her precious baby from the incubator, expertly juggling wires and tubes to prevent tangling, to place him onto her bare skin. He was just above her breasts, on his tummy with his arms and legs spread out and even his tiny fingers and toes splayed.

'He looks like a little tree frog,' Abby whispered. She touched his head with her finger so gently she could almost feel the individual hairs of the fluff covering his scalp. 'But you need to channel your inner lion, sweetheart. We've got stuff to get through today.'

'He's going to be fine.' Noah was right beside her. 'Did you understand everything they said about the procedure?'

'Not really,' Abby admitted. 'My training only included a fairly basic cardiac course and… I'm not sure it would help to know more. The idea that they're putting things into Leo's heart is terrifying enough.'

She was touching her baby's back now. Feeling the tiniest bumps of his spine. She could feel his heartbeat against her skin and it was all too easy to imagine just how tiny his heart was. How on earth could anyone repair something so small?

Of course Noah was confident. His whole life was spent operating on structures that were just as tiny. It was his passion but Abby couldn't understand why he wanted to talk about the procedure now, when he could be sharing the joy of this small miracle of being able to touch Leo properly for the first time. To count those tiny fingers and toes and touch the tip of his nose and marvel that something so small could be so utterly perfect.

But that was precisely why Noah was seeking an escape, wasn't it? This felt like the hardest challenge Abby had ever faced but it had to be harder for Noah and she had to factor in that heartache to the emotional battle between joy and fear that was currently tumbling inside both her head and her heart as she soaked in every second of being this close to their baby.

'But maybe it would help,' she found herself saying. 'If you tell me again.'

If nothing else, Leo could listen to his father's voice for a few minutes. And Abby could stroke his soft, downy skin at the same time, to try and let him know just how much he was loved.

It was like being able to find a new handhold or somewhere to put your foot to take some of the weight that was threatening to make it impossible to climb this cliff and could send you tumbling God only knew how far or what was at the bottom.

This handhold was no more than a piece of paper and a pen but it provided something that Noah could focus on and, while he could still see their baby sprawled against Abby's much paler skin, it was only in the periphery of his vision and that was much easier to cope with.

His sketch was rapid but accurate enough to be useful and he was explaining at the same time as drawing the diagram.

'So this is the heart. You've got the two ventricles there, and the two atria on top and you've got these arteries, here… This is the pulmonary artery that takes deoxygenated blood from the right ventricle to the lungs and that's the aorta that takes the oxygenated blood from the left ventricle to the rest of the body. With me so far?'

He could see Abby's nod but she wasn't looking at him. Her gaze was firmly on Leo and she was touching one of his cheeks, softly tracing the outline of one of the strips of tape holding a tube in place—the nasogastric tube that was allowing him to be fed some of his mother's milk now, which was a step forward from only having intravenous nutrition.

'Before a baby's born, the lungs aren't going to be providing oxygen because they're full of fluid so the ductus arteriosus is an extra blood vessel that lets most of the blood go straight to the aorta and bypass the lungs. After birth, it closes up and becomes a ligament rather than a blood vessel. That's why it's a common problem with premmie babies and, if it's big enough, it can present significant issues, like it has with Leo.'

Noah paused to take a breath. He'd just made this suddenly so much more personal by using Leo's name instead of explaining something in terms of babies in general.

'But they're not going to cut his chest open, are

they?' Abby's question was only a whisper but he could feel her fear hovering in the air between them.

'No. And he'll be sedated so he's not going to feel any pain. They'll make a very small incision to put a catheter into an artery in his groin and make sure it gets to exactly the right place in his heart by using X-rays to follow it. They can take measurements and pressure readings and then they can thread in another catheter that has a closure device on it. They position that and implant the device and it fills up the blood vessel and seals it shut.

'Then they take out the catheter, close the incision and make sure that there's no bleeding from the entry site. I'm not sure how long it will take and he'll need to go into a recovery area afterwards for close monitoring so it might be a while before you're back in here and able to hold him again.'

One of the nurses looked up from where she was adjusting settings on the incubator. 'It's nearly time to tuck him up again,' she said gently. 'His oxygen sats are dropping a bit. We'll probably get the call to take him up to Theatre soon, anyway.'

Abby was nodding. It looked like her lips were pressed together too tightly to let her say anything. She bent her head, just enough to touch the top of Leo's head with her lips and it seemed to startle him because he lifted his arms. One of the miniature miracles of a hand had come even closer to Noah and, without thinking, he lifted his own hand to touch it—as if he wanted to check that something so small and perfect could be real. He touched it just with the very tip of his forefinger on the palm of his son's hand but, almost instantly, Leo closed his hand and gripped Noah's fingertip in a tiny, determined little fist.

Noah froze.

It felt like time froze as well and the whole world stopped turning for a heartbeat. And then another and another.

That, oh, so tiny hand was touching way more than Noah's fingertip. It was reaching inside his body. Into his heart. It was touching those walls he'd built so carefully to protect his heart and that touch was all it took for them to crack and begin to crumble. He could feel the cracks widening so that what was behind them was about to escape. A tsunami of... *feeling*...

Feeling the joy and hope and dreams of loving someone so much.

But also the fear that came with knowing what it would be like to have it all snatched away from you.

He could drown in that tsunami. But, even if he didn't drown, he would be swept off his feet and be unable to be strong for Abby while she faced up to her own fears as she waited for Leo to come out of Theatre. He caught her gaze at that moment, while his finger was still being held, and what he saw in her eyes was the final push on those walls.

He couldn't do this.

He couldn't *not* do this...

Noah had no idea what might have happened if his pager hadn't sounded right then. The loud sound was enough to startle Leo again and he let go of Noah's finger as the nurse carefully scooped him up from Abby's chest to put him back in his incubator.

'I…ah… I have to get this…' The pager message had come with a priority of something urgent.

Abby simply watched him as he got to his feet and moved towards a phone at the nurses' station to make an internal call. Noah's legs felt as if his whole body had been shaken by something and he could feel Abby's gaze following him. A curious gaze. Maybe a hopeful one? Was she wondering if she'd really seen what she'd thought she'd seen when his son had been holding his finger? That moment when he'd realised that it was only his own fear that was holding him back from loving someone absolutely. Not just Leo but Abby as well. *Especially* Abby…

The phone call was from the emergency department and Noah listened only for a very short time.

'I'm on my way,' he said.

A few rapid steps back towards Leo's corner of the NICU where he was being settled for when the call to transport him to Theatre came through. Abby had just put his woolly hat back on his head.

'I have to go,' Noah told her. 'I'm sorry. There's an emergency in ED. Someone's come in having split their hand in half with a circular saw.'

If there'd been anything like hope in Abby's gaze, it faded now into something very different. Resignation, maybe. Sadness? Or perhaps it was simply determination.

'We'll be fine,' she told him. 'Go. That person needs you.'

So did Abby and Leo. But Noah went—because he had to.

Because he needed to. Because this urgent summons was giving him the chance to escape and get to higher ground in the last moments before that tsunami arrived. A chance to take control back and, if he couldn't repair those protective walls in his heart, he could at least stay out of an overwhelming wash of emotions. He had to, because if that wave caught him, he might not be of any use to anyone and letting that happen would not only be selfish, it would be completely unacceptable. Someone was waiting for him in ED. Someone who was probably desperately hoping that Noah could help stop their injury from turning their world upside down for ever.

And he *could* do that. Or as much as it was possible to do and maybe, by doing that, he could save his own world from falling apart as well.

This waiting room was the loneliest place ever.

Lisa and Hugh were on their way to the hospital but they'd been in central London this morning, choosing Amy's first cot because, at nearly seven months old, she had grown too big for her bassinet and now they were caught in a traffic jam that didn't look like it was going to clear anytime soon.

Abby didn't know where Noah was. Probably scrubbing up for some incredibly long and challenging surgery to save his patient from losing his hand. The only thing that really mattered to her right now was that he wasn't here.

She was alone.

More alone than she'd ever been in her life. She'd followed Leo's incubator as far as she was allowed—to the theatre anteroom where a specialist paediatric anaesthetist would be sedating her tiny baby so that he could undergo a procedure that might well be perfectly safe but it still seemed unbearably invasive, especially for a baby who wasn't even developed enough to be able to breathe on his own.

Rolling away from that room had felt like her heart was being ripped out and left behind. And now she had way too much time to sit here and feel that fear and the loneliness that was making it so much worse.

It was well over an hour since Noah had rushed out of the NICU to go to St John's emergency department but there'd been a delay in getting Leo up to Theatre. It hadn't been so hard waiting down in the unit because Leo was still safely enclosed in the plastic walls of his incubator and in the care of the amazing nursing staff who'd been watching over him almost from the moment he'd been born. So Abby had felt safe, too. More than that. She'd been able to sit there quietly with Leo, with her hand through the porthole and feel that exquisite pressure from the tiny fingers wrapped around hers.

The way he'd been holding his father's fingertip a short time ago.

And, oh... Abby could have sworn she'd seen straight through the barriers that Noah had kept up for as long as she'd known him. Straight through to a place where the glow of being able to love was shining so brightly it had almost blinded her for an instant.

She'd seen a place that made her own heart break more than a little because it had dark corners where things like fear and tears lurked but the brightness of happiness and love and just...*hope*...could win if it was allowed to—for most of the time, if you were lucky—because it shone so much more brightly than the opposite side of that coin.

A member of staff from the surgical suite had been sent to keep Abby company in the waiting room but Abby had told her she'd rather be alone. It wasn't true, of course, but what she didn't want was to be with someone who didn't know her. Or Leo. Someone who had no understanding of just how agonising this waiting was, with every passing minute making it harder.

Why was it taking so long?

Had something gone wrong?

Why had she signed that consent form that had given them permission to do whatever might be needed if a complication arose—like opening up that tiny chest to do more major surgery?

Maybe that was what was happening right now. Abby could hear the footsteps of someone approaching this waiting area and they weren't the soft squeaky ones of the nurse who'd been wearing trainers. These steps sounded heavier. More urgent? Abby's heart was in her mouth as she turned to face the door and whatever bad news was on its way.

But the person filling the doorway was Noah and the expression on his face was...was as raw as she'd ever seen anybody look. Ever.

'I can't do it,' he said as he came towards her. He

hunkered down so that his face was on the same level of Abby's and balanced himself by putting his hands on her wheels. 'I have to go and scrub up in a few minutes and I'll probably be in Theatre for hours but I had to come and tell you because, otherwise, I don't think I could focus on what I need to do. So I came. To say that I can't do it.'

If Abby's heart had been breaking earlier, it was now in a million pieces that were raining down into a chasm so dark she didn't want to know how deep it was. She could get a sense of how deep it was, though, by what she could see in Noah's eyes. And she couldn't hate him for protecting his own heart. If she'd had a choice, she'd be protecting both his and Leo's from any of this.

'I know,' she said softly. 'I do understand, Noah. This is hard enough on me and I can see how impossible it would be to put yourself through it all over again.'

But Noah was frowning now.

'No...you don't understand, Abby.' Noah took hold of Abby's hands, which had been resting in her lap. 'What I can't do is *not* go through this. I can't not feel...*everything*. I can't *not* love Leo. Or you, Abby. It's been there all along but I couldn't reach it.' His eyes were shining with what looked very much like unshed tears. 'But something changed today and... I can feel it all. The fear and the pain but most of all... I can feel what it's like to love somebody this much and there's no going back from that. I can't be away from you— or Leo. I just can't do it.'

Those shattered pieces of Abby's heart were magically coming back together, as if someone had put a video on reverse and things were speeding backwards. It felt like there were more pieces than there'd been before, too, because her heart was feeling as if it wasn't going to stop getting bigger. As if it was so full it was in danger of bursting.

'I know how that feels,' she said, her voice cracking. 'I know exactly. Because it's how I feel about you. How I've felt for such a long time—before we even knew that Leo was on the way.'

Noah's arms were around her now. Holding her so tightly it was hard to breathe, but that didn't seem to matter. This was the only place that Abby needed to be at the moment. In Noah's arms, with her head tucked into that space beneath his collar bone, where she could hear, and feel, the steady beat of his heart. And feel his lips pressed against her hair and when he spoke she could hear the words but she could also feel them rumbling against her cheek.

'We'll get through this, Abby. Whatever happens— now or in the future—we'll get through it together, okay?'

Abby could only nod. The promise in those words and her faith in that promise had made her throat too tight for her to breathe properly, let alone find any audible words.

She could hear someone saying something, though. A female voice. And now the weight of emotional overload made it seem as if it was too hard for her heart to keep beating as she looked up and saw the woman with a theatre gown still over her scrubs and a mask dangling by its strings around her neck. It was the cardiologist who'd been doing the procedure on Leo.

And she was smiling.

'It all went perfectly,' she told them. 'Your little boy came through with flying colours and he's absolutely fine. You can come and see him in Recovery.'

Abby turned at the exact moment Noah did and they held each other's, gaze which was far more intimate than handholding could ever be. And they both had tears escaping to dampen their cheeks. They were in this together and they always would be. And there was love there. So much love that Abby felt sure that even if there were darker things to face in the future, the glow from that kind of love would never be extinguished.

They were together now, she and Noah. As committed as any couple could ever be.

More than that, it really felt like they were a family already.

And it was time to go and see their son, even if it would only be for a minute or two on Noah's part because he had an important job to go and do. Other people needed him as much as Abby and Leo did. They needed him more right now, in fact, and that was okay because Abby and Leo and Noah had the rest of their lives ahead of them to be together as much as possible.

And even if they weren't in the same room together, that love would still be there and Abby knew it was going to keep her as strong as she needed to be until they could take their baby home.

CHAPTER TEN

FACING CHALLENGES IN life with another person always held a risk that it could test a relationship too much and force you apart, but a tough patch could also do the opposite and build a foundation that felt like it would be strong enough to withstand anything and everything that life could throw at it in the future.

Getting stronger was exactly what the next ten weeks did for Abby and Noah as they lived their lives centred on the neonatal intensive care unit until baby Leo was big and strong enough to go home.

There were milestones along the way that neither of them would ever forget, even if they didn't have some special photographs that had captured the memories— such as the day Leo had been able to come off the ventilator and breathe for himself after the corrective surgery on his heart meant that his condition had improved enough so he'd only needed some supplementary oxygen.

It was Noah who was holding him this time. Sitting with his shirt open so that he could have skin-to-skin bonding time with his son, leaning back in his armchair so that Leo was lying flat with his arms and legs out—doing what Abby called his little tree frog impression. Abby had positioned her wheelchair as closely as possible to where Noah was sitting because, that way, she could touch both of them, with a hand resting on Noah's leg and the palm of her other hand taking the weight of Leo's tiny foot with those precious little toes.

It wasn't just that their baby was almost hidden by being cupped by Noah's hand. Or that he had his eyes open and seemed to be not only taking in everything that was happening around him but content in knowing how much he was loved.

For Abby, this was filling her heart even more because, despite still being in the unit, this was one of those deeply private experiences that was bringing her closer and closer to Noah every time they happened. She knew how significant this one was because she could see the tears in Noah's eyes.

Not like that night—in the early hours of the morning after Leo had had his heart surgery—when Noah had come home to Abby's apartment after spending such a long time in Theatre with the man who'd very nearly amputated half his hand. That day had been the turning point of their whole relationship—the day they'd become a family and one that had been baptised by many tears when they'd finally had the chance to be together properly. When Noah had come home simply to hold Abby in his arms.

To tell her how being able to love her was making him feel so many things all over again and he'd realised that maybe he'd never processed his grief properly all those years ago. Abby had encouraged him to tell her all about Ellen and she'd learned how they'd been so young when they'd met and how much they'd loved each other. He'd told her that, because Ellen had loved him that much, he knew that she would be happy that he'd found Abby and that she'd want him to love her and be loved in return. For them to be together to bring up their baby. And Abby had wrapped her arms even more tightly around them and promised that that was exactly what was going to happen and that they were going to make the most of every moment.

On this milestone, when Noah was holding Leo for the first time, there were more tears but they didn't need to share anything tragic. This was just something else that Noah needed to tell Abby about so that there were no secrets between them. No barriers to them being as close as it was possible for a couple to be.

'I was so scared to give him a name,' he said, so softly that nobody around them could hear. 'Ellen and I had chosen a name for our baby as soon as we found out she was on her way. We didn't tell anybody, though, and it was only at the very end, when I was holding her…like this…that I told them.'

Abby leaned sideways in her chair, so that she could rest her head against Noah's arm. So that he could tilt his head to touch hers. And they were both touching their baby, which made the connection so powerful that Abby's heart ached.

'What was it?' she whispered. 'Your daughter's name?'

'Grace.' Noah had to clear her throat. 'I spoke her name aloud and…just minutes later I lost her.'

Abby had to catch a tear with her fingers before it fell onto Leo.

'She's still part of you. Like Ellen is. And that makes them part of our family, too. We'll never forget them. Have you got photos?'

'Somewhere. Packed away like so many things were before I met you.'

'Let's find one. As soon as we've finished the painting in the house we'll start a family wall somewhere and we'll put them up. And...' Abby raised her voice a little as a nurse walked past the end of Leo's incubator. 'Jenny, have you got a moment to take a photo for us? Our first family photo?'

Leo learning to breastfeed was another milestone after a journey that began with no more than a lick and ended with him being able to latch on and suck for several minutes before tiring. The nasogastric tube that had been used to give him Abby's breastmilk for his early weeks was added to the growing pile of other tubes and monitoring wires that were no longer essential. Noah was by her side for that first proper feed and they had both been so happy with the progress.

'We'll be like normal parents in no time.' Noah had grinned. 'You'll be poking me when it's my turn to get up for a night feed.

He was there for Leo's first smile as well, and happy didn't begin to cover how that made them both feel, even though there'd been no chance of capturing the moment in a photograph. It was enough to know that there would be many, many opportunities to do that in the months and years to come. They were both going to ensure that their tiny boy had plenty to smile about.

Moving out of Abby's apartment and into the house was a huge step forward into their new life together and, while the renovations were not quite complete, both Noah and Abby had wanted to be settled into their for ever home before Leo came out of the hospital. The photo taken that day was a selfie when they were finally alone in the house and they'd curled up together, exhausted, on one of the couches that had come from Abby's apartment.

'I still think we should have upgraded these couches,' she said. 'They're getting old.'

'Are you kidding? This couch has history and I'm keeping it for ever.' Noah pulled his phone from his pocket and held it above them to take a photograph.

'Oh...' Abby laughed. 'How could I forget that first time... I can't believe I actually confessed that I was a virgin when I hardly knew you.'

'And I still can't believe that you *were*. That somebody so incredibly beautiful and clever and kind and... well...pretty close to perfect really...hadn't already had her heart won.'

He dropped his phone and pulled Abby into his arms and kissed her. Such a long, slow, tender kiss that when she finally came up for air, it felt as though her bones had melted.

'I'm so lucky it was you,' she whispered. 'That you were my first. That I never need to go looking again because I know I'd never find anyone I could ever want to be with as much as you.'

The look in Noah's eyes as he got to his feet and gathered Abby into his arms made her completely forget how tired the moving in had made her.

'I think we need to check that they've put our bed in the right place, don't you?'

'Oh, yes…' Abby wrapped her arms more tightly around his neck. 'Absolutely.'

The glossiest photographs that were taken in the weeks before Leo finally came home weren't taken by Noah or Abby. Or even Leo's doting aunt and uncle on the many visits from Lisa and Hugh. They were photographs taken by a magazine and they weren't even the subjects of the article, although Steve and Pauline had tried to convince the journalist writing the article that Noah and Abby were the real heroes in the story of the toe that had become a thumb.

'It wouldn't have happened without both of them,' Steve told the journalist as they were grouped together for a photo. 'Dr Baxter for the incredible surgery he and team did for me. And Abby, of course. She kept me on track for all those early months and kept me going until I was good enough to get back to the job I love.'

Steve could see that the journalist was eyeing Abby with interest—as if she'd sensed another angle to the story she was writing.

'I know, right?' Steve nodded. 'Who wouldn't be inspired by a physiotherapist who knows what she's talking about because she's obviously been through more than a few challenges herself? I said that right from the start.'

'And you're still having therapy on your hand?'

'Nah… I'm pretty much discharged from care now. Unless I have a problem, of course. I'd be back like a shot to these two if that happened but I might have to wait until Abby's back at work and that might be a while from what we've heard.'

Pauline was smiling at Abby. 'We heard about your baby,' she said. 'That he arrived too early and that he needed an operation on his heart. That must have been so terrifying for you both.'

'It was,' Abby agreed. She couldn't help looking up to catch Noah's gaze. 'But we've got through it and Leo's doing really well. They're starting to talk about letting him come home.'

Noah was smiling back at her and the journalist and photographer exchanged glances themselves.

'So you're together?' she asked. 'You're married?'

'We're not married,' Abby responded. They could have been, of course, but she knew she'd done the right thing in refusing Noah's proposal when it had only been about being together as parents and not as two people who loved each other as well as their child. They'd been too busy since then, wrapped up in caring for their sick baby, work responsibilities and the renovations of their family home to even consider the idea of marriage again, and this question out of the blue made Abby think that if he asked her again, her answer might be very different.

Maybe she would ask him.

Or maybe they didn't need anything formal to advertise their commitment to each other.

'But we're definitely together,' Noah added. He caught Abby's gaze again and it was her turn to smile.

'Yeah,' she murmured. 'Definitely together.'

'Did you meet at work?' The journalist had her notebook out again. 'It didn't have anything to do with Steve being your patient, did it? That would make such a lovely extra angle to this story.'

'Yes and no,' Abby admitted. 'It was Steve's first operation when I realised that Noah was St John's new specialist hand surgeon.'

'I knew there was something going on.' Pauline smiled. 'You could feel it in the air when they were in the same room together.'

'But we'd met before,' Noah added. 'And that hadn't had anything to do with Steve. You could say it was more of an accident than anything.'

'Oh?' The journalist looked eagerly towards Abby, hoping for more details.

Abby kept her face as straight as Noah's. Their story was their own and they weren't about to share it with the world at large. They weren't about to forget it either, however. An accidental meeting that was going to shape the rest of their lives.

So she simply shrugged as the silent communication between herself and Noah was full of laughter. And love...

'It's no big deal,' she said. 'We just kind of bumped into each other.'

EPILOGUE

One year later...

'THIS HAS TO be the most romantic place on earth for a wedding.'

Abigail Phillips grinned at her sister. 'You should know. It's where you had yours. Where you got engaged *and* where you had your first date.'

'Mmm...' Lisa Phillips smiled dreamily into the mirror as she put the finishing touches to her hair. 'I'm just so happy to be back here. And for the best reason ever.'

'I was never intending to copy you. You know that, yes? I would have been more than happy to get married in the local registry office. It was Noah who had other ideas.'

'I'm pretty sure that was Hugh's doing. You remember that night you came around to dinner? When that magazine article had come out about that guy with the toe for a thumb and you told us that the journalist had assumed you were married?'

'Of course. And when we went out to the kitchen I

told you that it didn't really bother me at all whether we got married or not. That I would always be happy as long as Noah and I were together.'

'Yeah…well, it was then that Hugh showed Noah the picture of where we got married. *This* place.'

'I know. He was still going on about it when we got home that night. The south of France, he kept saying. That view from that terrace. Those stone floors and walls…that grapevine…'

'It wasn't just the picture,' Lisa confessed. 'Hugh told me later that he'd told Noah that there was something magic about this particular restaurant. That it was only because he'd been clever enough to bring me here on our first date that I fell in love with him and we began our happy ever after.'

Abby laughed as she took the last sip of the glass of champagne she'd been given as she made her final preparations to marry the love of her life.

'It might be true. You *are* happy, aren't you?'

'Couldn't be happier. Especially now that the morning sickness is fading. I didn't get any the first time around with Amy. Hey…maybe that means it's going to be a boy this time. It would be nice for Leo to have a boy cousin.'

'Speaking of Leo. And Amy…it's about time we went to find my flower children, isn't it? If Hugh and Noah are playing with them, they're probably grubby already.'

'Let's see…'

Lisa gave Abby a searching glance from head to toe that took in her wheelchair with the tiny bunches of delicate, white gypsophila attached to the wheels' spokes with silk ribbons. Abby's dress was white and lacy but fitted enough to be elegant and she had a red sash around her waist to match her matron of honour's dress—a nod to the pact that the sisters had made when they were very young, that they would wear red despite the different shades of their hair because it was their happy colour. Abby's long, golden red hair was in loose waves, threaded with tiny white roses, fragrant orange blossom and single sprigs of gypsophila.

'Yep,' she pronounced. 'You're ready.' She looked around them. 'Where are the baskets of rose petals for the kids?'

'Over there. What's the bet that Leo just sits down and tries to eat them?'

Lisa smiled. 'They're edible. I checked.'

'Do you think he should be walking better by now?' Abby couldn't help the anxious question as they reached the door of the bathroom they'd been using for final preparations and she could see her son in his uncle's arms as he came towards them. 'Look at that. He still loves to be carried everywhere and he's nearly fifteen months old.'

'Don't forget he arrived nearly three months early so he's actually spot on with his milestones. Plus, he's the most adorable little boy in the entire world.'

Lisa stepped through the door to give Abby room to manoeuvre her wheelchair to the start of the aisle that had been created by shifting all the wrought-iron tables to one side of the terrace, where the wedding breakfast would be served later, and putting chairs—

decorated with silk ribbons and more small clouds of the ethereal gypsophila—into rows for the select group of close friends and family who'd travelled to France to share this celebration.

Lisa smiled at her husband, who would be returning to his best man duties as soon as the children had been delivered back to their mothers to play their part in this intimate wedding ceremony.

'I should warn you, though…' she said, seriously. 'I can only keep saying that about Leo if it turns out that Amy's getting a little sister.'

Amy, at nearly two years old, was delighted with her task of being a flower girl and she was beaming as Lisa straightened her headband of white daisies and gave her the small, silk-lined basket of rose petals.

'You'll need to hold Leo's hand, sweetheart,' she told her daughter. 'You can go down to where Daddy and Uncle Noah are waiting and throw the petals on the ground on the way.'

'C'mon, Leo.' Amy turned to her cousin. 'Let's go…'

But Leo stayed where he was, standing there with his cute short trousers and braces over a white shirt with a red bow tie. And then he sat down on his well-padded rump and looked at his mother—those dark eyes looking huge in that perfect little face framed by dark waves just like his father's.

'You want a ride?'

Leo's face split into the biggest grin ever and he held up his arms. Abby laughed and expertly adjusted the position of her wheelchair so that she was close enough to lean over the side and scoop Leo into her lap.

Hugh was standing beside the groom now, in front of the stone wall of the terrace, where an archway covered with white flowers had been placed to offer the best possible view of the forests covering the mountainous terrain that flowed from this medieval French village towards the blue streak in the distance that was the Mediterranean.

Lisa walked ahead of Abby, helping Amy to scatter rose petals. Abby rolled across the big flagstones that made the floor uneven enough to bounce Leo on her lap and make him giggle. He hadn't been in the least bit upset that Lisa had taken his basket of petals to help Amy. He had his lion lovey blanket firmly in one hand, just in case he might need comfort in strange surroundings.

Not that he was looking anything less than perfectly happy, cuddled against his mother as she approached the man who was waiting for them both.

Noah.

The man she always thought she couldn't possibly love any more than she did right now but then, almost every day, she discovered she was wrong.

Her lover.

Her best friend.

The father of her baby and now he was about to become her husband.

The enormity of it all stole Abby's breath away but that was okay. She'd never really needed words to be able to communicate with this man, had she?

She could tell him now just how much she loved him. And she knew, without a shadow of a doubt, that he would say exactly the same thing back.

* * * * *

COMING SOON!

We really hope you enjoyed reading this book. If you're looking for more romance, be sure to head to the shops when new books are available on

Thursday 16th April

To see which titles are coming soon, please visit
millsandboon.co.uk/nextmonth

MILLS & BOON

MILLS & BOON

Coming next month

UNLOCKING THE EX-ARMY DOC'S HEART
Juliette Hyland

Rafe's phone continued to ding. Apparently, a late-night ice cream post was popular. He ignored it, but the world invaded their private heaven with each buzz.

—*I also want you. The real Rafe. The swing dancer, who has a midnight sweet tooth and gets cold easily. Not the persona that makes an algorithm happy.* Annie swallowed the words as she spun her pint to him and grabbed his. "My turn for the chocolate."

A smile pulled at Rafe's lips. Lifting his spoon, he laughed, "I don't want cookie dough. *En garde*, Annie."

Giggling, she defended the chocolate from the swipes of his spoon as he dove for the pint. This was belonging. Laughing over ice cream, late at night, with no audience. How could she make him understand?

Finally, she pushed it to the middle of the table. "Guess I can share." The bottom of the pint appeared too quickly, and Annie waved away Rafe's offer to let her have the final bite. Looking at the clock, she reluctantly pushed away from the table. *If she didn't leave now...* "Thanks for keeping me company. We have a full schedule tomorrow. I think we both need some sleep."

Annie's fingers brushed his as they reached for the empty ice cream containers at the same time. Lightning flashed between them, and Annie didn't care about the buzz of the phone, or anything else. She just wanted, needed, to know how he kissed.

"Rafe," ignoring the tension racing through her belly,

she leaned forward. He tasted of chocolate, heat and summer. Her heart gasped at the tender way his mouth shifted under hers, accepting her exploration. If she took his hand, he'd come with her to bed. The thought excited her before panic rushed into its place.

Stepping away she stared at him, "I—"

Rafe placed a finger against her lips. "Don't apologize. Please."

Pursing her lips, she grabbed the containers, holding them before her, an empty sugar wall between her and temptation. "I wasn't going to apologize." Annie held her breath, wishing she had the courage to ask him to follow her, and hating the uncertainty that kept the words buried.

Rafe soft lips brushed her cheek, "I'll see you tomorrow."

His words held a promise and an escape.

Continue reading
UNLOCKING THE EX-ARMY DOC'S HEART
Juliette Hyland

Available next month
www.millsandboon.co.uk

LET'S TALK
Romance

For exclusive extracts, competitions
and special offers, find us online: